The Man With Five Minds

He was the ...
all the Confed...
When the impos...
tect the security ...
one called. Then his mind was wiped, and he was given a luxurious vacation until brought back for the next job.

Not this time, however! This time they needed to transfer his mind into the brains of four criminals sentenced to the mysterious Warden worlds, the Confederacy's dumping ground for dangerous criminals. Return from the Warden worlds was impossible because of a strange organism that invaded every living thing—and most other objects, as well. Only his mind could insure the assassination of the Four Lords of the Diamond, the rulers of those worlds, who were in league with aliens who threatened the existence of the Confederacy.

Now the four criminals were gone, and their activities were being beamed back to him—each in a sense reflecting the assassins actions, each criminal somehow the assassin himself. And they were not doing what he knew they should do.

To his horror, he found his own mind changing as he lived their lives with them. The Confederacy depended on him—but he was rapidly losing himself!

By Jack L. Chalker
Published by Ballantine Books:

THE WEB OF THE CHOZEN
AND THE DEVIL WILL DRAG YOU UNDER
A JUNGLE OF STARS
DANCE BAND ON THE *TITANIC*
DANCERS IN THE AFTERGLOW

THE SAGA OF THE WELL WORLD
Volume 1: *Midnight at the Well of Souls*
Volume 2: *Exiles at the Well of Souls*
Volume 3: *Quest for the Well of Souls*
Volume 4: *The Return of Nathan Brazil*
Volume 5: *Twilight at the Well of Souls:*
                The Legacy of Nathan Brazil

THE FOUR LORDS OF THE DIAMOND
Book One: *Lilith: A Snake in the Grass*
Book Two: *Cerberus: A Wolf in the Fold*
Book Three: *Charon: A Dragon at the Gate*
Book Four: *Medusa: A Tiger by the Tail*

THE DANCING GODS
Book One: *The River of Dancing Gods*
Book Two: *Demons of the Dancing Gods*
Book Three: *Vengeance of the Dancing Gods*
Book Four: *Songs of the Dancing Gods*

THE RINGS OF THE MASTER
Book One: *Lords of the Middle Dark*
Book Two: *Pirates of the Thunder*
Book Three: *Warriors of the Storm*
Book Four: *Masks of the Martyrs*

CHARON:
A Dragon at the Gate

Book Three of
THE FOUR LORDS OF THE DIAMOND

JACK L. CHALKER

A Del Rey Book

BALLANTINE BOOKS • NEW YORK

A Del Rey Book
Published by Ballantine Books

Library of Congress Catalog Card Number: 82-90379

ISBN 0-345-29370-3

Printed in Canada

First Edition: November 1982
Eighth Printing: May 1991

Cover Art by David B. Mattingly

For Art Saha, longtime member of First Fandom, anthologist of exceptional taste and discernment, and a Good Man

Contents

THE WARDEN DIAMOND

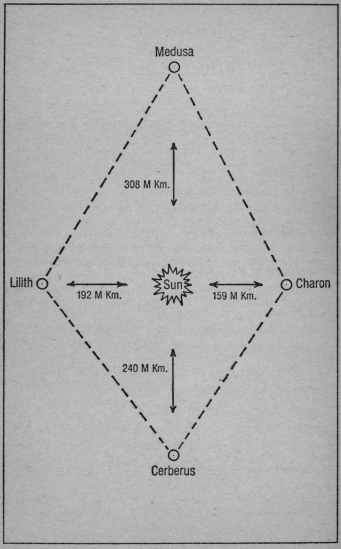

A Time for Reflection

1

The naril circled and positioned themselves for the kill against the backdrop of the onrushing *al*-wind. Opening their razorlike runners, which squeezed out through slits in their skins, the naril started down.

The man looked around frantically without breaking his desperate run. There was little shelter in the desolate desert landscape, and the cracked desert floor was harder than concrete.

The naril were great creatures of the air, huge, speeding black ovals with great egg-shaped eyes that made up what little face there was, tentacles behind shifting subtly to aid in flight as if a solid tail and rudder. Underneath each black horror were the two curved bony plates, almost like rockers, out of which came the deadly sharp steel-like blades with which it would slash its prey.

The man realized that there was no place left to go and decided to make what stand he could here, in the flat open land. One naril swooped down on him, impossibly fast, but he dropped to the ground and rolled an instant before the sharp blades struck, and the naril almost bit into the hard earth and spilled. No such luck, though, and the man was quickly to his feet once more, cursing that he had delayed so long. Taking a quick check of both naril, he knew that he needed both of them in front of him, not flanking as they now were, so he summoned a reserve only impending death could call up and ran at an angle to the two circling monsters.

The naril were quite intelligent, but also overconfident. They had several square kilometers of open country to play around in and never doubted the final outcome. In the meantime, this was fun.

The man stopped once more and whirled again to face his tormentors. As he had hoped, the pair had joined again and seemed to be almost hovering there in the air, their yellow, expressionless eyes watching him and concealing, he had no doubt, some great amusement.

He knew he had very little time.

From the naril point of view he seemed just to stand there, facing them, eyes closed, hands outstretched. They took this act as a gesture of surrender and submission, and, since this sort of thing was boring, moved in for the kill.

They dropped very low, only a meter or so off the desert floor, and sped toward him, relishing the kill. As they neared their intended victim there was a rumbling sound and the earth itself seemed to rupture. Around the man grew a wall of solid stone as he himself sank down into the earth behind it. The predators were so taken by surprise that each struck an opposite side of the still-growing wall. There was a shower of sparks as their sharp runners ground into the stone, but both had sufficient balance to stay aloft and veer off.

Inside the sudden pit, in the darkness surrounded by four meters of stone wall, the man heard the naril hiss in defiance and frustration. He was nearly spent; he had used up half a day's water. The fort would *have* to hold. He sank down, relishing the cool relief his tiny fortress afforded, and listened.

The naril adjusted quickly to the new conditions and tried to break down the walls, hitting them hard and at careful angles. While they managed to do some damage to the rocky fortress, they did even more damage to themselves, since their blades were of bone. They soon gave up the attempt.

Settling down on top of the structure, they blocked what little light was left to the man. He saw that he had judged the side of the pit well; both were too large to get down the chimneylike opening to him.

Ultimately, of course, one of the creatures sat on top of the opening, trailing its long tentacles down into the pit.

Again the man had been exacting in his measurements, although it was terrifying to lie there in the bottom, with all light blocked, and hear those tendrils slapping and searching about just a bit above him. Finally that, too, stopped, and he relaxed a bit. He had come so far, so very far, and although momentarily safe, he felt his reserves nearly gone.

He heard the naril shift again, and then he was subjected to the ultimate indignity. Unable to reach him in any other way, they were trying to flush him out by defecating on him.

There was an angry, frustrated growl from above and then the naril moved off, allowing some light inside. He did not kid himself that they were gone. At least one still lurked outside, waiting for him to come up, while the other was most likely now up and away into whatever clouds there might be, soaking up moisture as only naril could. He would have given anything for some of that moisture in a form other than that he now wallowed in.

Clouds . . . He tried to think. What had the sky been like? His attention had been on more immediate stuff. Still, there were always *some* clouds around. High ones, of course, which contained less moisture than he would like, but *some* . . .

Concentrate . . . concentrate! If only he had the strength! With supreme effort he closed his eyes and attempted to shut out all but his sensitivity to the *wa*, an attempt made doubly difficult by the slimy naril feces being baked even more in the heat of the sun and stinking all the worse for it. He too would bake, he knew, if he did not succeed, for his crude fortress was also a crude but very effective oven.

Think . . . think! Think only of the *wa* . . .

He felt the *wa* that built his fort from the start, of course, but those he needed now to shut out. He reached out, *wa* to *wa*, his to those others, and broke free his vision onto the desert floor once more.

Of the naril there was no sign, but there were two bar-bushes nearby that hadn't been there before. Inwardly this made him smile, although he had little to smile about. The naril were intelligent animals, it was true, but barely that.

It would never occur to them that bushes in a place like this were as conspicuous as the naril themselves—which is what the bushes most certainly were.

The fact that both waited, so still and patiently in the heat, confirmed his worst fears about them. Trained and under orders they most certainly were, possibly Yatek Morah's own personal hunters.

He felt the *wa* of the thick desert air around them all, but again he ignored it, reaching up, up, ever higher, hoping, praying that somewhere within his range was enough cloud to form what must be made.

It was there, of course, but terribly sparse and high up. He hoped it was enough. It *had* to be enough.

Slowly, carefully, he reached the *wa* of the cloud, of the water molecules, reached and talked to it and carefully guided and cajoled it into patterns, clumps, groups growing thicker and thicker, bringing it together centered on the tiny instant fort far below.

He wasn't sure if he had enough power, but it was all his strength and power could muster. It *had* to be enough. It just *had* to be . . .

Now fly, *wa* of the clouds, fly upward, rise toward the sun your nurturer. Rise . . . rise . . .

The two "bushes" lying in wait outside trembled, shimmered, and were naril once again. They did not quite understand what was happening, but they saw the shadow on the ground and felt its coolness. Great yellow eyes looked skyward and beheld the clouds gathering together, coalescing at hundreds of times normal speed, growing thicker and darker as they did so. The naril did not understand why it was happening, but they knew, could smell and sense, that a small but powerful thunderstorm was building just over them most unnaturally, and they felt real fear. For a moment they were poised between their fear and natural instincts and their command to pursue and kill this man, but as thunder boomed out of the strange, unnatural cloud and echoed eerily across the vast desert, fear and instinct won out. They rose into the air and sped away, toward the sunlit desert outside the boundaries of the clouds' shadow.

The rain came now, falling not heavily but steadily on the small fort and an area of approximately eighty or so meters around it. The man wasted no time in commanding the *wa* of the walls to return to form, and as the walls shrunk, he rose until he stood once more on the desert floor with no sign of structure. The naril feces still clung to him, and he shed all but his empty water flask and black skin belt, letting the rain wash him. For a minute or two he just stood there enjoying the rain and the cool relief it brought, but he knew he dared not linger. There was not much water up there, and it could give out any time.

The recovered naril, understanding that their quarry had somehow caused the storm and regaining their confidence, hovered just at the edge of the clouds, waiting for the rain to end.

The parched ground, which had seen rain perhaps two or three human generations ago and not since, could not absorb the water, and this made the hard ground slippery and treacherous going. As the man moved, the center of the storm traveled with him, keeping him in its center, while at the edges the naril moved at his pace, waiting for the rain to give out. The rain itself would foul the naril's delicate membranous wings, invisible in flight or hover, but once the rain stopped they would move once more.

The man prayed the rain would hold, and it almost did, getting him to within a hundred meters of the mountains before it started to give out. All the *wa* in the world could not conjure more rain if there was no more water to use, and he hadn't time to take the evaporation from behind him and recycle it into the diminishing cloud.

The naril, wary of more trickery and fearful that he had stopped the rain only to lure them in, held back, though, and this extra time gave him the opportunity to run for the rocky outcrops just ahead.

Seeing him sprint, one naril forgot its caution and, hissing, shot out after him, overtaking him just at the base of the rocks and striking him in the back. He flew against the rocks from the force of the blow and gave a terrible scream, but the naril had forgotten to extend its blades, and while the blow was crushing, it neither cut nor sliced.

Though dazed, he managed to crawl into a cleft in the rocks and wedge himself in as tightly as possible. Even so, he knew he was done in, out of strength at last, his bag of tricks used up, the cleft far too shallow to protect him from the naril tentacles. He was done, though; he almost didn't really care anymore. He passed out there, in the rocks, with a last thought that death at least would give him rest.

"Jatik?"

The voice seemed to come from far away. *Go away!* his mind shouted. *I am dead! Let me have my peace!*

"Jatik, you must listen to my voice," it said again, closer now, more commanding, harder to ignore. "Jatik, this is Koril. You must speak to me."

"I die," he muttered, almost angrily. "Let me go."

"Yes, you are dead," Koril's voice agreed. "You are beyond my power or anyone's to save you. Yet while your *wa* still burns and struggles against extinction within you, we may yet communicate. Please, Jatik, you were a brave man and a loyal one. Do not pass until your bravery is given meaning by your words."

He struggled, tried to remember. The words . . . The mission . . .

"Where are the others, Jatik?"

Others? "Dead. All dead."

"Then you are the last. Hurry, Jatik, for time grows short and my power to hold you weakens quickly. I must know. Did you get in? Did you see the meeting?"

Meeting . . . what meeting? He struggled. Oh, yes, the meeting. Oh, God! The meeting . . .

"I—I saw," he managed. "The Four Lords at Diamond Rock. The Four Lords and the others. Oh, God! The others!"

"Those others—think, Jatik! Hold on a bit more! The others! What were they like?"

"Horrible . . . Monstrous. They wore the cloaks of men but could not hide from us. They are terrible, Koril, terrible to behold. Spawns of some hell beyond man's imagination. Slobbering, horrible . . . Such as they were born in some hellish place far removed from man."

"The Four Lords—there is an alliance?"

"Yes, yes! Oh, God! You must destroy them, Koril! You must not let them sell man out to such as these! Horrible! You cannot know! I pray to God you never know. Their very sight was enough to drive Latir and Mohar mad."

"What do they look like, these spawns of hell? Think, Jatik! Hold on!"

"Look like! My mind holds what little it still has by putting that likeness from it. Monstrous . . . Pulp . . . Slime . . . They are evil, Koril! Evil in ways no human can comprehend. They will devour man and then they will devour the Four Lords and us. You must . . ."

"*Jatik! Jatik! Hold on!* Just a little more! *Jatik!* Come back! I need to know . . . Oh, hell, what's the use? He's gone."

Koril sighed and shook his head, then got up from beside the dead man and looked around his desert domain. The bodies of the two naril still twitched nearby where he had slain them.

He spent the better part of an hour restaging the death scene. Sooner or later he knew that some party from Diamond Rock, even now covering the trail of chase and capture, would happen here, and he wanted to make it absolutely certain that any such party would draw the obvious conclusions. Essential to him was that party's belief that the naril and Jatik had finally finished each other. They would believe it. To get even this far required one of enormous power, and even so, only seeing the dead man's rainstorm from afar and recognizing it for the signature it was had brought him here. Too late, alas, too late for poor Jatik . . .

Still, he had learned much from the dead man. Or, more properly, Jatik had confirmed his information and his worst fears. But Koril was old—old and alone now. Power he had in abundance, but there were limits to an old man's endurance even with the best of powers.

He needed a new Company, he knew, and that would not be easy to assemble, particularly under Matuze's watchful eye. While she would assume that his messengers had all failed to report, there was no question that she would recognize the dead for who they were and guess who had sent them.

Still, he knew his course was already set and his resolve was firm. No matter what the odds, it must be done. There was no getting around the shock and revulsion of Jatik's last utterances. Both he and the dead man had been born and raised on worlds far from this one, and both had seen a lot in this universe before being exiled to this hell.

Hell . . . That was Charon, true enough. Every horror in the mind of man from the beginning of time to now was here, along with a physical landscape, climate, and plant and animal life appropriate for the worst of Dante's hells.

Koril knew this for a fact, and he knew that Jatik also knew and felt it.

What could a man already in hell see that so frightened him?

What sort of thing could cause a criminal imprisoned in hell with thousands of other criminals to label something unimaginably evil?

What was so monstrous that even the denizens of hell were repulsed and frightened by it?

Jatik had been a sadistic mass murderer without the slightest sense of good and evil. The very concepts had been alien to him. And yet, and yet—even he had now seen something so terrible that he *had* known evil before he died. There was a certain symmetry in that, anyway.

Still, the Four Lords had made a compact with whatever it was here on Charon. Their egos would protect them, Koril reflected sourly. For a while, anyway.

The Four Lords were evil by human standards. They were evil personified to many, including the confederacy itself. But they had not been evil to Jatik, not in the slightest.

Just what *had* Jatik seen? Into what terrible bondage had they sold themselves and mankind on their own egomaniacal delusions of grandeur?

It was almost as hot as a human being could stand there on the hard, desolate desert, yet Koril felt a sudden chill as he turned and walked away from the body of the dead man.

2

The most frustrating thing to a great military force is to discover that it is at war only long after the first blows of the enemy have been struck. Even more frustrating is when, even after the discovery of enemy action, you simply can't find the enemy.

The Confederacy was the culmination of all human history and culture. In the distant past, man had determined that expansion to the stars was the most interesting and preferable means of advancing civilization without racial suicide. Somehow the sporting instinct overrode all else in the human condition when the proposition was put correctly. National competition was something all people, regardless of background or ideology, could understand. They could work for, root for, and cheer on their home team against all comers.

As politics became dirtier and more and more irrational in the twentieth and twenty-first centuries, and total global annihilation grew more and more certain, man remembered that he had first set foot on the Moon because it had been sold as a sporting wager—a space race. Not that space had been ignored since—in fact, every country had been involved—but it had been a slow technocratic and military growth that sputtered here and there for lack of popular participation and support. Anybody with the spirit could try the Oregon Trail in the nineteenth century, or carve a city out of frozen Siberian tundra in the late twentieth, but the very people who were the pioneers of ancient times were excluded from this new frontier, no matter how limitless it was. The poor, the destitute, and the refugee as well as idealistic dreamers had settled and tamed the old frontiers, but they couldn't even get a ticket to the Moon in the age of space. Only the highly skilled specialist was able to get into space—or the very rich. The masses of Earth, even if they wanted to go, could not, nor did the dull and plodding development of space offer the same excitement that the space race had generated in the early explorer.

The governments of Earth came to understand this, and also saw a world of ever-increasing population and incredibly diminishing resources grow more and more apathetic toward life in general. A steady decline in living standards worldwide was something that every computer forecast as inevitable, and each group's demand that *its* country not be the one in decline put tremendous pressures on even the most totalitarian regimes and increased the pressure for total war.

Technology, however, offered a way out, a way that the various nations took reluctantly but with the realization that there was little else to do. Researchers had ultimately done the impossible and broken the universal speed limit. It was complex, and involved physics that did not contradict Einstein so much as deal in totally different areas where he was simply not relevant. The stars were open to exploration. Not that the distances were shrunk to nothing: within the first century, there were so many new places to go over such vast distances that it still took more than three years subjectively to travel from one end of man's domain to the edge of the frontier. This was still a far smaller price to pay than the generations such trips would otherwise have taken. It had, after all, taken some of the early American pioneers four to six months to reach California. But this new system had another big advantage. Building the ships and great engines needed took a lot of capital, but once built, they cost very little to operate, and size was not a factor in cost beyond air and food.

Only one world in a thousand was even terraformable, but there were *still* a lot of habitable worlds out there, and the nations of the world began to compete for them instead of for more tufts of worn-out Earth—and colonizing with incentives, so the poor and the dreamers finally got to go. It took the pressure off and provided a new spark to humanity. There was excitement and discovery in the air once more and all could be a part of it, and the resources were infinite.

But as generations were born on new worlds, generations who had never seen Earth and had only an abstract concept of what a Russia or an America or a Brazil or a Ghana was, the old concepts of nationality began to blur. Three generations later they were no longer Americans or Soviets or Brazilians but were natives of their own worlds, the only worlds they knew. Nor did the distance between worlds and the burgeoning numbers of worlds lend themselves to effective colonial government from afar. Fearful now less of destroying one another than of being left behind, cast off by the new populations on alien worlds, the old governments began to cooperate more than compete, to merge, over little more than another century, into what was in effect a single ruling instrumentality, the Confederacy, with a bureaucracy dominated by those old powers but presiding over a congress where each new world was represented.

The pooled resources and ever-expanding technology remade world after world, many into great paradises of which the people of old Earth had barely dreamed. Many diseases were wiped out; genetic manipulation made man and woman beautiful and nearly perfect. Careful genetic and cultural nudging produced a population each of whom had an equal but large slice of a very huge pie. People were bred and raised to do specific jobs, and they were the best people to do those jobs, too. It was a civilization without tension or fear—nearly a paradise. Worlds that reached such perfection were called the civilized worlds. Though wonderful places to live and work, these worlds were spiritually and culturally dead—totally stagnant.

Obviously the Confederacy could have totally controlled population and settled into this stasis, but they were the heirs to all of Earth's own history. Humanity might last in paradise for a million years, but once the spark of excitement and creativity was extinguished, it was dead, an extinct race. The answer, of course, was never to stop. Scouts would continue to be dispatched, scouts that would discover more and more worlds to settle, tame, and remake by the oddballs and misfits that even the civilized worlds occasionally created. The frontier became not merely the edge of expansion but a religion, an article of faith among the

Confederacy, something that could never be allowed to stop because it alone provided the safety valve, the creativity, the spark, the purpose to human existence.

As man filled up almost a quarter of his galaxy, he ran into some alien races. Not too many—and not nearly the number many had expected—but some. There were ones that inhabited worlds that no human could ever use, and these were simply watched for signs of future threat and generally ignored. Others used the same sorts of material as man, and these were treated in an age-old way. Those that could be modified and adapted to the Confederacy's way of doing things were welcomed into it, whether or not they wanted to come. Those that could not be culturally assimilated for one reason or another were ruthlessly eliminated, as many of the Indian tribes of America and the aborigines of Tasmania had been eliminated in ancient times. Many alien worlds were primitive and some were quite advanced, but all had one thing in common: the Confederacy was bigger and stronger and more ruthless than they were.

Then one day the powers that be in the Confederacy woke up to the fact that the moment they feared had finally arrived—somebody smarter than they were had found them first.

A robot so sophisticated it was beyond the Confederacy's technology—although only by a hair—managed to impersonate a security clerk in Military Systems Command. Managed to impersonate that clerk so well that it fooled the man's friends of many years, his co-workers, and even the very sophisticated security systems in Military Systems Command. It had gotten in, had stolen vital military secrets, and had almost made it out. One tiny slip was all it made, but that was enough. Still, this robot managed to survive two vacuums, crush thirty-centimeter armor-plate walls, shoot up into space and actually attain escape velocity, then to steal a ship in orbit and blast off. Military Systems Command managed to track and finally destroy it after they figured out where it was reporting.

The Warden Diamond.

Even in a society like the Confederacy, there were the superior misfits. For all of humanity's perfections in environment, genetics, and culture, there was always the by-product of such manipulation—the perfect criminal. They were few, but they existed, and because they could operate even in such societies as the civilized worlds, undetected in many cases for years, they were in fact the best of the best—those with that great spark the Confederacy nurtured and cherished. The petty ones could be "reeducated" or mindwiped and given a new personality. But these master criminals, these geniuses of crime and villainy, were far too valuable to be thus squandered. And yet no civilized prisons could hold them so the frontier would become their unrestricted playground.

Catching them was not the real problem, although some managed to do great damage before they were apprehended. All the Confederacy did was breed a new kind of super cop, a master detective type perfectly matched to the quarry. There were few of them, too—the Confederacy feared them almost as much as the criminals they caught—but they did their jobs well. They and their personally tailored and custom-matched self-aware analytical computers found the politically corrupt, the master crook, the psychopath, the most dangerous men and women ever produced in human history. But where could these people be put?

The Warden Diamond provided the final answer.

Halden Warden, a legendary space scout even in his own time, discovered the system nearly two hundred years before the robot was discovered in Military Systems Command. Warden disliked almost everything about the Confederacy, most of all other human beings, but only such an antisocial personality could stand the loneliness, the physical and mental hardships that came with deep-space scouting.

Warden, however, was worse than most. He spent as little time as possible in "civilization," often just long enough to refuel and reprovision. He flew farther, longer, and more often than any other scout before or since, and his discoveries set all-time records for their sheer volume alone. Unfortunately for his bosses, Warden felt that discovery was his *only* purpose. He left just about everything else, including preliminary surveys and reports, to those who would use his beamed coordinates to follow him. Not that he didn't do the work—he just didn't send the information back to the Confederacy until he felt like it, often years later.

Thus when the signal "4AW" came in, there was enormous excitement and anticipation—four human-habitable planets in one system! Such a phenomenon was simply unheard of, beyond all statistical probabilities, particularly considering how rare it was to find even one. They waited anxiously to hear the names the laconic scout would give the new worlds and his preliminary descriptions of them.

Then the report came, confirming their worst fears. He followed form, though, closest in to farthest out from the newly discovered sun.

"Charon," came the first report. "Looks like hell.

"Lilith," he continued. "Anything that pretty's got to have a snake in it.

"Cerberus," he named the third. "Looks like a real dog."

And, finally, "Medusa. Anybody who lives here would have to have rocks in his head."

The coordinates followed, along with a code confirming that Warden had done remote but no direct exploration—that is, he hadn't landed—and a final code, "ZZ," which filled them with some fear. It meant that there was something very odd about the place, so approach with extreme caution.

They cursed Crazy Warden even as they assembled the maximum-caution expedition. A full-scale science team, with two hundred of the best, most experienced Exploiter Team members aboard, backed up by four heavy cruisers armed to the teeth. They knew that Warden's reports were almost always right, but you never found out how until it was almost too late.

The huge F-type star had a massive solar system that included eleven gas giants, eight of them ringed spectacularly, as well as large numbers of comets, asteroids, and some large solid planets of no use. But the system had four worlds—four jewels—that stood out from all the rest, four worlds with abundant oxygen, nitrogen, and water.

And when they looked first at those four worlds, they

were almost exactly at right angles to one another in their orbits.

The Warden Diamond.

Of course, as the planets were in far different orbits this diamond formation was quite rare. In fact it has not been precisely duplicated since man first saw it.

Still, there was an uneasy feeling that somehow the Warden Diamond was not a natural thing. The Exploiter Team was suspicious, as Warden himself had been, and doubly cautious.

Charon, the world closest to the sun, was a hot and steamy world. It rained a lot of the time there, and the dominant life seemed to be reptilian, almost dinosaurlike. Seas covered much of the hothouse world, but although the atmosphere was hardly pleasant, man could live on it un-aided.

The second world, Lilith, was almost textbook perfect. Slightly smaller than Charon, it was roughly seventy percent water but far more temperate and gentler in the landscape. Mountains were low, and there were broad plains and swamps. Its axial tilt was so slight there were few seasons anywhere on the planet, and while it was warm to hot, it was comfortably warm, almost resort-type warm. It was a blue-green world, rich in plant life that was different but not *too* different from what man knew elsewhere, and its creatures were insectlike, from almost too small to see up to behemoths that still seemed harmless, perhaps even useful. It was the kind of world that terraformers aimed for and almost never achieved—and not a snake in sight.

Cerberus was harsher, but not much. Although it had great seasonal variations, none were all that unmanageable, and in the large tropical zones there was plenty of room for settlement—or there might have been if there had been some land. The trouble was, the entire world was covered by a great, deep ocean. Still, there was a strange sort of plant life there, which rose up from the ocean floor to break the surface and almost reach for the sky. Giant plant colonies, so huge, strong, and clumped together that they formed large, almost landlike masses. The seas held promise, though, of huge and vicious predators. It would not be an easy world to live on, and they could see why Warden called it a dog, particularly when compared with Lilith.

Finally, farthest out, there was Medusa, a hard, cold, rocky world with frozen seas, blinding snow, and mountains broken with the only evidence of vulcanism on the four worlds. There were some forests, but mostly tundra and grasslands. It was an ugly place.

But back on old Earth, man had lived and built in lands at least as bad as Medusa. In the temperate zones people, with a lot of hard work and a lot of time, could even build a civilization there. Still, to want to go to a place like that and make it your home, well—you had to have rocks in your head.

Four worlds, from steaming hell to frozen tundra. Four worlds that still had temperature extremes that could be borne and air and water that could be used. It was incredible. Fantastic. And it was for real.

Not being crazy, the Exploiter Team chose Lilith as its main base, settling in on a beautiful island in a tropical lagoon. After a week or so of preliminary setup, smaller teams were sent out to the other three from Lilith to set up provisional base camps.

Once down, the Exploiter Teams were placed in strict quarantine from the military and all commerce with the Confederacy. It would take at least a year with the team serving as the guinea pigs, poking and probing and testing, before others would set foot on any of the worlds. They had shuttlecraft capable of traveling between the four planets, if need be, and ground and air transportation for their own work, but nothing interstellar. The risk was too great; man had been burned too many times to take any chances.

It took Lilith's snake about six months to size up the newcomers.

Scientists eventually gave it a long, incomprehensible name, but everybody referred to it as the Warden organism—or, often, as the Warden beast. It was a tiny little thing, not really life as we knew it, and so it hadn't been recognized as such until far too late. And yet it was pervasive. It was attached to almost every solid and liquid molecule on Lilith, organic and inorganic, almost as a component of the molecular structure itself. It was not sentient—nothing that small and that elementary could be—but it was omnipresent and it knew what it wanted. It didn't like molecules that didn't have it inside, and it did a very nice job of dissolving almost everything alien to Lilith, leaving all the equipment, even the clothes on the scientists' backs, as so much fine powder. Lilith's little beast could not cope with any synthetic compounds, and almost everything the Exploiter Teams used or wore was in fact synthetic. The scientists themselves, and some of their plants, were nonsynthetic carbon-based organic stuff, and the Warden organism could cope with that. It quickly invaded every cell and set up housekeeping, modifying each cell to suit itself in a nicely symbiotic relationship. This was scant comfort to sixty-two stunned, stark-naked scientists that they never again had to worry about colds and that even minor wounds would heal themselves.

Thanks to the expeditionary bases on the other three worlds, the Warden organism, it was theorized, had been carried there by the first to settle. Of course, the three other planets were quite different from Lilith—different gravities, different levels of radiation, different atmospheric balances. The Warden organism could not adapt those whole worlds to its Lilith standard, but the submicroscopic creature had a hell of a survival instinct. On Medusa, for example, it adapted the host organism—the people, and, quickly, the plants and animals—so as to ensure their, and its, survival. On Cerberus and Charon it struck a balance in the hosts that was to its liking, but which produced by-products of physical change not relevant to it but rather resulting from that balance it found most comfortable. This produced strange by-products in the humans so infected.

A cure was sought, but to no avail. The Warden organism, it seemed, so changed the host's body chemistry that the host could no longer live *without* the Wardens there—but the Wardens required more, something else, something not clear. When you removed a Warden-infected person from the Diamond, the organisms died—and so did its unfortunate host.

The mutation was so complete that those on one Warden world *could* move from world to world, but could not move outside the system—ever. Humans *could* live, work, and build in the Warden Diamond, but once there, they could never leave.

It became the perfect prison for those master criminals.

So first had come the scientists, then the criminal elite. Over two hundred years a large indigenous human population had arisen on the four worlds as well—by far the majority. But the criminal element was the elite and the rulers. They hated the Confederacy for what it had done to them, and thanks to the Wardens within them, no longer felt human but something quite apart, alien, having no loyalty or kinship to the civilized worlds. Quickly they established control over their worlds, and quickly, too, they took advantage of interstellar communications to reestablish contact with their far-flung criminal empires and even with the Confederacy itself. They were quick to realize that the Warden Diamond not only kept them *in*, it also kept the Confederacy *out*. They controlled the fate of all sent to the Warden Diamond, and even the best Confederacy agent not only was at their mercy but was also, like them, changed and trapped there forever.

It usually took very little time for such agents to realize on which side their bread was buttered.

Their old cronies Outside in the rest of the Confederacy were quick to note that, except for Lilith, one could steal the *Mona Lisa* and by remote courier could leave it in the Diamond in plain sight—and no one could touch it, let alone recover it. But since the *Mona Lisa* was made of natural pigment and canvas, and was inanimate, it could not "die" should the thief ask for its removal, retrieving it beyond the range of Warden life. The Warden Diamond was the perfect repository, for the cops couldn't even confiscate the evidence.

It became the safe-deposit box for the rulers of the Confederacy, because of its total inaccessibility. Much of the wealth and many of the secrets of the great interstellar empire went through the Warden Diamond, which gained more and more by proving itself reliable and secretive.

To the leaders of each of the worlds—the best of the best, the criminal elite, the top crooks evolution could produce—accrued tremendous power and wealth that reached to the far limits of the Confederacy and far exceeded their powers back in the old days. These four leaders of the four Warden worlds were probably the most powerful human beings alive.

The Four Lords of the Diamond.

And yet so much did they hate the Confederacy for their exile that they were prepared to do almost anything to get back at it.

And now an alien race of unknown form and unknown size, power, and intent had discovered humanity before humanity had discovered it. Discovered and poked and probed until that alien race understood the system man had built very well indeed.

Seeing how other alien civilizations had been treated, they knew war was inevitable, but were by no means sure they could win it. And thus had the aliens contacted the Four Lords of the Diamond, and thus had they made a spectacular deal.

They took out a contract on human civilization.

The Four Lords, motivated by revenge and by unknown inducements from the aliens, would have full access to the alien technology and their own far-flung criminal networks as well as to the experiences of all those exiles on the four Warden worlds. The aliens would remain unknown, unseen, while the Four Lords would be so powerful as to be untouchable.

"You have a tough problem," the young man sympathized. "You don't have any reliable people on the Warden worlds, and anybody capable of doing what has to be done goes over to the other side. What *can* you do?"

Commander Krega, head of Confederacy Security, nodded in agreement. "Exactly. You see where this puts us.

Now, of course, we *do* have some people down there. None
are a hundred percent reliable, and all of them would slit
your throat in an instant if doing so was in their best interests. But there are occasional inducements, small payoffs of
one sort or another, even a little blackmail on ones with
close relatives back in the Confederacy, that give us a little
edge. A little, but not much, since the Four Lords are
pretty ruthless when it comes to what they perceive as treason. Our only advantage is that the worlds are still fairly
new to us and thus relatively sparsely settled. There is no
totalitarian control on any of them, but different systems
and hierarchies on each."

The young man nodded. "I have the uneasy feeling that
this is leading up to something, but I must remind you of
what you told me about past agents, and also that I'd be
but one man on one world."

Commander Krega grinned. "No, it's not quite like that
at all. You're a damned good detective and you know it.
You've located people in places nobody else looked twice
at. You've outmaneuvered and outguessed sophisticated
computers and some of the best criminal minds ever
known, despite the fact that you are still quite young. You
are the youngest person with the rank of Inspector in the
history of the Confederacy.

"We have two different problems here. One is that we
must identify this alien force and trace it back whence it
came. We must know who they are and where they are and
what their intentions are. Even now it may be too late, but
we must act as if it were not. Also, we must neutralize
their information conduit, the Four Lords. How would you
do it?"

The young man smiled thoughtfully. "Pay the Four
Lords more than the aliens are. Put 'em to work for us."

"Impossible. We already thought of that," the commander told him. "No, making a deal is out. We have no
cards."

"Then you need somebody good down there on each
world, looking for clues to the aliens. There has to be some
sort of direct contact: they have to get their information
out and their little playtoys like that fancy robot pro-

grammed and in. An agent might turn traitor, but he wouldn't be motivated by revenge if he were a volunteer, and he'd sure as hell feel closer to humanity than to some aliens of unknown looks and designs."

"Agreed. And it would have to be the very best for all four. Someone who could survive, even prosper under their conditions while having the ability to collect enough data and get it out. But how do we buy the time we also need?"

The young man grinned. "Easy. At least easy to say— maybe nearly impossible to do. You kill all four Lords. Others would take their places, of course, but in the interim you'd buy months, maybe years."

"Our thinking exactly," Krega agreed. "And so we ran it through the computers. Master detective, loyal, willing to volunteer, and with an Assassin's License. Four needed, plus a coordinator, since they all would have to be put to work simultaneously and would, obviously, have no likely reason or means to contact one another. Plus, of course, spares for insurance who could be sent in if something happened to one or more of the others. We fed in all the attributes and requirements and you popped out."

The young man chuckled dryly. "I'll bet. Me and who else?"

"Nobody else. Just you."

It was an elaborate and complex project—and the most closely guarded secret of the Confederacy. Called the Merton Process, after its inventor, it involved actual personality transfer. It was a rather messy affair, and the new personality not only totally destroyed the old but "took" in only one out of thirty or so cases. The others died, sometimes quite horribly. But the Confederacy had a number of expendables for such purposes and didn't really think twice about it. Originally conceived of simply as as a way of securing immortality for the rulers of the Confederacy and the best and brightest brains it had, the Merton Process was now to be put to a more rigorous test.

One very special man's entire personality was recorded, digitalized, quantified, and stored in the Merton computers, which would then be used to create four new hims—all with his personality and intellect but in four very different bodies. Meanwhile the original himself would be out there in space, in his special module with his complementary computer partner. A tiny organic transmitter implanted in the brains of his counterparts on the Warden worlds would send all that they saw and did back to the module, the raw mass of data going into the computer, then filtered through the original detective's own mind to form a subjective report. The combination—the objective raw data and the subjective report—would allow dispassionate analysis of all the data gathered by the counterparts below.

The young man was thoughtful for a moment. "And what if I refuse after all this? Or to put it another way, what if I say to go ahead and my, ah, alter egos decide once down not to follow through?"

Krega grinned. "Consider what I'm offering. We have the capacity to make you immortal—if you succeed. If you succeed, no reward would be high enough. You are an atheist. You know that when you go, you go forever— unless you succeed. Then you and, because of the soft imprints, your alter egos as well will continue to exist. Continue to live on. I think it's quite an inducement."

The young man considered it. "I wonder if *they* will see it that way," he mused.

Four Lords of the Diamond. Four clever, enormously powerful people to kill. Four keys to an enigma that could well spell the end of humanity. Five problems, five puzzles.

Krega didn't really have to offer a reward. It was irresistible.

3

He reentered his command module from the great picket ship that was always on station near the Warden Diamond, just beyond the life range of the Warden organism. Totally protected, it was a great city in space with all the amenities, offering both comfort and security. Still, none of the thousands aboard the combined research and quarantine enforcement ship knew what the man was doing there, nor could they enter or in any way discover the secrets of the module.

"You have been away more than three days," the computer chided him. "We have had an incoming data report from Charon all this time."

"I know, I know," he grumbled. "I just . . . needed some time, that was all. I needed a little contact with the Confederacy and its people." It shamed him a bit to admit that last, even to himself, such a blow was it to his self-image, but he was not the same man who had first entered this module so long ago. The experience he had shared with his counterparts on Lilith and Cerberus had changed him greatly, and he really didn't like it one bit. It wasn't as if he were getting reports from agents down there: hell, those people were *him*.

The sociopathic worlds of the Four Lords were a contradiction of every single principle and belief he'd always held so dear. It wasn't so much seeing the Confederacy and its values the way the criminals did—that was excusable, since he was dealing with psychopaths of one sort or another. But when he himself down there on those worlds began to doubt and finally fractured all those bedrock ideals—well, that was something else again.

The Confederacy did not look so good, so much like paradise, when viewed from outside, and that view was difficult to refute. He feared for his own sanity most of all, and that made him fear another report, another secondhand life, yet another insane challenge to his orderly universe. He knew it, understood it, but that didn't help much at all.

The fact was, he most of all didn't like discovering that he was as human as all the others in the human race, subject to the same fears, emotions, and failings. He had always thought himself superior, above all that. No more, no more . . .

Nor had it escaped him that he was learning too much, knew too much even at this point. He was a tool of the Confederacy, just as a saw, drill, hammer, or—well, computer—was a tool. Useful to get the job done; then, as if such a tool grew, say, radioactive, readily destroyed when the job was over. He wasn't kidding himself. They didn't even have to worry about keeping any sparks alive within him—four of him were already down there, on each of the Warden worlds.

The moment he solved the riddle of the Four Lords of the Diamond he was a dead man. His faithful computer might jettison the module into the sun or explode it, might supercharge it with electricity. The worst part was, he couldn't even opt out now, not even with a mindwipe. They'd just trot out the Merton recording, make another him, have that new him go through the same experiences—and reach the same point he was at right now.

But *he* would have to solve the puzzle first. He and he alone—not even the computer—would decide that terrible moment. It was an ironic, terrible box, and he knew it. The fate of human civilization, perhaps human life, was very much in his hands. Yet he could save them or himself—not both.

His final, agonized decisions were nonetheless a compromise. First solve the puzzle. *Then* decide what to do with that solution. What troubled him most was the nature of that decision. He suspected even now that the nature of this alien threat was not as good and evil as he had originally believed.

He sat down at the lab screen and thought a moment. "Put up a wide scan of the Lilith organism," he told the computer.

The screen in front of him lit up and showed a strange enlargement. Its closest relative was a virus, yet it was infinitely smaller, an alien abstract design of tiny lines and pits actually able to combine on an atomic level with actual molecules—*molecules*! It wasn't a real creature but a few extra chemical ingredients on the end of a molecular formula, extras that somehow didn't really change what the molecule was but nonetheless controlled it. Once organism and molecules were linked, to remove the organism from inorganic molecules was relatively simple—they were always on the end. But in carbon molecules the Warden was not at the end at all but in the middle. Remove the Warden from a carbon chain and the chain fell apart—and so did the individual it helped make up. In much the same way, the synthetics with their odd and unnatural chains attracted the Wardens as carbon molecules did, but while the Wardens wormed their way in, they couldn't stick. Synthetics disintegrated.

There was an advantage to that, from the Confederacy point of view. It kept the Four Lords and their worlds technologically far behind the Confederacy, and limited their industry to what they could take from their own worlds and from the asteroids and other space junk in the system that the Warden somehow recognized as "natural." In fact there were no important heavy metals on any of the Diamond worlds; mines on the asteroids and on the moons of the nearest gas giant, Momrath, provided the raw materials for the Warden worlds that could use *any* machines. Many down there could easily build an interstellar spacecraft, but they didn't have the materials to do so.

And yet, and yet . . .

That *thing* on the screen couldn't possibly be alive, not in any sense that any biologist understood life. More than that, it didn't *fit*, not on the Diamond. The four worlds down there were very different, yes, but every one of them—*every one*—was composed of logical, rational, carbon-based life. Most of it wasn't nearly as exotic as life on most planets in and near the Confederacy itself, yet it was consistent and logically there.

But nowhere was there any sign of anything else like the Warden organism. It didn't belong there, not on those worlds. It had no clear ancestors, no relatives, no dead ends. In fact, it had no place or reason to evolve down there.

"The remote probes—the ones that preceded the initial landings on all four worlds. Why didn't those core samples show the Warden?"

"The instruments were not really designed to look for something like it," the computer replied. "Only after they knew something was there could they find it.

"Mighty poor procedures," he noted. "The whole idea of an exploration is to find just such new threats as this."

"If a question has not been asked it will rarely be answered," the computer responded philosophically. "In other words, nobody can think of everything. Still, why the interest in the old samples? Surely you don't think the Warden organism itself can be the aliens?"

"No, of course not. It's an incredibly odd and alien thing, but even in its collective mode it's hardly capable of a consciousness. You know, there are worlds in our catalogue where this thing wouldn't really shock me or any of the scientists one bit—but not here. The thing doesn't fit here. It's as if an iceberg were suddenly found on a tropical world—it just doesn't logically belong there."

"A number of researchers and theorists have noted as much. Some have even theorized an interstellar origin—it arrived, perhaps in a meteorite, and set up housekeeping. That is the prevailing theory."

He nodded. "But why just on Lilith? Or was it just on Lilith? How do we know we were the carriers to the other three worlds? Perhaps by the time we found the thing all four had already been contaminated, if they were."

"It has been postulated that the Wardens existed on all four worlds, too," the computer told him. "Sampling work was taken from a base ship that was actually beyond the life range of the Warden organism. However, since plant life did not disintegrate in the Warden manner it was simply assumed that the Wardens were not yet there."

"Assumed . . . I wonder. What about the plant samples from Lilith, then?"

"I just checked on that. The fact is, all vegetation died in the samples from Lilith, but there were a thousand natural explanations and it was not taken as a terrible sign. It wasn't unusual enough in general surveys of alien worlds, really. Many alien plants are interdependent on organisms and conditions requiring exacting biospheres to survive—a minuscule change in pressure or temperature, for example. Although Lilith's samples died first, all of the samples died within a period of a day or two at most. This is normal and expected. You can't possibly hope to duplicate every exact condition for totally alien forms of life. Still, your proposition is now beyond proof. All four worlds have the Warden organism."

"Still, it is an interesting speculation."

"Why? If the alien-spore theory is correct, and it seems most logical, it might easily hit all four as one. That proves nothing."

"Maybe not," he murmured to himself. "Maybe . . ." He got up and walked forward to the control area. "Who's in?"

"Charon."

"Too bad. Most of all I want Medusa now, I think. I'm beginning to think the confirmation of my theories must lie there—and perhaps beyond. I suspect that Charon's not going to add any new pieces."

"You're sure you just aren't trying to avoid the experience?"

He stopped and looked around quizzically. Was he? He *did* dread this new experience, it was true, but was he kidding himself, or the computer?

He sat down in the master command chair and adjusted it for maximum comfort. The computer lowered the small probes, which he carefully placed on his head; then the thinking machine that was part of the module itself administered the measured injections and began the master readout.

For a while he floated in a semihypnotic fog, but slowly the images started forming in his brain as they had before. Only now they seemed more definite, clearer, more like his own thoughts.

The drugs and small neural probes did their job. His own

mind and personality receded, replaced by a similar, yet oddly different pattern.

"The agent is commanded to report," the computer ordered, sending the command deep into his own mind, a mind no longer quite his own.

Recorders clicked on.

Slowly the man in the chair cleared his throat. He mumbled, groaned, and made odd, disjointed words and sounds as his mind received the data and coded, classified, adjusted, and sorted it all out.

Finally the man began to speak.

CHAPTER ONE

Rebirth

After Krega's talk and a little preparation to put my own affairs in order—this would be a long one—I checked into the Confederacy Security Clinic. I'd been here many times before, of course, but not knowingly for this purpose. Mostly, this was where they programmed you with whatever information you'd need for a mission and where, too, you were "reintegrated." Naturally, the kind of work I did was often extralegal—a term I prefer to "illegal," which implies criminal intent—and much of it was simply too hot ever to be known. To avoid such risks, all agents had their own experience of a mission wiped from their minds whenever it involved sensitive matters.

It may seem like a strange life, going about not knowing where you have been or what you've done, but it has its compensations. Because any potential enemy, military or political, knows you've been wiped, you can live a fairly normal, relaxed life outside of a mission structure. There's no purpose to coming after you—you have no knowledge of what you've done or why or for whom. In exchange for these blanks, an agent of the Confederacy lives a life of luxury and ease, with an almost unlimited supply of money and with all the comforts supplied. I bummed around, swam, gambled, ate in the best restaurants, played a little semipro ball or cube—I'm pretty good, and it keeps me in shape. I enjoyed every minute of it, and except for my regular requalification training sessions, four-to-six-week stints that resemble military basic training only nastier and more sadistic, I felt no guilt at my playboy life. The training sessions are to make sure that your body and mind don't stagnate from all that good living. They have sensors

in you that they constantly monitor to determine when you
need a good refresher.

I often wondered just how sophisticated these sensors
were. The notion that a whole security staff could see all
my debauchery and indiscretions used to worry me, but
after a while you learn to ignore it.

The life offered in trade is just too nice. Besides, what
could I do about it, anyway? People on most of the civilized worlds these days had such sensors, although hardly
to the degree and sophistication of mine. How else could a
population so vast and so spread out possibly be kept orderly, progressive, and peaceful?

But when a mission came up it wasn't practical to forgo
all that past experience. A wipe without storage simply
wouldn't have been a good idea, since a good agent gets
better by not repeating his mistakes. So in the Security
Clinic they had everything you ever experienced on file,
and the first thing you did was get the rest of you put back
so you would be whole for whatever mission they'd
dreamed up this time. I was always amazed when I rose
from that chair with my past fully restored. Just the clear
memories of the things I'd done always surprised me—that
I, of all people, had done this or that.

The only difference this time, I knew, was that the process would be taken one step further. Not only would the
complete me get up from that table, but the same memory
pattern would be impressed on other minds, other bodies—
as many as needed until a take was achieved.

I wondered what the others would be like, those four
versions of myself. Physically different, probably—the offenders they got here didn't normally come from the civilized worlds, where people had basically been standardized
in the name of equality. No, these people would be from
the frontier, from the traders and miners and freebooters
that always existed at the edge of expansion. They were
certainly necessary in an expanding culture, since a high
degree of individuality, self-reliance, originality, and creativity was required in the dangerous situations in which
they lived. A stupid government would have eliminated all
such, but a stupid government quickly degenerates and

loses its vitality and growth potential by standardization. Utopia was for the masses, of course, but not for everyone—or it wouldn't *be* Utopia very long.

That was the original reason for the Warden Diamond Reserve in the first place. Some of these hard frontier people are so individualistic that they become a threat to the stability of the civilized worlds. The trouble is, anybody able to crack the fabric that holds our society together is most likely the smartest, nastiest, meanest, cleverest, most original sort of person humanity can produce—and therefore not somebody whose mind should idly be wiped clean. The Diamond, it was felt, would effectively trap people like that forever, yet allow them continued creative opportunities, which when properly monitored might still produce something of value for the Confederacy.

Of course the felons down there were anxious to please as well, since the alternative was death. Eventually such creative minds made themselves indispensable to the Confederacy and ensured their continued survival. That possibility had been foreseen, but it wasn't altogether unwelcome. Like all criminal organizations in the past, they provided services that people were convinced should be illegal or were immoral or some such, but that masses of people wanted anyway.

The damned probe hurt like hell. Usually there was just some tingling, then a sensation much like sleep, and you woke up a few minutes later in the chair yourself once again. This time the tingling became a painful physical force that seemed to enter my skull, bounce around, then seize control of my head. It was as if a giant fist had grabbed my brain and squeezed, then released, then squeezed again. Instead of drifting off to sleep, I passed out.

I woke up and groaned slightly. The throbbing was gone, but the memory was still all too current and all too real. It was several minutes, I think, before I found enough strength to sit up.

The old memories flooded back, and again I amazed myself by recalling many of my past exploits. I wondered if my surrogate selves would get similar treatment, considering that they couldn't be wiped after this mission as I could. That caused me to make a mental note that those surrogates would almost certainly have to be killed if they did have my entire memory pattern. Otherwise a lot of secrets would be loose in the Warden Diamond, many in the hands of people who'd know just what sort of use to make of them.

No sooner had I had that thought than I had an odd feeling that something was very wrong. I looked around the small room in which I'd awakened and realized immediately the source of that feeling.

This wasn't the Security Clinic, wasn't anyplace I'd ever seen before. A tiny cubicle, about twelve cubic meters total, including the slightly higher than normal ceiling. In it was a small cot on which I'd awakened, a small basin and next to it a standard food port, and in the wall, a pull-down toilet. That was it. Nothing else—or was there?

I looked around and spotted the most obvious easily. Yes, I couldn't make a move without being visually and probably aurally monitored. The door was almost invisible and there was certainly no way to open it from inside. I knew immediately where I was.

It was a prison cell.

Far worse, I could feel a faint vibration that had no single source. It wasn't irritating; in fact, it was so dim as to be hardly noticeable, but I knew what it was. I was aboard a ship, moving somewhere through space.

I stood up, reeling a little bit from a slight bout of dizziness that soon passed, and looked down at my body. It was small and lithe, almost wiry, but there was muscle there and no fat at all. I had a few rough-looking scars, but aside from the evident fact that they had been more crudely treated than by a meditech they didn't look all that unusual. The skin was naturally dark, with an almost olive complexion that was unusual but apparently quite natural. A natural-born body, then, and not one that had been genetically engineered. It would be psychologically difficult to adjust to being not merely short but small. I could only stand there, stunned, for I don't know how long.

I'm not me! my mind screamed at me. *I'm one of them*—one *of the surrogates!*

I sat back down on the cot, telling myself that it just wasn't possible. I knew who I was, remembered every bit, every detail, of my life and work.

My shock gave way after a while to anger—anger and frustration. I was a copy, an imitation of somebody else entirely, somebody still alive and kicking and possibly monitoring my every move, my every thought. I hated that other then, hated him with a pathological force beyond reason. He would sit there comfortable and safe, watching me work, watching me do it all—and when the mission was over, he'd go home for debriefing, return to that easy life, while I—

They were going to dump me on a world of the Warden Diamond, trap me like some kind of master criminal, imprison me there, hold me there for the rest of my life—of this body's life, anyway. And then? When my job was done? I'd said it myself upon awakening—passed my own sentence. The things I knew! I would be monitored at all times, of course. Monitored and killed if I blew any of those secrets. Killed anyway at the completion of the mission just for insurance's sake.

My training came into automatic play at that point, overriding the shock and anger. I regained control and considered everything that I knew.

Monitor? Sure, more than ever. I recalled Krega saying that there was some sort of organic linkup. Are you enjoying this, you son of a bitch? Are you getting pleasure from vicariously experiencing my reaction?

My training clicked in again. It didn't matter, I told myself. First of all, I knew just what he must be thinking—and that was an advantage. *He* of all people would know that I would be a damned tough son of a bitch to kill.

It was a shock to discover that you are not who you thought you were but some artificial creation. It was a shock, too, to realize that the old life, the life you remembered even if you personally didn't experience it, was gone forever. No more civilized worlds, no more casinos or beautiful women or— And yet as I sat there, I adjusted. That was what they picked men like me for from the start—our ability to adjust and adapt to almost anything.

It was not my body, but I was still me. Memory and thought and personality were the individual, not his body. This was no different than a biological disguise, I told myself, of a particularly sophisticated sort. As to who was really me—it seemed to me that this personality, these memories, were no more that other fellow's than my own. Until I got up from that chair back in the Security Clinic I'd really been somebody else anyway. A lot of me, my memories and training, had been missing. That old between-missions me was the artificial me, the created me, I thought. He, that nonentity playboy that presently did not exist, was the artificial personality. Me—the real me—was bottled up and stored in their psychosurgical computers and only allowed to come out when needed—and for good reason. Unlocked, I was as much a danger to the power structure as to whomever they set me against.

And I was good. The best, Krega had called me. That's why I was here now, in this body, in this cell, on this ship. And I wouldn't be wiped and I wouldn't be killed if I could help it. That other me, sitting there in the console— somehow I no longer hated him very much, no longer felt anything at all for him. When this was all over he'd be wiped once more—perhaps get killed himself if my brother agents on the Diamond and I found out too much. At best he'd return to being that stagnant milquetoast.

Me, on the other hand . . . I would still be here, still live on, the *real* me. I would become more complete than he would.

I was under no illusions, though. Kill me they would, if they could, if I didn't do their bidding. They'd do it automatically, by robot satellite and without qualms. *I* would. But my vulnerability would last only until I mastered my new situation and accustomed myself to my new and permanent home. I felt that with a deep sense of certainty, for I knew their methods and how they thought. I'd have to do their dirty work for them, and they knew it—but only until I could get around it. They could be beaten, even on their own turf. That was why they had people like me in the first place. To uncover those who had expertly covered over their whole lives and activities, who had managed to totally vanish from their best monitors. To uncover them and get them.

But there'd be no new expert agent sent to get me if *I* beat them. They'd just be putting somebody else in the same position.

I realized then, as they had undoubtedly figured, that I had no choice but to carry out the mission. Only so long as I was doing what they wanted would I be safe from them while still in that vulnerable position. After—well, we'd see.

The thrill of the challenge took over, as it always did. There was a puzzle to be solved, were objectives to be accomplished. I liked to win. Doing so was even easier when you felt nothing about the cause, just the challenge of the problem and the opponent and the physical and intellectual effort needed to meet that challenge. Find out about the alien menace. The outcome no longer concerned me either way, since I would be trapped on a Warden world from now on anyway. If the aliens won the coming confrontation, the Wardens would survive as allies. If they lost—well, it wouldn't make a damned bit of difference, only maintain the status quo. That meant the alien problem was purely an intellectual challenge and that made the situation perfect.

The other assignment created a similar situation. Seek out the Lord of that particular Diamond world and kill him if I could. In a sense this would be more difficult, for I'd be operating on totally unfamiliar ground and would therefore require time and possibly allies. Another challenge. And if I got him, it could only increase my own power and position over the long term. If he got me instead, of course, that would solve everybody's problem, but the thought of losing is abhorrent to me. That set the contest in the best terms, from my point of view. Trackdown and assassination was the ultimate game—either you won or you died and never had to live with the thought that you lost.

It suddenly occurred to me that the only real difference that probably existed between me and a Lord of the Dia-

mond was that I was working *for* the law and he—or she—
against it. But no, that wasn't right, eigher. On his world *he*
was the law and I would be working against it. Fine. Dead
heat on moral grounds.

The only thing wrong at this point, I reflected, was that
they were starting me at a tremendous disadvantage and I
disliked having more handicaps than absolutely necessary.
The normal procedure was to program all pertinent information into my brain before setting me off on a mission,
but they hadn't done it this time. Probably, I thought, because they had me once on the table for four seperate missions, and the transfer process to a new body was hard
enough without trying to add anything afterwards. Still, the
outcome put me in a deep pit. I thought sourly that somebody should have thought about that.

Somebody did, but it was a while before I discovered
how. About an hour after I had awakened a little bell
clanged near the food port and I walked over to it. Almost
instantly a hot tray appeared, along with a thin plastic fork
and knife I recognized as the dissolving type. They'd melt
into a sticky puddle in an hour or less, then dry up into a
powder shortly after that. Standard for prisoners.

The food was lousy, but I hadn't expected better. The
vitamin-enriched fruit drink with it, though, was pretty
good. I made the most of the drink, keeping the thin, clear
container which was *not* the dissolving type in case I
wanted water later. The rest I put back in the port, and it
vaporized neatly. All nice and sealed. You couldn't even
draw more than a thimbleful of water at a time from the
tap.

About the only thing they couldn't control was bodily
functions, and a half hour or so after eating my first meal
as a new man, say, I just had to go. On the far wall was a
panel market *Toilet* and a small pull ring. Simple, standard stuff, the same sort of thing you might get in a cheap
cabin on a passenger liner. I pulled the ring, the thing
came down—and damned if there wasn't a paper-thin
probe in the recess behind it.

So I sat down on the john, leaned back against the panel,
and got a brief and relief at the same time.

The thing worked by skin contact—don't ask me how. I'm not one of the tech brains. The system was not as good as a programming, but it allowed them to talk to me, even send me pictures that only I could see and hear.

"By now I hope you're over the shock of discovering who and what you are." Krega's voice came to me, seemingly forming in my brain. It was a shock to realize that not even my jailers could hear or see a thing.

"We have to brief you this way simply because the transfer process is delicate enough as it is. Oh, don't worry about it—it's permanent. But we prefer to allow as much time as possible for your brain patterns to fit in and adapt without subjecting the brain to further shock. Besides, we haven't the time to allow you to 'set in' completely, as it were. So this will have to do, and I profoundly regret it, for I feel that you have an exceptionally difficult assignment."

I felt the excitement rising within me. The challenge, the challenge . . .

"Your objective world is Charon, nearest to the sun of the Diamond colonies," the Commander's voice continued. "If there is a single place in the universe that will drive sane people mad and insane people to ecstasy, it is Charon. There is no way to adequately explain the effects of being there. You will have to find that out for yourself, and you will receive a thorough orientation briefing from Charon itself after you land.

"The imprint ability of this device is limited," he continued, "but we can send you one basic thing that may or may not be of use to you on Charon. It is a physical-political map of the entire planet, as complete and up-to-date as we could make it."

That puzzled me. Why would such a map *not* be of use? What kind of place was this, anyway? Before I could mull that over further and curse my inability to ask Krega questions, I felt a sharp pain in my back, then a short wave of dizziness and nausea. But when the discomfort cleared, I found the complete map was clearly and indelibly etched in my mind.

Following this came a stream of facts about the place not likely to be too detailed in any indoctrination lecture.

The planet was roughly 42,000 kilometers at the equator—or from pole back to pole, allowing for topographic differences. Like all four Diamond worlds, Charon was basically a ball—highly unusual as planets go, even though everybody, including me, thinks of all major planets as round.

The gravity was roughly .88 norm, so I'd feel a bit lighter and be able to jump further. That would take a slight adjustment in timing, and I made a note to work on that first and foremost. Charon was a tad richer in oxygen, not really enough to matter, but it was overloaded with water vapor, which probably accounted for that extra oxygen in the first place.

The planet had a reasonable axial tilt, which normally would have meant strong seasonal changes, but 158,551,000 kilometers out from an F-type star it was basically a choice of hot, hotter, still hotter, and hotter than hell. There were no polar caps—the circulation of warm ocean water prevented it—but there *was* sometimes ice in the dead of winter in the arctic or antarctic circle regions, so even on a tremendously tropical world you *could* freeze, but as both polar regions were entirely water, it wasn't likely you'd ever get there.

Equatorial temperatures were almost at the limit of human endurance: temperatures of sixty degrees centigrade or more had been measured there, along with near-lethal radiation levels for brief periods near the time of the sun's direct rays. There was sufficient land in the more temperate zones for the mere eleven million or so people who inhabited the place. Not that the temperate zones were all *that* temperate—in the latitudes with the largest populations temperatures still reached above fifty degrees centigrade at midsummer and rarely fell below twenty-five degrees in the dead of winter—but they were better than that equator. The three major continental land masses, however, were spaced above, on, and just below the equator, thus keeping everybody in the hothouse. A day was about twenty-nine standard hours, not enough of a difference from that to which I was accustomed to be a real factor, and a year was a short 282 Charon days.

Three continents—one not very useful that was mountainous and had large stretches of desert blocked from rain by the landforms; the other two basically tropical rain forests where the rain damn near never stopped. Not a cheery place at all, I reflected, remembering that old Warden had named this his vision of hell. Not far off the mark.

Well, I'd better get used to loving it, I told myself. Short of suicide, I had no way to avoid calling it home.

"Charon is the only one of the Diamond worlds with a female Lord," Krega continued. "I would not, however, count on your considerable charm to tame Aeolia Matuze. She is something of a political genius, and as hard and cynical as a human can become. At one time she was actually on the Confederacy Council, and it's a sure bet that a lot of the aliens' information on our political and military structure came from her. Her crime might best be called an excess of ambition; she skillfully manipulated whole governmental forces and key individuals in the governments and military and was well on the way to pulling off something of a coup d'etat, which would have in effect substituted her for the Council. Don't laugh—she came very close. Needless to say, she was well enough connected to be sent to the Diamond, where she was fifteen years into the system before taking complete charge only four years ago. It appears that her predecessor actually retired, although we consider this so unlikely that the retirement was almost certainly forced by Matuze. Do not underestimate her! In another age and time we would probably all be worshiping her as a goddess."

Aeolia Matuze. I remembered her from the distant past and from some of my history indoctrinations. I also vaguely recall that she had died and there had actually been an official period of mourning back when I was still a kid. So now at last I knew the truth about her, and it was fascinating. A formidable opponent indeed. I had to wonder if the aristocratic beauty my mind recalled was still as stunning after nineteen years on Charon.

The rest of the briefing was pretty much routine, and after it was over I simply got off the john and pushed it back into the wall. I heard a flushing sound and, the next time I used it, discovered that my waste wasn't the only thing flushed. The direct neural transmission had taken less than a minute to transfer all the information they could pack into it. Extremely efficient, the security boys, I told myself. Even my ever-vigilant jailers on the other end of those lenses and mikes would have no idea that I was anybody other than who I was supposed to be.

As to who that was, I'd gotten my first mental picture of myself from the briefing. My impression of myself as small was very true—barely 157 centimeters tall, and a mere 46 kilos. Physically, my mind had to go back to childhood for a really good word—*elfin*. Small, thin, wiry, with a sharp, stern-looking face set off by ears slightly too large for it and pushed back and a healthy shock of jet-black hair trimmed almost in a pageboy style. I appeared to have little or no body hair and no facial hair beyond the dark, V-shaped eyebrows. The truth was, with some nondescript clothing I would look more like a young girl of eleven or so than the mature twenty-seven-year-old the dossier said I was. Perhaps that had been part of his problem.

For the body was that of Park Lacoch, the Butcher of Bonhomme. I remembered Park's case from recent press reports—recent to the old me, anyway. He had a real thing about women, and on the frontier he'd been an insidious terror.

The odd thing was, he'd been a colonial district administrator—that was the only reason it had taken so long to catch him. One of his duties was heading the local cops who were all-out to capture him, and he had mastery of the computer records and lab facilities of the whole place. He was by all reports a superior administrator: always in under budget, never needing excuses, well-liked by the people under him. A charmer. His big problem was that he liked to play with women in a most unapproved manner. He would abduct them, often from frontier farming areas, take them to his private labs, and systematically mutilate and torture them to death. He had done so seventeen times in one year until finally hard deductive detective work by one of his colleagues, brought in, ironically, at his own request, finally tracked him down and nailed him.

He was a textbook case for the psychs, of course. Looking like this, he had been the butt of every cruelty while growing up and had had a hard time being taken seriously by anybody. But he had a keen mind and graduated first in administration—no mean feat for a natural-born frontier human, not a genetically and culturally generated individual of the civilized worlds—and he made them pay attention by doing everything just right. Why he became the Butcher was something the press had a field day with, but the causes were certainly far more complex than pop psych. Still, so revolting had been his crimes, so against all standards of civilized behavior no matter where, that only death or exile to the Warden Diamond would have been politically acceptable. The publicity alone made his face and name notorious throughout the Confederacy, so that even a totally psyched and wiped Park Lacoch could hardly have fitted back in anywhere.

He was in fact a perfect Diamond candidate for those reasons and for his brilliance. As such, he was a near-perfect cover, but he would also be something of a liability if his notoriety followed him. Hell, *I* liked women in a more normal way, but it would be damned difficult to make friends with any of them if they knew Lacoch's criminal history. Well, perhaps I could devise a decent cover story to attain some degree of normalcy if it came up.

I lay back down on the cot and put myself in a light trance, going over all the briefing information, filing, sorting, thinking it all out. Particularly important were the details, large and small, of Lacoch's life and work, since I would be most vulnerable to tripping up in those areas. I also studied my host's mannerisms, nervous habits, and the like, and tried to get myself into the mind-set of a small, effeminate-looking man in a big, rough world.

By the time I reached Charon, I'd better be perfect for my own sake. Lacoch—me—would have one more lady-killing to his credit before it was all over, but I wasn't for a minute going to underestimate Aeolia Matuze.

CHAPTER TWO

Transportation and Exposure

Except for the regular meals there was no way to keep track of time, but it was a fairly long trip. They weren't wasting any money transporting prisoners by the fastest available routes, that was for sure.

Finally, though, we docked with the base ship a third of a light-year out from the Warden system. I knew it not so much by any sensation inside my cloister but from the lack of it: the vibration that had been my constant companion ceased. The routine still wasn't varied; I suppose they were waiting for a large enough contingent from around the galaxy to make the landing worthwhile. All I could do was sit and go over my data for the millionth time and occasionally reflect on the fact that I probably wasn't very far from my old body (that's how I'd come to think of it). I wondered if perhaps he didn't even come down and take a peek at me from time to time, at least from idle curiosity— me and the three others who probably were also here.

I also had time to reflect on what I knew of the Warden situation itself, the reason for its perfection as a prison. I had not, of course, swallowed that line whole—there was no such thing as the perfect prison, but this one had to come close. Shortly after I was landed on Charon and started breathing its air I would be infected with an oddball submicroscopic organism that would set up housekeeping in every cell of my body. There it would live, feeding off me, even earning its keep by keeping disease organisms, infections, and the like in check. The one thing that stuff had was a will to live, and it only lived if you did.

But it needed something, some trace element or some such that was present only in the Warden system. Nobody knew what and nobody had been able to do the real work to find out, but whatever it needed was found only in the Warden system. Whatever it was wasn't in the air, because in shuttles run between the worlds of the Diamond you breathed the purified, mechanically produced stuff to no ill effect. Not the food, either. They'd checked that. It was possible for one of the Warden people to live comfortably on synthetics in a totally isolated lab like a planetary space station. But get too far away, even with Warden food and Warden air, and the organism died. Since it had modified your cells to make itself at home, and those cells depended on the organism to keep working properly, you died, too—painfully and slowly, in horrible agony. That distance was roughly a quarter of a light-year from the system's sun, which explained the location of the base ship.

All four worlds were more than climatologically different, too. The organism was consistent in how it affected an individual on each planet, but—possibly due to distance from the sun, since that seemed to be the determining factor in its life—it did different things depending on which world an individual was first exposed. Whatever it did stuck in just that fashion even if you later went to a different world of the Diamond.

The organism seemed to be vaguely telepathic in some way, although nobody could explain how. It certainly wasn't an intelligent organism; at least it always behaved predictably. Still, most of the changes seemed to involve the colony in one person affecting the colony in another—or others. You provided the conscious control, if you could, and that determined who bossed whom. A pretty simple system, even if nobody had yet been able to explain it.

As for Charon, all I really knew about it was that it was terribly hot and rainy. I cursed again not having been fed the proper programming to fully prepare me—learning the ropes would cost time, possibly a lot of it.

Almost three days—eight meals—after I'd arrived at the base ship there was a lurching and a lot of banging around, which forced me to the cot and made me slightly seasick. Still, I wasn't disappointed. The disruption meant that they were making up the consignments and readying for the in-system drop of these cells. I faced the idea with mixed emotions. On the one hand, I wanted desperately to be out of this boring little box. On the other, when I next got out of the box it would be into a much larger and probably prettier box—Charon itself, no less a cell for being an entire planet. And while it would be more diverting, challenging, exciting, or whatever, it would also be, unlike this box, very, very final.

Shortly after the banging about started, it stopped again and, after a short, expectant pause, I again felt a vibration indicating movement—much more pronounced than before. I was now either on a much smaller vessel or nearer the drives.

Still, it took another three interminable days—nine meals—to reach our destination. Long, certainly, but also fast for a sublight carrier, probably a modified and totally automated freighter.

The vibration stopped and I knew we were in orbit. Again I had that dual feeling of trapped doom and exhilaration.

There was a crackling sound and a speaker I'd never even known was there came to life. "Attention all prisoners!" it commanded, its voice a metallic parody of a man's baritone. "We have achieved orbit around the planet Charon in the Warden system," it continued, telling me nothing I didn't already know but probably informing the others, however many there were, for the first time. I could understand what they must be going through, considering my own feelings. A hundred times mine probably, since at least I was going in with my eyes open even if no more voluntarily than they.

"In a moment," the voice continued, "the doors to your cells will slide open and you will be able to leave. We strongly recommend you do so, since thirty seconds after the doors open they will close again and a vacuum pump will begin sterilization operations within the cells which would be fatal to anyone who remains."

Nice touch, I thought. I couldn't help wondering whether anybody would choose death.

"Immediately after you enter the main corridor," the

voice continued, "you will stand in place until the cell
doors close once again. Do not attempt to move from in
front of your cell door until it closes or automatic security
equipment will vaporize you. There will be no talking in
the corridor. Anyone breaking silence or failing to obey orders precisely will be dealt with instantly. You will receive
further instructions once the doors close. Ready to depart—*now!*"

The door slid open and I wasted no time in stepping out.
A small white box, complete with marks for feet, showed
you where to stand and I did as instructed, galling as all
this was. There was something about being totally naked
and isolated on a ship controlled only by computer that
humbled you more than was right. It produced a sense of
total futility.

I could still look around and I saw that I'd been right.
The ship was basically a long sealed hall along the sides of
which little cells had been attached. I looked up and down
and counted maybe ten or twelve prisoners, no more. The
cream of the crop, I thought sourly. A handful of men and
women—mostly men, it seemed—naked and bedraggled,
beaten now, about to be dropped off and left. I wondered
why they had been chosen rather than wiped, considering
the transportation costs alone. What had the computers and
psych boys found in these dejected specimens that dictated
they should live? *They* didn't know, that was for sure. I
wondered exactly who did.

The doors snapped shut. I waited expectantly, as the air
was pumped out, to hear the scream of someone who
hadn't moved fast enough, but there was no hint of melo-
drama. If anyone had taken that way out, the fact was not
evident.

"At my command," the voice barked from speakers
along the ceiling, "you will turn right and walk slowly in
single file, as far forward as you can. There you will find a
special shuttle that will take you to the surface. You will
take forward seats first, leave no empty seats between you,
and immediately strap yourselves in."

I heard some muttering from a few of my fellow prisoners, and instantly a brief but very visible spurt of light shot

from a side wall. It did not strike anyone but hit with an audible hiss just in front of the offenders' feet. They jumped slightly at this demonstration of power. All the grumbling and mumbling immediately ceased.

The voice, which had paused for this digression, now took up its instructions with no reference to what had taken place. None was needed.

"Right turn—*now!*" it commanded, and we did as instructed. "Walk slowly forward to the shuttle as instructed."

We walked silently, definitely in no hurry. The metal floor of the corridor was damned cold—at least the shuttle would be preferable to this damned refrigerator.

The shuttle itself was surprisingly comfortable and modern, although the seats weren't made for naked bodies. I sat about three rows back and attached the safety straps, then waited for the rest to enter. My first impression had been close, I noted. The shuttle itself could seat twenty-four, but there were only eleven of us, and only three were women.

The hatch closed automatically, followed by the hiss of pressurization. I felt a violent lurch and knew we were free of the transport and on our way down.

The shuttle was much too modern and comfortable for mere prisoner transport, I told myself. This had to be one of the interplanetary ships regularly used for transportation between the worlds of the Warden Diamond.

The overhead speakers crackled, and a much nicer female voice that actually sounded human came on. It was a great improvement.

"Welcome to Charon," the voice said, sounding for all the world like it meant it. "As has no doubt been explained to you, Charon is your final destination and new home. Although you will be unable to leave the Warden system after debarking on the planet, you will also no longer be prisoners. Rather, you will be citizens of the Warden Diamond. Confederacy rule ended the moment you entered this shuttle, one of a fleet of four shuttlecraft and sixteen freighters owned in common by the Warden Worlds. The System Council, a corporate entity fully recognized as internally sovereign by the Confederacy, has a seat in the

Confederacy Congress. Each of the four worlds is under a separate administration and the government of each planet is unique and independent. No matter who you are or what you have been or done in the past, you are now citizens of Charon and nothing more—or less. Anything done prior to this moment is past history that will neither be remembered, filed, or ever again referred to. Only what you do from this point on, as citizens of Charon, Warden System, will matter."

It—or she, I wasn't really sure—paused for that much to sink in. The contrast between the attitude and tone taken now and what we'd all been subjected to previously was enormous. But if she expected me to believe that the powers-that-be on Charon didn't know anything of our past she had a very low opinion of my intelligence.

"We will arrive at the spaceport at Honuth in approximately five minutes," she told us. "You will be met there by representatives bringing clothing and then taken to an orientation center where all your questions will be answered. Please be prepared for hot, wet weather and for a level of technology below what most of you have come to expect. This is still very much a frontier world, with even more restrictions than on any frontier world you have ever known. But please don't be unduly upset by that. Charon is not without its comforts. Again, welcome to Charon."

Although the lid was off, nobody really said much for the rest of the trip. Part of the reason was that we were still conditioned by our recent imprisonment; the rest was nerves, mine included. This was it, I told myself. Here we go.

There were a few bumps on the way down, particularly once we were firmly in the atmosphere; but, overall, the ride was smooth and efficient. Then came a level-off, a slow descent, and a glide right up to and into the dock.

In less than a minute I could hear the airlock door mechanisms operating, and the indicator moved from red to orange to green. Following a pneumatic hiss, the doors rolled back.

For a moment, none of us moved, but finally those nearest the hatch stood up and walked out the open door. Sighing, I did the same.

The docking area was small but quite modern and fully air-conditioned. Walking along the glassine tubelike egress arm, I could see Charon, which did nothing to improve my spirits. It was raining like crazy, so heavily I could hardly see a thing.

The terminal was quite small but nothing like the log hut I had been expecting. The air-conditioning was positively chilling. Two very ordinary people, a man and a woman, waited for us. They were both dressed in pullover black shirts and briefs and wore thick, rubber-soled sandals. They looked more like a couple that had just gotten rained out at the beach than officials of a planetary government.

"Welcome to Charon," the woman said, and I recognized the voice as the same one in the shuttle. Remote controlled from the ground, then. "Please step over to that table, pick out clothes and sandals in your size, and put them on," she instructed in a businesslike tone.

Part of my briefing had included Park Lacoch's sizes, but I quickly discovered that all the men's clothing was too large and that I would have to go to the women's section to outfit myself. It didn't really matter—it all looked the same anyway—but I did get some idea of how Lacoch developed his nasty complex and bad identity problem.

The modified beachwear was apparently standard attire, at least here—where was it? Honuth, that was it. I wondered if the stuff was waterproof.

I dressed and was standing around waiting for the others to get similarly set when the fact really hit me. I was here, on Charon—and even as that first blast of air-conditioning had hit me, my body was being systematically invaded by an alien organism that was to be my permanent jailer.

CHAPTER THREE

Orientation

After getting dressed, we were gathered around the two greeters in the small terminal.

"All right—listen up!" the man called out, his voice almost lost in the sound of the heavy rain hitting the roof of the building. "We're going to leave here and go into town where we have set up temporary quarters for you. I strongly recommend that you follow us closely, since Charon is a world that can kill the newcomer in a minute. Mechanized transportation is not allowed in town, so we'll have to go in two coaches that are parked outside now. Don't be startled at what's pulling them, just get in the nearest one."

"Got any umbrellas?" somebody called out. The man and woman both smiled a bit but didn't reply.

I became acutely aware of my physical disadvantage in the group. Everybody, male and female, was taller than I, and so I was forced to watch our hosts from a small break in the gathering that opened and closed. The whole thing was very frustrating.

"Come on!" the woman called to us. "Don't run or rush—those sandals have fair traction, but on the slick pavement just outside they'll slip on you." With that both Charonites turned, and the man started leading us out, the woman bringing up the rear.

It wasn't just bad outside, it was worse than I had imagined—incredibly hot, almost like a steambath. The rain seemed to be pouring out of some giant faucet in the sky, so thickly was it coming down. The rigid awning to the street offered little protection thanks to a hot wind, and we

were all soaked in moments. Still, the ugly climate wasn't
the real shock—it was what waited for us at the curb.

Two huge wheeled coaches made entirely out of what
appeared to be wood, were there: pulling each of them was
a pair of monster lizards, each almost four meters tall.
Well, they weren't *quite* lizards, but that was the closest
you could come. They were bipedal, standing on enormous,
muscular legs, balancing themselves by use of a long, thick
tail. Their saurianlike heads, with unblinking eyes of burning red, were not only enormous but looked full of row
after row of sharp teeth. Two small arms ended in handlike
appendages now flexed in apparent anticipation—or boredom. Those hands, smaller versions of the enormous feet,
were composed of three, long jointed fingers connected by
webbing that made them look like giant leaves. The fingers
ended in suckerlike tips. The splayed hand and foot was, as
I later learned, a feature of many of the animals of
Charon. Instead of having reptilian scales, the great creatures were smooth-skinned, and colored a uniform and
ridiculous-looking perfect baby blue.

Each wore an elaborate looking bridle, with a network of
reins rivaling a marionette's strings in number and complexity, that stretched back into a raised driver compartment above the coach proper. The driving compartment
was completely enclosed, and included a windscreen with a
huge windscreen wiper.

I jumped into the nearest coach, almost slipping on the
smooth paving despite the warning—that rain was so fierce
it almost hurt—and found myself jammed in with five
other prisoners and the male Charonite. The coach was
quite comfortable, with soft, padded upholstery but it
would have been a lot more comfortable with two less people.

After closing and locking the door, our coach, the lead
one, started off with a strong jerk. The ride was *not* at all
comfortable; extremely hard and bumpy all the way, with
the coach lurching this way and that, more like a ship at
sea in a storm than basic ground transportation. I saw the
Charonite looking at us with some amusement, probably
wondering if any of us were going to get seasick. "Don't

worry, it's not a long trip. Sorry about this, but it's considered deluxe transportation here on Charon."

"This ain't Lilith—machines operate there," a big man sitting next to him grumbled. "How come all this primitive shit?"

"*Some* machines operate here, when they are permitted to," the native responded somewhat enigmatically. "Fact is, most of this misery is a sort of compromise. Machinery's so easy to foul it isn't worth a damn here anyway, so we go with what we can. For the most part though, it's this bad or worse. Better get used to losing a couple of thousand years, 'cause that's what you just did."

"Damn foolishness," the big man grumped, but the rest of us remained silent, either because we didn't know enough or out of real depression.

Within five minutes the coach rolled to a stop with a jerk even worse than the start. I thought to myself that these vehicles could use seat belts more than the space shuttles, but said nothing. My situation was still too new and I was far too green, not to mention soaked and perspiring from the heat.

It was a relief when the door was opened, since at least it let in a breeze with the rain. The Charonite emerged and stood there, almost oblivious to the rain, helping us all down and pointing to a nearby door, which we made for. Once inside that door we were all dripping wet again and a little dazed, but after a half a minute or so I got my bearings and was able to look around.

When they said the place was primitive they weren't kidding. The buildings seemed to be made mostly of various kinds of native wood, along with other plants of the area. They were well-crafted but very utilitarian, that was for sure. Along the walk of polished mosaic in front of the buildings on this side of the street, were what appeared to be wick-lamps, burning oil of some kind magnified through polished glass. The reason they didn't fall victim to the rain was ingenious: between the walk and the street a wall of some glassy substance ran the length of the street and had a roof attached to the roofs of the buildings themselves. Although there was some seepage through cracks in the walk, it was pretty well watertight—a clever idea. There was also some airflow, which felt oddly chilling, although I couldn't figure out where it came from.

Our host, as soaked as we, examined us with a sour smile, and I knew we probably looked worse than he did.

The second coach arrived shortly after, and the rest of our party joined us and went through the same drying out—not that we were dry by any means.

"It doesn't rain like this *all* the time, does it?" I asked the native.

He laughed. "No, not like this. Usually it's no more than an hour or two, but in early spring and late fall the rain sometimes lasts two, three days at a clip, dumping up to three centimeters per hour." He paused a moment for that to sink in, then added, "We do have a *good* drainage system."

They'd better, I thought, more amazed than anything else. Three days of such a downpour at that rate would come to almost *two meters* of water.

"What season is it now?" someone asked sourly.

"The middle of spring," our guide responded. "It's gonna be getting hot soon." Unfortunately he didn't say it like he was joking.

The group was led into the nearest building, which proved to be—well, rustic. It was composed of logs of some kind, including log bracing for the log ceiling, which was very high. There were wickerlike chairs around, some tables, and very little else. The building was also lit by those basic lamps, and they did a very good job I had to admit, despite the slight flickering that took some getting used to. The floor was carpeted with a rubbery-feeling tilelike substance with an elaborate grooved design—to allow water run-off, I supposed. Still, if this place didn't flood it must be well designed indeed.

Groaning, we sank into the chairs, feeling as if we'd put in a full day already despite the fact that we had actually done very little. The tension was beginning to wear off, producing a general lethargy.

"This is normally the lobby of the town's hotel," the woman told us. "We requisitioned it for a few days so that you could get acclimated. We reserved the top floor rooms for you—although I'm afraid you'll have to share two to a room for the most part. We need the lower floor for regular guests, and they're cramped as it is. The guests and townspeople will not come in here while we are using it, and for the first stages of orientation we'll take all our meals here as well. I would recommend that, pending our series of talks, you avoid any of the townspeople you might meet in the lavatory or on the stairs. Don't be mean, just don't strike up any conversations or get into any arguments. Most of them are natives here and won't understand your lack of familiarity with Charon and it's no use getting into trouble before you know what you're getting into."

Several of us nodded in agreement on that. "What about getting out of these wet clothes?" I asked.

"We *all* have wet clothes," she replied. "We'll try and get some dry ones for you as soon as we have your sizes down, but for now you'll have to make do with the ones you have."

A pretty young woman in our party shivered slightly and looked around. "Is it my imagination or is cold air blowing in here?"

"It's not really all that cold," the man told her. "But, yes, cooler air is circulated through a system of pipes that blows cool air from below ground, where there are natural underground river caverns, and some man-made ones as well. The blower system is powered by windmills located on top of the buildings, and it keeps us from frying or strangling in stagnant air."

Pretty ingenious, I had to admit, although I couldn't help wondering why the ban on machinery. The spaceport terminal was tiny, it was true, but it was quite modern, electrically powered and air-conditioned, all the rest. Technology then wasn't so much impossible on Charon as it was *banned*. By whom? Matuze? No, she hadn't been in power long enough to produce this sort of thing. This town and the culture reflected by the male native was long-term. By the Lord of Cerberus, that was for sure—perhaps long, long ago. That made some sense if the ruling could be enforced on a planetary scale. If only the Lord of Cerberus

and those he or she designated had access to technology
and the training to use it, they would be assured of absolute
control.

"We'll let you go to your rooms first for a while," the
woman was saying. "There are towels and such there, and
you can get fairly dried out. We also have robes there, so if
you want to change into those you'll probably be more comfortable. Top floor, pick your own rooms and roommates,
and meet us back down here in—say, an hour for food. I
know you don't have watches, but we'll make sure you get
called."

We made our way to the rear of the lobby area and discovered an alcove in the back with a spiral wooden staircase. From the other side of the alcove, beyond two closed
wooden doors, came the smells of food cooking and people
talking loudly. The bar? The restaurant? Well, it didn't
matter—yet.

I hung back. I had decided the easiest way to guarantee
either that I'd be alone in a room or at least get a random
shot at it was to be last, there being an odd number of us.

No such luck on the single, though. The big, gruff man
who had made all the sour comments along the way staked
out a single and nobody seemed inclined to argue with him.
Everybody else, including two of the women, paired off,
and by the time I reached the top of the stairs only one
person remained—the pretty young woman who had asked
about the air system downstairs. I saw her down at the end
of the hall looking slightly worried and more than a little
confused. She cautiously opened the last door on the right
and looked inside then turned back to see me approaching.
I could tell by her expression that she wasn't thrilled by the
situation.

"Looks like we're stuck together," I noted.

She thought a moment, then sighed. "What the hell—
what does it matter, anyway?"

"Thanks a lot," I responded sourly and walked into the
room. It was surprisingly spacious and contained two large
comfortable beds, mattresses and all, some closet space and
a sink with a cold water tap. I was surprised at that, having
expected to have to go down to a well someplace. The beds

were not made, but clean linen was folded at the foot of each along with washcloths and towels and, as promised, a robe each.

I saw her hesitating, a little nervous, and I sympathized. "Look, if I'm offending your morals I'll step into the closet. Somebody my size could practically live in there."

"No, no, that's not necessary. After all, we were all naked on the shuttle coming in."

I nodded, relaxed a little, and peeled off the wet clothes and stuck them on the towel rack to dry. I then took the towel and dried myself as best I could, particularly my hair, which was a tangled mess, then tried the robe. As I suspected, it was quite a bit large for me. So much for standardization. Still, I decided I could manage in it without breaking my neck.

During this time she just stood there, watching me. I began to wonder if she knew who her roommate was. "Something wrong?" I asked her.

For a moment she said nothing, not even acknowledging my comment or existence. I was beginning to suspect I had somebody really ill but she finally snapped out of it and looked at me.

"I—I'm sorry, but it's been hard for me. I feel like this is all an ugly dream, that I'll wake up from it sometime."

I nodded sympathetically. "I know what you mean. But you can't let it get to you. You have to figure that you're alive, and you're still you and not some psych's dream, and that you've got a whole new start in a whole new life. It isn't as bad as all that." But, of course, it was. She was from the civilized worlds and probably had never even seen a frontier settlement. Her world, a world she not only had loved but had taken entirely for granted, was now totally and irrevocably gone.

Come to think of it, so was mine.

She walked over and sat on the edge of her bed. "Oh, what's the use? It seems to me that being dead would be better than *this*."

"No, death is never better than life. Besides, you have to consider that you're really pretty special to the Confederacy. There's only eleven of us out of the—what? Hun-

dreds?—convicted at the same time. They saw something in us that they didn't want to lose. In a sense, they're
saying we're better than almost all the people in the Confederacy."

"Different, anyway," she responded. "I don't know. I
just don't. Spending the rest of my life in this rotten place."
She looked me straight in the eye. "What makes you so
special? What did *you* do to get here?"

Well, here it was—acid test early on. I decided to take a
very mild gamble, but first a proper priming. "You know
you aren't supposed to ask that."

She was beginning to relax a little now, and moved to get
rid of her own wet clothes. "Something you're ashamed
of?" she asked. "Funny. I never thought it mattered."

"It doesn't matter to you?"

She thought a moment as she dried her hair. "No, not
really. I'm Zala Embuay, by the way."

"Park Lacoch," I responded, tensing a bit to see if it got
any reaction. He—I—was pretty damned notorious.

She let it pass without a glimmer of recognition. Well,
that was something, anyway.

"Well, Park Lacoch, weren't you some sort of criminal?"

"Weren't we all?"

She shook her head. "No, not me. I'm different. I may
be the only person ever sent to the Warden Diamond because I was an innocent victim."

I was finding it hard to take her seriously. "How's that?"

She nodded seriously. "You've never heard of the Triana
family?"

It was my turn to betray ignorance. "Nope."

"Well, the Trianas are the ranking political family on
Takanna. Ever been there?"

"No, can't say I have," I admitted.

"Well, you know at least what it's like to be a ranking
political family, don't you?"

You bet I did—but Lacoch would have been a little
more removed. "I understand it, although I'm a frontier
man myself. I've been to many of the civilized worlds but
I've never actually lived on one."

"That's what I mean. You're much better equipped for someplace like this."

"The frontier's not as wild and primitive as you think," I told her. "In comparison to the civilized worlds, yes, but it's nothing at all like this. Believe me, our backgrounds may be very different but they're much more alike than either of us is to the people who were born here."

I'm not sure she accepted that truism, but she let it pass. "Well, anyway, I was raised in a government house, had a happy childhood and was being prepared for an administrative slot. Everything was going right when all of a sudden, the Security Service came in one day and arrested my designated mother and me."

I understood what she meant by that. All people of the civilized world were born *in vitro*, perfect products of genetic engineering, predesigned and predestined for their lives and careers. Each career on a civilized world was a Family, and when children were five they were given to a designated member of that Family unit to be raised and educated. "What was the charge?" I asked her, really interested now. I wondered whose territory Takanna was in.

"Well, they charged *her* with unauthorized genetic manipulation," she told me. "They claimed I was a special product—*product!*—illegally created and born."

I sat up, all ears. *This* was interesting. "You look perfectly normal to me," I assured her. "Just what were you supposed to be that you weren't supposed to be?"

"That's just it! They wouldn't tell me! They said it would be better that I didn't know, and maybe if I didn't the truth wouldn't make any difference. That's what's so frustrating about it all. How would you like to be told one day that you're a freak, but not told how or in what way?"

"And you haven't a clue? Your mother never indicated anything?"

"Nothing. I've searched and searched my whole childhood, and I haven't come up with anything that anyone found odd or unusual. I *do* admit I found the whole business of administration pretty boring, but a lot of it *is* boring. And I never saw her after the arrest, so I never got a

chance to talk to anybody else who might know and would
tell me."

"And for that they shipped you here?"

She nodded. "They told me it was for my own good; that
I'd do all right here, that I could never fit into the civilized
worlds. Just like that, I'm a convicted criminal—and here I
am."

I studied her face and manner as she spoke and came to
a conclusion. The tale was pretty bizarre, but it had a ring
of truth to it. It was *just* the kind of thing the Confederacy
would do. It would be interesting to know why she couldn't
have been recultured or simply shifted elsewhere. There
was no such thing as a criminal gene, of course, but there
were hormonal and enzyme causes for a large number of
physical and mental tendencies, from violence to anger to
schizophrenia. If her story rang true all the way, it meant I
might be sharing a room with a ticking bomb. Still, if she
ever learned the complete truth about Park Lacoch she
might think the same thing—and be wrong.

"Well, if it's any comfort to you, I'm something of a
freak myself, as you can see," I told her. "You get cases
like me out on the frontier, where there's all sorts of com-
plications in the different planetary conditions—radiation,
you name it—and most births are the old-fashioned kind,
of mother and father. By 'like me' I don't really mean exactly like me, just—well, unusual."

"You do look—well, unusual," she said cautiously. "I
mean, most of the frontier people seem to be so big and
hairy."

I chuckled. "Well, not quite, but my small size is only
part of it. Tell me, just seeing me in the clothes and now,
what do I look like? How old would you say I was?"

She thought a moment. "Well, I know you're a lot older
just by the way you talk, but, well, to be honest, you look
like . . . well . . ."

"I look like a ten-year-old girl, right?"

She sighed. "Well, yeah. But I know you aren't. Even
your voice is kinda, well, in between, though."

That was news. My voice sounded like a sharp but definite tenor to me. [I had the advantage of all that informa-

tion Krega had fed into my fanny, and I was beginning to understand Park Lacoch a little more.]

"Well, I'm twenty-seven," I told her, "and I've looked this way since I was twelve. Puberty brought me pubic hair, a slightly deeper voice, and that was it. It wasn't until I was sixteen, though, that my folks were able to get me to a really good meditech. They found out that I was a mutation, a real freak. A hermaphrodite, they called it."

"A—you mean you're both sexes?"

"No, not really. I'm a man, but I'm probably the only man you'll ever meet who's a man entirely by choice. Inside I have the makings of both, but the psychs and meditechs struck a balance, and that's the way I'll stay— because I wanted it. They could have adjusted the other way and, with a minimum amount of surgery, I'd have wound up female." Poor Lacoch, I'd reflected more than once. Confused totally about his sexual identity, hung up in a limbo not of his own making, permanently small and girlish. No wonder he went nuts. The file said he even masqueraded as a young girl to lure his victims away. I wondered if he'd have been different, perhaps better off, if he'd chosen to be female instead—but he hadn't, and while seventeen victims was a terrible price, here and now, in his body, I was damned glad to be a man.

"Then, in a way you and I are alike," Zala said, fascinated. "We're both genetic freaks. The only difference is, you *know* what's wrong. I wish I did."

I nodded. "Maybe you will now. Or maybe this Warden organism will just wipe out the problem. It's supposed to do that."

The idea sobered her a bit. "I'd almost forgotten about that. Funny, I don't feel . . . well . . . *infected*."

"Neither do I, but we are. Bet on it."

Then without warning, she returned to the original conversation. "Ah, Park?"

"Uh-huh?"

"What did you do to get here?"

I sighed. "What I did I won't do again," I told her. "It was a terrible sickness, Zala—mental illness that came from a lot of things, including my physical condition. The psychs cured me of that, though, and I've never been more sane in my life. That alone is really worth the price. I was in real hell, Zala, back home. I may be a prisoner here, but I'm free for the first time in my life. I was a district administrator, by the way, so we do have a little more in common."

She wasn't buying the stall. "Park, why won't you tell me what you did?"

I sighed. "Because if I did you wouldn't get a good night's sleep while we were together, that's why."

She thought for a moment. "You . . . killed somebody, didn't you?"

I nodded.

"A woman?"

Again I just nodded.

She hesitated. "More than one?"

Again I could only nod and wish this conversation hadn't come up.

"A lot?"

I sighed and sat back up on my bed. "Look, let's stop playing games. I really don't want to remember that part of myself. It's like I was somebody else, Zala. It was a terrible, terrible madness, a sickness. Looking back on it makes me more nauseated than people who remember it or were there. I swear to you, though, that they *have* to terminate anybody they can't cure of such madness, and the fact that I'm here proves that I'm cured. They could have sent me back on the streets with perfect confidence and in perfect safety, but my case was so notorious and I'm so physically distinctive that I would have been lynched, or worse. The Diamond was the only way out for me and, believe it or not, I'm grateful. For the first time I can be a whole human being—and that means a lot to me, even here on this pesthole."

She smiled. "Then I'm your acid test, because I don't *want* to be here. If you're lying, and you kill me, well, at least it'll be over. And if you're telling the truth, both of us will know it and maybe, together, we can survive this place."

"Sounds fair to me," I told her sincerely. A temporary

alliance, anyway. I *did* have a woman left to kill, but it wasn't Zala Embuay.

They knocked on our doors shortly after that, and we trooped downstairs again like a convention of bathhouse enthusiasts. I had some trouble with the robe on the stairs, but I managed to keep from tripping.

Our hosts, in fresh black clothes of the same kind we'd been issued, but looking dry and prim, were waiting for us. In the center of the lobby area a table had been set with a lot of steaming dishes on it, and eleven place settings.

The food was all natural, which was bizarre enough, but the tastes and textures were also rather odd. I won't go into a catalogue of the meal, but I had the feeling that, with the stew anyway, we really didn't *want* to know what was in it. For the six civilized-worlds prisoners, Zala included, it was probably the first nonsynthetic, non-computer-balanced and -prepared meal they had ever had, and they showed it. The rest of us rude frontiersmen and women ate with gusto. As I said, I really didn't want to know what the stuff was, but it *was* good and highly but delicately spiced. At least the food was going to be decent here.

Our native guides obviously had either already eaten or would eat later. They busied themselves setting up a large chart stand and adjusting lights and the like until we were through.

Eating mostly in silence but feeling for the first time a lot more human, we finally finished and waited anxiously on our hosts.

The man began. "I am Garal," he introduced himself, "and this is Tiliar. We've been assigned this job by the Honuth District Supervisor, acting for and at the command of the planetary government. We are both former prisoners ourselves, so we know what you're going through. Let's start out by saying that you must have fears and odd superstitions about the Warden Diamond, and we want to assure you that those fears have no basis. You're not going to get sick—in fact, you will most likely not notice any real difference between yourselves before and yourselves here. It is true, though, that your bodies are even now altering in minute and undetectable ways. Within a few days you and the Warden organism will reach a state of what we like to call 'alliance.' Let me emphasize that you are not sick. In fact, in the five years I've been here I've *never* been sick, not once. The Wardens are far more effective than any body defense in killing off viruses and any other disease organisms you might have brought with you—the ones native here are too alien to do you any harm—as well as infection and a host of other ills. You can appreciate the fact that, in a climate like this, nobody ever gets a cold."

That brought a small chuckle from us, but it was an important aspect of this world. Back in the civilized worlds people never got sick much either, but that was due to the immediate access to the best medical facilities. Here, if Garal was to be believed, doctors and the like were simply not necessary.

"Some of you may find a little discomfort in one or two areas," Tiliar put in, "because you aren't healthy enough. Anyone who has chipped or lost a tooth, for example, may find it growing back, which can be an irritating thing. Anyone who has vision problems might experience some dizziness or slight headaches as whatever problems you had are corrected. The Warden organism doesn't just keep you from getting worse, it makes you better. And it keeps you that way. Cuts heal quickly and rarely leave a scar; even whole limbs are often regenerated if lost."

"You make it sound like we're immortal," the big prisoner with the single room commented.

"No, not immortal," she replied. "Fatal wounds Outside are fatal wounds here. The Wardens use your own body's natural abilities to keep you healthy and whole, but if your body can't fix it, well, neither can they. However, more people on Charon die from external causes than natural causes. With the Warden ability to repair and even replace brain cells, your potential lifespan in a healthy body is longer than in the civilized worlds."

Most of those at the table, Zala included, heard only the second part of that statement and seemed pleased. I was much more interested in the implication that a lot of people died here from unnatural causes. I couldn't forget the teeth on those baby blue lizards.

Our guides followed up with a general rundown of the planet, much of which I already knew. It was interesting in the context of the torrential rains to discover that there were a few deserts on the central continent, often the only places where blue sky was seen for more than brief periods. Water, it seemed, was feast or famine on Charon—mostly feast. But in those dry areas it might rain once a century. Additionally, there were violent storms, tabarwinds they were called, that were quick and deadly and could strike out of nowhere with tremendous lightning charges and winds of over 160 kilometers per hour. Much of the weather, including these storms, could not be accurately predicted since a layer in the upper atmosphere had an odd field of electrically charged particles that fouled most conventional radars, infrared cameras, and the like, while artificial electrical fields on the ground attracted the full fury of tabarwinds. I began to see a practical reason why they kept technology at a minimum level. The spaceport was immediately shut down at the first sign of such tabarwinds, and, even so, it had been hit and destroyed twice in the memory of these two people. The shuttle had special protection against many of these electrical fields, but was not totally immune.

As with all the Warden worlds, a "research" space station was maintained in orbit well outside the range of any nasty stuff, but it was closed to unauthorized personnel. It was an interesting fact that on those space stations the Warden organism would infect anyone that it came into contact with, but would leave all the inorganic material alone. Its full properties were operative only on one of the planets, and then only on people affected with the same breed of organism.

That brought us to what we really wanted to know. "In addition to the total lack of technological comforts," Garal told us, "there is a by-product of the Warden affiliation that is, well, hard to accept even after you've seen it. There's a different by-product on each of the four Diamond worlds, all relating to the fact that the tiny Wardens are, somehow, in some sort of contact or communication with one another. On Lilith, for example, some people have the power literally to move, build, or destroy mountains with a thought, by telling *their* Wardens to give orders to *other* Wardens in the rocks, trees, other people, you name it. But the degree of power an individual has is arbitrary. On Cerberus this communication is so bizarre that people can literally exchange minds with each other—and it's so universal that they often do so without meaning to. No control. On Medusa, the Warden communication is so limited that it's really only within one's own body, and causes rapid and involuntary shape-changing to meet whatever environment the person finds him or herself in. Here—well, things are a bit different but still related."

We were all silent now, raptly intent on the speaker. Here was the heart of the Charon experience—what we would become.

"As on Lilith, we have a certain power over objects and people," Tiliar jumped in, taking up the talk. "As on Cerberus, it is a mental ability rather than a physical one, and mind-to-mind contact is possible. As on Medusa, physical change is possible, but in a different sense. And, while these powers are *not* arbitrary—that is, everyone has these abilities—it takes great training and discipline to be able to use them properly, while those with the training and control *can* use them on you. That's why we cautioned you to avoid the locals for a while." She paused for a moment, carefully considering her words.

"You see," she continued after a moment, "Charon is a world out of children's stories and fairy tales. It is a world where magic works, where sorcs—sorcerers and their spells have devastating effects. And yet it is a world where none of the laws of science are violated."

This was a hard concept to digest, and several of our company muttered and shook their heads.

"I know, I know, it's hard to accept," Garal said after a while, "but the more hardheaded of you will quickly grasp the reality. Let me ask you first how you know you're here.

How do you know this place looks like this place, that you look like you and we like us? How do you know it's raining?"

"We got wet," somebody mumbled, and we all laughed.

"All right, but how do you *know* you got wet? You—your personality, your memories, the thinking part of you—are really all locked up in the cerebellum and cerebral cortex. Your brain is the only real *you* that you know—and the brain is totally encased in your skull. It has no way of directly knowing what's going on at all—it doesn't even have pain centers. Every single thing you know comes to you, your brain, by remote sensors. Vision. Smell. Taste. Touch. Sound. The five senses. Each transmits information to the brain, and supports the others to tell the brain what's going on. *But what if those five senses were wrong?* There are methods of torture—and a lot of psych work, which may be the same thing—that capitalize on this. Sending you false information. There is, in fact, an ancient human religion called voodoo—that might explain it."

"A practitioner of voodoo," Tiliar explained, picking up the lecture, "took samples of your fingernails, hair, even shit, and put it on a doll. Then whatever that magician-priest did to the doll was supposed to happen to you. And why has voodoo really survived the space age? *Because it works.*"

"Aw, c'mon," the big man scoffed.

She nodded seriously. "Yes, it works. But only under two conditions. First, the intended victim must believe that the priest has this power. It doesn't even have to be strong belief, just a subconscious fear that maybe it *does* work. And second, the intended victim must be made aware that he or she is being hexed. People have been crippled, physically and mentally, and even killed by this method, as long as those two conditions are met. And it's easier than you think. Even the most rational-minded have, deep down, a streak of superstition or doubt about unknown powers. The voodoo priests are master psychs, and every visible success reinforces the belief in their powers among others."

"Of course the priest doesn't really *do* anything," Garal

noted. "They just establish the psychological conditions and you do it to yourself. In a sense, you might say that voodoo is a magic force that violates no known scientific laws."

"You mean this is a voodoo world?" I asked jokingly.

They did not think me at all funny. "In a sense, yes," the man replied. "But here you can eliminate the variables completely and go a lot further. If you'll remember, I said that the Warden organisms can communicate, so to speak, with one another, even outside the body they inhabit. But it's a passive thing. They communicate, but they don't actually *say* anything. But, because they are a part of you, they can talk to you as well—and you to them. That's the trick. How well you can master communication between your own Wardens and others. In a sense, Charon is the ultimate voodoo world where belief and preparation are not really necessary."

Tiliar thought a moment. "Look, let's put it this way. Suppose some powerful person decided to turn you into a uhar—one of those big blue things that pulled the coaches. If he has the power, the training, and the self-control, he contacts the Wardens in your mind through *his* Wardens. He sends out a message—you are a uhar. Not being trained, or not possessing the mental control needed, or any combination of these things, you have no defense, no way to tell your *own* Wardens that they are receiving false data. So this idea, that you are a uhar, gets pounded into your brain, much like a forced hypnoprobe. Your senses are fooled, all the information coming into the brain now confirms that you are a four-meter-tall blue lizard—and, from *your* point of view, you *are*."

I saw Zala shiver slightly and felt some perspective was needed. "So all we are dealing with is a powerful form of hypnotism, the same kind we can achieve with machines, only we've dispensed with them to make the contact mind to mind."

"Sort of," Tiliar agreed. "But it doesn't stop there. Remember, your Wardens are in constant communication with all the other Wardens. Your own perceptions and self-image are 'broadcasting,' so to speak, to everyone else. What this means is that if *you* think you're a uhar, well then, so will everybody else. Even uhar will perceive you as uhar, since they, too, are Warden affiliated. *Every single thing will act as if the command, or spell, is real.* And since we depend on our senses for all our information, what we and everybody else perceive as real *will* be real. The more training and self-control you have in this ability, the more protected *you* will be and the more vulnerable everyone else will be. It's that simple."

"Needless to say, the better you are at it, the higher you will rise in Charon society," Garal added.

I'm not sure any of us really believed what we were being told, but we kept an open mind as it was information on how the place operated. Before I believed in any magic though, I'd have to see it demonstrated myself.

If this ability took training, it was worth going after. "Just how do we get the training needed to develop this?" I asked our hosts.

"Maybe you do, maybe you don't," Garal replied. "First of all, there's that self-control, a certain mental ability and attitude-set that you just can't teach. The fact is, most people can't handle the discipline involved, or can only handle it to a degree. Needless to say, it's also not in the best interests of the powers-that-be for everyone to develop this ability, even if they could. It is this way all over. There are few wolves and many sheep, yet the wolf rules the sheep. There are masses of people, nearly countless people, in the Confederacy, yet their entire lives, from their genetic makeup to jobs, location, even how long they will live, are in the hands of a very few. Please don't expect Charon to be any different."

That we could all understand at least. There was a government here, a government headed by the worst kind of power-mad politicians and super-crooks, and they had to preside over a society that was at least five percent as crooked and nasty as they were, or the children and grandchildren of the same sort. Such a government would not willingly share any of its power, nor dare to make it easily available. Still, I reflected, my own self-discipline and mental training and abilities were engineered to be way

above the norm, and what an Aeolia Matuze and lesser
lights could do, I most certainly could do as well. And
there was always somebody ready to beat the system. Unofficial training would be around someplace—if it could be
found, and if its price could be met.

In a way I suspected this might be something of a test.
We had come to Charon with nothing but our wits; those
who could secure the method and means for training and
its protection and chance for upward mobility would do so.
The rest would join the masses in the endless pool of eternal victims. That was, I felt sure, the challenge they were
issuing us here.

Back in our room, Zala and I talked over what we'd
been told the first day.

"Do you think it's for real?" she wanted to know.
"Magic, hexes, voodoo—it all sounds so ridiculous!"

"Ridiculous perhaps, when put in that context, but that's
the context of science. Look, they're not saying that anybody on Charon can do anything that a good psych with a
battery of mechanical devices couldn't do. Believe me, I
know." And I *did* know—but not from being on the wrong
end of them as she believed.

"Yes, but that's with machines and experts . . ."

"Machines, yes," I agreed, "but don't kid yourself that
the experts are any less expert here than back there. There
are even psychs sent here—they're the most imaginative
people you can find, but they go out of their heads more
often than those in any other job. No, the only difference
here is that everybody's carrying his own psych machine
around inside of him—an organic machine, but still a
gadget, a device."

She shivered. "What's wrong?" I asked her.

"Well, it's what you said. Psychs are the people most
likely to go nuts, right? I guess it's because they not only
get involved in hundreds of messed-up people's minds, but
their machines give them a god complex."

"That's pretty fair," I agreed.

"Well, what you just said is that we're on a world of
psychs and *everybody* is under their machines and can't get
disconnected. I mean, if a psych goes nuts back home,

there are other psychs and computer monitors and all the rest to catch it, pull the plug, and get him out of you, right?"

I nodded.

"But, Park—who's the monitor here? Who's around to pull the plug on these people?"

And that, of course, was the real problem. Loose in a Bedlam with the psychs crazier than the patients, and nobody to pull the plug—and no plug to be pulled. Nobody except . . . me.

It hadn't been a very trying day, but the release of tension added to the fact that none of us had gotten any real exercise for weeks, made it pretty easy to turn in fast. I had a little trouble figuring out how to extinguish the oil lamp in the room without burning myself, but I finally discovered the way the globe was latched. A tiny little cup on a long handle hanging next to the towel rack proved the easiest way to extinguish the light. It was not until days later that I found out that this was exactly what the little cuplike thing was for.

Despite my near exhaustion, I couldn't fall asleep right away. I kept thinking about Charon and the challenge it posed. Obviously I could do nothing until I was able to experience this pseudo-magic first hand and get a measure of what I was up against and what I had to learn. After that I'd have to get a job, I supposed, to develop some local contacts, to find out what I needed to know about training and rogue magicians. I would be totally ineffective until I had enough experience and expert instruction to hold my own on this crazy planet. It was entirely possible—likely, in fact—that the top politicians like Matuze weren't the top powers in magic here. I suspected the skills involved were quite different. But she would be flanked and guarded by the absolute tops, that was for sure; and the only way to her would be right through them. As a top agent, I had no doubt that I could eventually master the art enough to get by the best, but I was pragmatic enough not to think I could get through *all* of them single-handedly. No, I would need help—local help. The one thing I could be certain of was that a system like this would breed a whole raft of enemies for Matuze, and they'd all be either as criminal or as psychotic as they come—or both. The trick was to find them and organize them.

"Park?" Her voice came to me in the darkness, through the sound of the omnipresent rain on the roof.

"Yes, Zala?"

"Can I . . . would you mind if I got into your bed? Just for a while?"

I grinned in the dark. "Not afraid I'll strangle you or something."

She got up and walked over, almost stumbling, and sat on the edge of my bed. "No, I don't think so. If I really ever thought so I wouldn't have stayed in here a minute." She crawled into bed with me and snuggled close. It felt good, oddly comforting, but also a little disconcerting. I wasn't used to women that much larger than I was. Well, I'd better get used to it.

"What makes you so sure about me?" I teased, whispering. Still, it was reassuring to have the uncertainly settled so quickly.

"Oh, I don't know," she replied. "I've always been able to tell things about people."

"Things? Like what?"

"Oh, like the fact that Tiliar and Garal are a couple of hoods who don't really give a damn about us. Or that that big son of a bitch would enjoy breaking people in two just for fun."

"And what can you tell about me?"

"I—I'm not sure. There's a hardness in you somewhere, that's for sure, but you're no psycho. It's almost as if, well, if I didn't know it was impossible I'd say you weren't Park Lacoch at all but somebody very different, somebody who didn't belong in that body at all."

Her observations was dead on, and my respect for her intuitive abilities, if that's what it was, went up a hundred notches. Still, a smooth, glib cover was called for.

"In a way you're right," I told her carefully. "I'm not the same man I was all my life. Mentally, I'm the man I *should* have been all along. I owe them at least that much.

The old Lacoch's dead and gone, never to return. He was executed in the psych rooms with my full and hearty cooperation." *That* was true enough, although not in the way it sounded.

"Do you still have any doubts about what you are?" she asked. "I mean, ever think of maybe having the operation?"

I laughed. "Not anymore," I told her, and proved it, both to her and to my own satisfaction.

CHAPTER FOUR

Interviews and Placement

Over the next few days we got down to learning the basics of the planet through a series of lectures that would normally be very boring—and really were—but which even the most thick-headed of us realized we needed before we took our place in this new society.

The economy of Charon was almost entirely agricultural, a combination of subsistence and plantation farming. The service industries were still very primitive. While little could be brought into the Warden Diamond from Outside—the general term for every place *except* the Warden system—the planets themselves were not without resources, and material from one world could be shipped and used on others. There were sea creatures that could be caught and eaten that were rich in protein and minerals, and many creatures of the land could also be carefully raised for food. The skins of some of these reptilian creatures were also useful. Shipped to Cerberus, where they apparently had elaborate manufacturing facilities, they could be made into everything from the best waterproof clothing you could find to roofing and insulation materials.

I couldn't help but wonder about my Lilith counterpart. I myself was having a tough time with this nontechnological culture on Charon; I wondered if I would even survive in a world whose denizens were rabidly antitechnological. "I" was probably doing far better on Cerberus and Medusa, both of which had a technological level which, if below what I was used to, was nonetheless closer to my element.

Another export was the woodlike material that made up the rain forests and provided the foundations for Charon's buildings. Its weather-proofing properties and hardness made it desirable even on worlds that had their own trees.

So they exported a great deal of it to Medusa to pay for raw materials. Medusa controlled the asteroid and moon mining industries. The raw materials were sent to Cerberus where they were made into things they needed and could use under their peculiar conditions. All in all it was a neat and interdependent system.

The political system on Charon was also a good topic, and a most revealing one. I remembered Krega's comment that Matuze would become a goddess if she could and I was thus not as surprised as the rest.

The vast majority of the eleven million or so inhabitants of Charon were, of course, the workers who were mere citizens. In a nicely feudal arrangement, they worked for Companies—a euphemism for plantations basically—in exchange for which the Companies guaranteed their safety and all their basic needs.

There was a small town at the center of every dozen or so Companies, and the townspeople were also organized, this time into what were called Unions, based on trade, profession, or skill. The political head of each town was, interestingly but logically, the Town Accountant, whose office kept all the books not only on what the town produced or provided but what the Companies owed for those services. Although it was a barter system (until you got to the very top anyway), some money was in circulation—coins, made of some iron alloy. They were a good small currency, since without any significant metals the supply was strictly controlled by trade with Medusa.

In the Companies, the coins were used basically as rewards for exceptional work, so there was very little money there. In the towns, however, each Union had a set wage and a varying scale of who got paid what based on a number of factors; the money was used to buy some necessities—the Unions provided housing—and all luxuries, which weren't many. The Transportation Union, of course, was planetwide and centered in Honuth; and it used the coins to buy what was needed along the way. Honuth, being the spaceport, was the largest city on Charon— although there *was* a freightport on the southern continent, a land just now starting to be developed—and greater Honuth consisted of maybe five thousand people. The average town was a tenth that size.

Companies and Unions were run by Managers who lived pretty well as long as they produced. The Town Accountants kept tabs on them all, and *that* tab was forwarded to the Board of Regents which collectively kept track of everything and got the requirements from the towns and Companies and the raw materials and finished products they needed from off-planet. The head of the Board of Regents was called the Director, and he was the top government official on Charon. A simple system, one that seemed to work.

However, there was a parallel system as well, and this one was a little bit off the beaten track. It was composed of the small number of men and women who were in command of the Warden organism and its uses. These were the people to watch. As I'd suspected, the political and "magical" ends were not necessarily the same.

At the low end of this parallel system were the apts, the students of the art, who studied under and worked for journeymen magicians, usually referred to as sorcs, which was short for sorcerers. The sorcs were represented in every Company and Union and in every Town Accountant's office, too. They protected the people who had to be protected, enforced the rules and laws, and generally gave advice and consent when asked.

Basically, the magicians and their students were the cops. They reported to a board of Bishops whose responsibilities encompassed whole planetary areas. Collectively this group was known as the Synod.

Interestingly, the Bishops were appointed by the Director, who could hire or fire them at will. I wondered how the hell Matuze could make a firing of somebody that powerful stick—and why the Bishops were in any way obedient to her in the first place—but they were. The reason was something to be found out later. Still, the system confirmed my basic idea that Matuze herself, while probably schooled in those magical arts and reasonably competent, wasn't the top witch or whatever in terms of magical power.

Sooner or later I'd have to find out just what the Director's base of power was.

One thing was sure—Matuze had not only all the political power but all the respect and pomp as well. She was almost invariably referred to in ancient royal terms, such as "Her Highness" or even "Her Worship"; but she was nevertheless, the Lord, not the Lady, of the Diamond.

She liked to have her picture everywhere, that was for sure. Four different full-size portraits adorned the lobby. When the rain actually stopped for periods and we had walking tours of the town, I found her likeness almost everywhere, even on many of the coins we were shown— but not all. Older coins showed several men's faces, different men, and while I was sure she hated them I could see she was practical enough not to go to all the trouble and expense of replacing all the old currency until it was worn out—not when the mint was 160 million kilometers away.

All the portraits showed her much the way I remembered her—fairly young, attractive, somewhat aloof and aristocratic. Even though she was from the civilized worlds and conformed to the norm, there was something in that personality that even portraits caught, something that made her stand out. I couldn't help but wonder, though, if she still really looked that good.

The animal life on Charon was too diverse to keep track of, and was quite strange depending on which of the three continents you were on. Difficult as it was in rain-soaked Honuth to believe, animals existed on the parched central continent for whom rain could be disabling, even deadly.

The most important thing, from a survival viewpoint, was that the animals also possess a certain power for magic. It was on a primitive level, of course, but the carnivores, in particular, could quite often make you think they were a tree, a bush, or even a pretty flower, until you came too close. Some of the carrion-eaters in particular could project whole landscapes, disorienting and confusing travelers as well as instinct-driven herbivorous prey, causing bogs to look like rocks or land water.

"In a very real sense," Garal warned us, "walking along unprotected on Charon in broad daylight in good weather is like walking blindly in pitch-dark night, never knowing what is waiting for you, never knowing what is real and what is not."

This situation, of course, reinforced the feudal Company system. Nobody dared walk away, nor even travel from town to town, without the protection and abilities of a sorc. Charon was a deadly place indeed, well-suited for easy population control and political domination.

But Charon didn't worry me because in the long run its least common denominators were the same socio-economic factors that supported every world, even the Confederacy itself. Here, you got the training to use the power if you could—the easy way up, like being born to power or position elsewhere. Failing that, you found somebody who *did* have the power and rode up with that individual, using that person's power as your own—a slower and more delicate method than the first, but one that worked.

I realized, of course, why we were being kept in this hotel in this rain-soaked town for so long. Our hosts were waiting for the final "set in" of the Warden organism in order to demonstrate its effects—and powers. We were the cream of the criminal crop; we had to be shown explicitly who was boss first.

With one exception, that is. Zala continued to be more and more of an enigma to me. I realized very early on that she had been lying about herself, at least in part—she was never trained to be an accountant or, for that matter, in any similar profession. In just routine conversation and in discussing the briefings it became clear that her counting ability only slightly exceeded the capacity of her fingers and toes; her reading ability was similarly quite basic. That put her well outside any government, business, or scientific areas of expertise. It confined her, in fact, to the lowest job classes, not at all unusual for the frontier but very unusual for one of the civilized worlds.

But lies were the stock in trade of people sent to Charon, so the problem wasn't that she was lying but that she was a bundle of contradictions. The ego, the sense of self-worth in the job you were born to do, was central to the social fabric of the civilized worlds. Everyone had a job they did

well and knew was important, even vital, and something
few others could do as well. Sex was casual and recrea-
tional. There were, of course, no family units and everyone's egocentrism kept the concept of individualism a core
idea. You had a circle of friends certainly, but no depen-
dency on others in a psychological sense. The slogan "Inter-
dependence in work, independence in self" was everywhere
and was always being drummed into you.

But not Zala. Zala *needed* somebody else, and I do mean
needed. She latched onto me immediately despite the distinct possibility that I was still a mass murderer of women.
I had enjoyed our sexual encounters; she had required,
needed them. She was simply incapable of existing, let
alone surviving, on her own for very long—and that was an
incredible idea for someone like me from the civilized
worlds. Timid and passive, she lacked any of the egocentrism I took for granted. I didn't have any illusions that she'd
chosen me because of some innate magnetic charm or superior radiance I gave off. She'd chosen me because I happened to be there, was convenient, and therefore the one.

But once I was chosen, she was totally solicitous of my
welfare to the exclusion even of her own, as if she had no
thoughts of her own but simply awaited my pleasure. Although her behavior was demeaning in my eyes and bothered me in the extreme, nonetheless I have to admit I got a
certain charge from it, since it certainly fed my own ego
beyond anything I had come to expect short of service robots.

And yet, and yet . . . How the hell did somebody like
her her ever get to *be* at all, particularly on the civilized
worlds? And why was she sent to the Warden Diamond?

Late in the evening of the fourth day on Charon I decided to confront her. Her response, which was both embarrassed and nervous at being caught in so obvious a lie,
did little to answer my basic questions about her.

"I—well, you're right," she admitted. "I'm not an administrator. But the rest is true. I am, well, what they call
a bioslot Entertainer, but that isn't really quite right either.
Basically, well, the planetary administrators often have

guests from other planets and from the Confederacy itself. There are banquets and entertainments of course for the bigwigs—and I'm part of it. My job is—was—to provide those important people with just about anything they wanted. Keep them happy."

Now I knew what she meant. I'd seen a number of her type in just such circumstances while working on cases involving business and government bigwigs. The very sameness of the civilized worlds made them pretty dull. When you saw one you saw them all. Even the entertainments, meals and the like were standardized—in the name of equality, of course. It was a perfect and proper system, but there were still men and women in incredibly high places who had to be impressed when they dropped in on your little world, and those in the Entertainer class were the ones to do it. They planned and set up banquets that would be unique and offer exotic delicacies. They planned and performed unusual entertainments, including live dancing and even more esoteric demonstrations. And if even sex was boring they could provide really exotic demonstrations there too. So that's what Zala was—literally programmed and trained and raised to do anything and everything for other people. Cut off from that, she'd naturally latched onto the first person that would make her feel valued—me.

But these facts didn't explain what she was doing here, or why she had lied.

"As for the lie, well, it seemed better *here* to be an administrative assistant than an entertainer. They would have just thrown me in some kind of frontier-style brothel and that would have been that. I am not a whore! My profession is a valuable and honorable one—back home." Big tears started to well up in her eyes, and I found myself somehow on the defensive instead of the attack. She was really good at that.

Still, she stuck to the rest of her story. She was supposedly a genetic illegal, of what kind she hadn't been told, and she had been shipped here without a clue as to why. Shifting her to the right slot in life had cleared up one of my mysteries, but left her big one still unanswered.

* * *

On the afternoon of our fifth day, we got a taste of what was to come on Charon. Some minor tests had been performed without our knowing about them; they proved we were now fully "affiliated"—or seasoned—and ready to face the cold, cruel world. One of the tests, I discovered, involved the excellent soup we'd been served for lunch. Everybody had had some, everybody loved it; the only trouble was there hadn't been any soup.

At the end of the meal it came as a big shock when Garal stood up and announced, "We will need no service to clear this soup from the table." He waved his hand, and the soup—bowls, spoon, and tureen—suddenly and abruptly vanished. Even the spots where some had spilled a little on the tablecloth instantly vanished.

Although we'd all been warned to expect this, I'm afraid my jaw dropped as low as any other. The demonstration was incredible—unbelievable. That soup had been as real as my own right hand. And yet, we had all sat there, in reality eating absolutely nothing, and raving about it.

"Now, at last, you see what we mean," Garal said smugly. "But we need a few more examples just to give you an idea of the range." He pointed at a young, sandy-haired frontiersman. "You. Float up and over the table and hover there."

Immediately the startled man rose from his chair, still in a sitting position, floated over to about a meter above the dining table. He grew panicky and started flailing away at the air as we all gaped.

Mogar, the big brute with the single room who was sitting next to the man, reached over to the now empty chair and felt around. His IQ was obviously higher than I'd thought—it's exactly what I would have done. "Th—he's not in the chair!" the big man growled in amazement. To prove it, even to himself, he moved down one and sat in the chair.

"Stop thrashing about in the air!" Garal snapped, but the hapless floating man didn't heed him. Finally Garal, in a disgusted tone, said, "All right then—get down from there!" He snapped his fingers. The man fell into the cen-

ter of the table with a loud crash, almost knocking it over.
Soup wasn't the only course we'd had, and he got up a little
dizzily covered in leftovers.

We were all stunned. Levitation? "I thought you said the
magic wasn't real," I remarked suspiciously. "If that wasn't
real—what is?"

Garal smiled. "*Now* you're getting the true measure of
Charon. What *is* real here? Did that man float up, then
fall? Or did he climb up under the *impression* he was floating and then fall into the food? Do *you* know?"

"Do *you*?" somebody grumbled.

He smiled. "In this case, yes, I do. But I don't always
know. You have to be a real master of this always to tell
what's real and what's not—and usually, even then, there's
somebody around at least as good as you who can fool you.
The point is, you can't trust anybody or anything on
Charon. Never." He snapped his fingers once again, and
we all fell smack on our behinds. The chairs we had been
sitting in had all abruptly vanished.

Garal laughed. "You see? Real or illusion? Because *I*
will it even *I* see what you see, perceive it as you perceive
it. A perfect check on my own handiwork. Had someone
come in who'd never met any of us before while you were
sitting eating your soup, that person would have seen you
all sitting there eating soup. They would see what you
saw, smell what you smelled, the works. Why? Not because
I willed the illusion, but because you believed it—and radiated it."

Zala picked herself up a little painfully and then helped
me to my feet. We were all more than a little shaken.

"Enough of these children's games," our host proclaimed,
"you now know exactly what you're in for. It's not really all that bad—nor is it all that easy. Spells and coun-
terspells, mental control and discipline, those are the keys
and they aren't easily learned—and even less easily
tamed."

"Well how do we know what's real, then?" somebody
asked.

He took the question seriously. "There is only one way to
survive and prosper on Charon. Only one. You must act as

if *everything* is real—even magic. You have to discard all
your notions of the past and live as if you were part of a
children's fairy tale. You're in a world where magic works.
You're in a world where sorcery, not science, reigns, even
though it knows and understands scientific principles.
You're in a world where science, natural law, and even
logic and common sense can be suspended at the whim of
certain people. It doesn't matter if we're dealing with reality or illusion—it doesn't matter one bit. No matter what it
is, *it is real to you,* and to everyone else. Look—see that
pitcher of fruit juice on the table?"

We all looked at it, expecting it to vanish. It did not.
Instead, Garal concentrated, half shutting his eyes, and
pointed to the pitcher.

Slowly the yellow liquid inside seemed to churn, to bub-
ble, to run through with many colors, while smoking and
hissing. It was an ugly brew now, and all the more so because we had all drank from that pitcher earlier.

Garal opened his eyes and looked at us seriously. "Now,
that pitcher contained one hundred percent *nui* juice and
nothing else. I have just changed the contents into a deadly
poison—or have I? You all *see* and *smell* the stuff, don't
you?"

We all just murmured assent or nodded.

"All right, then. Stand back a bit." He walked up, carefully lifted the pitcher, and spilled a small drop on the edge
of the table. It hissed and bubbled and began eating
through the tablecloth and into the finish. Then he replaced
the pitcher on the table.

"Now, *did* I just change that into a deadly acid, or is
that still a pitcher of fruit juice?"

"It's still fruit juice," somebody said, and reached for it.

"No! Don't touch it!" Garal almost yelled; the man hesitated. "Don't you understand? It doesn't matter what it
really is! It doesn't matter a bit! You all perceive it as
acid—and so for you it *is* acid. If you got some on you it
would burn a hole in you. Why? Because you'd subconsciously tell the Wardens in your own body that it was
acid, and your cells and molecules would react accordingly.
We believe it's acid, and so our Wardens tell those in the

tablecloth and top that it's acid, and they, having no sensory apparatus of their own, believe it too, and react accordingly. Don't you see? Whether it is illusion or not, this is not simple hypnosis." He waved an arm at the room as a whole. "See all this? It's not dead. *It's alive!* The rocks and trees outside are alive. The table, walls, clothing, *everything* is alive. Alive with Wardens. And so are you and so am I.

"Wardens don't think, but they hear what you are thinking and they act accordingly. They broadcast that to all the other Wardens, and those Wardens act accordingly. That is acid because your senses tell your brain it is acid—that's hypnosis. But your brain tells the Wardens, and the others that it is acid—and that's not hypnosis. That *is* acid."

Tiliar entered from the rear accompanied by a distinguished-looking man, in his forties perhaps, wearing a long black robe adorned with golden and silver threads. He was gray-haired, an unusual sight in one so young, and had a ruddy complexion, as if he'd spen a lot of his time in a hard outdoor climate. Not *this* climate, though—he certainly was dry enough.

Garal stepped back and bowed slightly in deference to the newcomer. Both he and Tiliar treated the man with respect, the respect of subordinates to the boss.

He stopped and looked around at us, then at the acid still sputtering in the pitcher, and smiled. With no sign of concentration or effort at all, he mumbled a word and pointed to the pitcher, which immediately ceased bubbling and quickly began to transform itself back into fruit juice. Once its normal, healthy yellow color was restored, he walked over to it, picked it up, materialized a glass from somewhere, and poured juice into the glass. He then drank about half and looked satisfied, then put the glass back down on the table.

"My name is Korman," he introduced himself, his voice a mellow and pleasant baritone with an air of extreme confidence in its tone. "I'm what the locals would call the sorc—the town sorcerer. I'm also one of those who sit in the Synod, so I'm here as the official representative of the government of Charon and Her Worship, the Queen Aeola, Lord of the Diamond. Welcome."

That was a new one. So she was queen now? Could goddess be far behind—or would that be too much even for the Synod?

"My assistants here will be setting up an interview table in the rear while we chat," he continued, "and I hope I can answer some of your questions." He paused a moment. "Oh, how inconsiderate of me!" He snapped his fingers and the chairs reappeared. In addition to ours, an almost thronelike wooden monster appeared at the head of the table. He sat in it.

We all eyed the chairs with some suspicion, which gave Korman some amusement.

"Oh, come, come," he admonished us, "please have a seat—or has nothing Garal told you sunk in as yet? Face it, *you* don't know if the chairs were always there and only seemed to vanish, or whether there never were any chairs. And does it make any difference? These chairs are solid and comfortable. They will support you. You can go completely mad here trying to decide if things like that are real. Accept what your senses tell you. Sit down, please!"

With a shrug, I sat down, and slowly, the others followed suit. Korman was right of course, it made no practical difference whatsoever whether or not the chairs were real. However, I had a pretty good idea they were—Garal just didn't look like the type to exert himself to actually carry the things out, and they had been real the previous four days.

"That's better," the wizard approved. "Now, let's begin. First of all, none of you are ordinary to us. Oh, I know, it sounds like a political snow job, but I mean it. We have a lot of ordinary people to work the farms and fields. Some of the other worlds of the Diamond waste resources like you, would just throw you together with the peasants and forget about you, but not us. Each of you is here for a reason, each of you has special skills learned Outside that would take years to learn here. We don't propose to throw away any valuable talents and skills you might have just because you're new here. We don't get many Outsiders these days—you're the first small batch in more than three years—and we don't propose to have you out there picking fruit if you have something we can use."

That was something of a relief to me and probably to most of the others at the table. None of us had any desire to be peasants, and we all, for good reasons and bad, had pretty high opinions of ourselves. But Korman's statement also had an element of insecurity in it, for the challenge was clear—they would make good use of us only if we could show them a talent or skill they needed. What if everything one knew proved obsolete at Charon's quaint technological level?

"Now," he went on, "when you arrived here you were told your past was behind you, that no reference to it would be made. That is the stock speech everybody gets on all the Warden worlds, and there is a measure of truth in it. If there is anybody here who does not wish his or her past to be brought up ever again and wants a totally clean start, you are free to tell me now. We will destroy your dossier back there and you will be assigned as an unskilled laborer under any name you wish. That is your right. Anybody?"

People looked at one another, but nobody made a move or said anything. For a moment I thought Zala might, but she just took my hand and squeezed it. Nobody in this group wanted to spend the rest of his life as a melon picker in a swamp.

After a suitable pause, Korman nodded to himself. "Very well then. Your silence is consent to reopen your past—just a little. Now, one at a time I would like to interview each of you. Do not lie to me, for I will know it, I guarantee you. And if I am lied to, I will place a spell of truthfulness on you and keep it there so you will be forever incapable of lying again. You can appreciate how embarrassing that would be."

Uh-oh. I didn't like *that* at all. Still, not lying was not the same thing as telling the truth. If I could fool some of the best machines, I should have little trouble fooling a real person.

"Now, before we begin, are there any general questions you want answered?"

We looked around, mostly at one another. Finally, I decided to be the brave one. "Yeah. How do we get trained in the, ah, magical arts?"

He looked amused. "A good question. Maybe you do, and maybe you don't. Not right away, certainly—there's a certain mind-set you have to acquire over time before the training will do you much good. As long as you are in any way concerned with what is real and what is not it's hopeless. Only when you accept this world and this culture on its own terms can you begin. Your entire lives have been rooted in science, in faith in science, in belief in science and experimental evidence. Empiricism is your cultural bias. But here, where an experiment of any sort will always come out the way I decide it should, that's not valid. We'll know when—or if—you're ready, and so will you."

Somebody else had a good question. "These things we see that you and the others cause—I know everybody here sees 'em, but what about anybody not from here? Somebody from a different Warden world, maybe. Or a camera."

"Two questions," Korman replied, "and two answers. The easy one first, I think. Cameras. Cameras down here will take pictures, and no matter what is actually photographed the picture will be perceived as what was believed to have been photographed. Say I turn you into a uhar. This fellow here then takes your picture. He looks at the picture, and he sees a uhar. He takes the picture to a different town and shows it to somebody else. They see a uhar because you see a uhar, so the question's moot. Incidentally robotic devices don't work well down here—the electrical fields and storms of Charon will short out any known power plant I've heard of in fairly quick order. The same properties disrupt aerial or satellite surveillance. But even if a robot worked here, it would be nothing more than a guide for the blind, and one you could never fully trust because you wouldn't know all the questions to ask it."

"And somebody not from here?" the questioner prompted.

"Well, that's more complicated. Our Wardens are a mutated strain of the other Wardens. Our Wardens don't talk to the Wardens of the other three planets, just to those like themselves. So a visitor here from Lilith, say, would see things as they really are. However, on Charon our wishes have a way of partially coming true. A building must be a building, or the winds rush through and the storms will get you. It may not really be as fancy as it looks to us, but it's a building all the same. Organic matter, however, is a different story. If I turn you into a uhar, as my previous example shows, you'll believe you're a uhar. So will the Wardens in your body. Now, we don't know how they get the information, let alone the energy, but, slowly, the illusion will become the reality. Your cells will change accordingly, or be replaced. The whole complex biochemistry of the uhar is suddenly available to your Wardens. Perhaps they just contact their brethren in a real uhar, I don't know, but they draw all the information they need, and they draw energy from somewhere outside themselves and convert it to matter as needed; so, over a period of time, you will *be* a uhar. Really. And then even our visitor from Lilith will see you as such."

This was a new, exciting, and yet frightening idea. Transmutation was not something I relished. Still, something very important was involved here. The Wardens could get information, incredibly complex information—more complex and detailed than the best computers—and then act upon it, even converting energy to matter to achieve it. I mentally filed the information for future reference.

Korman looked around. "Anything else? No? Well then, let's begin. I'm sure you are anxious to get out of this place and pick up your lives. We are just as anxious to give this hotel back to its regular patrons, who are none too happy about the arrangement." He stood up and walked back to his two assistants, who had set up a folding table and placed a stack of thick file folders on it. He walked behind the table, sat down on a folding chair, and picked up the first of the dossiers. "Mojet Kaigh!" he called out.

One of the men in our group walked nervously over to the table and sat down at another folding chair placed in front. They were just slightly too far away to hear them when they talked in low tones, but normal conversation carried sufficiently so that we were all more or less in on the interview.

It was pretty routine really. Name, age, special skills and backgrounds—things like that. Then right in the middle I experienced something odd, as if, somehow, a second or two was lost—sort of *edited out*. Nobody else seemed to notice it and so I said nothing, but it was eerie nonetheless—either this was something I should know about or it was me, and the latter worried me the most.

The same thing happened during the second and third interviews—a sense of following along, hearing the routine procedure when, *blip*, there was a sudden slight difference in the scene—people slightly out of position, something like that. The more it happened, the more I became convinced that something not apparent to everyone else was happening.

Interestingly, the occurrence was repeated with each interview except one—Zala's. I followed what was going on particularly keenly, not only looking for the telltale blackout but also to see how well Korman's records jibed with Zala's own version of her life. It was pretty close, I had to admit—and there was no disorientation.

I fidgeted irritably as the boring process continued, although it was not completely without interest. Our big bully upstairs with the private room had been something of a dictator, it appeared, on an off-the-beaten-track frontier world; he had a particular fondness for grotesque maimings and the like. Although this information confirmed the man's chilling aura, it also reminded me that big, brawny, and nasty did not necessarily mean stupid. Anybody who could pull off a virtual planetary takeover and hold on for almost six years was definitely on the genius side—which is why he was here at all. Aeolia Matuze would love him—but whether he'd play ball with her was something else again.

I was kept for last, and when Korman called my name it was with a great deal of curiosity that I approached the table. Would I too suffer an "edit"?

He was pleasant and businesslike enough, as he had been with the others.

"You are Park Lacoch?"

"I am," I responded.

"You have no objections to your past being reviewed?"

I hesitated for what I judged was an appropriate length of time, then said, "No, I guess not."

He nodded. "I understand your apprehension. You are a most colorful character, Lacoch—did you know that?"

"I hardly think that's the word most people would use."

He chuckled dryly. "I daresay. Still, you're in a long line of mass murderers from respected backgrounds. They color human history and make its humdrum aspects more interesting. I gather they solved your basic problem?"

"You could say that. I was in deep psych for quite a long time, you understand. I emerged as what they call sane, but because of my notoriety I could hardly be returned to society."

"You see what I mean about colorful? Yes, that fits. Also, we could hardly ignore the fact that you've shared quarters here with a woman and have now spent a week in a town full of them and you've been nothing but civilized to all. Tell me, though, honestly—do you think that any conditions might set you off again, even the most extreme?"

I shrugged. "Who can say? I don't think so, not any more than you or anybody else. I'm pretty well at peace with myself on that score, so much so I can't even imagine myself doing such things, though I know I did."

"What about killing in general? Could you kill somone under any conditions?"

That was pretty easy. "Of course. If somebody was trying to kill me, for example. They didn't take that route out with me, sir. I wasn't programmed—I was cured."

He nodded approvingly, then looked up suddenly and straight at me, eyes wide, almost burning—a hypnotic gaze, an amazing one, but it flared for only a second and then was gone. Korman sighed and relaxed a moment. "There, we're alone now."

I jumped. "Huh?" I looked around at—well, nothing. There appeared to be a huge, smooth black wall right in back of me.

It was clearly too routine a thing for him to even be amused by my reaction. "A simple thing. When we return to the real world once more none of your compatriots will even be aware of any gap."

"So that's what happened! I noticed the jerkiness."

"I'm impressed. Almost nobody does, you know. The brain fills in the gap or explains it away. You say you noticed it with others?"

I nodded. "The first time I thought I was going a little crazy, but when it happened again and again I knew something was up."

"You noticed it with every one of them?"

I smiled, seeing his probe. "All but Zala. You didn't take her aside like this, I don't think."

He nodded approvingly. "You're quite correct. I don't think I've underestimated you, Lacoch. With training, you might even gain and control the Power yourself. You have demonstrated an abnormally early affinity."

"I'd like to give it a try," I told him sincerely—and *that* was no lie.

"We'll see. Chance has placed you in a most fortuitous position, Lacoch, and now you show even more interesting abilities. You've got a golden opportunity to go far on Charon."

"Oh? In what way?" I was both curious and a bit suspicious at all this interest. I didn't like having attention called to myself quite this early in the game.

Korman thought a moment, seeming to wrestle with some question in his mind. Whatever the dilemma, he seemed to resolve it and sighed.

"A little more than five years ago the Lord of Charon was Tulio Koril. He was a wily old rogue, and tremendously powerful. He had little stomach for the routine affairs of state—when one can be a god, how much more do bureaucracy, paperwork, and routine decisions weigh on him?"

"Why did he keep at it, then?"

"A sense of duty, of obligation, mostly. He derived no joy from it, but he saw the potential for terrible abuse in the position and felt that any of his logical successors would be a disaster—his opinion, of course, which has to be balanced against the egomania necessary to get to be Lord in the first place."

"A *Warden* man with a sense of duty and obligation?"

"There are many. I fancy myself one, in fact. You are as much an outcast as any of us, yet far more than we, you are the product of the society that cast you out. It is a society that aims overall for the common good, but to achieve that aim it requires all its citizens to take a certain viewpoint that is not necessarily the only one. Many of us are criminals by any lights, of course, but many more are criminal only because we dared take or develop a different viewpoint than the one the Confederacy favors. Throughout man's dirty history 'different' was always equated with evil, when 'different' is—well, simply 'different.' If *their* system is perfect, why do they employ detectives, assassins, and, for that matter, how the hell can they produce *us*?"

It was not a question easily answered, nor profitably responded to at this time. I said nothing.

"When first the Confederacy system was imposed, they set their assassins to execute those few who would not or could not adapt. That was centuries ago, and many millions of lives ago, and yet the unadapted are still here—and they are still out there killing. You know something, Lacoch? No matter how many they kill, no matter how many they reprogram, no matter what means they develop to control mind and body—we will still exist. Those who would shape history never learn from it, and yet if they did they would see in people like us the greatness of man, why he's out here among the stars instead of blown away by his own hand back on some dirty fly-speck of a home world. No matter how many enemies tyranny would kill, *there is always somebody else*. Always."

"I wouldn't exactly call the Confederacy a tyranny. Not when compared to the old ways."

"Well, perhaps not, but there, new ways mask the old. A society that mandates absolutely the way people must

think, eat, drink, whom to love—and whether to love—is a
tyranny, even if cloaked in gold and tasting of honey."

"But if the people are happy—"

"The people of the greatest tyrannies are usually
happy—or, at least, not unhappy. No tyrant in human history ever governed without the tacit support of the masses,
no matter what those masses might say if the tyrant was
ever overthrown. Revolutions are made by the few, the
elect, those with the imagination and the intellect to penetrate the tyranny and see how things could and should be
better. It is a lesson the Confederacy understands full
well—that's why people like Koril and myself are here.
And, no matter to what lengths they go, the Confederacy
will eventually follow all other human empires and fall,
either from external factors or from sheer dry rot. They
are staving off the fall, but fall they will, eventually. Some
of us would prefer they fall sooner than later."

"You sound like an embittered philosopher," I commented.

He shrugged. "Actually, I was a historian. Not one of
those official types teaching you all the doctored-up versions of the past you were supposed to learn, but one of the
real ones with access to *all* the facts, doing analyses for the
Confederacy. History is a science, you know—although
they don't really let you know that either. The techs are
scared to death of it and put it in the same category as
literature, as always. That's why hard science people are
the most ignorant of it and so easily led. But, I digress
from my point."

"I find this all fascinating," I told him truthfully—
knowing my enemy was vital—"but you were speaking for
some reason of Koril."

He nodded. "Koril is one of the old school intellectuals.
He knows that the Confederacy will fall one day of its own
weight and he is content to allow natural forces to do just
that, even if it might be centuries in the future. There is
another school, though, that believes that a quick and, if
need be, violent push to oblivion will, overall, save lives
and produce positive results for more people. A man can
die in agonizing slowness or nearly instantly—which is

more merciful to him? You see the difference in positions?"

I nodded. "Evolution or revolution—an old story. I gather this is behind Koril no longer being Lord?"

"It is. He was an evolution man in power at the wrong time."

I was becoming more and more interested. "The wrong time? That implies that such a revolution on such a scale is suddenly possible, something I find very hard to believe."

"About five years ago," Korman told me, "Marek Kreegan, Lord of Lilith, called a special conference of the Four Lords of the Diamond. We had been contacted, it seems, by an external force that wanted our aid in overthrowing the Confederacy."

"External force?" I could hardly believe it. A week on Charon and already I was finding out a lot of details I thought I would have to dig out with a sword.

"An alien force. Big. Powerful. Not really more advanced than the Confederacy but unhampered by their ideological restraints, which means they have a lot of stuff we don't. They are also—by design, we think—far fewer in number than humankind. They have a long history of getting along with other kinds of life forms, but their analysis of the culture and values of the Confederacy said that together we would just out-and-out crush them. They feel they must destroy the Confederacy, but they have no wish to destroy humankind as well."

"Do you think they could? You just said how small they were compared to us."

He shook his head sadly from side to side, more in wonder than in reaction to my question. "You see? You make an easy mistake. It's not *numbers* that are important. The Confederacy itself could destroy a planet with ten billion on it with *one* simple device, and do it with perhaps only one man and two robots. Three against ten billion—and who would win?"

"But they'd have to get to all those planets first," I pointed out.

"Any race smart enough to meet and attempt an alliance with the Four Lords—and pull it off under the noses of the picket ships and the other devices our prison system contains to keep us isolated—and who even so remains virtually unknown to the Confederacy would have few problems doing so."

I had to admit he had a point there, but I let it pass for the moment. "And the Four Lords went along with the deal?"

He nodded. "Three of them did. Kreegan came up with the master plan; the aliens will provide the technology and access; and the other worlds contribute their power, wealth, and expertise."

"I assume the one who didn't was Koril."

Again he nodded. "That's the story. He was just flat-out against the plan. He feared the aliens were only using us for a painless conquest which once undertaken, would enable them to enslave or wipe out mankind. In this he was pretty well alone. Of course, emotionally, to be a party to the overthrow of the Confederacy within your lifetime is almost irresistible, but there is an overriding practical reason as well. The Warden worlds that help will share in the rewards, even the spoils. There is very good reason to believe that these aliens are capable of curing, or at least stabilizing, the Warden organism. You understand what *that* means."

I nodded. "Escape."

"More than escape! It means we, personally, will be there to pick up the pieces. Quite an incentive! But, as I said, there is overriding practicality here. Charon is probably the least necessary of all the Warden worlds. Mostly political criminals, wrong thinkers, that type are sent here, and the plot, quite frankly, could proceed without us. Could—and would. We would be isolated, cut off as things proceeded without us. But if anything went wrong, we would be blamed along with the others, even though we took no part. That might result in the Confederacy literally destroying the Warden Diamond. But, if things succeeded, the other three would be on the winning side, with all those IOUs and means of escape, and we would be stuck here, consigned to eternal oblivion. Therefore, since we were not important to the plot, we either joined it and gained or we didn't and lost whatever the outcome. *That* was what caused the unprecedented removal of a Lord of the Diamond."

"This Koril—I gather he didn't take this lying down?"

"Hardly! It took the entire Synod's combined power to oust him, and even then he was horrible in his power. He fled, finally, to Gamush, the equatorial continent, where he had already prepared a retreat and headquarters so well hidden none have been able to find it. Consider—a lowly apt in the magical arts could kill you with a glance. One of the village sorcs could level a castle and transform all the people into trees if he or she felt like it. The combined Synod could make a continent vanish and rearrange the oceans of the world. But that same combined Synod could only oust, not kill, Koril—and cannot locate him now. Does that give you an appreciation of the old man's power?"

I had seen little but parlor tricks on this world so far, but I could accept his examples at least as comparative allegory. "And he's still working against you."

"He is. Not effectively of late, but he is more than dangerous. He retained good friends in high places, and some of his agents even managed to penetrate meetings of the Four Lords themselves. At one point, they got past tight security of kinds you can not imagine to witness a meeting with our alien allies themselves. The spies slipped up before they could do any harm and were all eventually tracked down and killed, but it was a *very* close call. Koril came within a hair's breath of killing all Four Lords and two of the aliens as well—and he wasn't even there! He was still safe down in Gamush."

It was my turn to push now. "All this is well and good— but, tell me, why are you telling me all this? I would assume it's far from common knowledge."

"You're right. Koril's fall was pictured publically as a move to save Charon from evil ambition. We created, in the minds of the people, a portrait of him as a devil, a demon, a creature of pure powerful evil. It has been quite effective, and even useful—a force of opposition based on fear and power. It keeps the masses in line, and he can be blamed for just about anything that goes wrong."

"A bogeyman." So much for tolerating other points of view, I thought to myself.

"Yes, exactly. But a real one who remains a real threat. We would much prefer to have him be merely a myth. He's used our own propaganda against us too, to attract those unhappy with us in any way, employing the trappings of devil worship and the rest, creating an effective cult of opposition, in both senses of the word 'cult.' We can not be truly safe and secure until Koril is destroyed."

"But I thought you said you had tried that and failed."

"Well, not exactly. There was no concerted effort to destroy him when he wasn't already forewarned and forearmed. After all, we didn't hate him or covet his job—we merely wanted him out because we could not change his mind. Had we foreseen what sort of enemy he would make—but that's hindsight. We *can* kill him—if we face him down. But to do that we have to know where he is, where that redoubt is."

I knew all this was leading somewhere, but it wasn't clear why I was the one being led there. "What's all this have to do with me?"

"I'm coming to that. First of all, he has a large minority following in his demon cult, but they are mostly useless except as information gatherers because they really believe that guff. In the aftermath of his botched assault we pretty well wiped out his effective force. He needs new people—level-headed, unclouded with superstition, and yet with some residual ties to the old values of the Confederacy. People who would be useful commanders of his demonic troops, bring fresh ideas and approaches to him, and take his side against the aliens even if they had no particular love for the Confederacy."

I began to see. "In other words, newly arrived inmates like me."

"You're the most logical. We get few newcomers these days—none of the Wardens get many, and we get the fewest of all. The nature of our atmosphere prevents most clandestine communications, and even blocks basic surveillance of us on the ground by remotes. The Confederacy has agents of one sort or another all over the Warden Diamond, but they are of almost no use here since messages are nearly impossible to get in or out except by spacecraft, which are rigidly monitored. You're the first small group we've gotten since long before Koril was deposed, so you're an absolute natural for him to approach. And of course there is a different reason as well—the real reason why we got *any* prisoners this drop. You see, due to the inevitable slip-up, the Confederacy is finally wise to the fact that we and our alien allies are plotting against it. That's *all* it knows though, and it's too little to act upon—and, I think, too late. Still, they are not stupid. They have already sent at least one top assassin to the Warden Diamond—we know that."

"*What!*" I felt a cold chill. Was I being led down the garden path to the guillotine? Had my cover been so easily blown?

He nodded. "And while we are sure only of the one, it's reasonable for us to assume that they would send more."

"But what for?" I asked, steadying my nerves as best I could. "You just said it would be nearly impossible to get information out. And anybody they'd send here would be stuck, just like us."

"It is our belief—Charon's, not the Four Lords, I might add—that they will send their best men available to each of the four worlds with the intent of killing each of the Four Lords. Doing this will, they feel, cause some disruption, and the new Lord will be a lot less sure of him or herself and perhaps less disposed toward treason. It is not much of a hope, I admit, but it's the only logical thing they *can* do while they try and find the alien enemy first."

He was uncomfortably close to the mark, and I could only feel I was being toyed with. Something inside kept shouting "*He knows! He knows!*"—but my more controlled overmind kept saying that the best way to proceed was to play along, at least for now. "And you think that one of us is a Confederacy fanatic?"

"I *know* it," he responded. "I knew it the moment I met the agent face to face."

He paused for a moment and I braced for the inevitable denouement to our little play.

"The Confederacy's agent," he said, "is Zala Embuay."

CHAPTER FIVE

A Plot, a Deal, and a Potion

"*Zala?* You've got to be joking!" I could hardly contain my emotions at this point, a mixture of incredulity, relief, and a still-lingering suspicion that I was being had. "You've got to be kidding. Without protection she wouldn't last ten minutes outside this hotel."

"That's partly the point," Korman responded, and he didn't seem to be joking. "Have you ever seen anyone so innocent, so confused, so totally *dependent*? Not the Warden Diamond sort at all. Not even the Confederacy's."

"You're saying it's all an act? A plant?" I found it hard to take this seriously from *any* viewpoint.

"Oddly enough, no. Zala is, I'm certain, exactly what we see. She's shallow, weak, more an outline of a real person than a whole human being. There is no doubt in my mind that she believes herself to be what she is utterly and has no inkling whatsoever of her true nature and purpose."

I had to laugh. "This is impossible."

"When I saw her I was immediately aware of the anomaly. The Wardens, you see, congregate in every cell, in every molecule of our being. They permeate our existence. With some training you can even see them. Sense them. *Hear* them. I'm sure you'll one day experience what I can only inadequately verbalize. But the Wardens become as highly specialized as the molecules they link up to. The brain is particularly odd. Wardens there organize in specific ways, so specialized that you can actually see a diagram of the parts of the brain. When I look at anyone—you, for instance—I see those parts distinctly, and even how they interconnect and interact. The cerebrum and the

cerebral cortex are easy to define. In you, in everyone—
but not in Zala."

"Huh? How's that?"

"I can't really explain it. It is outside my experience in
every way. Outside anybody's, I'd guess. But organically,
Zala's cerebral functions are organized very differently. It's
almost as if there were *two* forebrains in there, two totally
different operative centers linked to the same cerebellum,
medulla, spinal cord and nervous system—but not to each
other. It is definitely organic. Deliberate. And unprecedented as far as I can tell."

"You're telling me that there are two minds in one body?
That's hard to swallow, although I've heard tales of multi-
ple personalities."

"No! Not in that old sense. Multiples as we know them
are psych conditions. Psychologically induced—and cur-
able. This is not a psych condition. I'm talking about two
real minds, Lacoch!"

I couldn't shake the oddest feeling that either I was
dreaming this whole illogical and improbable conversation
or that I had really gone suddenly insane. The thought
suddenly came to me that all this was illusion, some way
in which they were pulling some sort of sophisticated
psyche job on me. Still, I had wits enough left to realize
that no matter what the situation, my only choice was
to keep playing along, at least for now. "You will understand," I said carefully, "that I find both the idea and
your means of confirmation rather, ah, improbable."

He nodded. "Still, it's true and it must be acted upon.
The implications of a dual mind with unknown powers are
ones we can't ignore, and must know more about it. Within
a matter of hours, I can get a set of master defense codes
for the Confederacy, even a list of the top fifty assassins
now on assignment along with the actual assignments of at
least half. Our information conduits into the Confederacy
are not only beyond their belief, they are almost beyond
mine. Yet we have heard nothing whatsoever about a project like this, which must have been—what?—twenty years
plus in the making. The perfect agent. She can be hypnoed,
psyched to the gills, tortured beyond endurance and she

wouldn't know or give away a thing. If we had telepathy she'd pass *that* test too. All the while the other mind, the assassin's mind, would be there, beyond reach, gathering data and picking its own time to assume control. It must be something else—it has nothing to do *but* its job. Cold, analytical genius set to one task and only one."

I thought about it. If all this were real, I could not only see his point I could almost doubt myself. Krega had never said that I'd be the only agent, and Zala might well be part of an independent effort. Telling myself I was really crazy for starting to believe all this, I still had to press on. "So you just kill her and that's that," I commented dryly.

"Oh, no! Then we would never see this other mind, never know its capabilities—and we might not catch the next one, or the next dozen, or hundred, or whatever. Not to mention that they'll be ticking bombs back in the Confederacy when all hell breaks loose and we return. We need to know a great deal more about her new type. Of course, we'd like to know just how much they really know about us at this stage."

"I thought you just told me their secrets were an open book."

He glared at me. "Some. But we—the Four Lords—are a special target of a special group. Their plans are so secret that even those who formulated them have been wiped now." He sighed. "And that brings us back to what we have dubbed 'Operation Darkquest'—which brings us back to you."

I nodded, beginning to see how all this was fitting together. Still, I couldn't resist a mild jab. "It seems to me that for a man with the powers of a god you're sounding pretty human."

Again the glare, but it softened, and his eyes lit up with just a trace of humor. "You're right, of course. It *is* something of a humbling experience, but the mind is always the best weapon no matter what sort of power one acquires."

"Now—do you mind getting down to specifics?" I pressed.

"All right, all right. We are going to assign Zala to you

and you to a minor but conspicuous village post down south where Koril's cult is very strong. We feel certain Koril will contact you, indirectly of course, and sound you out. Now that you know the situation, we want you to go along with him, feed his prejudices. You and Zala will ultimately accept his deal to join him, and that will mean getting you to his redoubt."

"You feel sure he'll contact us? We'll be pretty obvious, I'd think."

"He'll contact you, all right. Maybe not right away, but he'll come. Eventually he'll contact all of you, but not all will go his way."

"I see. And you want me to somehow get the location of that fortress to you."

He nodded. "That and his future plans."

"You have some gadget for me to do all this with, I presume?"

He shook his head from side to side. "Sadly, no. Most of the usual ones won't work here, and anything I might add by my powers Koril would detect. He's that good. No, I suspect we'll have to wait until he sends you out on your first errand, or mission, or whatever. Call it a test of your resourcefulness."

I considered it. "And how am I supposed to make sure this message gets to you without getting my head blown off either by your people or Koril's?"

"Koril is your problem. As for the other, the key word is 'Darkquest.' Village sorcs and those above will know the term but not what it means. What it will do is make certain that you are not killed and that word of your capture or whatever will reach the Synod."

"It seems to me Koril's going to know at least the signal word himself—if he's as good as you say."

Korman nodded. "He will, but it will do him no good. He won't know what it means, and any of his people using it other than yourself will simply walk into capture."

That part pretty well satisfied me. "How good is this Koril in psych terms though? Am I likely to go through some sort of exercise that will betray the plot when I'm down there in *his* domain?"

"He himself is powerful enough to turn your mind to almost anything, which is the reason for the length of our session here. I have been creating blocks in your mind, selective traps and guards that will go up should he try any such thing. And if he *does* try any mind-turning, it won't take. Not for long anyway."

"But he's likely to sense the blocks," I noted.

"On most attempts, certainly," Korman agreed. "But *you*—you have been through three years of intense psych before coming here, remember. Your mind now shows many, many blocks and rechannelings to me. The extras I add won't be noticed, and that alone is what makes you so uniquely qualified—you see?"

I *did* see. Of course, the psych blocks Korman saw weren't from any Lacoch psych treatments but from my own breeding, training, and Krega's Security; but it explained a lot. If Korman could sense those blocks—but not remove them—it not only reinforced my assumed identity but quite possibly prevented him from doing some of that mind-bending on me. I remembered that earlier hypnotic gaze. "All right, I understand the plot," I told him. "What about Zala?"

"Take her along, by all means!" Korman urged. "Find out all you can from her, particularly from her alter ego which you will almost certainly see. And if you can manage it, when *you* are in position to use 'Darkquest' see if you can't manage to have her with you."

I chuckled. "This is *some* job you're giving me. I was a planetary administrator, for god's sake! Now I'm instantly supposed to be a master spy, secret agent, and the rest, pitting myself against the top power on the planet and a Confederacy assassin!"

"You don't have to accept," he said calmly. "I admit your overall qualifications aren't very good. Against the perfect psych cover and an interesting and agile mind, we must balance your lack of experience. Do you remember your old self all that well?"

I gave the required shudder. "Yes, I remember him."

"You were a master of disguise and you baffled the best

police for over five years. You're not as rank an amateur as you think."

I considered that. "Still, I'm going to have to make every move right—no mistakes of any kind. One goof and I'm done, maybe for a very long time. The odds are I'm going to get killed."

"Well, that's true," he admitted casually, "but consider that you have alternatives. First, you can refuse categorically. I'll find another candidate, team Zala up with him or her, and wipe this entire conversation from your memory. You'll then be sent north, out of the way, and can spend the rest of your life toiling in the fields getting in the harvest. That's safe. Or you can accept—and get killed. Or you can accept, accomplish the mission, and find yourself very abruptly a man of immense rank and power at the right hand of Aeolia Matuze and the Synod, a participant in the coming revolution, and sure recipient of its fruits."

I looked at him cautiously. "And I could accept, contact Koril, and really join his side."

"You could," he admitted, "and yet—why? If you win you'll be a big shot on an isolated and primitive world forever. More likely, you will not win, and will either grow old in frustration as we go ahead anyway—or die in some foolish attempt on the Synod. If you can't see that Koril has nothing to offer worth the risk, then you're not much good to me anyway."

I nodded. "All right, I'll be your boy. Overall, you don't give me much choice, and it beats boredom. Besides, I'm kind of curious about all this myself."

Korman smiled. "I knew you would see reason. Just remember this: don't underestimate Koril a whit, and under no circumstances try to take on the old boy himself or even run to us while he's anywhere in the neighborhood. Nobody's that good. It'll take the whole Synod to nail him. Bet on it."

"I fully intend to live through this," I assured him.

He laughed evilly. "Lacoch, if you blow this, death will be the *best* you can expect. Now, I'm going to lower the barrier and continue asking routine questions once more. None of the others, not even my associates, will know that this conversation has even taken place. You'll be assigned later today and be on your way early in the morning. It's a long trip, but one you'll find interesting. Once in Bourget, the town we're sending you to, you'll be under the wing of Tally Kokul, the local sorc. He's a good man and he'll orient you properly, but he won't be in on this at all. Keep it that way—and watch out for him and his apts. We're not so sure of the apts, and any of them have more power than you can imagine."

"I'll remember," I assured him.

There was a sudden feeling of disorientation that lasted only a fraction of a second. I didn't turn around, but I could hear the rest of the inmates whispering and rustling behind me.

"I think we have a number of openings for administrative types like yourself," Korman said, now very business-like. "You may return to the group."

I got up and went back to the rest of them, searching for signs that any of them were in any way aware of just how long we had been talking, but detected nothing. Still, there were a few knowing smirks, and I remembered that Korman had had private conversations with most of the others as well. I wondered if they had gotten the same offer that I had. I somehow doubted it—unless some of them also had unique qualifications. It was unlikely that the sorcerer had put all his eggs in one basket.

I had to look at Zala again, with new insight, but what I had just heard still didn't seem possible. And yet . . . It was also unlikely that the Confederacy would have put all *its* eggs in one basket either. If what Korman suspected was true, it would place me in a very interesting position. I too wanted very much to meet this other Zala—if indeed she truly existed.

We were fed again, and then relaxed, playing some basic games, just snoozing or sitting in the lobby waiting for our hosts to return. Several times I got into conversations, but either I was too subtle or nobody wanted to discuss his experience. Finally I wound up in a corner with Zala.

"What do you think will happen to us now?" she asked me.

I shrugged. "They're going to give us jobs, I think."

"They knew I wasn't an administrator," she said nervously. "I guess they have the official records no matter what they said. He said there wasn't much call for my talents here."

"Don't worry. It'll all work out."

"I wonder if they'll split us up?" she went on, playing out her petty fears. "I wouldn't want to be split up. Not from you."

"We'll see," was all I could reply, knowing the verdict ahead of time.

It was a couple of hours before Korman returned, this time with a clipboard. He took his seat again behind the table, thumbed through some sheets, then looked up at us. We all stood, expectantly, waiting for the word. Zala seemed extremely nervous and squeezed my hand so hard she was almost cutting off circulation; some of the others looked a little anxious themselves, but others did not. I found that an interesting fact in itself.

One by one, Korman called out our names, not in the order he had used at the start, and told the various people the names of towns and jobs they were assigned to. About halfway through, he called both Zala and me, whereupon my suffering hand got squeezed even tighter as we approached.

"Park Lacoch, you were a planetary administrator, and that's quite good and useful experience, although here you won't have your fancy computers and large staffs. It'll take some getting used to, so we're going to start you off small. The town of Bourget on the southeast coast just lost its Town Accountant. It's a bit larger than we'd like to start somebody green at, but the position's open and you're here. You'll deal with four industries, twenty-one Companies. There's a civil staff there that'll break you in and get you oriented—depend on them until you learn the ropes."

"Won't there be some resentment that I got the job ahead of them?" I asked him.

"Probably a little, but not much. It's basically a local staff, all native, and they're a pretty contented lot. They do what they're told. If you're good to them and respect their experience they'll accept you."

"Sounds fair," I told him, meaning it.

"As for you, Zala Embuay," Korman continued, "you present us with a problem. Your nonaugmented literacy rate is very low, your grasp of figures basic. The best position we could find to fit your unique talents would be barmaid or chambermaid. Your entertainment and planning skills might be considerable, but they are all tailored to augmentation. Without the standard computer devices, these skills are mostly useless here. In fact, the more we considered it, the more we realized that you would be out of your element even in the bar or chamber service. You would have to learn skills taken for granted here."

I felt her tremble through the clutched hand as this was being said, all the more so because it was true. A product of a society in which robots did all the basic work and everything from the lights to the music was controlled through machines, she simply had no skills to offer here.

"Therefore, the most logical occupation for you here would be an agricultural field worker. But we feel that such a radical change to basic menial labor without some intermediate steps might not be best for you; your outworlder status could cause some disruptions among your fellow menials." Zala looked blankly at him when he said that, but I understood what he meant. Workers are happiest when they don't know what they're missing. Zala's memories and tales of the wonders of the Confederacy, while they lived with no hope of change in the wretched and primitive condition, would foster resentment—and cause all sorts of local disruptions, not to mention perhaps more converts for Koril.

"So, Zala Embuay, what shall we do with you?"

"I—don't know," she wailed, so pitifully that neither of us could be completely unmoved by her evident misery and low self-esteem.

"The best we could come up with, I'm afraid, is a rather outdated concept where you both come from," Korman continued, sounding cold and businesslike. "With Lacoch's permission, I'd like to propose you become his wifemistress."

She gave something of a gasp and I kind of started myself. "Wifemistress?" I echoed.

He nodded. "I'm rather embarrassed to bring it up. In effect it's a sort of chattel slavery. You would be pledged to Lacoch absolutely. You would live with him and be totally dependent on him for your living quarters and provisions. In exchange, you will learn and practice basic skills—cooking, cleaning, mending. Many of the villagers will take you in hand and show you these things. You will also clean and run errands in his office, whatever he requires you to do. And if need be, you may be called upon by any of the Companies or the town for supplementary labor in the harvest or maintenance."

She looked startled. "That almost sounds like a service robot."

"Something like that," Korman agreed. "But there are no robots here. Other than as a subject for experimental research, there's little we can do with you."

She started at that. "Exper . . . you mean like some kind of animal?"

He nodded gravely, then looked over at me. "Would you accept this arrangement?"

I was in something of a quandary. For anybody but Zala it sounded horrible, dehumanizing, demeaning in the extreme—but what else could she do? "If she's willing, I'll go for it," I told him.

He shifted his gaze back to her. "Well?"

"I—I'd like to go with Park, but I don't know whether I *can* . . ."

Korman grinned, made that magical wave and produced a vial of reddish-colored liquid. He handed it to her. "The oldest sorcerer's gift in magical history," he said. "If you decide to go along, both of you go up to your room and when alone, Embuay, drink this. It is pleasant-tasting and won't hurt a bit, but it'll make things a lot easier on you."

She took the vial and looked at it curiously. "What—what is it?"

"A potion," he replied. "As I said, the oldest basic for-

mula. A love potion, the ancients would call it. Just be sure
to drink it when the two of you are alone, maybe just before going to sleep."

Suddenly, again, that wall of silence and isolation came
down and Korman and I were effectively alone.

"Is that *really* a love potion?" I asked him.

He chuckled. "Not to you or me if we drank it. Tastes a
little like licorice. But I have prepared her mind for it, and
it'll be quite effective with her because she will believe in it
and that will trigger my patterns in the Wardens of her
brain."

"Which one?" I couldn't resist it.

"Actually, that should be interesting," he replied, taking
no note of the sarcasm. "The emotional centers and hormonal responses are in the animal, not the human part of
the brain. Theoretically it should affect her no matter
what—I hope. But don't count on it. If that other brain's as
good as I think, it can probably control and suppress almost
any emotional response." He paused for a moment. "See
that she drinks it. And—well, good luck."

"I'll need it," I assured him, and I sure would. Still, all
in all, things had gone better so far than my wildest
dreams. If what was going on could be taken at anything
close to face value, they suspected someone other than me
of being, well, *me*; and they'd assigned me to keep watch
on their mistaken notion. They had practically forced me
into the camp of what would seem to be a natural ally—
Koril—and given me the option of joining a local super-
powerful resistance devoted to my own cause or betraying
it, giving me entré into the presence of my quarry, Aeolia
Matuze, as a trusted confidant. Hell, I couldn't lose!

Zala, though, was still and always the unknown factor.
The more I analyzed her, the more I began to believe that
she *couldn't* be what she seemed. Such a weak ego was
unthinkable on the civilized worlds.

Later, back in our room, we sat and talked for a while.
It had not been pleasant having her low self-worth so
coldly and completely analyzed in the open, even if it was
obvious.

"I want to go with you," she told me sincerely, "but—

people as property! It's barbaric!" She took out the vial and looked at it oddly.

"You don't have to take that," I assured her. "Just come along."

She shook her head slowly, still looking at the vial. "No, I know what would happen. I'd rebel, or go crazy, and wind up worse than I am now. Maybe . . . maybe this is best for me."

"That stuff might not even work," I noted. "Not only is the idea pretty insane—a love potion—but it seems to me that it's like everything else on this crazy world—a love potion only if you think it is."

"I wonder what he meant by love potion, anyway?" she mused. "As in making love?"

"No, I don't think so. It's an ancient romantic concept. Somehow I doubt that any little bottle is going to revive that."

She removed the stopper and sniffed. "Smells like candy."

I sighed and relaxed back on the bed. "Look, stop it up for now and let's get some sleep. Bring it with you it you want. But let's get some sleep—we've got a big day ahead tomorrow."

"I—I suppose you're right. But damn it, Park, I'm scared! Scared of me, scared of that town, scared of . . . living." That last was said slowly, strangely, as if only now she was accepting the truth. I watched, curious, as she suddenly pulled the stopper back off and raised the bottle to her lips . . . and froze solid. It was odd, as if she'd made the decision, started to drink, and then become petrified in mid-motion. Still, there was movement, of a sort. Her hand, and only her hand and arm that held the vial, trembled, the little vial rising ever so slightly, then falling slightly more, as if it were at war with itself, receiving two totally different sets of commands.

I rose a bit and watched, fascinated. Two minds, Korman had said. Two minds, one central nervous system. Abruptly, the struggle stopped, and, without a word, her body seemed to relax, but her face seemed vacant, expressionless. Wordlessly she stood up, walked over to the basin, and poured out the contents of the vial. Then, after putting the vial on the commode, she turned, returned to her bed, and lay down.

"Zala? Are you all right?" I asked gently, finally getting up when I had no response and going over to her. She was asleep, breathing regularly and rhythmically.

I stood there a few moments, just staring. Finally I said, aloud, "Well I'll be damned," snuffed out the light, and got into my own bed. I found it hard to sleep. It had started raining again, but the regular sound of the drops hitting the roof hardly bothered me at all.

What the hell had I just witnessed?

CHAPTER SIX

The High Road to Bourget

In the morning, Zala had no memory of the internal struggle I had witnessed, and she seemed surprised to see the goop still in the basin, practically accusing me of doing the deed.

"You did it—I watched you," I assured her. "It's for the best anyway."

She stared at me in disbelief. "*I* did? You're not just kidding me?"

"No, no kidding. Honest."

She shook her head for a moment, as it trying to remember. Finally she just sighed and shrugged. "Well, let's get on with it."

"At least packing's easy," I noted. "I hope they have more clothing at Bourget."

We went down to breakfast, a fairly ample one as usual, but Garal, our host for this, our last morning, cautioned a few of us, Zala and I among them, to eat lightly. "You're gonna have a long trip and traveling isn't very smooth around here."

Both of us took his advice. I was never much of a breakfast eater anyway, but I put away several cups of café, a very good hot caffeine drink, and a sweet roll.

When we were finished, Garal stood at the head of the table. "We will be going out individually or in small groups as transportation is available," he announced. "The rain has stopped, which means that some of you will be flying, which is a good thing. Overland to some of your villages might take days."

"Flying?" I couldn't resist voicing the surprise that everyone felt. "I thought there were few machines here."

"Well, we use the shuttle, for extremely long hauls—like intercontinental ones—but we have other means here as well," Garal responded enigmatically. "Just hold on. You'll find out soon enough."

He reached down and checked his clipboard. "All right —take nothing with you except the clothes on your back. You'll get everything you need when you get where you're going." He looked around at all of us and smiled a little evilly. "So far you've had it soft and easy. Now you're going out into the real world there, and it's gonna be a shock, I promise you. Keep your noses clean, take the advice of any locals, and take it real easy until you get the lay of the land, I warn you. That sounds like the usual advice, but it goes double here. Just remember that scrawny kid you knock down might be an apt who'll get a little irritated and wrench your guts around or at the very least cast a spell on you. And don't stare at the changelings! Just remember that anybody who happens to look funny or different got that way for a reason and the same thing could happen to you."

This last meant little to us at the time.

As the morning wore on, official-looking men and women came by and called out a name, sometimes two, and out they'd go. We were not the last to be called, but in the bottom half, which made me start to regret how lightly I'd eaten.

Our initial transport was a small enclosed buggy pulled by a single toothy uhar. It wasn't nearly as comfortable as the coach—very basic board and putty insulation—and we could feel every little bump in the very bumpy road. The uhar carts, no matter how fancy or plain, would take some getting used to; the big lizard's gait tilted you first to one side, then to the other, rather quickly, while seeming to draw you forward in tiny and continuous fits and starts.

We quickly cleared the town, then took a branch road to the north. Zala and I said very little during the journey, for there was very little to say except to voice the anxiety we both felt. With her ego it was really bad; at least I not only had a full reservoir of self-confidence, but knew in what direction the future was leading. Never had two more dissimilar people started out on an epic journey together, I reflected.

We had broken through the rain forest to a vast clearing when Zala looked out her window and gasped. Frowning, I leaned over and looked out at what she was seeing—and did a little gasping myself.

I saw a great, sleek, jet-black body topped by a head that looked like an enormous black triangle, with an enormous hornlike bony plate going back from the top of that weird head to almost halfway down the body. The head itself seemed to consist of an enormous beak and a pair of huge, round eyes that appeared to be lidless. But the real stunning part of the creature was its wings, which were barely folded and ran almost the length of the body. The wings were supported, somehow, by an apparatus and guy-wires. The thing appeared to be eating something enormous and bloody, gulping it down easily. As our buggy pulled to a stop and two people ran to get the door for us, I heard an enormous belch.

We both jumped out of the buggy and stood there, transfixed by the sight. A young woman dressed in tight, leathery black clothes and boots approached, joined us, then turned and looked back at the beast. "Magnificent, isn't she?" the newcomer enthused.

"That's one word for it," I responded. "What the hell *is* it?"

"They have a long scientific name, but we generally call 'em soarers around Charon. They're very rarely found on the ground, because it's so hard to get them aloft again. They live up above the clouds around most of the planet, just floating there above the clouds and using surprisingly little energy."

"Is the beast down here for the reason I think it's down here?" Zala managed nervously.

The woman laughed. "Oh, yes. We use the soarers for transportation. They're very useful, although only certain areas have enough clearing, wind, and elevation to get them aloft again. They're quite friendly and intelligent, if they're raised from eggs."

"I'll bet," I replied. "And it can get back in the air from here?"

"Oh, sure. Silla's an old vet to this kind of thing. Still, they're not practical for mass transportation, and we use 'em mostly for the high-ups. You two're gonna get a real treat. Most folks never get to ride on one and the sight of one of 'em dropping through the clouds scares most folks silly."

"The thought of riding on one doesn't do wonders for me," I said uneasily, no longer regretting the light breakfast a bit.

"What do we do—climb on her back?" Zala wanted to know.

The woman laughed. "Oh, no. See? The crew's putting the passenger compartment on now. It's strapped on tight and fits between bony plates just forward of the wings—see?"

We *did* see—a fairly substantial-looking compartment, like a small cabin, was being hoisted into position with a manual winch. Two members of the ground crew, looking like tiny insects on that great body, positioned the contraption into place and then dropped straps to the ground, where others crawled under the beast and tied or buckled the straps together. A few sample pushes to make sure it was seated right and the people on top seemed satisfied and started down ladders on either side. The operation shifted forward, where a smaller compartment was being similarly mounted just in back of the thick neck.

"What do they *eat*?" Zala asked, still incredulous at the sight.

The woman shrugged. "Practically anything. They're omnivores, like us. Actually, they need very little. They're hollow-boned and amazingly light; once they catch the currents and get some altitude, they use very little energy. A ton of mixed stuff every two days or so is the usual—mostly the tops of trees, stuff like that, along with whatever's in 'em—but we give Silla extra, a couple of uhars or some other big animal, because of the energy take-off requires. They're quite effective in controlling the wild animal population, thinning forests, you name it, and they fly in heavy rain as easily as in sunshine. The wild ones just about never land, but they do come in close. Don't worry about 'em, though—they know better than to nab people, who generally don't have enough meat on 'em to be worth paying attention to, anyway."

I was very happy to hear that. "How's it flown—guided, I mean?" I asked her.

"The pilot—that's me—sits up there in that control cabin. I've got basic navigation instruments there, and the floor on both sides opens up. The early pioneers tried bridles, but they don't work and the soarers are smart anyway. A well-trained one like Silla knows what to do just from how I press my feet on which side of the neck, when to do it, and when to stop." She paused a moment, then added, "Well, it's a little more complicated than that—but I'll be in complete control."

Looking at her—she was no larger than I was and probably weighed less—and then at the soarer over there I was not reassured, but this wasn't my party, not yet.

A crewman came running up to her. "Word is it'll start pouring again in less than twenty minutes," he told her. "Better get everybody aboard and away."

She nodded.

"I thought you said it was fine in the rain," I said.

"She is," the pilot replied, "but taking off in those winds can turn us upside down at the very least. Better get on board." She ran for the pilot's cabin.

I looked at Zala, who looked nervously back at me. "Think you can take it?" I asked her.

"I'll—try. If *she* can fly one, I can sure ride one."

We walked quickly over to the creature, following the crewman. The ladder to the passenger compartment was still in place, and he steadied it as first Zala and then I climbed up and went through an open door.

The interior was actually quite nice—heavily padded, manufactured seats much like those on the shuttle, complete with seat belts; the whole thing was lined and carpeted with what looked like fur of some kind. Aft a small compartment was clearly marked as a rest room. Although it lacked lights, some sort of self-luminous chemical tubing ran all around giving off a sufficient glow to see by and we felt pretty comfortable.

We were not the only ones in the cabin. Although I hadn't noticed earlier, an elderly woman and a tough-looking young man had climbed aboard. They were dressed in very fancy raingear, obviously of offworld design. Following them were three ground crew people, two men and a woman, including the man who had taken us "aboard," as it were. He pulled up the ladder, made a last check, then closed the door and spun a wheel locking it securely in place. The other crewman stood facing us, while the woman checked in back.

"Please fasten both lap and shoulder belts," the man told us. "While the flight's basically a smooth one, you never know what you're going to run into. Keep them fastened at all times. If you have to walk back to the lavatory, hold onto the rail and strap yourself in even in there. The cabin is not pressurized, so be prepared for a pressure differential in the ears. We have gum and mints if that troubles you. Occasionally we have to fly very high to get by some bad weather, and in that case I'll tell you to remove the oxygen masks under your seats and put them on. They are fed by manual pressurized tanks. Keep 'em on until I say it's okay."

A sudden violent lurch really shook us up; it was followed by the most chilling screech I've ever heard in my whole life. Both Zala and I jumped nervously; the crew and the two passengers took no real notice.

"Take-off positions!" the crewman yelled, and the three all strapped themselves into their seats very quickly. "Hold on, everybody! Here we go!"

At that moment I felt a sudden, violent lurch, and we were abruptly pushed against the back of our seats and simultaneously jarred up and down so hard it almost hurt. I suddenly realized that the damned thing was *running*. I glanced over at Zala, but she was all tightened up, eyes closed. Then I looked out the tiny round window to my left. It was possible to see the ground just ahead of that incredible wing, going up and down with that terrible bouncing, and then, all at once, the damned thing jumped off a cliff I hadn't known was there—and sank like a stone, throwing us forward in our seats.

As a certified pilot, both air and space, I'd experienced far worse than this, which may be why I was holding up so well. But *then* I'd been in control of a machine whose properties were known. To be perfectly honest, in that moment of forward fall all I could think was *"Well, this is it—you're dead."*

But almost as abrupt as the plunge was the sudden and violent turn and rise. At that moment I could see, with a kind of horrible fascination, just how close we'd come to the ground below.

Now we were lifting, with an eerie, rocking motion that first threw us forward, then back, as the enormous, powerful wings took us up, then paused to rest on a current of air. In another minute or two we were in the ever-present clouds, getting really bounced about. I glanced around and saw that Zala, eyes still closed, appeared very, very sick; the two other passengers were sitting quietly with no real reaction, while the crew was very relaxed. One was eating a fruit of some kind.

That terrible bouncing seemed to go on forever. Finally, we broke free, above the clouds, and into bright sunshine. Within another minute or two the creature caught a comfortable current, adjusted its course, and settled down. The experience was really strange now—after such a violent upheaval, the ride was now as smooth as glass, and nearly silent.

I looked over at Zala. "You can open your eyes now, and catch hold of your stomach," I told her. "It'll probably be like this the rest of the way." I just hoped and prayed this was an express.

One eye opened, then the other; she looked at me rather mournfully. "I'm sick," she managed.

All I could do was be sympathetic. "Just relax, calm down, and don't worry. That was a pretty rough take-off, but it's going to be like this until we get where we're going."

She didn't seem to be any more relieved. "I keep wondering what the landing is going to be like, if that was the take-off."

Good point. How the hell would something this size brake to a stop? Still, I had to have confidence since the pilot and crew did this all the time and none of the crew seemed worried.

At one point one of the crewmen took out a small carton and offered us fruit. Zala turned green at its mere mention. I almost took one, then decided for her sake that I could spare her the sight of me eating for the duration which, the crewman told us, would be a little more than five hours if we didn't run into weather problems. The thing managed an average airspeed in excess of 250 kph, a pretty respectable rate over the long haul for something this big.

The smoothness was interrupted every fifteen minutes or so by one or two sudden jolts, as those great wings compensated or switched currents, but that was about the only problem it presented.

The sky of Charon was nothing if not spectacular. Below were the dark, swirling clouds that seemed to never leave; above our clear place wasn't the sky I'd been expecting, but an odd band of reds and yellows all swirling about, almost as active as the storm clouds below. Some kind of gaseous layer that acted as a protective filter, I guessed, allowing a human-tolerable temperature below. The sun, a great, bright glob in the sky, was hot and visible through the upper layer. I guessed that the upper layer rather than the clouds below prevented much surveillance from orbit and blocked transmissions to and from the planet. I wondered what the stuff was.

Aside from my ears popping every so often, and the occasional screech from the soarer as we passed another soarer somewhere near us—I never did get more than a vague glimpse of black so I didn't get to see one in full flight—the voyage was uneventful. I took note of the other two passengers though—still fairly well-dressed even after removing their rain gear. They were obviously together, but the woman, who seemed to be going over some paperwork, rarely acknowledged or talked to the younger man. I smelled boss and bodyguard, but had no way of knowing just who they really were.

Even Zala managed to relax after a while, although she never did move during the entire trip and never really seemed to recover her color.

Finally my ears started popping a bit more regularly, and I saw that we were turning and descending very slowly. The crewmembers checked all their boxes and small hatches to make sure all was secure, then returned to their seats and strapped in.

I looked out at what I could see of the ground in front of the big wing, and was surprised to see breaks in the clouds not far off, and large patches of dark blue below. Hitting the clouds was similar to hitting them in an airship, and we experienced some rocking and a number of violent jerks as the wings worked harder to compensate for downdrafts, updrafts, and the like. The window showed moisture as we descended through a gray-white fog, then we broke suddenly into clearer air and the ground was visible below. Aside from seeing that it was green and somewhat mountainous down there, I couldn't make out much of anything.

The soarer circled, slowing a bit each time, then dropped and put its wings at an angle, abruptly braking hard. There were three or four jolts as the wings suddenly beat hard, and then one big bang—and we were down and, incredibly, motionless. For something this big, I had to admit it certainly could land much easier than it could take off.

I had to tap Zala and assure her we were down in one piece and that it was all over. She could hardly believe it, but finally opened her eyes and looked around. For the first time, she looked across me to the window and finally seemed to relax.

"Not as bad as take-off, was it?" I said cheerfully.

She shook her head. "I'll kill myself before I get on one of these again, I swear it, Park."

The wheel was spun, the hatchlike door opened, and a blast of really hot, sticky air hit us. Still, after five hours in that hotbox of the cabin, it was welcome, and it didn't seem to be raining.

The two other passengers gathered their things together and departed first. We followed, although Zala was more than a little shaky, and made it down the ladder.

I looked around the open field. A wagon was heading for the soarer with what looked like an entire butcher shop in the back—the fuel truck, I thought, amused. Off to one side, a small group of people and two coaches waited. Our fellow passengers had already reached one of them and were being greeted by very officious-looking men and women, some of whom bowed as they greeted the woman; others opened the coach door for her, while still others rushed to the soarer and retrieved what had to be baggage from a compartment under the passenger unit. Other cargo was also carried, and several buggies came right up to the soarer for it.

We just stood there, not quite knowing what to do. Finally I went over to the crewman who had been our host aboard. "Excuse me—but is this Bourget?" I asked him, praying that it was.

"Oh, yeah," he responded. "This *is* where you wanted to go, wasn't it? Our next stop's Lamasa."

"This is the place," I assured him, then thanked him and turned back to Zala. "Well, I guess we go over to that group and see if anybody's expecting us."

We walked cautiously over to the second coach, then looked expectantly at a couple of the people standing around. One young man—hardly more than a boy—grasped our situation and came over to us. "You the new Accountant?" he asked.

I felt relieved. "That's me. Park Lacoch."

He looked over expectantly at Zala. "You?"

"Zala Embuay. I'm his—assistant."

"Yeah, sure," the boy responded knowingly. "Well, if you two'll get into the coach there we'll get you into town and squared away." He looked around. "Any luggage?"

"No," I told him. "We're new to Charon. We're going to have to pick up everything we need here."

He seemed mildly interested. "Outside, huh? Funny they'd stick you here."

I shrugged and climbed into the coach. "They gave me the job and I took it. I wasn't in any position to say no."

We rode into town in silence, there not being much to say. The boy was not the driver, but stayed topside with him.

Bourget was not quite what I expected. A small village set against a very pretty bay, it was up and around low hills covered with trees. The buildings were all low and mostly painted white with reddish-brown roofs. There was nothing like the glassed-in sidewalks of Montlay or its more modern architecture. It was more like a small peasant village on one of the better frontier worlds, with the buildings made mostly of adobe and stucco of some kind, many with thatched roofs of that reddish-brown plant. Despite the clouds, it clearly didn't rain as much here as farther north, which was well and good from my point of view. There were many boats in the harbor, most with masts.

But it was *really* hot, easily over 40 degrees Centigrade, and both Zala and I were sweating profusely. I didn't know about her, but I needed a long, cold drink of something— anything.

Zala, however, was impressed. "Why, it's really *pretty*," she commented, looking out the window at the scene.

The town was organized around a central square that had a little park in the middle and four large multipurpose buildings—each a square block around although all two stories tall—which were obviously markets, shops, and stalls. The coach pulled up across from the one of the four buildings that had a more or less solid front and stopped. The boy jumped down, opened the door, and helped us both down.

The place was lively, I'll say that. People rushing this way and that, stalls open to the outside displaying lots of fruits, vegetables, clothes, and handicrafts, and doing a fair business from the look of it.

"Come with me now," the boy instructed, and we followed. I could see that Zala had completely recovered from her flight for she was showing some anticipation at touring the market.

We entered the solid-facade building and found ourselves in a wide entry hall with a large wooden staircase
situated directly in the middle. Corridors led off in all directions with what were obviously offices along them. The
boy stopped and turned to us. "You wait here. I'll see if the
Master is in." And with that he bounded up the stairs and
was off.

Zala turned to me. "Who do you think he means?"

"Probably the local wizard," I replied. "Remember to be
respectful to him. I want to get off on a good note."

"Don't worry."

We waited for the boy to return. A few people walked
here and there on unknown business, but none gave us
more than a passing glance. Civil servants looked the same
anywhere. The one oddity was that the place was cool—at
least a lot cooler than it was outside. There was certainly
some kind of air circulation system at work, although what
type I could not guess. Not regular air-conditioning, that
was for sure—the temperature was down, but not the humidity.

Before long the boy was back. "The Master will see
you," he told us, and we followed him upstairs. It was a bit
warmer there, as would be expected, and as we walked to
the rear of the large building I was conscious of the temperature rising.

We were ushered into an office with nothing on the
door. There was an antechamber, like a waiting room, with
nobody behind the desk; we went straight back to a second
door which the boy opened.

We felt a surprising blast of cool, dry air as we entered.
The office was large and very comfortably appointed, with
a huge carved wooden desk in the center. Behind that desk
sat a rather large man with an enormous white beard, as if
in compensation for his mostly bald head. He was smoking
a pipe.

He smiled as we entered and nodded. "Please, take seats
in front of the desk here," he said pleasantly, gesturing.
The chairs, large and high-backed, were modern and quite
comfortable, although as the man surely knew, it's impossi-

ble for a person sitting opposite anyone behind a desk to feel
on an equal footing.

The bearded man looked at the boy. "That'll be all, Gori.
Shut the door on your way out."

The boy nodded and did as instructed.

"A good lad, that," the man commented. "Might make a
good apt someday, if he gets over his hangup."

I couldn't imagine what the fellow was talking about, so
I said, "Hangup?"

"Yes. He wants to be a fish. Oh, well—I'm Tally Kokul,
chief magician and high muckety-muck of this little speck
of humanity."

"Park Lacoch," I responded, "and this is Zala Embuay."

He looked at Zala, and I saw a little puzzlement come
over his face, but he recovered quickly. Whatever Korman
had seen, though, Kokul had just seen as well.

"I knew you were coming, Lacoch, but nobody said anything about the lady here. I—" He was about to continue
when there was a knock at the door. The boy Gori entered
and placed a brief-pouch on his desk, then turned and left
again. "I was *wondering* about this," he muttered, as he
opened it, removed two file folders, discarded one and
opened and looked through the other. I could guess pretty
well that those folders contained everything known on both
of us, along with orders and recommendations from above.

"Humph. I'm not sure I like your status, Madame Embuay," he said almost to himself. He looked up at her.
"Bourget is a pretty conservative village. Other than myself, you're the only two people here not native to Charon."

Zala looked blank, so I hazarded a guess. "Religious?"

He nodded. "Fifty, sixty years ago the Diamond had a
near invasion of missionaries from all sorts of sects. The
Confederacy more or less encouraged it—got the fanatics
out of their hair and voluntarily exiled here for life. Bourget wasn't much of anything then—it still isn't all that
much, although we now rate as a sort of local capital. This
one group, the Unitites, were real fanatics and were pretty
much run out of all the established towns. But their leader,
a fellow named Suritani, was a real lady's man who was
also pretty well practiced in the Arts. He was able to get a

pretty good following, mostly female, and came here and established Bourget as a religious colony of sorts. Most everybody here's a cousin of everybody else."

"Sounds pretty liberal to me," I noted. Zala said nothing.

"Oh, it was—for the big man. But not for everybody else. The usual story. Understand, I'm the only one around who can get away with talk like this. You better respect the local beliefs so you don't step on any."

I nodded, and he went on.

"Well, anyway, you'll find most everybody stops twice a day—at eight and six—and prays together for a couple of minutes. Men and women have clearly defined, but different jobs, very strict, and men can have up to three wives. We still have more women than men by a long shot."

"Can a woman have three husbands?" Zala asked, seriously interested.

"No. I told you it was an old-style, almost throwback religion—one big god, who supposedly lives at the center of the universe, and assorted godlets who are the messengers between people and this one god. All very complex, and very strict."

"Sounds like this isn't a very good place for loyalty to the central government," I noted. "Not with a woman as Lord of Cerberus."

"You're very perceptive, Lacoch. I can see why they sent you. You're right—they simply don't accept the prevailing politics, which is always a headache to me. One of several this sect gives me, frankly. Most of them just prefer to believe Aeolia Matuze has a man who does all the thinking for her, making her a bridge, like the godlets. So far that's been okay, although there've been rumblings that our leader is going to declare her divinity and impose her own religion on the planet. If it comes to that, they may have to get a new population for Bourget, even the Company chiefs. I'm hoping that, at least, I can get a soft-pedaled exemption here."

I sympathized with his problem, and it didn't escape me that the chief sorcerer of Bourget was a ripe candidate for somebody like Koril.

"This religion is a hundred percent, then?" I asked.

He shook his head. "Nothing's ever a hundred percent. I'd say about half the people are really devout and really believe all of it, another thirty percent just do it because it's the way they were raised, and another ten go through the motions just to avoid trouble."

"That's only ninety percent," I noted.

He nodded. "The other ten are with the opposition."

"The opposition?"

"Most religions have a devil, a demon, somebody who represents evil and on which everything bad can be blamed. This one's no exception. It's called the Destroyer. Some personalities are just naturally attracted to the side of evil in such a strict society. In addition, it's a natural place for people in Bourget who chafe under the strict society— women, mostly, who have some or a lot of the Art, and know either by experience or direct knowledge that the rest of the worlds allow women not only equality, but occasionally superiority. It used to be pretty local, but lately similar cults have been cropping up all over Charon, and there's some evidence that they've been co-opted by a political opposition to the rule of Matuze."

"I'm familiar with the politics of the situation," I told him. "Still, it seems funny that the logical order's been reversed here. The establishment, which backs the existing order on Charon, is prejudiced against women in leadership positions yet has a woman at its head; the opposition, which wants women made equal like everywhere else, is falling in with a group designed to put a man back in power."

Zala followed the conversation but said nothing. I had pretty well given her the entire outline of recent history on Charon, so she at least knew the players even if she didn't seem quite able to understand the game.

"Well, it's not that simple," Kokul came back. "On most of Charon it's different, although some towns have pockets with even crazier beliefs and systems than Bourget. What we have is a three-sided system here, as in most places. Our cult with its value system; the opposition, which ties

into the overall opposition; and governmental authority—
which right now is you and me and just about nobody
else."

I understood what he meant, and although it wasn't comforting to me, I could well understand why I'd been sent to
Bourget. The stricter the local social system, the more
likely that the opposition—and Koril's strength and
agents—would be powerful and well-organized as well,
particularly with its south-coast location and general isolation.

Although Kokul seemed casual and not a little cynical
about Matuze, I was under no illusions that he could be
trusted. Like me, he was from some other world and culture—and had been sent here for a reason. No matter how
casual he was about the central government, there had to
be the suspicion that they would hardly send a traitor or an
incompetent to such a sensitive spot as Bourget.

"Enough about that," the wizard decided. "As for Bourget—well, if you can tolerate the social structure, which
really isn't all that bad once you get used to it, the citizens
are a pretty good, hard-working lot. We're self-sufficient in
food and building materials, have a lively local handicrafts
industry, and generate a fair amount of surplus income
through exports. Not bad for a village of less than 5000.
The climate has two seasons—hot and hotter—so outside
of official circles you'll find dress ranges from little to less.
We have good ground water, which is safe for all purposes,
and back in the hills some really nice waterfalls, which
we've harnessed as best we can for everything from cooling
systems to pumps and the like—all direct mechanical,
though. About the most modern machine you'll find here is
a solar watch, although we do generate some minor steam
power for the big jobs, mostly out in the Companies. It's
surprising what good engineering will do, even without
modern power sources."

I accepted his point, since it was self-evident—early man
had built some stunning empires on the most basic of
power sources. "So what's *my* job here?" I asked him.
"And how do we get set up and get started?"

"Well, it's basically supervision, but as you're responsible for overall efficiency, the accuracy of all data and will be held accountable for any problems or errors, it's very much a hands-on job. Within a day's journey of Bourget are nine Companies, employing upwards of a thousand people and producing very valuable commodities. In town, there are thirty guilds which produce everything from clothing to handicrafts. All of them need things and I don't just mean raw materials. You are, basically, the head of the local bank. The government's syndicates meet four times a year in Montlay and decide on a fair price and profit margin for everything, and you get the official rates in a big book. The job of your office is to maintain a balance between what they get and what they provide according to the set table of values. All Company orders come to you, as do orders for their products. The trick is to make sure the Companies get only what they have paid for in products, but receive enough to get by on. If there is an imbalance in their favor, they are paid in money."

I nodded. "Sounds pretty direct. But who pays my salary, my staff, and my operating expenses?"

"Well, that's simple. The bank takes ten percent of all transactions at the time of the transaction. Half of that is your take, split along mutually agreeable lines. Naturally, in good times you make more than in bad, with each employee getting a share. The rest gets sent on to Charon's government."

I nodded. "So the more I encourage business and make it easier, by advice, suggestion, whatever, to increase production, the more we all make. A very interesting system."

"That's about it," he agreed. "If somebody's got a real problem you can send for an expert to help—paid out of your overhead, though."

That, perhaps, explained the elderly woman on the soarer. I wondered how somebody used to being the boss would like this culture, even for a short time. Still, I had a few more questions.

"Where will we live and how are we going to pick up the basics?"

"Oh, that's easy," he responded. "The share account for the T.A. kept operating in the two months since the old one

died, so there's a fair amount in there now. You can draw
on it downstairs—they'll be expecting you. Then just buy
what you need. A house goes with the job, already furnished—Tudy, that's the boy who met you, will show it to
you. It's on the bay, an easy walk from here."

"Out of curiosity—who pays *you*?" I asked him.

He laughed. "Oh, nobody. The last thing I need is
money." He grew more serious. "Now, the staff will break
you in during the next few days—take it easy until you get
the hang of it. Your first month you can use learning the
ropes, since any minor mistakes can be blamed on the past
two month's vacancy. We open at eight each morning, the
markets and stores at nine, and we close except for a night
accounting staff at four. The businesses stay open until
nine or ten, the cafés a bit later, but the nightlife's pretty
poor around here. For one thing, they drink only weak beer
and light wines, and the entertainment's mostly home-
grown and not very good. We go for six days, then take
three off, then go again."

"I would guess a small town like this is full of gossip and
rumor," I noted. "I doubt if it's going to take very long to
get to know these people."

"Oh, it'll be easier than that. We'll introduce the two of
you at your wedding."

"What!" That was Zala.

"I *said* it was a conservative place. You have no job, no
means of support—and you're quite attractive. I assume
that you'd rather marry Park here, than be forced to marry
some local with one or two others around."

"I don't want to marry anybody. I don't believe in it."

He sighed. "Look, it doesn't matter *what* you believe.
You're not back on the civilized worlds now. You're not
even in some freewheeling town like Montlay or Cadura.
Remember, you don't have to take the ceremony very seriously since it's just for the locals' consumption."

"Then why not just say we're already married?" she
wanted to know.

"Because this is the easiest way to get in with the locals.
They'll get to know you, will like you respecting their local
customs and beliefs, and they'll be much more likely to

accept you. Just let me arrange it all, and go along. Other than that, just keep your mouth shut when you see something you don't agree with. Antagonize these people and you can find yourself in a world of trouble. I'm the strongest and most feared wizard in these parts, but I'm hardly the only one who can cast spells and work magic. There's a lot of home-grown talent around, and a lot more than can be bought. Some of them are pretty good. Unless you can develop your own powers, it's best to go along with them no matter how backward or ignorant they may seem. This is literally the key to your survival—you have to live with these people and depend on them for your necessities. It can be pretty lonely if you antagonize them from the beginning."

She seemed slightly unnerved, but a little chastened. "I'll try," was all she could promise.

CHAPTER SEVEN

Settling In

Things actually went off rather nicely, if I do say so my-self. As it turned out, the accumulated back pay was more than generous, and we were both able to buy suitable toilet-ries, wardrobes, and the like.

The wedding took place in the town square, officiated at by one of the local priests who did a lot of prerehearsed mumbo-jumbo, and by Kokul as State's Witness and certi-fier. Zala made a beautiful bride, and there was a real fes-tival afterwards with lots of singing, dancing, presents, and goodies of all sorts, plus some nice socializing. Kokul was particularly helpful in pointing out the important people in the crowd, and I was taking careful mental notes. Even Zala, who had been expressing extreme misgivings right up to the ceremony, seemed to get into the swing of things, for later she noted that weddings were something she thought everybody should do every year or two.

As for me, I was most interested in settling down, learn-ing the job, and doing it well. There was no percentage in acting any other way. Koril was unlikely to pop up right away, knowing certainly that Matuze would figure we were prime recruiting targets and keep a careful watch on us.

The staff was friendly and helpful, and the system, once fully laid out and demonstrated in practice, was primitive but quite effectively organized. Solar calculators and small solar computers helped, but the basic work was all done by hand and typewriter on endless sheets of accounting paper.

Zala, too, seemed to adjust, after a fashion. Local women taught her how to use the wood stove without burning her-self or the house down, and the basics of domestic work.

Since nothing much could be stored in this heat and under these conditions, she went to the market daily and even learned the art of bargaining. What particularly fascinated her was the very concept of handicrafts—nothing in her world or background prepared her for clothing made from scratch, designed and sewn by individuals on individual machines, or pottery hand-made on potter's wheels and hand-decorated with brush and glaze. Suddenly flung back thousands of years in cultural time, both of us were very surprised to learn that there were whole art forms devoted to such things. The products had a special sort of quality machine and mass production at its best just couldn't quite match.

My job though took more time than I'd figured, since it included trips out to the Companies to see their accountants, to plan for the future, and to examine and get to know their operations and see if there were new and better ways to do things. Money was tight because the system really wasn't designed for one person supporting two. Zala, to her credit, solved that problem by learning to use the hand loom and joining a Guild in town in which many women and some men weaved intricate patterns into blankets, bedspreads, you name it, and then sold them to the Guild for a set price per piece. The Guild, through my office, then sold them all over Charon.

The people were friendly, open, and seemed reasonably happy, and neither of us gave them any cause to get mad at us, particularly after we saw a few of the cursed and the changelings. The cursed were more prominent since they weren't bad off enough to be able to drop out of society. Mostly they just covered up as best they could, but you could always tell. A club foot, a withered arm, a scarred face, or some deformity even worse stood out rather well in a society so well protected by the interior Wardens that cuts always stopped bleeding and never left scars and even amputated limbs grew back.

The knowledge that many of our fellow townspeople could throw curses like these wasn't very comforting, and the discovery that you could actually *buy* curses in the marketplace didn't help either. One old woman who sold them in a small stall explained to me that it didn't pay as well as weaving, for example, but it was a living.

The changelings, which were beyond the power of an untrained or self-trained local (or so I was assured) were far more bizarre. Many were former apts themselves who had literally done it to themselves, either for psychological reasons or because something got away from them, or they had displeased Kokul or others of great power and training. Kokul was the best around, as he said, but each of the Companies also had a sorc of considerable power to add to the changeling population—and since, unlike Kokul, the Company sorcs were employees of the Company and not the government, they were often willing to do the cruel bidding of their employers, meting out reward and punishment with equal ease. I ached to learn something of that power, but I had neither the time nor the teacher—not at this stage of the game.

For example, there was this two-meter frog that sat on a rock just down from the town staring out to sea and smoking big, fat cigars. Well, actually, I hadn't a notion what a frog really looked like, but I read the fairy tales just like everybody else and this one sure looked like a fairy-tale frog, standing on its hind bow legs, balancing on big webbed feet.

There were others around too—halflings that were half human and half something else, almost anything else it seemed, and probably more that I never fully recognized as such because they were so completely transformed. They never came into town, though, and were generally shunned by people, although I suppose somebody had to trade with them on at least a barter basis—how else did the frog get his or her cigars? There was supposedly a small colony of them out on the point north of the town, but nobody ever went there that I could find.

I saw more of them on Company lands, since people there were more at the mercy of Company officials and the local sorc and apts. I was out at Thunderkor, a Company that was basically involved in softwood logging and milling, when I had my first direct encounter with a changeling. I was on my way back from the mill after checking production schedules, and I'd decided to walk rather than ride back to Sanroth Hall, the Company headquarters, because it was a nice day and I felt I was getting soft, when I ran into her.

She was a halfling and at one time had obviously been a very beautiful young woman. The woman's body remained, down to the lower chest, but from that point it became the bottom part of a uhar or uharlike animal, with powerful saurian legs and, coming out from the spine, the long, thick saurian tail. Her color was a leaf-green rather than the blue of the uhar clan, including her long hair which was, however, a far darker green in color. She walked with the peculiar angle that showed that the tail was needed as a counterbalance, and she was walking up the road about ten meters in front of me. At first I took her for some kind of animal—there were a great number on Charon—and she heard me despite the fact that I stopped in my tracks; she herself stopped and turned around. Her face showed more annoyance than surprise at the sight of me, and certainly no fear. Hers was a pretty face, even in its shades of green, exotic and quite sensual, though she *did* have a long, sharp horn protruding from the center of her forehead.

She stood there, and I stood there, and finally I decided that it was the better part of valor to keep on. Besides, I was more curious than fearful or repelled.

"Good morning!" I said cheerfully as I approached. After all, what else *do* you say to a half-woman, half-lizard standing in your way? "A nice day, isn't it?"

She stared at me strangely for a moment, and I wondered if she could still speak—and which half, the human or animal, was in control. That thought hadn't really occurred to me until I was too close to run.

She was large, in proportion to her saurian half, and almost towered over me. Almost everybody did, of course, even Zala, but I was used to *that* disproportion. This was more than the usual—she was certainly over two meters, even slightly bent like that.

"You're the new T.A. from Outside," she said, her voice sounding deep but otherwise quite ordinary. I was relieved.

I stopped near her, just out of range of that horn, and nodded. "Park Lacoch."

"Well? What the hell you staring at?" she snapped.

I shrugged sheepishly. "Remember, I'm new here—not just to here, but to Charon," I reminded her. "Let's just say you're a bit, ah, different, than most of the people I meet."

She laughed at that. "That's true enough. Am I the first changeling you've ever seen?"

"No, but you're the first one I've *met*," I told her.

"And?"

I wasn't sure if she was fishing for a compliment or spoiling for a fight. "And what?" I responded. "I find you—and the whole idea—fascinating."

She gave a sort of snort. "Fascinating! That's one word for it, I guess."

"You work here for Thunderkor?"

"What else? They hitch me up and I pull things they want moved. My arms aren't much use but I've got real pull in the legs."

I looked at them and wasn't in any mood to argue that point. "What did you do—before?" I asked as delicately as I could.

"Before? Hah! I was a riverwoman. Ran log floats, that kind of thing. Takes more skill than strength."

I was impressed. "I would have thought you'd have been up at Sanroth," I told her. "With your looks . . ."

She smiled grimly. "Yeah. My looks. That's what got me into trouble. I was born and bred on the river, into a family of river people. I had the talent and loved the work, ever since I was little, but everybody said I was too pretty for it, that I should get married and make babies. Hell, I loved that job. Even the men admitted I was the best—that's why they wanted me out of there. I embarrassed them."

I could see the situation in this particular culture.

"Well, anyway, one day this old guy, Jimrod Gneezer, comes down from Sanroth and sees me. Next thing I know I'm ordered up to the Hall—never been there in my life. Real Mr. Ego, too."

"I think I've met him," I told her, recalling a distinguished-looking man of middle age.

"Well, he thinks I'm supposed to swoon all over him. I tell him where to go. He gets real mad, tries to force himself, and I belted him one—knocked him cold, walked out, and went home. Next thing I know, Simber, the dirty sorc, comes down, tells me I better go back. He reminds me that he could cast a spell and I'd be Gneezer's willing slave. I tell him to go ahead, that that was the only way I'd go back to the bastard, but it turns out that the guy's got such a big head he don't like no spells for that. His pride's hurt. So Simber takes some hair and nail clippings—I couldn't stop him, he being a sorc—and the next thing I know this little brat of an apt, Isil, shows up and tells me all about how I've been given to him now and he's very creative. Yeah, very."

I whistled. "That's rough" was all I could think to say.

"Oh, I could reverse the spell, probably, by going crawling to Gneezer, but I'd rather be like this than do that. Someday I'll get even with 'em, you can count on it. But it's not so bad. They didn't mess with my head, if you know what I mean. But he sure got even. I mean, the only thing I could marry would be a bunhar, and who wants to play sexy with a lizard?"

I saw her point, and assumed a bunhar was the kind of creature she half was.

"No chance of having a different, more powerful sorc undo it?"

She shook her head. "Naw. First of all, they got a brotherhood, a code. Even the women. None of 'em will undo what another has done no matter how much they want to, because if one breaks it they all will, you see, and then where'll they be?"

It was a good point. "And none of the unofficial ones can help?"

Again the head-shake. "It's a good spell. Them amateurs can only make things worse. Besides, there seems to be something in the spell that makes it tougher. Tried it once—and that's when I got this horn. That's enough."

"Are there others like you around?" I was genuinely curious.

"Like me? Not exactly. Some others got some of the

same bunhar parts, I guess, and a lot of other stuff. There's a few dozen around the Company, I guess, of different kinds. It's a big place, so we don't see much of each other, and some of 'em are really messed up in the head by what was done to 'em. They don't do this all that much—we're the examples, see?"

I *did* see, and it made me even happier to be both a townsman with a degree of freedom and on the good side of Tally Kokul and the Charon government.

"Did you ever think of leaving?" I asked her. "I hear there are places where changelings can live together. It would probably be—easier."

"Oh, yeah, there's lots of that," she agreed, "but here's where the dungheads who did it to me are, and here's where they could remove it—or I could remove them." She flexed her very human arms and hands, and I could see that at the end of each finger was not merely a nail but a sharp, long curved talon.

"Well, I've got to be getting on," I told her, not making excuses but being honest. My transportation back to town was waiting. "It was nice, and interesting, talking to you. And if I catch your Mr. Gneezer with his hand in the till I guarantee I'll remember you when I turn him over to Master Kokul."

She chuckled evilly. "Wouldn't *that* be something, now!" She paused for breath, then said more gently, "Hey, look. If you get back over this way, stop by and see me, won't you? Most of the people here, they treat me like dirt. You're the first person in a long time who's been nice to me and treated me like—well, like a human being."

"I'll do that," I promised her. We started to go our separate ways, but I stopped and turned. "Hey—what's your name, anyway?"

"Darva," she called back. "With no family now I'm just Darva."

She took a branch path and walked away from me. I stood there for a moment, watching her lumber off—rather gracefully actually. I also made a mental note of the names Gneezer and Isil. One of these days there would be an accounting.

* * *

Months passed, and I settled in very well and really enjoyed the job. Zala taught me how to swim more expertly
than I had learned as a kid, and we took full advantage of
the warm bay. I also learned how to sail, although I
couldn't afford a boat and had to beg or borrow one for the
lessons. Zala saved up enough from her loom work to buy a
pair of bicycles, obviously made off-world—on Cerberus,
as it turned out—and this extended my range and gave me
some much needed exercise when it didn't rain.

Large sailing ships occasionally came into the bay to
pick up manufactured goods and nonperishables and drop
off what we needed, and I was very impressed by them.
Although strong steel ships could be built on Cerberus,
which I understood was a water world, the cost of shipping
that size and weight here was prohibitive. Charon's ships
were made out of native hardwoods and were the more
impressive for it. I noticed that the crews of these ships
often contained a disproportionate number of changelings
—every kind and variety I could imagine and many I
couldn't. But certain forms and variations were particularly
useful in rigging and setting and taking in sail, and in
cargo management. The shipping guilds apparently didn't
care who or what you were if you were best for the job.
They mostly remained on board when in port, although
once or twice I thought I saw longboats heading for Par-
hara Point where the changeling colony was supposed to
be.

Tally Kokul I saw very infrequently—he kept mostly to
himself and his "studies," and I almost never needed him.
His apts occasionally got playful in the wrong places
though, and I'd have to send him a note or drop in if he
was there and get him to control them. They were mostly
young boys—with more power than young boys should
have. I wondered what he did with the talented girl apts,
then reflected that somebody who could turn a young
woman into a hybrid creature could easily disguise the sex
of an apt if she were really promising.

I also heard very little from the central government of
Charon, other than the routine correspondence and man-

uals necessary to my job, and that suited me just fine as well. It was with some surprise, then, that a clerk came in one day and told me that a very important visitor had arrived, and he wanted to see me in Kokul's office as soon as possible. "I'd make it possible right now," he added, shuddering slightly. "You haven't seen *him* yet."

That was enough to get me up there on the double.

Just walking into the inner office I knew what he had meant. Even before I saw the man, I could *sense* something, something decidedly wrong. It wasn't my old agent's "sixth sense" or any kind of apprehension—it was a real, tangible feeling of unease, almost of dread, like you feel just before you have to stick your hand in a damp, dark hole without knowing what's on the other side.

He was large and lean, dressed from head to foot in black leather trimmed with silver and gold designs. His face, peering out of a black hood, was lean, hard, even nasty-looking. What really struck me, though, were the eyes—there seemed to be something wrong with them, something odd and not at all human. It was as if his pupils were not solid black, but rather, transparent, like windows into some unfathomable other dimension. It was the damnedest effect I'd ever seen and it was extremely unnerving. Kokul sensed it too, and looked uneasy in his big office chair for the first time since I'd known him. This man was no ordinary man—he was Power, raw, tremendous power of an unknown sort. I noticed the man remained standing even though there were enough chairs, the better no doubt to negate the man-at-the-desk feeling. I, however, just nodded at Tully and sat down. I only came up to the strange man's chest, anyway. Never, not even with Darva, had I felt so totally small, puny, and weak.

"Park, this is Yatek Morah, from the Castle," Tully introduced us and I noticed a feeling of unease in his voice.

I stood up again and offered my hand, but Morah ignored it. I sat back down. "Any problem?" I asked as casually as I could.

"I am making a survey," the strange man replied in a voice as cold and emotionless as an assembly-line robot's. Coming from a living man it was unnerving, particularly on this planet where robots were impossible. "We are having severe security problems in most of the coastal areas. Ships have been pirated on the high seas and never been seen again. Soarers with important, even vital cargo have vanished, or suffered attack. Important people have been imperiled. As Chief of Security it is my job to put a stop to this."

I looked at Tully in genuine surprise. "First I've heard of it."

"I've had rumblings," the sorc responded. "But nothing in this area."

"That is exactly why I am here," Morah told us. "Sixty coastal settlements along the south and east have been hit, either directly or indirectly, in the last three weeks. There have also been more than two dozen incidents in the interior. Practically every community within two thousand square kilometers has been touched—except Bourget. Messages, records, you name it have been destroyed or disrupted all over—except material to or from fat, rich Bourget. Interesting coincidence, is it not?"

"I'll agree it sounds anything but a coincidence," I replied, "but I haven't a clue as to who or where. I've been here now the better part of—what?—five months and I've never seen a straighter, more basic and open culture than this."

"A culture that refuses to recognize the Queen and festers the largest cult of the Destroyer on the planet," Morah snapped back. "A culture with the resources and means to mount a widespread rebellion."

"Except that all the Unitites want is to be left alone," Kokul noted. "As far as they're concerned, they're on another planet and they'd just as soon keep it that way."

"That's about it," I agreed.

"You have made no attempts to break the Destroyer cult," the Chief of Security noted.

Kokul shrugged. "What can I do? It's a safety valve for this kind of culture, and the ones I've caught have been genuine fanatics. They have someone of great power at their heart though—they know and completely change and move as soon as I get a clue. It's as if they had somebody right in my labs."

"Perhaps they do," Morah replied. "Perhaps you have been here too long, Kokul."

The wizard's face turned red, and he stood up. I had never seen him angry before, and he was a fearsome sight. "Are you questioning my loyalty? Even *you* have no right to do that, Morah!"

The big, weird man was unmoved. "I have every right to do whatever is necessary," he replied. However, he seemed to realize he had overstepped his diplomatic bounds if he hoped to get cooperation with a minimum of trouble, and added, "However, I am not questioning your loyalty. Were I, you would be brought up before the Synod, as you know. No, I merely reflect that you have been here a *very* long time. You *like* Bourget and its isolation, and as you are intimate with the people, they are also intimate with you. You may or may not have the power necessary to do what needs to be done, but you lack the will in any case. I have no such problems."

Kokul was only partially mollified, but he sat down.

"You will call a series of assemblies of all townsmen," Morah told him. "Groups of 500, in one-hour intervals— and I don't care if it *does* disrupt things for a day or two. I will make similar arrangements with the Companies. If I read these Unitites correctly, they would be more intolerant than even we of anyone discovered to be in the cult of the Destroyer. We will bring them into the open. We will let your precious villagers discover just who is who. And then we will stamp out this cult in Bourget."

"Just what are you going to do?" I asked him, still trying, and failing, to look directly into those weird eyes.

"My best troops are even now in the process of sealing off the town by both land and sea," he told us. "There will be no escape for this band of traitors. Be there for the first assembly tomorrow morning. It will probably be the only one required. I think both of you will find the exercise an educational experience."

CHAPTER EIGHT

All Hell Breaks Loose

"Who's this Yatek Morah, anyway, that he can come in and order us around like this?" Zala wanted to know.

"Chief of Security, he says, and I know little more except that Tully is scared stiff of him and he comes directly from Aeolia Matuze."

"Well, I don't think he's got any right doing this. I've got half a mind not to show up."

I stared at her, wondering a bit at her sudden show of spunk and bravado—or was it? She wasn't very good at hiding things, and in her eyes I saw a tinge of fear and uncertainty. For a brief moment I wondered if maybe there was more going on here than I realized.

"You have to go," I told her. "We all do. Anybody on the list who doesn't show up when ordered will automatically be branded an enemy of the people, and they can take whatever action they want. Besides, you saw the ships out there?"

She nodded nervously.

"I don't know how many troops he's got with him, but they're a nasty bunch and very well trained and efficient— and according to Tully they're *all* at least apts." I paused a moment to let that sink in. "Besides—aren't you just the least bit curious to see what they're going to do?"

"I—I suppose. Well, let's do it."

We left the house together and walked up the road toward the square. Everything was closed today, even the bank, and there was the general feeling of a community under sudden siege. I didn't like it—the eerie stillness, the tension so thick you could feel it, like cobwebs or dense fog

147

oozing around, despite the fact that this was one of our few bright, rainless days.

Most of the first group had already gathered in and around the square, which nonetheless looked oddly barren without the vendors and café tables. A small stage had been erected in the center of the square, on the grassy plot where Zala and I had been ceremoniously married only five months before. The four streets leading into the square were all filled with men in the black and gold imperial uniforms of Charon. I was struck by their tough, nasty appearance and by the fact that they were all armed with very ugly-looking rifles of unfamiliar design. I looked around on top of the market buildings and the town hall and saw indications of movement, reflections in the light, everywhere. Morah was taking no chances. I had no idea what those rifles shot or their rate of fire, but I was pretty sure that, in a pinch, this force could probably mow down everyone in the square. Not a comforting thought.

Zala looked nervously at the troops and gulped, grabbing and squeezing my hand for reassurance. "Park?"

"Yeah?"

"Let's stay close to Tully in this. At least we'll have some measure of protection."

"Good idea—if we can find him in this mob." I looked around but the wizard was nowhere to be seen. "Let's try the town hall. That'll be where Morah will come from."

She nodded, and we made our way through a sea of worried faces; the people were milling around, looking at the troops, but not talking very much. We had almost reached the front door when it opened and Morah and Kokul emerged, flanked by four more troopers. Zala stopped at the sight of the security chief and gave a slight gasp as, for an instant, she saw those strange, terrible eyes. But Morah paid us no notice and, using his troopers—all four female, I noted, deliberately chosen to thumb his nose at the Unitites—to clear a path, he made his way to the stage. He really didn't need the troopers—nobody was going to stand in *that* man's way.

Tully followed him to the foot of the stage, but did not climb up on it. I started to go to him, but Zala pulled me back. "No. Let's stay against the building, near the doorway," she suggested hopefully. I looked around and could see her point. If any shooting started it was the best exit available and one I knew well.

Morah was, if anything, more imposing than ever, standing alone in the center of that platform. I could see his weird eyes survey both the crowd and the positions of his troops. There was an air of tense expectation in the crowd, as if everyone knew that something, something explosive and, perhaps, evil, was about to begin. Even Zala seemed to sense it and feel that way. As for me, hell, I was a member of the party in good standing—I could hardly wait to see how the big boys operated here. Things had been dull for too long.

Finally, Morah seemed satisfied. I suspected that he was delaying things, letting everybody become as nervous and jumpy as possible, for good, psychological reasons. This was a tenth of the town, including almost all the bigwigs, and they were going to be the example.

"Citizens of Bourget," he began, his voice tremendously amplified and echoing off the walls, lending an additional alien quality to his presence. "Thank you for coming. Charon has long valued Bourget and its industrious people who are so valuable to the whole of the planet for their products. We deeply regret these measures, and I, Yatek Morah, Chief of Security, wish to assure those of you who are loyal citizens that you have nothing to fear today. In fact, I am here precisely because there is a threat to your peace and well-being, a threat you did not know existed but one that might consume you should it go unchecked. After today enemies both of Bourget and of Charon will be unmasked, exposed, and dealt with, and we can all feel safer because of it."

He paused a moment to let that sink in. I found the softening up very impressive and quite good human psychology. Of course, very soon would come the still-hidden knife, but these were simple people and most of them probably didn't know that yet.

"I come today to tell you of treason," Morah continued. "I come today to tell you of ships falling victim to piracy, treasuries looted, important officials kidnapped and assassinated. It is a scourge that has enveloped our beloved land, although it has not as yet touched Bourget." Again the dramatic pause. "And, of course, we had to ask ourselves, why not Bourget? Is it not the richest, fattest, and most tempting target for such enemies? And yet we could not bring ourselves to believe that Bourget itself would be a party to such things. Bourget has been good to Charon, and Charon has been good to Bourget. What, then, are we to think of all this?"

Some rumblings, mumblings, and whispers could be heard in the crowd. I noticed, too, that at least a few people started looking around very uncomfortably, or were edging toward the back of the crowd. Very, very interesting.

"Obviously," the security chief continued, "our enemies are in Bourget, *of* Bourget, but unknown to the loyal and peace-loving people of Bourget. And if such enemies are amongst you, living amongst you, while they perpetrate such monstrous crimes, they are growing stronger, richer, more confident. Eventually, they would have taken over and dominated this community. Today we will end this threat."

More rumblings and whisperings, and I noticed the troopers coming to full alert. I was now beginning to get an idea of what Morah had in mind, remembering Garal's original statement back in orientation that a curse is only good if the victim knows about it. Well, anybody in this crowd who was involved in the underground movement sure knew—and had no way out, as a couple of women who started walking toward one of the streets found out when they were blocked and turned back by the troopers.

"What *is* he going to do?" Zala whispered to me.

"He's going to cast a spell on the evildoers," I told her. "At least, I think so."

"I am Chief of Security," Morah reminded them, "and as befits one of my titles and responsibilities, I have great power." He raised his arms up over his head and began chanting what sounded to me like nonsense syllables—but I'd witnessed such a thing before. "Concentration aids"

Tully had called them, but the people called them spells.

Slowly the arms dropped, and those eerie eyes seemed to fill the stage. He stretched out his arms to the crowd, which reacted by nervously pulling back. I noticed that Tully Kokul was viewing the scene with interest but was taking no part in the proceedings.

Morah stopped his chant and froze in position, pointing both arms at the crowd. "Now and in the presence of you all," he intoned, "I do hereby curse those who would follow the Destroyer, Lord of Nothingness, and do his bidding. Let their evil traitorous presence be known to all good men and women—*now!*"

It was an amazing show. Bright yellow sparks seemed to fly from his fingers and reach out in all directions for the crowd, many of whom screamed or cried out. Many in the crowd really let out yells and raised hands to foreheads. One woman near us let out a screech and turned in fear and shock toward us, whereupon I let out an involuntary gasp. From her forehead protruded two short, stubby, demonic horns.

"Look at that!" I exclaimed, turning to Zala. "I—" then stopped dead. Zala, looking shocked and scared to death, was feeling her own pair of horns. "Oh, no! Not *you.*" She looked at me in mixed fear and bewilderment. "No, I—"

But the comment was suddenly cut off, and I watched in amazement as an odd, bizarre transformation seemed to take place within her. Her body seemed to be all in motion as some power reshaped muscle and transformed her into someone else before my very eyes. I thought for a moment it was part of the spell, but a quick glance around showed that it was not. Shots rang out, and I saw several people who had rushed for one of the streets near us go down in a hail of gunfire and lie there, writhing and moaning.

"Get them, honest citizens!" Morah was ordering. "Hold them for us!"

When I looked back, the woman next to me was only barely recognizable as Zala Embuay. She seemed larger, stronger, and the face, even the eyes, while still hers, seemed to belong to someone else, someone I did not know at all. She looked at me—horns still present—and said in a crisp, low voice, "Get inside the hall—*fast*! For your own sake!"

"What the hell?" was all I could manage. Roughly she picked me up as if I were a rag doll and shoved me in the doorway. It didn't take a genius to realize that, for the first time, I was in the presence of the other, hidden Zala Embuay—but not for long. Before I could say another word she ran into the town hall and was quickly gone. For a moment I debated running after her, but I realized there was little I could do—and few places for her to run, with troops on the roof and, surely, stationed at the side exits as well. So, keeping well inside the doorway, I returned my gaze to the street.

The massacre was starting on schedule. I estimated thirty or forty people, perhaps, had suddenly sprouted horns—all female as far as I could see. The crowd, primed, acted as Morah expected, actually jumping on their erstwhile friends and relatives and helping the efficient troops to capture them.

Suddenly a series of tracerlike blasts shook the square, and there were explosions and concussions everywhere, followed immediately by the steady sounds of something I knew well. Laser pistols! But they weren't supposed to *work* on Charon!

Stun rays were playing down the square, collapsing people into little heaps by the dozens, but not far away, on the rooftops, a deadly gunfight was obviously taking place between the troops and—who? I realized I didn't know and, from my protective vantage point, I couldn't really see either.

Near the stage I saw Tully Kokul's mouth sag as he watched the scene in total amazement. The rays playing the square seemed to have no effect on him at all, nor did he seem unduly worried.

On the stage, Morah was shouting instructions to his troops and trying to rally those he could. As with Kokul, nothing happening around him seemed to touch him in the slightest, a state that attested to both men's extreme powers—and one I, also, would have found especially useful and comforting right about then.

Suddenly all the shooting stopped. The square itself looked like the scene of a grisly massacre, although I knew from the nature of the rays and from experience on the sonics that most of the people had simply been knocked cold.

Morah, suddenly aware of the silence, stopped his commands and turned to look at the rooftops.

"All right, Morah! Stay where you are until we get our people out and no additional measures will be taken," came a deep, gruff voice. You too, Kokul. We've no desire to kill you—but we will."

The Wizard of Bourget seemed to smile a bit, then looked up at the security chief. Morah's face remained impassive as always, but his eyes and manner suggested that he was boiling inside.

"You dare face down *me*?" Morah shot back defiantly. "If that's you, Koril, I welcome the challenge. If not, I have little to fear from the likes of the rest of you!"

My heart jumped on hearing Koril's name. Koril! It was really beginning! In fact, I wondered if this wasn't all pretty well stage-managed to do just that. Maybe Matuze was becoming as bored and impatient as I was to get something moving. Well, they'd sure as hell gotten something moving now . . .

After a long pause, heavy weapons opened up from the rooftops right at Yatek Morah and the stage area. They were prevented from using real devastators since they wanted to keep the unconscious crowd alive, but the amount of ordinance that did open up would atomize anything it hit, and it hit Yatek Morah head on. Tully Kokul moved fast to the side as the entire stage area crackled, burned, turned suddenly white-hot and vanished, leaving a crater two meters deep.

Yatek Morah was still standing there where the stage had been, about four meters in mid-air. The stuff continued to pour into him, and for a moment he seemed not to notice and certainly not to be worried as he looked this way and that. I realized, however, that it was a frantic series of glances even for so impressive a power. He was holding off all that concentrated firepower by sheer force of will, aided, probably, by some very effective body-worn neutralizers, but they couldn't withstand that sort of concentrated power very long and he knew it.

Suddenly he seemed to grow and expand, becoming in an instant a huge, three-headed dragonlike monster rising up, up, out of an invisible cavity in the air just above the smoldering pit. It was a fearsome, terrifying sight as the thing grew and grew until it towered over the entire square and bathed the scene in its shadow. The firing wavered, but then picked up again and, with a defiant howl and hiss from all three heads, the terrible creature shot from sight as fast as a shuttle and quickly disappeared into the sky.

The firing stopped, leaving only a scene of incredible carnage and a vast, bubbling caldron where once the square had been. Some of the people who had been knocked out by the stun rays had been caught, inevitably, in the firing, but very few—most had drawn back during the excitement.

I had to admit I was stunned almost beyond thought, and had to call on all my training and experience to put myself back together. Things had happened very fast, and few of them were expected. First Zala—the fact that she was, perhaps had been all along, part of the opposition here and neither told me nor betrayed it in any way. And, of course, there was her transformation into someone quite different almost before my very eyes. Then the tables being turned on Morah, followed by his own incredible transformation into the terrifying three-headed dragon.

And now? I was acutely aware of how very alone I was at the moment—and how much on the *outside* of where I wanted to be *in*. I looked out into the square and listened carefully. No weapons, no sonics, no rays. It was over, whatever it was. They would come in and take their own out, now marked with the horns, and shift to new and unknown places and bases. Either I got left behind to rot or I got out there and tried to get inside.

I opened the door and walked cautiously into the street, being careful to keep close to the wall and exercising all my training and experience to make as small and difficult a target as I could for anybody who might get nervous. I admitted to myself that I would have felt much more confident with a laser pistol of my own.

Still, I had to be out here if only to make my contacts. I wondered where Zala was. If she were in this up to her neck, as it now appeared, she would be very handy—I needed some friend to bridge the gap.

For a few minutes nothing moved except a couple of the poor devils shot but not killed by the troopers near the street intersection. Obviously the ray hadn't gotten that far. The troopers themselves were mostly ugly messes, smeared over the nicely whitewashed walls.

But then, carefully, shapes began moving into the square—or what was left of it—starting with two nasty-looking things that flew down from the rooftops. Strange creatures covered with what appeared to be both fur and feathers of gold and brown. Their batlike wings did not fold into their bodies but instead semi-accordioned on their backs. Their heads were nasty, somewhat birdlike with large eyes and beaks but capable of an almost humanlike expression. They were horrors, and for a moment I feared they were some new kind of Charonese creature come to feed on carrion. But the deliberateness of their moves and their very human manner in going through and checking the unconscious and the dead showed them to be changelings. I was not really surprised at the changeling involvement, but to see two of them that looked like the same creature was more than interesting.

Huge, clawlike hands gestured beyond my line of sight, and from all four main streets they entered—a nightmarish parade of creatures that had never evolved except in the human mind. Shaggy, apelike things, things that crawled, things on four legs, walkers, hoppers, amphibians—the collection of human horrors seemed endless and terrible, all the more so because you could see in their movements and gestures, and sometimes in their features, the humanity that lay deep within them. But they were not all repulsive—some were quite beautiful and graceful, exotic creatures out of mankind's myths and imagination, as well as its nightmares.

I looked around for some sign of Zala or, perhaps, Tully

Kokul, but neither were anywhere to be seen. I was suddenly acutely aware of the fact that I was very much alone in that square, the only whole and conscious human being and not marked by the spell as a friend or ally. I began to think better of the idea and edged back along the wall toward the door once more, whereupon a couple of creatures, one tentacled and snakelike, the other a gray thing like a crude stone carving noticed me and pointed. I froze, and some of the others turned in my direction. There seemed little I could do—they had the guns—so I just stood up straight, walked away from the wall, and put my hands up.

"Wait! Don't shoot!" I called to them. "I'm not a bad guy. I'm Zala's husband! You know—Zala. One of your people!"

A creature that looked something like a walking tree turned to the tentacled, snakelike thing and said something I couldn't catch. The tentacled creature said something back. I saw some shrugs and indecision from several of the more humanoid ones around as they stopped for a moment from their task of identifying those with horns and carrying them off.

The frog-man came up to them and said, clearly, "He's the T.A.—the government man here. Get rid of him!"

One of the winged creatures nodded, pulled its pistol, and aimed it at me.

"Hey! Wait a minute!" I yelled, but then something hit me real hard and I lost consciousness.

CHAPTER NINE

Changeling

I came to, slightly, but felt dizzy, weak, and my head hurt as it never had before. I know I groaned, but I was only semi-conscious and still not really thinking. I was aware, though, that I was on a stretcher or litter of some kind and that I was being carried someplace very fast. I managed to open my eyes and was shocked to see that it was dark. How long had I been out?

I heard a sharp command and the stretcher bearers slowed, then stopped and put me down. There was very little light and I was in no condition to see straight, but I couldn't help thinking that the front bearer was a giant caricature of a big bird of some kind. Caricature. That was a good word for most of the changelings I had seen. The image of the white, feathered head with its huge eyes and wide, flat orange beak finally penetrated by still-foggy brain enough for me to realize the obvious—they hadn't killed me but had, for some reason, taken me with them! The game was back on track—if my head ever reassembled itself.

The bird-thing poured something into a cup from a gourd around its waist. "Drink this," it rasped in a guttural, nonhuman voice. "Go on—it'll make you feel better."

I managed to grab the cup and bring it, with the help of a humanlike white hand, to my lips. It burned a bit, but tasted much like a fruit brandy. My mouth was dry and parched and I badly needed something. I spilled a little, but only a little, then dropped back down on the stretcher.

"He'll be all right," the bird-man said to a companion I

hadn't yet seen. "That'll keep him until we get to the Old Woman."

"That's all I want," replied the other, a woman's voice that sounded vaguely familiar but wasn't one I could easily place.

"Zala?" I managed weakly, voice cracking.

"Forget her," the voice responded, and then we were up and off again.

My head didn't really clear very much for the remainder of the journey, although the pain subsided into nothingness. I was semiconscious, but not really able to move or say much of anything, and the whole world seemed to have a fuzzy, dreamlike quality. I had enough wits to realize that I'd been given a drug containing a light sedative, but whether to lessen my pain or to keep me from recovering—or both—I couldn't be sure. Nor, in fact, did I much care.

Time had little meaning for me, but it was still quite dark when we slowed and approached what appeared to be a cave from which a dull fireglow shone into the blackness. Thunder sounded in the distance, and told us all that the inevitable Charonese rains would soon be upon us once more. But the cave was the destination, and they managed to carry me into it before the heavens opened.

The cave itself had a small mouth but opened into a single large chamber, although exactly how large I couldn't tell. A fire burning in the center of the chamber was the source of light. Its smoke was rising straight up, indicating some kind of air vent. If it was hot outside, it was really broiling inside, and if I had been in anything other than a drugged condition I would have gotten out of there. As it was, I could only lie there, sweating profusely, visions of being roasted on a spit dancing through my fevered brain.

There was someone else in the cave—a very old woman, it appeared, dressed all in black cloth that virtually hid her entire body, which appeared to be extremely large. She doddered up to us using a crooked stick as a cane and gestured for them to put me down where I was, which they did. Bird-man turned to the one in back of me, "All right, we're even now, Darva. I hope this is really what you want."

Darva! I'd almost forgotten about her. I hadn't really seen or talked to her after that first time, although I'd looked for her when I was out at Thunderkor. Even in my drugged state, it made me feel a little better to know that I had yet another friend among the others, one who had probably saved my life.

She moved around to where I could see her, near the old woman. Darva towered over the woman in black, who had pretty good bulk herself, although she was almost certainly human.

"I bring you my heart, Grandmother," she greeted the old woman.

The woman stood back and looked at her with ancient, dark eyes. "It is good that you are well," the old one responded in a voice cracked with age and experience. "I feared the loss of many lives."

"There were twelve of us killed," Darva told her. "That is less than we thought. And almost two hundred of them."

The old woman nodded. "That is well. But they will bring down a terror now beyond knowing or understanding. All are even now scattering to the winds and will not regroup for many weeks in special places far away. And what of you? What will you do?"

Darva sighed. "You know Isil is dead and his masters flown."

"I know," the old woman replied, a tinge of sadness in her voice. "You are a changeling forever, and no old changeling may ever return to Bourget."

"I know," Darva told her. "But what I did, I did for revenge, not out of some loyalty pledged to ones I don't even know."

"You will not join the others, then, at the appointed time?"

She shrugged. "I haven't decided as yet, Grandmother."

The old woman looked over at me. "He is the one of whom you spoke?"

Darva nodded. "He was kind to me when no one else

would be. He is not like the others. I ask you now for a last favor, Grandmother."

Still fogged and semi-comatose, I could only follow the conversation, not analyze it or join in.

"Does he consent?" the old woman asked.

Darva turned and pointed to me. "See how they have hurt him? They were about to shoot him when I stopped them. Without me he would be twelve hours dead. Does that not give *me* the right?"

"Under our sacred law, it does," the old one agreed, "but he may not be the kind of person you think if your will is imposed."

"What choice will he have?" She paused. "Besides—if not he, then who? It is my reason to live."

The old woman gave a sympathetic smile. "Then that is more than reason enough." She waddled over to me and examined me clinically, like a doctor before an operation. "That's a nasty crack on the head. Skull fracture, some concussion."

Darva came over and looked down at me. She was still exotically beautiful, even the light green skin and dark green of lips and hair served to make her even more alluring. For the first time though, I noticed the nonhuman touches of the now-dead creature artist who had remade her: small pointed ears that twitched this way and that through the dark green hair, and hands that were far rougher and more beastlike than I remembered. That sharp, curved horn, perhaps fifty centimeters long, was actually a curved bone, layer upon layer presenting a sense of concentric rings leading to its sharp point. "You will be able to repair him?" she asked, worriedly.

The old woman nodded. "Oh, yes, yes. Although the blow's a serious one that would have killed many men. He has a very, very strong will to live. Good *wa*, strong *wa*, already rushing within him to repair the damage. We will help the *wa*."

"When?"

"Why not now? He is quiet. He has been given *osisi*, I perceive. That is good. He is heavily sedated, but conscious. It helps, his being awake." She turned back to

Darva. "A spell of the mind will be hard. He is protected by the town sorc from such meddling. I could give you potions, though . . ."

She shook her head. "No. That will be all right. I wouldn't want it to be like that anyway."

"That is good. I will have enough problems reworking parts of his body functions, reflexes, balance centers, that sort of thing, without having to worry about the conscious mind as well." She sighed. "Well, let's get it done."

Again, I can say little about how much time passed, or exactly what was done. I know that the old woman chanted and meditated over me for a long while, and occasionally seemed to knead various parts of my head and body. I also seemed to have a bad fever, with all sorts of strange, surrealist visions passing in and out of my mind. I would come down with chills, then hot flashes, and even oddly erotic sensations ran through my whole body. They had remarked on how bad off I was, and so I didn't fight any of it. Finally, I just lapsed into an incredibly deep sleep where no odd creatures, feelings, wizards and witches penetrated.

I awoke still feeling groggy, although with no pain. It was some moments before I perceived a wrongness, somehow, about myself. I looked around the cave, but aside from a now tiny fire and a sliver of light coming in through the opening indicating it was day outside I saw nobody and nothing unusual. I fought to clear the cobwebs from my brain, and, at last, I realized a couple of things right away. First of all, I was standing up. That was really odd, since there was no way I could imagine myself rising in the dark—unless it was part of the witch's healing spells or whatever. Second, I no longer felt the least bit hot. In fact, I felt a little chilly, which was ridiculous in a cave with the fire still going.

I was suddenly very wide awake and with a very bad feeling about all this. I raised my hand to rub the last bits of sleep from my eyes and saw what I feared.

The hand was green, rough, and taloned.

"*No!*" I shouted, my voice echoing slightly around the cave walls. "Damn it!" I took a step forward, and immediately knew the whole story. I turned and looked down and back at myself. I had big, taloned lizard's feet and thickly muscled lizard's legs, not to mention a bright green tail that was almost as long as my body without the legs. Frantically I looked around the cave, then saw over in one corner something that would do for my purposes—a large piece of shiny metal. I went over to it, picked it up, and looked at myself in the fire's reflection.

Horn and all, I reflected glumly. The face and torso retained some of my former appearance, but it was an odd hybrid, a combination of the features of Park Lacoch and Darva.

I heard someone enter behind me. I put down the shiny metal and turned. It was Darva. She stopped and looked at me, a mixture of pleasure and apprehension on her face.

"Darva, why?" I asked her.

She looked a little apologetic. "I saved your life," she reminded me. "I would think you would do the same for me."

"I—I would," I told her honestly, "but how is changing me into a near double of you going to do that?"

She sighed and looked a little sad. "The only thing I lived for was revenge, and I've had that, although not the way I hoped. Now, with all this, I'm completely alone and like this forever, unless I'm changed into something even worse. The only one of my kind, Park—and never able to go home again, to see my family, to be among the few I treasure." There was a note of pleading in her voice. "Don't you see? If I had to go on alone, I'd kill myself. And there you were, and Jobrun knocked you out, then drew his pistol to shoot you. I saw it, and knew, somehow, it was destiny and that the gods had put you and me there like that for a reason."

I shook my head sadly. The truth was, I had to admit even to myself, that what she was saying was totally understandable and even reasonable. How could I even argue with her logic, no matter how I felt? Face facts, I said to myself. You'd be dead without her, so you owe her. And this way, you are still in the game, still playing. If the changelings were the heart of Koril's movement, then it was with the changelings I belonged. If there was any doubt about that I should have just stayed out of that square and helped Tully pick up the pieces as a loyal T.A. Besides, there were a lot worse things I could have been turned into—I ought to know. I had seen them in the square.

I went over to her, almost knocking over some stuff with my tail, took her hand in mine, and smiled. "I *do* understand," I told her, "and I *do* forgive you."

She looked instantly happy beyond measure.

"But you might have gotten more than you bargained for," I warned.

She didn't seem to hear the comment, but two big tears welled up in her green eyes. "I'm glad we're not going to have a fight."

I sighed. "No, no fight. I admit this is going to take some getting used to in more ways than one, but I think I can live with it."

"Let's go outside," she suggested. "We're sort of cold-blooded."

Well, that explained the slight chill, I thought. I followed her out. It was the usual hot day, with heavy humidity and great clumps of white fog covering almost everything. The heat and humidity seemed to fade slowly away, though, and I began feeling very comfortable for the first time since arriving on Charon. Suddenly I was conscious of a great hunger. "What do we eat?" I asked her.

She smiled. "Almost anything living," she replied, and I had visions of tearing small lizards limb from limb. She caught my thought and laughed. "Oh, no. Plants, fruits, leaves, that sort of thing. Animals, too, but I prefer mine cooked the old way."

"Fair enough. Anything nearby?"

"There's a grove of fruit trees—cuaga melons—just down the hill here. Follow me."

She started off and I followed. "You say it's a grove. Any chance of our being seen? I'm pretty sure changelings aren't too popular right now."

"No, it's on the edge of Bindahar's holdings," she replied. "They won't be out this way for a couple of days, and by then we'll be long gone."

The melons were big, fat black and orange striped things, but they were very filling, although I had to get used to eating the rind as well. Either my taste sense had changed drastically—which was likely—or the humans who ate only the pulp missed something good.

We ate long and heavily. My old self—my original self—might have managed a whole melon, pulp only. The old Park Lacoch maybe a quarter of that. I ate seventeen, rinds and all, and still wasn't totally full.

"You eat a lot," Darva told me, "and whenever we can. We never get fat, though—just stronger, it seems."

"That's a fair trade," I admitted, feeling much better now. Once we'd eaten, it was time to talk of other things. Eating made me a little lazy and lethargic, and it was time to relax.

"Look—tell me a lot of things."

"Anything," she responded, obviously meaning it. "You don't know how very long it's been since I've had anybody to talk to, just friend to friend."

I nodded. "Okay. First of all, the immediate stuff. Who was the old woman who cast the spell?" Frankly, I wanted to know for more than one reason. She was the one who, at some future time, might also take it off.

"That was my great-grandmother—my real one," she told me. "She's had that power since I don't know when. Maybe since she was little. She studied with a Company sorc when she was very young, when there weren't the kinds of prejudice and tight unions they have now. But she never got the full bit. She had nine kids instead."

"I can see where that would slow you down," I admitted, "though she seemed powerful enough. But—why make me into your twin sister? Was that because her powers were limited?"

She hesitated a moment. "Well, that's not exactly true," she responded. "It's true that she had me for a model, and it's kind of tricky, making a changeling. Do it wrong and your brain's not right for the rest of you and you get crippled in the body or head. There's lots like that. So she used the same spell that bastard Isil used on me as her guide. That meant you look almost like me. But she had bunhars as models also. I was so excited I didn't even really think about it, but *she* did. You're still a male, Park—looks aside."

That was interesting. It was also ironically funny, and I had to chuckle.

"What's so funny?"

"Well, you know I wasn't born on Charon. I was sent here. Sent here by the law."

She nodded. "I know. It was the talk of Thunderkor."

"Well, I got into—trouble. I killed somebody, for no reason you—or even I, now—would think was right or sane. And the reason, when they found it, was that I was a hermaphrodite, a freak."

Her mouth formed a little circle. "Oh . . . So that's why you looked a little, well, funny."

I nodded. "But they got me straightened out and happily male," I continued. "And now—look! I'm a male who looks like your sister!"

She laughed at that herself, but it brought up an interesting question. All right, I was male—but a male *what*? I asked her about it.

"I wondered about that myself," she said. "According to Grandmother, if we were to, ah, make it, right now nothing would happen. But as soon as the *wa* inside you gets the rest of you straight, it might just be that we could reproduce our own kind. It's not certain, but it's been known to happen. We might start a whole new race!" She looked thoughtful. "*Darvus Lacochus.*"

"Sounds like a disease."

She laughed. "You know, this is wonderful, Park. I feel more alive than I have in two years!"

I could see her joy, and even feel good about it. I liked her, too. Her speech was a little rough, and occasionally became even rougher. She was uneducated and inexperienced, but she was a bright, intelligent woman whose potential had been blunted by a man's cruel ego. And she was certainly tougher and more decisive than Zala—the old

Zala, anyway. I idly wondered what the new Zala was like.

"Look," I said, "you're going to have to fill me in. What the hell happened back there in Bourget? And who did it? And why?"

She sighed. "Well, for a long time there's been a devil cult. You know that?"

I nodded.

"Well, anyway, it was mostly bored and frustrated women trying to get a little of the Power. But a year or two ago, things changed. How and who did it I don't know, but they got kinda taken over by this bigger group that wants to overthrow the government. It's got a real powerful sorc behind it is all I know."

"Koril," I told her. "Used to be Lord."

"Yeah, him, I think," she agreed. "Anyway, lots of folks liked him better. You didn't have any creepy guys like that security chief, and no troopers jumping out at you. Well, this sorc also contacted all the changeling colonies. He promised them that when he got back they'd be given Tukyan, the south continent, for their own. There's few people down there now, and it's mostly still unexplored, but it's at least as nice as here, or so I'm told. Well, this was great for the changelings, who have no real life and no future here. The humans went along, too, because we'd be out of their hair. See?"

I nodded. It was very logical—and good politics on Koril's part. I was beginning to see how formidable the man was, even without his reputed super magical powers. I had to wonder how Aeolia Matuze was ever able to oust him in the first place, and how she kept her power.

In a flash, I had it—the only logical answer. She was in the job because she backed the war against the Confederacy. The other three Lords couldn't care less about Charon—Korman said as much. Who did? The only logical answer was the aliens themselves.

You didn't have any creepy guys like that security chief . . .

Whose Chief of Security *was* Yatek Morah? Matuze's? Yes, but only so long as she followed the correct line. And that meant that it was very possible that the strange man with those strange eyes, that robotlike manner, that incredible power, was not human at all. And *that* meant that, while Charon was unimportant to the war, it was, for some reason, very, very important to the aliens. Why?

Aeolia Matuze, with her great ego and dreams of godhood—the aliens would feed that, and in exchange, she would follow the alien line right where they said. It made sense. I wondered if Koril, even now, realized it? What was one Lord of the Diamond to a race prepared to disrupt and take over a thousand worlds or more?

"What'cha thinking?"

I was startled out of my reverie. "Just putting a lot of pieces together in my head. I'll explain them to you later. We're going to be together a long time, and it's a long and complicated story."

"Together," she sighed. "You don't know how good that sounds."

"First, some basics. How come I don't trip over my tail when I walk or tip over on the run? I feel pretty natural in this body."

"It was a good spell, with all the necessaries."

I nodded. That was good enough for me. "Okay then—where do we go from here?"

"Far away," she responded quickly, "and fairly fast. This place is a day's march from Bourget, but it'll soon be crawling with government troops. Probably already is. We have a number of defenses—including the ability to stand absolutely still. You'd be surprised, but big as we are, if we're all surrounded by green and stay completely still they'll run right past us."

"Handy," I told her, "but the weaponry suddenly turned a lot more modern around here than I was used to, and the good stuff has heat sensors."

She laughed. "So what? They tried them in hunting. Our body temperature's pretty much the same as our surroundings. They're nearly useless."

I hadn't thought of that angle. "Still, I'd just as soon be away from here—fast. How well do you know the land beyond this region?"

"Fair," she responded. "Worse if we get more than a

hundred kilometers from here. I never traveled much. But I know where the roads are, even though we can't use them—and I have landmarks from maps in my head. They made us memorize a bunch of them."

"Good girl," I told her.

"You want to join up with the others, then?" She sounded almost disappointed.

I nodded. "I'll try and explain why as we go. There's a lot going on they don't tell you about."

"We've still got three weeks to get maybe 800 kilometers," she told me. "That's time enough to tell me everything. We were supposed to scatter and live off the land until then."

"Gives 'em plenty of time to capture some of us and force those locations out of us," I said worriedly.

"Oh, there's hundreds of rendezvous spots, and only a very small group was told of one and two alternates. Even if they pick up half the changelings, which I doubt, we still would have an even chance that one or more of ours was still good."

"Not the odds I like, but they're the only ones we have." I looked around. The fog was coming in even more thickly. "And now's the time to make tracks for far away."

She laughed. "And even those'll be bunhar tracks."

There were, in fact, advantages to this shape.

I looked around. "I think I'm going to have to find a friendly tree," I told her. "It goes right through you on an empty stomach."

She laughed and pointed randomly. I took her advice, picked a spot, and relaxed, looking down.

"Oh, so *that's* where it is," I said aloud.

CHAPTER TEN

Decision at the Pinnacles

It was, in some ways, an idyllic three weeks, and it bothered me a bit because I thought of it as such. The fact was, I really *enjoyed* Darva, person to person, and found within myself the stirrings of feelings I never even knew I had. It was a blow to my own self-image, really, that I should feel this way. The strong, solid, emotionless agent of the Confederacy, who needed nothing and no one—ever. Who was born, bred, and trained to be above such petty human feelings as loyalty, friendship . . . love? Hadn't I been the one who couldn't even pin down the meaning of the word to Zala only a few months ago? Was it possible, I found myself wondering, that loneliness was not something only inferior people suffered? Had I, in fact, been as much an alien and an outsider to my own culture as Darva had been to hers? That thought, I knew, was dangerous. It struck at the very value system of the Confederacy which I still told myself I believed in.

But had we, in our headlong rush to perfection, somehow left holes somewhere in the human psyche? Or was it rather just a new body, a new form, new hormones and whatever that created those holes where they'd never been before? For the moment, I preferred to think the latter—although, from a practical standpoint, it made no real difference when it was happening to me.

Several times during the three weeks we roamed the jungles of Charon, I was on the brink of telling her my real identity, my real mission, but I always held back. Nothing was to be gained from doing so now, and there was always time later on. I got to know her, though, as thoroughly as I knew anybody, and I liked what I found. She was a quick

study, too, entranced by my tales of the civilized worlds
and the frontier she would never see. She had less trouble
than I would have thought with the alien/Four Lords backdrop, although I suspect that she thought of the aliens only
as a new form of changeling. When you're bright green,
215 centimeters tall, have a horn and a tail, the concepts of
"alien" and "nonhuman" just don't come across quite as
well. But she understood that alien did not mean form as
much as mind. If, as I suspected, Morah was an alien, she
was all for saving a humanity she'd never see nor ever be a
part of.

Some aspects of the new form were definitely affecting
my mind, though. I found myself increasingly emotional,
and increasingly aware of that emotion. I still retained all
my training and its gimmicks, but I felt everything with an
intensity I'd never known before, both positive and nega-
tive.

Our new form, which I shortened to *darvas*, wasn't at all
bad, either. We were enormously strong, and despite being
large, we could indeed fade into any green underbrush,
then sprint faster than any human could run. The talons
were handy as weapons, although we hadn't had to use
them for that, and for cutting and slicing food of no matter
what sort, and they made no difference to us, since our
skin was extremely thick and tough—and it shed water like
a waterproof coat.

There was no question they were out looking for us,
though. We saw soarers on many occasions, some coming
very close to the treetops or open spaces, occasionally with
troopers spray-firing into clumps of growth just to panic
anything and flush it out. The roads were under constant
patrol by more of those nasty-looking troopers as well as
some locals. Still, as long as we didn't run into a sorc or an
apt and betray ourselves, we found it little trouble to stay
out of the way.

The only trouble, in fact, came near the end of our jungle exile. We had both become easily accustomed to the
jungle, a fearsome place for most humans. Our hides were
too tough for the insects to penetrate, and we were relatively immune to predators and strong enough to break free

of vines and mud. It was, in fact, a wondrous sort of place, the kind of place where there was endless fascination, endless beauty. Although we didn't really realize it, what we were doing in psych parlance was "going wild," totally adapting to an environment for which we were, quite literally, designed.

What brought it home to us was when we ran into the bunhar. Now, we'd seen and encountered many of the large creatures of jungle and swamp, including hundreds I'd had no idea existed before, but mostly we'd managed to steer clear of them—and they seemed to accept us as well. But this one was different. I will never be sure just what we did wrong. Maybe he was just horny and smelled Darva. But, anyway, he didn't avoid us; he challenged us with a great roar and snarling teeth. In fact, he looked to me like he was *all* nice, sharp, pointed teeth.

Despite some overlarge fanglike incisors, we had the omnivore's complement in a human-type mouth and face. It was a no-win situation, but try as we might to avoid him he challenged all the more, and we realized we had a fight on our hands. Oddly, I felt a rush of adrenalin or something similar like I'd never known before. While the big saurian sat there, snarling, I found myself overcome with anger and rage—and heard similar, animalistic snarlings from Darva. Without even thinking, both of us charged the brute, who was about our size, heads down and horns straight.

The bunhar had teeth, all right, but no horn, and I don't think he was quite prepared for our sudden charge. He reared back on his tail to protect his head, and both our horns penetrated his upper chest, while our talons ripped at him. Again and again we plunged and ripped into him, and he roared in pain and anger as his blood gushed all over his chest and us. Then Darva whirled around and kicked the creature behind his right leg with her own powerful leg, rearing back on her own tail for maximum effect, and the bunhar toppled.

In a moment we were both on him, plunging our horns into his vulnerable neck and ripping out flesh and limb. The poor creature never had a chance from the start, not only because of the horn but because, even in our animal rush, we had the advantage of human fighting tactics. The creature was killed outright, and neither of us received more than a slight scratch from the foot talons as we plunged in.

But when it was dead, the anger, the rage, the sense of power without thought, continued in both of us for some time, and we drank of the dead creature's blood and ripped off and ate chunks of raw flesh until we could eat no more and it was a bloody mess. Only when the eating was done and the feeling of satisfied lethargy overtook us, did we relax. The great emotions subsided, and rational thought returned.

For a while neither of us could say anything. Finally, Darva looked at me, as blood-spattered as she, then back at the carcass that was already drawing insects and would eventually draw carrion eaters. "My god, what have we done?" she gasped.

I looked at her, then at the carcass, then back at her again. I shook my head in tired wonder. "It looks like we're more animal than even you thought."

She looked dazed, slightly horrified. "It—it wasn't the bunhar. I mean, the damned thing asked for it. It was— after." She dipped her hand in a small pool of bunhar blood, brought it up to her nose, then licked it off her fingers. "My god, Park—it felt *good*! And it tasted . . ."

"I know," I replied wearily. The whole experience was wearing off now, leaving me feeling very tired, muscles aching a bit, and aware now of my scratches. I knew she was feeling the same.

She was still in that shocked daze. "I—I've been this way for over two years, and I never felt like that before, never did anything like that before."

I nodded wearily. "Your Isil was more creative than you thought. I suspect that this was to be the next stage if you didn't cave in, as you weren't—if your Gneezer even remembered you anymore. It was probably a good idea at the time, long forgotten. If the change wouldn't do it, they would put you off in the swamps, where your animal instincts would take over. You'd go wild, either winding up with a bunhar group or crawling back to them." I paused for a moment. "Still, it's not all bad."

She looked at me strangely. "What in hell is good about it?"

"Consider. We—the two of us—killed that mass of muscle and teeth, and did it pretty easily. We *instinctively* used all our best biological weapons against him. He outweighs us by a couple of hundred kilos, probably, and he was born a predator. But we're a more fearsome predator. That maneuver that toppled him probably saved us from serious injury. It's something you did almost automatically, but it would never occur to such a pea-brain as him. We're the bosses now. The king and queen of Charon's jungles, totally adapted to our element. We have nothing whatsoever to fear while we're in that element."

"But—the blood. God! It was like a shock, an orgasm. It was like a supercharge, the ultimate drug stimulant! Even now, repelled as I am, I crave the taste of it."

She was right. So did I, and it was something that was going to be hard to ignore.

I sighed. "Well, I'd say we'll probably keep it under control, but maybe have to give into it every once in a while. We're killers now, Darva. Natural predators. It's the bill that goes with this form and we simply have to accept it."

She looked dubious. "I—I don't know. Park—what if it had been a man? One of those troopers?"

My training was coming to the fore, my mind sorting and placing the new facts and choosing inevitable courses of action. It would be far harder for Darva, I knew, far harder, but she would have to eventually accept one basic fact and live with it.

"We're no longer human, Darva," I told her flatly. "We're something else entirely. Frankly, as long as the man is an enemy, I can see no difference between spearing him and shooting him.

"But—cannibalism!" She shivered.

"If I ate you, it would be cannibalism," I said realistically. "But a human is just another smart animal."

She shook her head. "I—I don't know."

"You'll have to accept it, Darv, or go nuts," I told her.

"But I wouldn't worry about it. Back with our own, back in intelligent company with ready food supplies, I doubt if our condition will be any problem at all. Only out here, in the jungle."

She said nothing for a while, and we more or less slept off the experience. When we awoke it was nearly dark, but we found a stream and washed the caked blood and remains from each other, feeling a little more like rational people and less like predators after we did.

Still, she could ask, "Park—those aliens you spoke of. Aren't *we* aliens, too? Particularly now?"

I didn't really have a ready answer for that one.

Despite the moralizing, we repeated our orgy the next day—deliberately. This time we found a small female uhar with a wounded leg who had been left by her herd to die because she could no longer hunt food. Such a target of opportunity was quite literally irresistible, incredibly easy, and also easy to defend to our consciences since the creature would have died more agonizingly anway. Still, the ease and quickness of the decision and the high emotion— "anticipation" I guess would be the word—of the kill actually bothered me more than Darva. My whole life and self-image was based on my absolute confidence in my ability to be completely in control at all times, to be able to analyze and evaluate every situation with cold, dispassionate logic. To be able to give in to such base, animal— literally animal—instincts so easily was disturbing. To enjoy the experience so much was even more disturbing.

As for the hunting and killing, humans had been doing that to animals since the dawn of time. Though the civilized worlds knew meat only as a synthetic, those on the frontier certainly knew it in the same way ancient man on ancestral Earth had. Here on Charon people made their livings hunting game and fishing and eating their catch, and those who did this work enjoyed it. The fact that the people of Montlay and Bourget, among others, had their meat ground or cut and cooked and seasoned so they no longer really thought of their meal as an animal that had to be butchered only eased their minds a bit. Darva and I were no different—we were simply eliminating the hypocrisy. Looking at it in that way we both found it much easier to move fully into our roles as predators.

The Warden organisms that governed everything inside us also seemed to take a more practical view. After only the third kill and feed I was aware of odd feelings, mostly numbness and a little discomfort in my mouth. I mentioned this to Darva, who had noted the same thing, and a quick examination showed that things *were* changing. Our teeth were becoming sharper, the front fangs growing longer and thicker. Without an additional magic spell or anything else, we were changing into true carnivores.

Such a modification could not have been in the long-range plans of an apt like Isil; the Wardens inside us, somehow, were sensing the change in our life-style and modifying us to adapt. But what exactly were they reacting to? I wondered. Was it the changed physical circumstances? That seemed unlikely—Darva had been this way for a long time, I a very short time, yet the transformation was taking place only now. It had to be the change in our *mental* attitude that triggered it, I decided. Korman said we all had the power. Maybe the process was more complex than even he thought.

But that brought up an even more mystifying question. How did the Wardens *know*? An apt like Isil, even a powerful soro like Korman, hardly had the kind of mind that could literally reprogram every cell, order speeded growth, put every cell and every molecule together in such a pattern as to create a biologically functioning changeling. The Confederacy's computers could do the job easily, of course, although doing so was illegal. But a man or woman could just wave a magic wand here, mumble some words, and somehow, force the transmutation of a human being into something else—something that functioned.

I had here a lot of pieces of a truly great puzzle but, as yet, nothing with which to put them all together. For the first time in a long while I wondered about my counterpart, my old self, out there, somewhere, off the Warden Diamond. Was he still getting his information even though I'd been transformed? And, if he *was* getting information

from all of us on the four Warden worlds, had he already
been able to put those pieces together with the superior
computer and Confederacy resources at his command?

I no longer hated him, certainly. Now, here, the way I
was, I wasn't even sure if I envied him.

Slowly, through it all in the final week, we moved cautiously closer to the rendezvous point Darva had selected as
the main target for us, the least likely to be betrayed. It
was about a kilometer off a main road, in a rock cleft near
a waterfall, and we approached it cautiously and in a round-
about manner. Darva was still hesitant about going at all,
particularly now.

"We're happy here," she argued. "You said it yourself—
we were made for the jungle and for this life. If we return,
there'll only be more fighting and trouble."

"What you say is true," I admitted, "but I'm thinking of
more than just you and me. For one thing, *I have to know.*
I want to find out just what the hell is going on here, and I
have a particular responsibility, since I know that all
Charon might be destroyed, we and our precious jungle
along with it. But there's more. If we win, and if this Koril's a man of his word, we can strike a blow for changelings and end this stupid discrimination. Changelings need
their own land and they need the Power. Otherwise, somebody will always control and threaten us. With the Power,
we could build a new race here, or many races."

I'm afraid she didn't really share my vision or my curiosity, but she understood, at least, that I could not be de-
nied—and she wasn't going to be left out, alone, again.

We approached the rocks cautiously. I let her take the
lead because she at least knew the lay of the land from the
maps. She was very cautious. Fifty meters or more from
the clearing, but within the sound of the roar of the falls,
she froze into the immobility we both could achieve and
still found hard to believe. Seeing her, I automatically froze
as well.

The falls masked most sounds, so I started looking
around, feeling a bit what she also felt—or sensed. It was, I
knew, another one of those animal attributes we were ei-

ther acquiring or discovering. There were others about. We couldn't see them or hear them but we knew with absolute certainty they were there.

Concentration on this one aspect produced an interesting sensation. I was aware that I was sensing something entirely new, outside any previous experience. For the first time, consciously, we were sensing our own Wardens—our *wa*, as the old woman had called it—and those Wardens were not isolated or alone. Somehow some threads of energy, incredibly minute, were sending and receiving signals in all directions. No, that wasn't right, either—not signals; more like an open communications link, waveforms of the most basic and microscopic sort; open channels to the trees, grass, rocks, stuff in the air—everything around us. This, then, was what the sorcs felt, what Korman could not explain to me.

The jungle was alive, both with the forms of life we could see and with the Warden organism itself. It was alive, and we were a part of it. What a glorious, heady feeling—unlike any I'd ever known.

Suddenly, I realized what exactly Darva and I were sensing. In us and most of the surroundings, the Wardens were usually passive, connected to all the other Wardens but sending and receiving nothing. But there were Wardens around through which things were now being transmitted. Not changelings—as far as Darva knew there were few with any of the Power and much of it had been blocked off by the spell. These were apts then, very minor apts, but apts nonetheless, and that meant humans.

Fine-tuning that sense of the Wardens as much as I could, I tried to locate the sources of these emanations— and did. One was about ten meters from Darva, behind a large tree. There was another about fifteen meters in the other direction and ahead of her. A third, at least, was near the waterfall—and a fourth was on top of it. It seemed absurdly simple to pick them out now, with their very different Warden patterns. But did that mean that they had also picked *us* up in the same way? Almost immediately I decided that they hadn't. Either they were totally unaware

of us or they took us for bunhars. If they knew, we would
have been jumped by now.

At that moment the one nearest Darva, the one behind
the tree, came into view, but he wasn't looking at us or
even in our direction. We were against the best natural
camouflage and remained incredibly still, so he might not
have seen us anyway.

He turned out to be a trooper in one of those black and
gold uniforms. Looking very relaxed and very bored, he
settled down under the tree, weapon still holstered. I could
tell from its shape that it was a laser pistol. How I wanted
one of those! Both Darva and I were efficient killing machines, it was true, but nothing could outrun a laser pistol.
If I had one now, I could knock the trooper off without
any personal risk at all.

I heard a short beeping sound, and the man reached to
his belt and picked up a tiny transceiver. He spoke a few
words into it, and I could make out that there *was* a reply,
although not what the reply was. Checking in, that was all.

Unfortunately, we were not small, delicate creatures.
The old Park Lacoch would have been better in this situation—tiny and catlike. We had to get away from here. I
was in no danger, but Darva was too damned close. Slowly,
carefully, I reached down and picked up a large rock, not-
ing idly that even the rock radiated the Warden sense.

Darva turned her head very slowly and carefully, saw
what I was doing, and gave me a careful nod; then she
turned back to look at the trooper.

Quickly I heaved the rock with all my might in the
opposite direction from where we stood. It was not a good
throw—my hands were tough and nasty, but my arms were
really very weak. Still, the rock made a clatter in back of
the trooper, and he jumped to his feet and whirled around,
pistol quickly drawn, then looked around suspiciously. The
rock, as I said, was weakly thrown, and though it *had*
landed beyond us the trooper began walking slowly toward
Darva. I seemed to see the man's Wardens almost "light
up," although that's not really the right word for it. I could
sense those channels of communication between his own
Wardens and those around him reverberating with a sense

of suspicion, a message of inquiry, as it were, although I could only guess that was what it was.

Darva was crouching a bit, flattened against broad-leafed trees and bushes of the same green as she; and she would have been nearly impossible even for me to spot had I not known she was there. It was the *Warden* sense that was to be feared, not any physical ones.

For some reason he hadn't yet picked her up—possibly we were involuntarily jamming in some way through our own apprehension—but I could see that he was soon going to be close enough to her that he couldn't miss her no matter what. It also hadn't escaped my notice that he had yet to call in on his communicator.

I made up my mind in a moment, only hoping that Darva would have the presence of mind to act correctly in the split second she would have.

The man stopped no more than two or three meters from her, turned slowly, and—I realized—saw her, first with Warden sense and then, knowing she was there, by sight. He grinned. "Well, well! A changeling with the Art," he said, obviously enjoying himself.

At that moment I popped up. "Hey!" I called, then gave my huge rear legs the kick of my life.

Darva whirled as the man's head and pistol turned toward me and struck him a blow that nearly cut off his head. Then his finger pushed the firing stud, and a beam of blue-white light shot out, burning a tree far over my head.

She didn't wait, but started for me, but I ran at her and at the dead body. She looked puzzled as I reached the man and tore the pistol from his hand; then I pivoted on my tail and headed for the jungle. I could hear another man's voice yelling behind us, and heard, rather than saw, the sound of laser pistol blasts.

Darva was still ahead of me dashing back into the jungle. When I saw she was safely out of the way I stopped, assumed my camouflage stance at a good spot, and waited.

Two troopers—a man and a woman—came running into the jungle, pistols drawn. I suddenly realized how off my timing was going to be with my oversized, taloned hands, but the comfortable feel of the pistol was reassuring enough. I was the absolute best—and this was like shooting targets at ten meters. Picking my time, I squeezed off two easy, well-placed shots, putting neat little holes in both chests. Both fell backward and were quickly still. As fast as I could, I went to them, took both pistols and both utility belts with their precious chargers, then turned and followed Darva's trail.

I handed her one of the belts and a pistol, power off, and we said nothing until we were deep into the jungle and felt safe. Finally we settled back on our tails, caught our breath, and relaxed a bit. "That was close!" she wheezed.

I nodded. "But worth it, anyway."

She looked puzzled. "Worth it? Why'd you take such a chance to get those pistols?" She flexed her talons. "*We* don't need them."

"You're wrong on that," I told her. "Neither of us can outrun a communicator or a well-aimed shot." I grinned. "But neither can they."

She shook her head in wonder. "He was so—weak. Puny." She lifted up her right hand. "I caved in his skull with one quick blow."

"That you did," I agreed. "And our arms are the weakest things we have. But don't get too cocky. Humans have always been the weakest and puniest creatures on any planet they've settled, and look who's boss."

She looked over at me. "Well, I guess that's it for any-place else. If they were at that place I'm almost positive they know the alternates."

I shook my head. "No, we've got to try them. One of them might still be good. If there's a chance, we have to take it."

"All right," she sighed, sounding disappointed; then she brightened a bit. "You know, I really did the right thing back there!"

"You sure did," I agreed. "I'm proud of you. There was no way for me to tell you what to do and you came through magnificently."

She beamed. "I guess maybe I'm cut out for this after all. You know—back there I was scared to death. And yet somehow I really enjoyed it."

"That's the way it is," I told her. "I hate to admit it, but it's fun to beat them like that. It really is."

"You know, you talk like you've done this kind of thing before," she observed. "A lot of times, just talking, you sounded like you did more than you told me about. And those two shots with that pistol! Wow!"

I sighed. "All right, I guess you should know the facts. You more than anybody." Briefly I told her about my real career, and why I had been sent to the Warden Diamond. She listened intently, nodding.

When I'd finished, she smiled. "Well, I guess that really explains a lot. And you're still on the job, even after . . ." She let the obvious trail off.

"More or less," I told her, "but not in the way you think. I wasn't kidding about reforms on Charon or the potential of the changelings. And I'm here for the rest of my life, just like you. There's very little they can do to me, although they *could*, as I said, destroy Charon. So you see why finding Koril is even more important to me. He's against the aliens—and so am I, at least from what I can see. He's my key to getting Aeolia Matuze, and also to our future here." I suddenly had a thought, checked one of the utility belts and found a communicator there. I picked it up and flipped it on.

". . . out of the bush, jumped Sormat—tore his throat out like some animal," a tinny voice said. "God! Two of 'em. Had to be. Only caught sight of one, though. Kinda looked like a bunhar. Creepy."

"What I want to know is how they managed to elude Sormie's *wa* shield," another voice came back. "Gives me the creeps. We should just get rid of these monsters."

Their signals were weakening—they were heading away from us, I could tell. The last comment made me a little mad. I looked at the communicator—a simple device, but not one I was familiar with. "Ever seen one of these before?" I asked Darva.

She came over and looked at it. "It's pretty much the same as the ones used to keep the Companies' headquarters in contact with the field workers," she replied. "A little different, but not much."

I nodded. "Military issue." I turned it over. Embossed on the back was a little logo—*Zemco, CB*. Cerberus again. The manufacturing center of the Warden Diamond. I predicted that my counterpart there would probably do quite well. "What's its range?"

"Huh?"

"About how far will it reach?"

"Oh. Well, the ones we used—maybe three, four kilometers."

I nodded. "This one's probably souped up just a little, but call it five at the top. If they're in common use on the planet, there would have to be some limits on them or nobody could talk to one another." I thought a moment. "I wonder if they're all using the same frequency?"

"You have something in mind?"

"Well, let's head for the first alternate—whichever's closest. It's possible we might be able to *hear* if it's occupied before we go in."

Some work with both belts and I managed to wrap one big combo belt around my torso, with two pistols, the communicators, and the rest all there. It wasn't very comfortable, but it was handy.

Using some vines, we managed to rig a carrier for Darva to wear the other pistol, although without practice it was more a psychological weapon than anything else. They were tricky to use.

We had a "window" of only thirty hours to allow for shifts to alternates. Every thirty hours the places would be checked to see if anybody was there or if they were staked out for the next four days, then—forget it.

We traveled, therefore, most of the night. During rest and eating breaks, we discussed what both of us had felt about the Warden organism. Our experiences were almost identical—and even the trooper she'd killed had sensed she had the power. We compared notes. She was not totally ignorant of the Warden sense from the start, although her understanding of it was cloaked in the ignorant mysticism of the natives.

"My great-grandmother, as you know, has tremendous

powers," she reminded me, "and much of her knowledge was passed down. As a kid I used to do the little exercises with her and it was really a lot of fun, but I never got too far with it. It was like the torgo"—a Charonese flute—"that my brother was given at the same age. For a while it was a toy, but it soon became boring and he never kept up his studies and practice. It's the same with the Art."

I nodded. "That doesn't explain my own sensitivity, though," I told her. "I don't think it came from the changeling spell, either. Korman said I had a natural aptitude for it and predicted I would sense the Wardens—the *wa*—as we did. That's important for a couple of reasons. It means both of us can learn it, and it means that changelings are no more limited than humans, which makes sense. We're built differently, but we're made of the same stuff and out of the same stuff." Since many of the changelings had been at least at the apt stage themselves, it was evident that what was needed was training. You could go only so far without that, after which it either wasn't usable any further or it backfired.

It was clear that the basis of the power was the ability to concentrate while sensing the Wardens in your object. Most people just wouldn't have the necessary self-control or self-confidence, but I was pretty sure I did, even now—and perhaps Darva did as well. An artistic bent and a mathematical aptitude would certainly help, of course, in doing elaborate things.

The place we were headed Darva called the Pinnacles, because of some odd rock formations. She'd never been near it, but had been shown a picture and assured me that, if she saw the real thing, she couldn't mistake it. Initially, she had rejected the spot because it was almost astride a main road and fairly close to an inland town called Gehbrat, but it was the closest.

We approached it in the late afternoon of the next day. I checked with my little communicator and found that there *was* some intermittent traffic on it, but it was mostly road patrols. Nothing was said about the Pinnacles as a staked-out place, and there was every indication that the frequency the things were on was fixed. That didn't mean somebody clever didn't have the place staked out using different frequencies or communicators, but the information we could get was a little reassuring.

We were more than a little cautious in approaching this time. She was certainly right—you couldn't miss the place. Four jagged spires of hard rock rose a kilometer or more over the surrounding jungle, like four great arrows pointing to the sky. Near the base of the second spire from the left would be the meeting place—if it were not already "spoiled."

We approached slowly and cautiously from opposite directions, ready to take any action required, but there was no sign or sense of any stakeout. If the location had been blown, the troopers were certainly far more professional than the ones back at the waterfall had been. It took a good two hours for me to satisfy myself that there were no dangerous troopers about, although when we linked up within sight of the rendezvous, we stayed just inside the woods. Having no timepieces, we could only settle back a little and wait, hoping for a pickup.

It grew dark quickly as night overtook us. Every once in a while I'd check the radio, but all signals were either faint or very intermittent; Pinnacles was never mentioned.

A bit after dark, we saw some movement in the area and froze. I drew one of the pistols and watched nervously. My night vision was extremely good—our eyes worked best in the murky twilight of the jungle, and were most sensitive to bright light—but it was by no means nocturnal vision. Therefore, I had difficulty seeing just who or what came into view. The Warden sense vaguely tracked the newcomer, but it was impossible to really tell much about its shape.

Whoever it was crept cautiously to the center of the clearing, seemed to stop and look around, then whispered nervously, "There is thunder in the south." That was the identifying phrase Darva had been told, but while our hopes rose our caution did not let down. If Morah knew of one hideout from captives, he certainly knew many of the passwords.

I looked at Darva and gestured at the pistol. She nodded,

moved away from me, then approached the dark shape. "The Destroyer builds," she whispered, giving the response.

I heard a sharp sigh. "Thank the gods!" a female voice said in low but clear tones. "Who's there?"

"Darva. Who are you?" She walked closer to the dark shape.

"I am Hemara," the other responded, "from the Valley of Cloud."

"I am from Thunderkor," Darva told her. "Come closer, so we may see each other clearly."

The other moved, and now I too could make out the shape. She was indeed a changeling, a large woman with a reddish yet very human face that differed only in that she appeared to have two large compound eyes of bright orange in place of the normal ones. She seemed to be carrying something smooth and round on her back.

Darva turned and whispered to me, "All right, you can come out. I think it's safe."

I moved from my hideaway and approached them. Up close, I could see that far more in the woman was changed than I had first noticed. Her body was black, hard, and shiny, like an insect's, and that round thing on her back was a huge black shell of some kind. She was standing on four of her eight legs—no arms—and these were also covered in a hard shell and had small pads at their tips ending in a single hard nail each. Still, she retained short-cropped humanoid black hair on her head.

The newcomer turned, looked at me, then back at Darva, then back at me again. "There are two of you?"

"Sort of," I responded. "It's a long story. Anyway, I'm Park and I'm the male."

Her very human mouth showed delighted surprise. "A pair! How wonderful!" There was a wistful note in that last, that I couldn't help but catch.

"Maybe," I told her. "For now, what's the plan to get out of here? I feel like a sitting duck."

She looked suddenly crestfallen. "I'd hoped that *you* . . ."

Darva sighed. "Just another refugee. Well, join the party and we'll wait some more."

She wasn't really constructed for the jungle, but down flat, or almost so, she could blend in pretty well with the rocks. Time passed as we talked, explaining where the pistols came from and telling her a little about ourselves— very little, really. As for Hemara, she'd been caught poaching by her Company—a very serious offense. As punishment, she was given to a Company apt as an experimental being on whom to practice. When not a plaything she was on public exhibition near the Company headquarters as a deterrent, and they had outdone themselves in providing a really nasty example. Without hands or claws she couldn't really manipulate much. Settling an interesting point, she said that the compound eye's multi-images resolved into a single image in her brain, but that she could focus on only one point. She could either see very far, but nothing close, or vice versa, and if she fixed on an object she could see only that object and its surroundings. That meant almost constantly changing focus to get a clear picture. She was a sad example of how far the cruel and insane minds that ran Charon could go, and yet she said she had seen and met worse. I probably had too, but the scene in that square after the fight had been so much of an overload that I found it hard to remember the shapes clearly.

We were joined later that evening by three more changelings. One was a man whose face was a hideous devil's mask and whose bent, winged body made him permanently bowlegged. His bat wings, however, were not functional. He was a good reminder of how volatile the Warden power could be. He'd been more or less stealing lessons, hiding himself and listening in while his local sorc instructed his apts. Then he tried experimenting on his own and had been doing very well, but one night he'd had a horrible nightmare . . .

The second creature was part long, gray limbless worm and part human torso topped by a hairless man's head. The body, perhaps five meters long, glistened and left a trail of ichor. He wouldn't tell us how he'd gotten that way, but we discovered he ate dirt.

The last one was surprisingly human, and decidedly uncomfortable with us. She was small, quite attractive, and had a distinctive pair of devil's horns. She appeared to be a nervous wreck and I'm afraid our all-changeling group didn't help her mood. Her name was Emla Quoor. She'd been in the group in the square, and she'd been terrified from that point on. There was little we could do to comfort her, except to point out that she must have some real guts and intelligence to make it this far undetected and in one piece. She looked like she'd been through hell, though, and I wasn't about to press her further. Others could do that— if we ever got picked up.

Suddenly a rumbling erupted all around us. "Oh, brother!" somebody swore. "You can't go three hours out here without getting dumped on." As the skies opened up for what promised to be the usual long deluge, everyone moved into the shelter of the trees. The way the wind whipped things up, though, there was no question but that everyone would be pretty well drenched.

Lightning swirled around the Pinnacles, lighting up the area intermittently in what, I had to admit, was an impressive scene. I looked out into the little clearing which was brightly lit by a lightning flash, then dark again. Then came a second bolt, but this time there was somebody—or something—there, standing in the middle. "There's somebody here!" I called to the others and drew my pistol.

All eyes peered nervously into the clearing—it was empty. They glared at me, but I stood firm. "Somebody *was* there," I assured them. "I do not see things." I flicked the power on the pistol to full.

Another lightning blast, and once again the figure appeared—a tall, thin human in a long black cloak and hood. Not a trooper, that was for sure. One of the others caught sight of it too, and mumbled confirmation of my sighting. All turned to look, nerves on edge.

The figure was certainly standing there now in the rain for all to see. Slowly it approached us. It came right into our midst and looked around. The impression was of a very dark human face inside the hood, but little else. Finally a woman's voice announced: "There is thunder in the south."

"The Destroyer builds," returned the stranger in a very deep female voice. She turned and nodded. "Is this all of you?"

"Us and the human girl over there," the worm-man responded.

"I am Frienta," the newcomer introduced herself. "I'm sorry to have kept you all waiting, but there are heavy patrols on the road and I decided to wait and use the storm for cover."

"You are from Koril's organization?" I asked.

"Master Koril is certainly involved, although it is not entirely his organization, or anyone's," Frienta replied curtly. "However, we have to move you and hundreds more out of the region, and that is a massive logistical effort. More than half of our people have already been caught or killed in this region, and you are not out of danger yet yourself. We must now get you quickly to an assembly point." She looked around. "Are you up to a long march in the rain?"

The human woman and the devil-man both groaned. Frienta took notice of them, then looked at our worm-man. "What about you? How fast can you travel?"

"I'll be fine," he assured her. "The wetter it is, the better."

"Well, then, our success depends on the two of you." She looked at Darva and me. "You're the biggest. Do you think you could each carry one of these?"

I looked at Darva, who shrugged. "Why not?" I replied. "But they'll have to hang on tight."

The devil-man gave a grotesque expression which I hoped was one of gratitude. The human woman seemed extremely nervous and uncertain. "Come on—climb up and get as comfortable as you can," I said, trying to sound as friendly and reassuring as possible. "I'm not poison, I don't bite—not people on my side anyway—and riding beats walking in this stuff."

The devil-man had little problem getting on Darva's back, but he apparently weighed more than he looked, given the expression on her face. Frienta went over to the human. "Come. I will help you."

She looked over at me. "I—I don't know. Maybe I can walk . . ."

"I have no time or patience for such prejudice," the strange dark women said acidly. "You too are nonhuman, as those horns attest."

The woman stepped back, obviously upset by the sudden attitude of the one whom she'd considered her only ally. Abruptly I was aware of a flaring of the Wardens within the dark woman's body, and I sensed complex message information flow from her outstretched arm to the scared woman. It was as if there were now thousands, perhaps millions of tiny weblike cords of energy linking the two.

Then, somewhat jerkily, the human walked up to me, and with Frienta's assistance, climbed on my back and clung tightly. Frienta nodded to herself, stepped back, and traced a few symbols in the air. "There!" she announced, satisfied. "You are bound there until I free you!" She turned to the rest of us. "Come! Follow me quickly! This is not the time to stay in one place!"

I was aware of the rigidity of the woman on my back, and said to Frienta, "You are an apt."

"A minor one," she responded crisply. Then we were off into the rain-soaked jungle in the midst of the darkness.

It was a long and arduous journey, taken at a good pace. Frienta, whose face I never could see clearly and whose body was masked by her black robes, proved extremely quick and agile—and apparently tireless. The extra burdens Darva and I carried soon proved to be wearing, but we had no choice but to go on. Worm-man and Hemara proved capable of some speed under adverse conditions, but none of us were cut out for this sort of thing. Frienta seemed to sense when one or more of us was spent and absolutely had to rest, and the breaks were well timed although not as frequent as we would have wished.

We walked all night through a wilderness so complete that after a while none of us had any sense of where we were, how far we'd come, or in what direction we were going. We finally reached a small clearing in the jungle where Frienta proclaimed a complete stop. We would be allowed to forage for food, each according to our own needs, then get some sleep. It was not well, she told us, to travel much in daylight and we still had a long way to go—more than two nights' march at the least.

Even relieved of our burdens, Darva and I felt exhausted, but we knew we needed strength now more than ever. We picked no fights, settling for catching and eating a number of small animals that were no real challenge and supplementing this with what wild fruits we could find. Then we slept through most of the day.

Frienta revealed no more of herself in light than in darkness—a fact that intrigued us all more and more. We felt certain she was some sort of changeling herself, but what sort we had no idea. We rotated guard positions while the others slept, but I kept the laser pistols. Most of the others didn't know how to use them and a couple simply couldn't. Besides, I didn't really fully trust anybody except Darva, who certainly didn't know how to shoot, and myself.

The next night was much like the first, although we got a break in the rain which certainly helped me a little. My human passenger said next to nothing during the entire journey, and I was glad for that. I was too tired to be conversational. During the middle of the third night we suddenly broke out onto a wide, sandy beach. We had reached the coast—the south coast again, as it turned out, but more than a hundred kilometers west of Bourget.

It was with relief that we realized that we were at the end of our journey. Our mysterious guide had taken us unerringly to the right spot through the jungle, avoiding all Companies and all but a very few roads—and also avoiding the worst of the jungle and swamps.

"We are safe now," Frienta assured us. "The encampment here is protected from interlopers by high sorcery."

I looked around. "Encampment?"

"Come," she beckoned, and we walked down the beach a little to where it curved inland, forming a small bay. It looked desolate, totally deserted, until we turned slightly inland on the bay's south side. Suddenly we found ourselves in a very large if primitive village, with tents, even fires and torchlight. It was so surprising that several of us uttered sounds of amazement; I, for one, stopped, then turned and stepped back a few meters and turned again. Desertion and silence. Walk a few steps forward, and there it was—a true camp with hundreds of beings, both changeling and human.

Frienta waved a ghostly arm. "Just find yourself a comfortable place and settle in," she told us. "Ample food to your requirements will be provided, but we are out of tents and other shelters, I fear. If you can make no arrangements, you can use the jungle in the rear. The spell covers the entire south side of the bay but only to a depth of ninety meters from the beach—so if you go beyond, into the forest, take care."

Our little group dispersed quickly as our fellow travelers found others they knew among the teeming throng of creatures on the beach. Our nervous human joined a small group of her own kind with evident relief.

Darva looked at me. "Well? What shall we do now?"

I shrugged. "Sleep, I think. Tomorrow we'll find out what comes next." I looked around at the various kinds of creatures on the beach, some of which were the stuff of real nightmares. Charon had taken criminal minds, insane minds, and given them great power. Much of that insanity could be seen reflected in its victims on the beach as well as in our former company, I reflected. Koril might prove more sympathetic, I knew; but he was still a politician, a king dethroned who wanted his position back and was willing to go to any lengths to get it. This system had been in effect when he was in charge before, and even before that, and he'd done nothing then to stop it. And that, of course, was something most of these people, the changelings in particular, would simply overlook; almost all were natives, and that alone accounted for a certain naivete to which was now added an exponential increase in trust borne of hope and desperation.

How were we different from the aliens, Darva had asked me—and I really wasn't sure of an answer. If I wasn't, then perhaps Koril saw few differences either. He would be unlikely to eliminate an external alien menace only to allow another to fester here homegrown. There was no question in my mind that these people were being used, as always. Sooner or later I knew, something would have to be done.

Darva had wandered off for a few minutes to see if anybody was around and awake whom she knew. When I saw her talking to a small group near a large tent, I decided to join her.

She looked over at me as I approached, smiled, nodded, and turned back to the trio by the fire—I saw one of them was frog-man, another the bird creature—and I strode right up to them. Before I could say anything, though, the flap of the tent behind me opened and I heard a familiar voice. "Why, hello, Darva! Hi, Park! My, you look stunning in your new suit!"

I whirled about in total surprise, and looked into the face of Tully Kokul.

CHAPTER ELEVEN

Koril's Redoubt

Tully and I walked along the beach. "Tell me," I asked him, "are *you* Koril?"

He laughed. "Oh my, no! I couldn't hold a candle to him! I'm really a very simple man, Park. In ancient times I'd be the parish priest, a man looking for rest and place to contemplate and experiment with a minimum of interference. Bourget was like a dream come true for me. Nobody around higher up to give me all sorts of orders, a peaceful village filled with good, profit-minded simple folk, and a very distant government that left us all alone. I was *extremely* happy there."

"So how come you're here, then?" I asked him. "Surely you didn't just come along for the ride."

He chuckled. "Oh no, but I'm like the pacifist who stays home, locks himself in his house while the war rages, then suddenly finds the opposing armies marching and shooting through his living room. I'm only a fair sorc, but I'm a *good* politician, Park. I knew what was going on in and around the village. I knew too that eventually the idyll would end, although I put off all decisions until the last minute. It was painful to lose—but when Matuze took over it was only a matter of time. She's a real nut case, Park. Morah keeps her protected from the Synod for his own purposes, and she's able to indulge her every crazy whim. She's sadistic, cruel, but very, very imaginative—and very ambitious. So when she took control, I more or less got my credentials from this group, although I kept a hands-off attitude almost to the last minute. It really wasn't until Morah himself showed up that I knew the game was up."

"Why not just go along with him and then settle back

like before?" I asked him. "You didn't have to cut and run."

"Oh, things will never be like they were before—not after that stuff in the square. Morah's been publically humiliated. Matuze will take it personally. If those people in Bourget have any sense—and the majority don't—they'll all cut and run. Even though they missed their targets, Bourget's going to become a big, ugly example. Permanent troops and a Synod sorc will be installed there from now on, bet on it. You won't be able to blow your nose there without permission."

I told him of my suspicions about Morah.

"Hmph. Morah an alien. Hadn't thought of that before, but it could be—providing we accept a couple of givens. One is that the aliens can catch the Warden bug themselves—Morah's just loaded and he knows how to use that power better than anybody I've ever seen. But if they *can* catch it the same as us, how'd that delegation five years back come and go without getting trapped?"

"They could have the cure," I noted. "Their whole deal with the Four Lords is predicated on that claim. What better way to prove it?"

"You may be right," he agreed, "but I'm not so sure. True, I know nothing of Morah's background, but that's not unusual. And then there's that fine show he staged at the end."

"You mean that monster he became?"

He nodded. "Get a good look at it?"

"Not really. Everything happened so fast. A multiheaded dragon, that's about all I can remember. Three heads. That's about it."

"That's fair enough. In fact, there were *four* heads, not three, and each of the four was extremely different. One was saurian, one like some great insect, one a creature of the sea, and one vaguely humanoid. See any significance?"

I shook my head. "Not really."

"Charon, Lilith, Cerberus, Medusa. The living sign of the Four Lords of the Diamond."

I gave a low whistle. "Symbolism to the very end."

"Almost the real end too," he noted. "Look, the only

reason he wasn't totally fried was that he wasn't really there at all. You couldn't sense it, but I saw. The moment the first shot was fired, the one that unfortunately missed, he was off that platform and into the crowd. I lost him at that point—he cast a spell on himself so complete I couldn't tell him from the victims."

I looked around nervously. "Then he could be here with us now."

"He could, but I doubt it. He would be the only one capable of coordinating the hunt, not to mention reporting to the government. Besides, he couldn't fool Koril, so once he got here he'd just have betrayed us anyway. No, don't worry about that part. But that was quite a show all the same . . . Say, speaking of shows—how the hell did you wind up like *that*, anyway?"

Briefly I told him the sequence of events.

"Fair enough. I thought you'd have sense enough to stay in the town hall, damn it, so I didn't pay any attention to you. I was far too busy trying to keep out of the line of fire while trying to spot Morah; then I got bogged down helping with the escapes."

"How'd you know it was me here?"

He smiled. "Your *wa*—your Warden brain pattern. It's unique, distinctive, as everybody's is. Not that I remember everybody's, but you were around for months in the same building."

"What about these spells, Tully? Are they really permanent?"

He stopped and turned to look at me. "Nothing's permanent, particularly not on Charon. But it's far, far easier to add than to subtract, if you know what I mean. When you cast a changeling spell, you form a mental set of instructions in your mind and transmit them to your subject's Wardens. Those Wardens then proceed to do whatever they're instructed to do. They draw energy from somewhere—external, certainly, but where nobody's ever found out. They draw the energy in, convert it into matter often at astonishing speed, and apply the redesign."

"Yeah, but it's not just changing shape," I replied. "Hell, I need a far stronger backbone; I have a different digestive system better adapted to this; a different balance mechanism—and a million other things, big and small, that make this creature that's the new me work. You can't possibly know or think of all the little details required. It would take an extensive biomedical library complete with full biological design capabilities to do that."

He looked at me seriously. "Want the truth? I warn you, it's something we don't tell everybody."

"I sure do."

"We haven't the slightest idea how it's done, and that's the truth. Some of it, I think—the basic stuff—simply borrows from the Wardens elsewhere on the planet. Information requested and exchanged in a way we can't comprehend—it's a whole different form of life. The bunhar parts of you, the pigmentation and so on, are probably borrowed like that. In fact, we know they are—one can sense the request for and flow into the subject of that information. But when there's no equivalent, or when you have to put bunhar and human together and make the new creature work, well, that's a whole different story. The Warden organism doesn't think. It's more like a machine, waiting for instructions. It's too simple a thing to think, even if you considered all of them on the planet as a single organism. Without instructions, it's totally passive."

I could only nod and file the information away—for now. I returned to the immediate subject at hand. "But basically once you're changed you're stuck."

"Fairly much so. It took very little time to remake you, but it'd be a ticklish operation and maybe take a year or more to put you back the way you were. First of all, you'd be destroying the homes of all those billions of extra Wardens, and they have a fair survival instinct. Second, the extra mass has to go somewhere, and in general the only place it can go is back to energy. Do that wrong, or in too much of a hurry, and you get a big flash and bang and you're dead. Far easier to modify you. In fact I think some modification may be in order. I can tell by looking at both Darva and you that your spell's become somewhat unraveled, and if that isn't checked, you'll have even bigger problems."

"Huh? How's that?"

"Well, the situation's unusual, but I've seen it before. Both of you have an abnormally high sensitivity to the *wa*, and it in turn listens to you. Without control, your subconscious, your animal parts, take over. If the trend isn't checked or modified, it'll turn both of you completely into bunhars. Tell me—have you been having any odd, ah, mental problems or urges lately?"

Sheepishly I told him of the hunting experiences in the wild.

He nodded gravely. "Well, we'll have to do something about that as soon as I can make a complete examination of you. It'll be tricky for several reasons. They're *your* Wardens, and *wa* will follow what it perceives as the will of its host first and foremost. We work by convincing it that you're some other way—by convincing *you*. In these reversions, the mind is the first to go since it's not only unnecessary to the ultimate goal but often gets in the way. The process is so slow only because it does not occur on the conscious level—and because you're around other people. If you'd missed us though, and stayed in the wild, the process would have accelerated. In a few months you'd have become a total bunhar, running with herd, and absolutely no different from a natual-born one. You were lucky."

I shivered. "Tell that to Darva, will you, Tully? That's what she wanted to do—and I almost caved in."

The changelings were being moved out in very small groups, usually by ship but occasionally even by air. Koril's network was far wider and deeper than I'd suspected.

Tully took the time we had there to work with us as much as possible. Our days were spent in a series of exacting and often extremely boring mental exercises, many of which gave us headaches. There were all sorts of effective blocking techniques as well, many based on simple self-hypnosis that I could do in a moment, that kept the growing understanding of the power within us under some sort of control.

The basics were simple. First, you couldn't make something out of nothing. There had to be Wardens there to

work with. Thus, one could not materialize something out
of thin air—it just wouldn't happen. But given something
very small, even a rock or pile of sand, you could cause it to
grow, multiply, and transform itself. You could not, however, give non-Warden life to something that had no life at
the start. You could create a lot of things with simple sand,
but you couldn't make it a living thing. You could, however, reshape it, then direct and motivate it, puppetlike, by
your own powers of concentration.

Darva was, in many ways, a quicker study than I was,
because she was taking up where she'd left off so long before. Tully warned us, though, that there was only a small
chance of us growing beyond very powerful apts, since the
younger you were the easier the Art was to learn. Still, *he*
had learned it starting at an age not far from mine, and
that spurred me on. Koril, in fact, had become perhaps the
most powerful and he'd learned it after he was forty.

You would think that the more you practiced a thing the
easier it would become, but in fact it became harder as we
progressed, since the more ambitious you became the more
complex the instructions and the more millions of Wardens
had to be contacted.

Finally though, when we'd been there almost four weeks
and the company had dwindled to only a handful—
meaning we were soon due to depart—Tully admitted he'd
taken us as far as he could under these conditions. It was
not far enough, of course, but we had far more self-control
and power than either of us could have hoped to have had
without his help. In point of fact, we were full-fledged, if
still minor, apts.

"You'll be leaving in two days," Tully told us finally.
"Going south, to Gamush, on my recommendation. You
should feel flattered—only apts with potential are sent
there. You might even meet the big man himself."

"What about the reversion?" Darva asked nervously.

"Well, you've stabilized it. I think we caught it just in
time, in fact. But down in Gamush you'll get the top professional help you need, extra training, and—who knows?"

"How will we be going?" I asked.

"Well, we've been having problems with the ships, of

course. Troopers are boarding and searching every one they spot, and they have effective aerial patrols out. We've been able to fake a lot—they don't have much of a list of names, let alone changeling descriptions, but it's a slow and risky process. No, we'll get you out by air. Rather direct, I'm afraid, but the best way."

Tully's "rather direct" turned out to be an understatement. We were not built for the compartments of a soarer, but a soarer modified and controlled by a sorc could be used to transport humans up top—and changelings by having the damned thing swoop down and pick us up in its huge prehensile feet.

Though we were both sedated for the sudden "pick up," it was still one of the most frightening things I'd ever experienced. Crossing an ocean held in the grip of a great flying creature's toes is *not* guaranteed to make anybody comfortable, although, it proved more comfortable than riding in that damned cabin. Not reassuring, though, when you looked down at countless thousands of square kilometers of open ocean and knew that you could be dropped in a moment if the big flying monster had an itch—and nobody would ever know.

Our sense of security was no greater when, several hours flying time later, we crossed the barren coast of Gamush. For one thing, this was the first time I had seen a broken sky and bright sun since landing on Charon. The sky was reddish-orange, with gray clouds, and it looked really strange. The gas layer was thin enough for the real sun of the Warden system to be clearly visible—and it was a real hot one. Since our body temperatures rose or fell to adapt to the outside temperature, I began to worry about just how high that temperature could go in our kind without boiling our blood. It really was that hot, or so it felt—and incredibly dry. Below, orange and brown sand, ridged and duned, stretched as far as the eye could see.

What a world, I remembered thinking. Tropical rain forests north and south and a desert baked almost beyond imagining in the middle.

Still, there *were* creatures about. We could see them

flying around; apparently wingless cylinders, but none came close enough for us to get a really good look at them. Somewhere down below, other things also must live, I realized, for those creatures to feed upon. Yet in the whole journey I never saw a single tree, shrub, or animal. Nothing but desolate sand.

We were rather rudely dropped at the end although we had trained as best we could and been prepared. There was no place for a soarer to take off from around here—not enough elevation on the dunes and no footholds—so it soared in low, stalled almost to a crawl, then dropped us a few meters into the sand. It then rapidly gained altitude until it was a small blot in the sky, and we saw those in the passenger compartment, mostly humans and human-sized creatures, parachute to the ground over a square kilometer or more. Parachuting was not a common art on Charon, but broken legs mended in a few days thanks to the Wardens.

We were met by a small group of men and women, all humans, dressed in thick yellow robes and wide-brimmed hats. They were quite efficient at moving about and gathering together the dozen or so humans and changelings that had been deposited by the soarer.

"How are you?" Darva asked, concerned.

I checked myself. "A little bruised and burned by the sand, but otherwise all right," I told her. "I feel rotten, though, and I need a drink. You?"

"Same here," she responded. "Let's see how we get out of this hole. This place is like something from the worst nightmare. It's hell itself." It was hard to disagree with that, although for her this was the first time she'd ever seen or experienced this sort of climate and desert terrain. But what she considered normal wasn't so nice, either.

One of the robed men holding a clipboard quickly checked our names, seemed satisfied, then brought us to a central spot in the sand not in any way distinguishable from any other point in the desert. They looked around, checked something or other, and suddenly we started sinking into the sand.

It was an eerie and unnerving sensation, although after

the flight it was pretty tame. I held my breath as I sunk to my mouth, then continued down under.

For a brief moment my entire body was encased in sand, and I had this horrible feeling of smothering, but it soon passed as I felt cool air hit my feet and hindquarters and I realized we were entering some sort of huge passage. Spitting sand and wiping my eyes, I managed to get hold of myself and look around.

What I saw was impressive—a huge hangarlike building, well-lit with very modern industrial lights, with a lot of people running around below apparently working on or servicing a lot of stuff. What struck me most was the machinery—this place could almost be out of the civilized worlds. It was at least as modern as the shuttle—the first time I'd seen such a technological level since arriving at Montlay in what seemed like a lifetime ago.

We were standing on some kind of translucent platform on a large pistonlike device that was gradually lowering us from the opening to the huge floor. Looking up, I had to gasp as I saw a huge roof apparently composed entirely of sand with no support whatsoever. How the effect was managed I never did find out, whether by some Warden sorcery or by some sort of force field, but this clearly was why the all-powerful Charonese and their alien allies had never found the place. Hell, I wouldn't be able find it myself again no matter what the inducement.

As we reached bottom, our greeting party quickly removed their robes and left them on the platform. A glance at them and at many of the personnel around the place showed that, down here, the mode of dress was closer to undress. I wondered how some of our moralistic Unitites were going to take that.

Another party arrived to greet us, dressed rather scantily though a couple had on medicallike garb. One of them approached Darva and me. "You are the two with the reversion problem?" she asked clinically.

We nodded. "I'm Dr. Yissim," she continued. "Follow me, please."

We followed her across part of the vast work area to a large tunnellike opening and went down it for a hundred meters or more, finally walking into a large, comfortable room that had large pads on the floor and little else.

"We're going to start your first treatment right away," she told us. "Otherwise you're going to have problems down here with fresh meat, among other things. Each of you please sit on a separate pad."

We looked at each other, shrugged, and did as instructed. The doctor stood back, looked at each of us in turn, then touched her temples and seemed to go into a light trance. I was familiar with the technique now, but it still surprised me. Hell, we'd only just arrived.

She stood still that way for several minutes, and I could sense her Warden power—her *wa*—reaching out to me. It tingled, sort of, as I suddenly felt myself under the most absolute of microscopes. Darva felt the same. Then the doctor came out of her trance, nodded to herself, and started mumbling into a small recorder I hadn't noticed before.

"Limik!" she called, and a young man came in also dressed in hospital garb. She wasted no time on amenities. "Six liters number forty," she told him, "for each of them."

He nodded, left, and in a short while returned with two large jugs full of a clear liquid. He approached us— without a flinch or without even staring oddly at us, I noticed with some satisfaction—and handed us each a jug.

"Drink all you can," Dr. Yissim instructed us. "It's basically water, which you need badly, with some additives. Drink it all if you can."

There was absolutely no problem in drinking it all. I seemed to have a bottomless reservoir.

"Master Kokul's analysis of the two of you was sent on ahead," she told us as we finished. "He's quite thorough. Now, you'll both start to feel a little sleepy, lethargic, and relaxed. Don't fight it. This is going to be a tricky series. If we don't get this exactly right from the start we could merely accelerate the process, and we don't want that. I realize you're both starved, but I want empty stomachs for now." With that, she turned and walked out of the room.

Darva looked over at me, already seeming a bit sleepy.

"She's the coldest person I've ever met. We might as well be two lumps of mud."

I nodded. "I've met a lot like that. Don't let it worry you. Her type almost always know what they're doing. Let's just help it, get into the relaxation mode, and let them do their job."

Using some of the concentration and relaxation exercises Tully had taught us, we needed very little time to reach a state of quasi-sleep. We were aware of what was going on, but floating in a cloud of peace and comfort, we just didn't give a damn. In many ways it was like the state I'd been placed into before the old woman had made me a changeling.

A wall flicked, and suddenly became transparent. I saw Yissim there, along with two men and three women, all sitting at a console of some sort. They looked at us then at the console; we could see only them.

It began. It began without any of the gyrations or mumbo-jumbo everyone before had always used. You could see it, sense it, feel it, as a tremendous concentration of Warden direction flowed out from those people behind the partition to us. It was blinding, overwhelming, all-encompassing, and within seconds it was in control of my mind. I found myself involuntarily resisting, and a minor fight ensued, made worse because, thanks to Tully, we knew the blocking techniques.

Somehow I managed a slight turn so that I could see Darva, and despite my drugged state I nonetheless had a fascination for what I was seeing, a fascination that was neither shock nor horror nor anything else but just that— fascination. I found I didn't really care. Darva's body was undulating, going through rapid, fluid changes. I knew that my body was probably undergoing the same. Her torso was thickening up, her arms becoming shorter and smaller, and merging into her head, which was also changing, flowing liquidly out, taking a whole different shape.

The Wardens in our bodies, aided by the animal foundations of our brains, were fighting the treatment, fighting it effectively by accelerating the change. We were turning

into true bunhars—and worse, we were gaining mass in the
head and torso as we did so, mass that would be very hard
to remove. This then was the loaded gun of the changeling,
the reason why it was next to impossible to change back.
Reversion . . .

I was aware my vision was changing. It was becoming
impossible to focus close in, although I could still see
Darva clearly and she could see me. I could see, blurrily,
that I had a snout and I realized that my eyes, like hers,
must be set much farther apart. It was becoming more and
more difficult, though, to think at all. My mind was dying;
I knew it, yet, eerily, even as it was lost I experienced less
and less a sense of any loss at all.

Darva looked completely like a *bunhar* now, and she appeared very natural and normal to me. Only her eyes, set
farther apart along that large, toothy snout, still retained a
curious human appearance. I had only three awarenesses
. . . I was hungry, yet sleepy, and there was a female over
there . . .

The next few days are all but impossible to remember or
describe. Basically, we were kept in a large pen with an
electrified barrier, and a pool of water; once a day, a large,
freshly killed creature was brought somehow into the enclo-
sure and Darva and I devoured it greedily. Eating was followed by a period of strained sleep, in which we were both
in this funny place, then we'd wake up again in the pen.
Both of us were bunhars, and we operated on the most
basic animal level and on no other. We had absolutely no
sense of time, place, or anything. We were barely self-
aware.

Slowly, though, we came out of it. Very, very slowly.
Memory returned first, but it was uncoupled with conscious thought, and thus useless. Finally, we came out of
one of the sleep sessions still in the strange room, and for
the first time, I could think again.

Yissim's voice seemed to float in to us. "If you can understand me, stamp your right foot," she instructed.

I turned, looked at Darva, and saw that she was still

very much a hundred percent bunhar. But she stamped her right foot—and so did I.

"Very good," the doctor approved. "Please do not try to talk to me or to each other. You don't have the equipment at the moment, and all you'd produce would be a loud roar. It has been a tricky, delicate operation to say the least. In order literally to save your minds we had to let the process take its course with your conscious selves decoupled. Believe me, this was necessary—but radical. You are only the third and fourth individuals we've had to use this procedure on, and we've had one success and one failure. Hopefully we will have two more successes here.

"Now," she went on, "we're going to try and bring you back, but it will be a slow, patient process. We have restored your minds, your basic humanity. Bit by bit we will restore the rest. We will be working with you, but you must do it yourselves. Our initial probe shows that we cannot impose the change on you. Were we to try a new series of spells, you would react in such a way as to literally alter your brain. Once your brain modified to the bunhar mode you would be bunhars and we could not restore memory, personality, or sentience. You must learn to control every Warden in your bodies. Every one. You must assume total control."

What proved most frustrating was that Darva and I could communicate neither with the doctors nor with each other since, I soon discovered, she was totally illiterate—a condition that simply had never occurred to me could happen.

If the situation was bizarre to us, it must have been more so to the doctors. Imagine going in every day and giving very elaborate lessons and exercises to a pair of bunhars. Still, I'll give them that much—they never once seemed to blink at the situation or treat us as anything except intelligent adults. I, for one, was more than anxious to do everything until I had it perfect—I had no wish to return to the zoo and the oblivious state of the simple saurian.

Still, it was a constant mental fight with those animal

impulses. I had to stop myself continually from roaring, charging, or doing other animal things in proper bunhar fashion. I realized that part of my trouble was my concern that Darva might not make it. I wanted both of us to succeed, desperately.

The day we concentrated on our larynxes was an exciting one. Each day I was gaining more and more control over my body and my actions—becoming, very definitely, the smartest and most self-controlled bunhar in all history. The spell was a complex one, but it still boiled down to *ordering* the Wardens in our bodies to form a voice mechanism that would work in our very primitive throats. I had no idea what one would look like, or how it would work, but I was like a small child with a new toy when I felt something growing, taking shape far back in my throat, and made my first, rather basic sounds that weren't roars and growls. Still, it was not a human voice, and it came from far back in my throat, independent of my mouth— which couldn't form the words anyway. It couldn't—but this new growth could.

Darva, I heard with excitement, managed it also, although the sound was more like a deep belching sound than anything else. We were stopped there and given a chance to practice. We managed in an amazingly short time to form crude words and sentences. It was a breakthrough, and one that said we were on the way. But how long would the rest take?

I discovered in talking that Darva had had a much rougher fight with her animal self than I, and was still having trouble. Dr. Yissim now knew this too, and in a separate session one day told me, "If we are to bring her all the way back, we may have to do another radical procedure."

"Of what sort?" I rasped, my new voice sounding odd— and yet appropriate to a bunhar, if bunhars could talk— even to me.

"You are now far enough down the line to control a great deal of your body. The *wa* is powerful and controlled in you. But if we were to remove you from lab conditions, both of you would quickly revert, simply because you are so far along. She would change much before you. You might even fight it off, but I doubt if she could. You need reinforcement and the only reinforcement around comes from each other. It's called a *wa* connection, and it may be her only hope—but only you can decide on it."

"There is danger then."

She nodded. "You know how the *wa* is really one, how it is in total communication with all other *wa*."

"Yes."

"But your consciousness contains the *wa* and directs it, and this is a method by which the *wa* of one consciousness is transmitted to the other and then stabilized. A permanent link is established."

"You mean our minds would *merge?*"

"No. The *wa* is directed by thought; it is not thought itself. No, your *bodies* would merge, on the *wa*, or metaphysical, level. Anything done to one, with the aid of the other, could be easily duplicated in the other body. Her mind would give you the little extra push you would need not merely to control, but to *direct* the *wa* in your body. And conversely, your having achieved this, the process could be easily reversed. However, such a total link, similar to casting a changeling spell but far more elaborate, has a drawback. If forged effectively enough to work on this level, it cannot be broken. The *wa* of one would be the *wa* of both. If you progress to the next stage of *wa* training, it could give you enormous power. Enormous. But you would be absolutely identical. Even an injury to one would be felt by the other."

"And the danger?"

"If her *wa* instincts overwhelm you, she could drag you down with her."

"And if this is not done?"

"Then we might well, over a long period, bring you back—but she would be lost. She simply doesn't have the mental training you seem to have."

"Then let's do it," I told her.

CHAPTER TWELVE

"The Wa Considers You One"

I had seen very little of Koril's redoubt since our arrival, for obvious reasons, but clearly several things were going on here that I would never have anticipated or even believed from my previous experience on Charon. Gone was the mumbo-jumbo, except for some general references to spells that seemed to be here more words of convenience than words implying some mystique. Down here was a thoroughly professional and scientific base where crisp, well-trained professionals examined and stretched their knowledge of the Warden organisms' powers and peculiarities almost to the limit. The technology, though, that supported it was basically from Cerberus, the only one of the four Warden worlds where efficient and modern industrial production was possible. This place remained in operation because of its unique below-ground desert location. Koril had surveyed and picked the one point on Charon that would allow such material and facilities to work and duplicated the precise conditions here.

Obviously the place hadn't just been thrown together in the last five years since he had been deposed. This was a far longer and more ambitious project than could have been assembled by some rebel, no matter how powerful he was, and it had to be sustained by clandestine traffic even between the Warden worlds. This refuge had been set up and outfitted in the years Koril was Lord of the Diamond, and *somebody*—certainly not the Four Lords—continued to supply it with spare parts.

The computers used here were hardly the equal of anything in the Confederacy—they were, in fact, incredibly primitive—but they were certainly better than the calculators and abacuses that I had used as Town Accountant.

The level of instruction we were given indicated an enormous amount of progress on understanding the Warden organism's mechanisms, even if the bottom line of knowing where their power and information came from remained a mystery. It was like gravity—centuries after gravity was first truly identified and quantified it was still not at all understood. Those who didn't understand *what* it was had discovered every effect and use of gravity despite their basic ignorance of just what really caused it.

The exercises were serious, complex and required an enormous amount of knowledge of a large number of disciplines in order to use them effectively. That, in fact, was why the most poweful users were either former prisoners from the Confederacy or natives trained as apts when they were very, very young. In my business, it was absolutely vital to know as much as possible—and at least a little about everything—and this gave me an enormous advantage in the training. Darva, on the other hand, had virtually no education and only limited experience with human behavior outside her own local group; that was the hang-up. My own mind control techniques and self-hypnotic abilities were crucial to the process, and my understanding of basic human behavior, particularly my own, gave me the advantage. But the spell that had made me a changeling was an imitative spell. I was locked into the spell originally used on Darva, and so the weaknesses in it, her weaknesses, were repeated in me. She could not control her *wa*, and so her *wa* was hell-bent on taking the path of least resistance. And what her *wa* did, mine duplicated, since her half-trained great grandmother had taken the short cut of linking my spell to hers. This was no matter of waving your hands and making chairs appear or disappear; I was dealing with a complex psychological and biological science involving the spin-off effects of a tiny organism that had no counterpart in human experience beyond the Warden Diamond.

Darva and I were led through as much basic training and instruction as we could take. *She* had to be "cured" before I could be, but I was the only one that could master the stuff well enough to do the job—and it was a job you really had to do for yourself. It was not simply a matter of removing the original spell either. That might have worked in the early stages, but things had gone too far. The Wardens themselves, freed from any spell, would just hurl us back into the animal world without restraint, dragging me with her.

I was certainly well enough advanced after two months to do the job, although I was also aware that mastering principles and exploring the potential to the utmost were two very different things. I could cast a spell, even produce a changeling—do just about everything Korman and his apts had demonstrated plus a lot more—but it might be years of experimentation and practice before I had it all mastered. I could read Isil's spell very easily—and the copy in myself—and even see where and how it was unraveling in the wrong direction. I even thought it was possible for me to break free myself, to sever my connection to Darva—but that would mean abandoning her. How funny! My old self wouldn't have hesitated a moment—she had been useful and good company, but she was no longer necessary to me. The old me would have discarded her at this point and concentrated on total mastery of the *wa* and the fabrication of a new, fine body. Logically that was the only course that made any sense.

And yet, I couldn't abandon her. I simply could not do it. I admit I agonized over the decision, but not because it was a hard one to make. What it would mean, though, was that I would be compromising my own mission—if, in fact, I still wanted to have one. It seemed equally logical that my best interests lay in the future course of Charon, not in the direction of the Confederacy—although, here, the two might be close. Aeolia Matuze must go, of course, and if Morah represented the aliens then he too must go. But did it have to be *me* who did it? From the looks of the place, Koril was more formidable than I could ever be.

That, of course, was the ultimate reason for my decision. My first loyalty was to myself, and I wanted Darva saved. If that somewhat compromised the rest—well, so be it. I was only part of a team here, and I had to wonder why the Confederacy even bothered to send me to a place like Charon, with so well-prepared and equipped a rebel organization.

Unless Koril too was not exactly what he seemed?

I had carried out the procedures so often in practice that when we came down to the real thing there seemed nothing to it. The staff, Yissim and the others, seemed amazed at my rapid progress. I discovered that there was a relative rating system for sorcs, I being the strongest they had seen (such as Koril and Morah), to V. Lower ratings were apts—VI to X. Tully Kokul, whom I hadn't seen nor heard from since that time on the beach, was a IV or V; Korman was a II. Normally, anyone could become a X with nominal training; apt VI was generally assumed to take one to two years for someone from Outside, like me, who had the necessary mental control, and perhaps ten years for a native raised as an apt from childhood. After VI it wasn't a matter of learning the procedure, but learning how to understand and use it, developing mental control, confidence, and accumulating knowledge to expand your range of influences. It had been barely three months since I'd begun training in Kokul's tent, and the staff easily rated me a V. Of course, the fact that I had nothing else to do, no distractions, the top instructors, and that mastering it was a matter of life or death—literally—for both Darva and myself had a lot to do with the speed, as did my own breeding, experience, and practice as an agent.

What I was going to do was, from my point of view, absurdly simple. I mentioned that the Warden sense was like open lines of energy, a communications net of infinite complexity, from me to everything around me. I was going to send complex prearranged messages—commands—to Darva's mind, to her controlling Wardens who were at the heart of our predicament. I was then going to direct her self-repair, point by point and area by area. In this I was aided by the redoubt's computer visualizations, which did a lot of the difficult preparatory work for me. It was a measure of the difference between, say, Morah and myself, that I couldn't have gone this far without the computer aids—everyone felt sure that *he* could.

I had taught Darva basic hypnotic techniques and now used them both on her and on myself. I was conscious of an audience for all this, but I couldn't see anyone. The experts would be there if needed, but otherwise would remain completely out of sight, and mind. I knew, though, that a lot of big shots were watching. Yissim had said they had learned an enormous amount of new material through our case—which, in the end, was the only reason all this was going on anyway.

The big problem had always been what to do with the extra mass. It could be reduced very slowly, over a period of perhaps years, but we hardly wanted that. I had almost 220 kilos to deal with—not an easy task. More importantly I wanted no trace of the old spell; I wanted no way that the Wardens could someday run wild again and reduce us to animals. So we had to become something with no equivalent outside my own mind.

Alone, in that now very familiar white room, I began. Hypnotized, Darva was far easier to take control of—but to be able to impose my spells so dominantly over the old that I could then wipe the old clean required tremendous concentration and mental effort. So much, in fact, that the experts believed it would be impossible ever to close those lines of communications from me to her and back again.

I cast the spell, using all the force at my command. The resistance was extremely hard and somewhat surprising. I saw immediately what the original sorcs had run into the first time they tried, and it was tremendous. But they hadn't been prepared for it, nor had they used this kind of force of will, backed by my total commitment to breaking it at all cost. What we were dealing with was, of course, at heart a psych problem—her romanticizing about the two of us in the wild—that any good psych could cure back in the civilized worlds. Here it simply had to be beaten back. I had to decouple and push back her subconscious control over her body's *wa* by making her consciously override it, then guide that force of will to my own. She was rated an apt 7, but she lacked the total commitment to break the pattern. I was supplying that.

It turned into an odd mental battle, almost a cross between a stubborn argument and rerouting points on a circuit diagram. At one and the same time I was constantly identifying and beating back her own subconsciously directed *wa* while, with her, I was trying to find any and all routes of *wa* communication between conscious mind and body and then tie them up, even dominate them, while isolating this strong, primitive influence, isolating it, and beating it back into submission. None of this had any effect on her mind or thought processes, of course; we were attacking only the *wa*, the Warden organisms giving out the wrong signal.

As the impasse became more obvious, I began talking to her, soothing her, trying to direct her, to convince her that she must not give in to this primitive, animal will. "Darva—if you have any regard, any feeling for me, you *must* help me! You must beat it back!"

"I do. You *know* I do," she responded.

"Darva—if you—love—me, let it go! You must!" The use of that word sounded odd to me, yet now I almost understood it. At least, I thought, I could *use* it. "Darva—I do this because I love you. If you know that and love me too, release! *Let it go!*" It was odd, what I had said for clinical purposes. Did I, in fact, love her? Was *that* why I was doing this?

Abruptly, the resistance broke—gave up, receded into the depths of her mind. It was so sudden and so unexpected that I wasn't prepared, and the whole force of my will flooded into her, so strong it almost knocked her out. I recovered as quickly as possible, retracing the pathways, seeing how the spell had been so neatly tied and then retied.

The rest was absurdly simple after that, I just followed the computer models I had memorized and practiced again and again. In what seemed like a matter of minutes, at best, although later I was told it was more than seven hours, we were done.

I pushed out the waste and fatty accumulations unnecessary for life rather easily, and did some internal rearranging to expel as much water and excess tissue as possible, getting the *wa* to treat it like common waste and thus assist its expulsion. The shift amounted to more than 30 kilos and looked and smelled horrible, but I was in no state at that point to appreciate it. 190 kilos were still a hell of a lot, but every bit lost made the job easier.

Diagrams, pictograms, three-dimensional views and designs both internal and external flashed through my mind from training and into hers and thus to the *wa* itself. And she was changing, flowing, redirecting to my commands. I could literally feel it, sense it, as if it were happening inside my own body.

When the job was finished I still couldn't relax because, thanks to the linkage, my body *was* in fact a mirror image of hers in every single respect, and that wasn't my intent. In fact, what took so very long was the attempt to differentiate my body from hers. There were a large number of false starts, as everything I tried to do to myself I found duplicating in her. We knew it might happen, and I hoped now she was up to the task. I could visualize only her; therefore, *she* must direct my own reconstitution while *I* concentrated on keeping her stable as she was. Doing so was difficult, because I was the stronger, but we finally worked out a system that would flow information both ways, an eerie sensation like trying to do three things at once, but one we finally mastered.

And when it was finally over, we both passed out for more than ten hours.

We both awoke, stirred, and opened our eyes. Somewhere an alarm buzzer sounded, probably to summon somebody when we awoke, I thought. Visions of computer diagrams and electrical signals pulsed in my brain, and I knew I was going to have a hell of a time getting rid of them.

"Oh, my god! It really *did* work!" Darva said, amazed. "Look at you!"

"Look at *you*," I responded. "I'm proud of you."

"We need mirrors," she decided. "Say—can you sense the *wa* between us?"

I hadn't really paid much attention, but now that she pointed it out I sensed what she meant. The links were still there, the lines of communication from nervous system to nervous system were intact.

A door opened, and Dr. Yissim and two others entered. One was a large, burly-looking man with rugged complexion and snow-white hair and moustache. I knew at a glance that he had at one time been part of the civilized worlds. He was dressed entirely in white, but not the medical whites of Yissim. His clothing was fine, tailor-fitted and almost a uniform. The other man was in every way weird.

He was small, had a goatee, wore horn-rimmed glasses— a real anomaly here, where the Wardens made certain of your eyesight and everything else—and he was dressed in a casual tweed jacket and dark blue slacks. That alone would have been enough to cause a stare, but there was something more dramatically wrong with him.

I suddenly knew how an animal that trusted its sense of smell above all else felt when confronted with its reflection in a mirror.

The man was patently there—I could see him, touch him, everything. But he had no *wa*, no Warden sense at all. On the level I had been learning to trust above all else, the Warden organism level, he simply did not exist.

"How are you feeling?" Yissim asked me.

"A little weak, otherwise fine," I told her. "We both would love a mirror, though."

"We expected that," she responded with a slight smile, then nodded to the far wall, the one that held the technician's booth. Instead of becoming clear, an indirect light made the surface a good reflector, with only a slight hint of the consoles in back. We both turned and looked at ourselves.

We were both giants, of course. That was mandated. 228.6 centimeters, the spec had called for, balancing off remaining mass. We towered over the more normal-sized people in the room, and particularly over the short little man who wasn't there.

The bone structure needed to support such a body properly, even in the slightly reduced gravity of Charon, was a bit different than the human norm, but none of it showed. Other than her size, Darva was an absolutely beautiful human-looking woman. I had taken my own visualization of what she must have looked like before Isil's changeling spell and produced what I freely admitted was an idealized version. I probably accented her female figure overmuch, but I plead guilty to doing so without shame. Hell, she'd done the same thing to me.

In fact, I hadn't the slightest idea who I looked like, but it was her idea of what the perfect man *should* be. We were both strongly over-muscled, of course—it was one fine way of compacting mass usefully—but hers only showed when she flexed, while mine showed all over. My face was broad and handsome, and overall we were very good personifications of some ancient god and goddess from man's primitive times. Both of us, of course, had tremendously long hair and I had a huge beard as well—more mass used up—but that was in an area that could be cut and trimmed.

But we were not human. She should weigh between 105 and 110 kilos, and I, perhaps 120, but we both had around 180 kilos to contend with and hair really doesn't take away that much. The balance I had placed in our tails; hers was a bit longer than mine. For pigmentation I'd selected, with her approval, a dark solid bronze, with the hair a reddish brown. She hadn't really cared—but we both agreed on anything but green.

I couldn't help but notice that her idealized man was as exaggeratedly endowed in one area as my idealized Darva was in the other. Even though the doctor was there, I had to admit I felt a little self-conscious. Well, something would have to be worked out, even with that tail in the way—but there was nothing to do about it now.

It was hard to tear our gazes away from the reflections, but finally we did and turned back to the trio, who were watching us with great interest.

"Tailed gods," the handsome older man in white commented in a pleasant, deep voice. "Fascinating. You could start a whole new religion, the two of you."

I chuckled. "I think there are enough of those as it is."

"Quite so," he agreed, then looked to Dr. Yissim expectantly.

"Oh, I'm sorry," Yissim said, sounding uncommonly flustered. "Park, Darva—this gentleman is Tulio Koril."

I felt a shock go through me. *Koril! At last!*

Yissim turned to the little man who wasn't there. "And this is Dr. Dumonia. He is a Cerberan."

We had problems with doorways made for smaller folk, and occasionally ceilings were just a tad too low. Darva bumped her head leaving the lab and I felt a shock. I hadn't bumped into anything, but I felt every ache she did. It quickly developed that there was more to our exchange than first met the eye—as we'd been warned. The lines of communication were permanent and intact, theory said, and that meant that whatever one felt, the other did too. A minor irritant, but a potential dagger at my throat nonetheless. Whatever was done to her was done likewise to me, no matter where I was. There *had* to be a range limitation— the energy channels were too tiny to carry—but as long as we were close enough to feel the *wa*, the *wa* in one body considered itself the body of the other.

"The *wa* considers you one," Yissim agreed. "You will have to be careful. Still, if you really *do* care for one another, you should be in for some unique physical sensations on the plus side, too."

I saw Darva's eyebrows rise and her lips form a slight smile. We hadn't thought of that angle—which really proved out, I might add.

We were led into a large office, the kind top executives have, complete with outer office staff, receptionists, the whole business, and we got a lot of stares. In the inner office, our tails proved useful for at least one thing. There were few chairs made for people our size but, with the tails, we didn't need them.

Koril took his seat behind a large desk in the center of

the room and Dumonia took a chair next to him, facing us. Yissim had left us in the outer office, assuring us that when we returned she would have already arranged to check us out physically, and for some sort of living quarters. She offered a barber but Darva just asked for barbering tools—no use somebody getting on a ladder to do us.

Koril looked at us for a few moments without saying anything. Finally he said, "Well, you two have become some kind of celebrities around here, I must say."

"I'll bet," I responded. "Still, it's good to be back among the living again, and maybe even be able to get out and see this great place you've built here. I am amazed by it all."

"A large share of the credit goes to the good doctor here," Koril responded, nodding to the little man. "Dr. Dumonia, you see, is the man who makes sure we get our share of Cerberan manufactured goods—and training in their use. He doesn't usually come along himself, though. In fact, this is the first time I think you've *ever* been here, isn't it?"

Dumonia nodded and smiled. "Things are going down all over the system. Matters are coming to a head. It was necessary to coordinate as much as possible with our friends elsewhere, and I could only do so in person. I will admit the trip has been both fascinating and—entertaining."

We stared blankly at him. "What's all this about? And what does it have to do with us?"

Koril looked at Dumonia, who nodded and sighed. "Three days ago, in a fluke, Marek Kreegan, Lord of Lilith, was assassinated."

My heart skipped a beat, and Darva looked at me in concern. *"What!"* I exclaimed, not even realizing that Darva's heart had also fluttered for no reason she could fathom.

The Cerberan nodded. "Despite its flukish nature, such a thing could never have happened without the direct intervention of a Confederacy assassin."

I couldn't suppress my excitement. So I'd done it! Or somebody had anyway. I kind of hoped it was the other me on Lilith.

"With Kreegan's death, the brains behind the alien plot

are dead as well," Dumonia went on. "But he was a good planner, so his death, in and of itself, will not affect much. His chief officer, Kobe, ran the basic system anyway and was not only in on everything but was in pretty fair agreement with Kreegan's aims, although he lacks his dead boss's imagination. Still, it is a blow. On Cerberus, I have high hopes that, within a matter of months, perhaps weeks, I will be able to gain control of the Lord of Cerberus. It is a tricky business, but I have several plots going at once and I'm confident at least one will succeed. You see, I'm the Lord of Cerberus's psych."

I burst out laughing. "You seem to be a one-man army," I told him.

"I only wish it were true," the Cerberan replied wearily. "Fortunately, you have a well-organized and equipped rebel force here on Charon—but you have additional problems. A—sorc, I think you call them—named Kokul, who knew you well, said you had a conviction that the aliens are physically here and behind the entire Charonese government. He reported this to friend Koril here, and we'd like very much to know if this is only conjecture or whether you have something to base it upon."

"A feeling, really," I answered truthfully. "But the more I'm here, the more I'm convinced of it. "I've been among the humans here, high and low, and I've been among the changelings. Even the most remote and terrible changeling monstrosity retains its basic humanity somehow—some inner something I can't really put my finger on that marks them as human."

"The soul," Darva put in.

I shrugged. "I'm not sure I know what a soul is, but that's as good a word as any. Even the animals here have a certain spark. Everybody and everything—except this man Yatek Morah."

"You mean he's like me—a Warden cypher?" Dumonia asked. "As you all are to me?"

I shook my head. "No, not that. Physically he's just a man, all right, but—inside—I don't know any other way to put it—he's just not there. That soul, that essence, that intangible—it's just not there. I'm not the only one who noticed it. Tully did, too."

"It's true," Darva put in. "I saw him only briefly and from afar, but even then you could sense something—different—about him."

"Like a robot?" the Cerberan prompted.

The comment surprised me, but I had to recall that "robot" was exactly the word I'd used. "Yeah. Very much like that."

Dumonia looked at Koril, and Koril looked back; both sighed. Finally the former Lord said, "Well, that's that, then."

The Cerberan nodded. "Not from Cerberus." He turned back to us. "You see, Cerberus is the source of those cute imitative robots that are playing hell with the Confederacy. Never mind how—our powers are quite different from yours. But this Morah's no Cerberan."

"No, he certainly is not," Koril agreed, then turned to us. "You see, I *know* Yatek Morah. Or, at least, I *knew* him. He was born on Takanna, one of the civilized worlds. We were sent here at the same time, so we got to know each other pretty well. That was forty-odd years ago, of course, but he owes his present position to me. He's a cold, cruel man—but he's human."

"He *was*," Dumonia added. "Now he's far more than that."

Koril sighed. "Yes, I think our friends here confirm that. It explains a lot. It explains almost everything."

"Well it doesn't explain anything to me," Darva put in, showing her old spunk.

It didn't explain anything to me either, but I was preoccupied trying to catch hold of something I couldn't quite corner. Takanna . . . What the hell was familiar about Takanna?

"The alien robots are extremely sophisticated," Dumonia told us. "They are of a sort unknown in the Confederacy, although theoretically possible. In effect, they are quasi-immortal superhumans with the memory and personality of actual human beings."

"And this Morah—he's one of these things?" Darva responded.

"It very much appears so," the Cerberan agreed, "but it's unheard-of. As far as we know, it will only work through a Cerberan. Cerberans, you see, can swap minds—or swap bodies, if you prefer, but only with each other and with these robots. We know of no way that a Charonese could do so—or anybody else."

I put Takanna to the back of my mind for a moment to percolate, then rejoined the discussion. "There *is* a way," I told them. "Even the Confederacy knows about it. It's called the Merton Process."

Both Dumonia and Koril seemed startled, but Dumonia most of all. "Merton! How do you know that name? She is a Cerberan!"

That was news to me. "No matter. They have a process for complete mind and personality transfer from one body to another. It's terribly wasteful of bodies, but it works. I know it works."

It was Koril's turn to get into the argument. "And how do you know?"

I took a deep breath and made a decision. Why not? If not to these two—then who? "Because I went through the process. I'm not nor have I ever been Park Lacoch. He died—and I took his body."

Although Darva had known I was an agent, she hadn't known before of the mind swap and looked at me rather oddly.

Dumonia, though, beamed and turned to Koril. "See?" he said smugly.

Koril sighed and shook his head. "I'll be damned how you knew," he replied.

"Knew what?" Darva asked.

"That your friend and partner here is a Confederacy assassin, come with the expressed mission of killing Aeolia Matuze," Dumonia told her.

"Oh, that," Darva said, surprising and befuddling the two men.

"*I'd* like to know, too," I added. "I haven't exactly been very conspicuous as an agent."

"Simple," Dumonia replied. "You see, once I found out that there was an agent on Cerberus, I suspected others. When another was involved in the Kreegan matter on Lilith, I had to assume that at least one agent had been infiltrated at the same time to each of the four worlds. I looked at who was dropped, got behavioral reports, and made my decision. It was only surprising that I found you already here. I thought friend Koril was going to have to track you down all over the planet to rope you in."

I nodded, feeling a bit relieved. "And *that's* why I'm here."

"Yes—and me, too," the Cerberan responded. "You see, I believe we're running out of time. I am convinced, and so are the Confederacy security and military authorities, that the war is less than a year away. The full war. Even now it may be beyond stopping—but we must try. Removing Cerberus may be impossible, but at least we can exert some measure of control there. But the aliens seem abnormally interested in Charon. As you noted, it is not central to the plan—but it is *vital* to the aliens, for some reason—or else why introduce Morah and topple Koril for Aeolia Matuze? Well, we must remove the danger. *You* must. I can give only technical help and moral support at this point."

Koril patted him on the shoulder. "And invaluable it's been, my friend. Otherwise I should be a crazy hermit in the desert now. We'll take it from here—and soon. Still, how do we kill such a man as Morah now is? He is as powerful as I in control of the *wa*—and far less mortal."

"He can be killed," Dumonia told him. "But it will take concentrated raw power weapons. Fry him completely—melt him down. Or blow him up with the most powerful explosive you can use. Nothing else will work Things like laser pistols, he will not only absorb but actually take in and use the energy. Melt him or blow him to bits. That's the only way. I've given you the rundown of just what these robots can do."

Koril sighed. "It is a problem. But Morah dominates the Synod, and Aeolia uses his power to rule Charon. No wonder I could not defeat them! You don't suppose . . . ? How many robots might there be?"

"Any number," Dumonia told him. "Who knows? Perhaps Matuze herself. But, remember your own power. Their minds are still the same, and their own Warden powers will be no greater than if they were human."

Koril nodded. "It's a terrible problem—here. Heavy weapons may be no good at all. Still we will work something out. We *will* act."

"Soon?"

"As soon as possible. As soon as we have even a half-decent chance to win."

"That, then, will have to do," Dumonia told him.

Suddenly I yelled, "Zala! Zala Embuay!"

Everybody turned and looked at me as if I'd gone mad. Darva's expression was even worse.

"What makes you think of *her*?" she snapped.

I didn't even recognize the tinge of jealousy. "She was from Takanna! The same world as Morah!"

Koril's eyes fixed grimly on me. "Who is this you speak of?"

"A woman who came to Charon with me," I told him. "We lived together in Bourget until the showdown there." Briefly I told him the rest—including her apparent involvement with the Destroyer's group there and her dual personality. "In fact," I added, "Korman was convinced that *she* was the Confederacy's assassin."

Koril looked at Dumonia. "Is that possible? Two of them—here?"

Dumonia shrugged. "Possibly. But nothing I know about, although, let's face it, the Confederacy and I trust each other equally—and you know what that means."

The sorcerer chuckled slightly. "This woman, then—she might be here."

"I didn't see her at Tully's encampment, nor any time since that shoot-out," I told him. "Still, if she's here, it might be time to get some answers to some questions."

Koril nodded. "I quite agree."

CHAPTER THIRTEEN

Kira

The huge complex beneath the desert of Gamush was indeed as impressive as it had appeared at first sight. Modern, efficient, and well-staffed, it was a mighty fortress, hidden completely from visual observation and also by more than a little subterfuge. Built as a modern lab and retreat while Koril was still in power, its location was deliberately obscured on maps and charts. Those who had been to it were saddled with spells of confusion that prevented their betraying, or even finding, the place again. By the same token, the isolated technical staff in the place was really stuck without Koril's supply missions and hardly able to betray him—or escape—even if so inclined. Tens of thousands of square kilometers of parched desert that all looked exactly the same, but in which nasty small sand predators lived—and above which the highly intelligent naril flew, ready to pounce upon and eat anything it could—were formidable barriers.

So, should Zala have been there, she was likely to be there still. Koril's clerks quickly located her. She had entered even before me and had been assigned mostly to maintenance. Poor Zala—even in the stronghold of the rebel headquarters she was deemed fit only to scrub the floors.

"Surely there can't be any connection between this woman and Morah," Darva protested as we walked down a long hall. "I mean, she can't be more than in her twenties—and Morah's been here since fifteen or more years before she was born. Their background has got to be just coincidence."

"That's pretty much what Koril figures," I told her, "but

I can't buy it. There's simply too many mysteries about her even without this new connection. Add to that a link between her and somebody high up in the Charonese power structure and I can't buy coincidence. There are too many worlds out there and too few prisoners sent here for that."

"You don't still feel anything for her, do you?"

I had to laugh. "Don't worry on that score. I never really did. Oh, at first I was fascinated—Korman's two minds, all the mystery. But when Zala stayed simple, mousy, little Zala she became boring pretty quickly. Besides, we're hardly even of the same race anymore."

"Still, I'd like to go in with you."

"No! This has to be one on one. Remember, I don't look anything like I did before, so unless she's got some really good spies she'll have no link between me and the Park Lacoch she knew. That gives me a big advantage. Still, we don't know what's going to happen, and I don't want to have to worry about you."

We reached our destination. I turned and kissed Darva, then smiled "Wish me luck."

"Depends," she responded cautiously, but let me go into the room without further protest.

The room had been set up according to my instructions, which meant one chair, a small table in front of it, and nothing else. I ducked my head, a habit I was getting used to, and entered the room.

Zala looked up. I could see a mixture of awe and fright in her face that couldn't be faked—or so I thought. I *was* pretty imposing, after all. I stood there a moment, just looking at her, as the door slid shut behind me.

She looked, I had to admit, no worse for wear. Aside from the loose-fitting blue slacks and shirt which marked her as a service worker she hadn't changed since the last time I'd seen her, there on the street so many months before. And she still had Morah's mark on her, the horns having settled in so well that they appeared almost natural.

"Zala Embuay?" I asked, sounding as officious as possible.

She nodded hesitantly, and I caught a slight gulp, but she said nothing.

"Zala, I'm going to give you some hard-fact ground rules right in the beginning," I went on. "First of all, you might notice in the far corner there two small devices. One is a camera—what is going on here is being recorded. The other is an automatic laser weapon that will follow you no matter what. The door will not open until and unless *I* say so, and it can only be operated by the person on the other end of that camera. Do you understand?"

She nodded weakly, but summoned up enough courage to ask, in a trembling voice, "Wha . . . what's this all about? What have I done?"

"I think you know. At first we thought you didn't know, but now it's been realized that you almost had to know, or at least suspect."

"I—I don't know what you're talking about."

"I think you do. Tell me, you were a member of the cult of the Destroyer in Bourget?"

She nodded hesitantly.

"Who was the leader of the cult?"

"I—I can't tell you that. It is forbidden."

"Zala, as you know well, *we* are the superiors of that organization. Hence, we already know the name."

"Then why ask me?"

I smiled. She wasn't quite as scared as she was pretending to be. "Because I want to see if *you* know."

"Of *course* I know. I *said* I was a member, didn't I?"

"Then tell me the name."

I could see thinking going on behind those frightened eyes. "I—I really can't. A spell was cast to prevent us from revealing it even if we wanted to. As protection."

Good ploy, I reflected. "You and I know that's not really true. I want the name. You won't leave here without giving it."

She shook her head in bewilderment. "I—I really can't. I *did* get a spell. I was scared . . ."

I smiled. "You can't tell me, it's true, but not because of a spell. You can't tell me because you really don't know. You don't remember any of those meetings, do you?"

"I—of course I do! That's ridiculous!"

"If you *did* remember, you'd know that the leader of the

cult was disguised by a spell, as were most of the members. You couldn't know who that head was—and no spell would prevent you from telling me that. You're lying, Zala Embuay. You were never a member of that cult."

"I—of course I was! See?" She pointed to the horns. "How else could I get *these*?"

"*That* is the question we're trying to answer here. You see, in the confusion there really wasn't enough time or organization to check *everybody* against the membership rolls. They had to take anybody who suddenly sprouted a pair of horns. We've already caught a few spies." That was a complete lie, although the thought had occurred to Koril and his staff and histories had been taken. The truth was, nobody *could* really be sure, so they were simply all under observation and in no case permitted to leave or even approach the cargo areas, Zala included. "They learned that death is the least punishment a spy can expect—here."

At that moment I reached out to her and touched her *wa*, effortlessly weaving a mild demand spell. She gave a sharp cry and stood up. I had to give a slight paralyzing stroke to her legs to keep her from involuntarily bolting. I had to be dramatic while being careful not to juggle mass, since this was to be a strictly temporary spell—but that was all right. The *wa* took days, even weeks, to complete a physical change, whereas the *perception* of that change was immediate.

She watched as her hands and arms shriveled, changed, became a mottled green and brown, then larger and heavier as they turned into perfectly repulsive suckered tentacles that, to her, weighed half a ton. "*No!*" she screamed.

"Want a mirror to see the rest of you?" I taunted, feeling less than wonderful about all this but realizing its need. Korman said she would break only under extreme pressure, and this was certainly that.

"*No! No! No!*" she wailed. "*Kira! Please help me! Kira! Kira!*"

I suddenly felt a little better. So she *did* know! I watched and waited to see what would happen next.

Korman had told me that I would one day perceive the

wa as he did—and I was well past that point. The two forebrains of Zala Embuay showed clearly, not just as two brains but as two distinct and particularly weird ones. From the odd, distorted *wa* sense they looked about equal, each smaller than the norm for a human. If a person had the Power, you could see the information flow from *wa* to *wa*. Zala didn't—but somebody did. Somebody, in fact, abruptly started doing the nearly impossible.

The message flares, terribly strong, flowed from the brain to the body and back again, measuring, checking the spell which showed as a spider's web of *wa* energy, then unraveling it in the same manner as I had unraveled Darva's spell and my own. Whoever was doing it—and it had to be Zala herself—was a stronger sore than the spell, which was, of course, a simple one but still a level VI or VII. I began to wonder if this mind might be more powerful than my own, and reflected that I just might have to find out. One thing was clear—not only was the mind powerful, it was extremely well trained. When? And by whom?

I made no effort to defend the spell and it broke easily, restoring Zala quickly to her former appearance. Very briefly I saw a vision of that stronger, Amazonlike Zala of those last moments on the streets of Bourget. But the vision was fleeting and quickly gone. Kira, it appeared, was still not quite willing to meet me face to face.

Zala sat down, looking weak and shaken. I did not intend to let her get off that easily.

"Zala, who is Kira?" I asked her.

She just shook her head and wouldn't look at me directly.

"She's inside you, isn't she?" I pressed. "Kira and you share the same body, don't you? And that's why you're here, on Charon—because of Kira, *isn't that right?* Zala, what is Kira?"

She put her hands to her ears, trying to block out my voice, but it wasn't going to be that easy.

"Kira, if you can hear me, understand me, you'd better put in an appearance," I said sharply. "Your spells are good, but that was a minor one for me and I'm hardly the most powerful sorc here. Any attempt to disable that laser by spell will be instantly detected and it will fire. *Wa* takes time to weave. I don't think anybody can beat the speed of light. You'll sit here until you come out, Kira. Sit here without food, without water, in a plain and empty room in a place in the desert from which there's no escape."

Zala's head turned and looked at the laser-camera combination, but she made no attempt at it. Finally she turned to me. "Damn you! Who the hell *are* you, anyway?"

I smiled. "Why, Zala, honey, it's your old loving husband, dear old Park, in his new suit of changeling clothes. Remember me?"

That got her, more than the threats or anything. "Park?" she managed weakly. "Is that really—you?"

I bowed slightly. "It's me, all right. And if it's any consolation, you were blown from the beginning. Korman actually assigned me to keep close to you and report. He thought you were a new kind of Confederacy assassin. Your rather unique mind shines like a beacon to all who can see the *wa*, I'm afraid."

She gasped. I could tell that this was genuine news to her—and to her counterpart too, I suspected. The fact is, self-control or not, we never accurately see *ourselves* in *wa* terms. *Wa* doesn't reflect in mirrors.

"What I'm telling you is all on the level," I assured her. "Koril's had a small team trying to figure out the unique part of your brain almost from the moment you arrived. There's been some debate on the science and security staffs about you. They've let you run, so far, to see what would happen—and nothing did. So we're making it happen. Now, don't you think it's time the truth comes out? If you're working for Morah, you might as well admit it and go from there. If you're working for anybody else, we want to know. And if you're not working for anybody, we want to know just what the hell this is all about."

She shook her head, as if to clear it. "I—oh, hell. What's the use of going on any further? I'm going to tell you—unless I'm stopped."

"By Kira."

She nodded. "By Kira."

"Zala, what is Kira?"

"She—she's my sister. What I told you—you *really* are Park?—at the start was mostly true. I was an experiment. *We* were. A whole different kind of brain, they said. Two of us. Two complete people in one body. It's really funny saying that, 'cause I don't really know what it's like not to have it."

I shook my head in wonder. "But why? What was the purpose? What was the aim? Surely somebody didn't take this kind of chance just to experiment? It wouldn't be worth the risk."

She chuckled dryly. "The risk. What risk? You have too high an opinion of the Confederacy, Park. That's your trouble. You see only what's on top, out there for show, and you swallow it whole, just like most of the jerks. You think the Four Lords just sit here and run their little worlds? Just because they're trapped here? That's a laugh. They run a lot you don't see all over the Confederacy. They're just the new examples of what's been around for thousands of years—maybe forever. A business. A business that sells things that nobody else does. Things that people say they don't want, but they really do: perversions, gambling outside the official casinos, special loans, even promotions. Fancy jewels, works of art, stuff like that is stolen or bought and a lot of it comes here, to the Diamond. They're everywhere and into everything. Drugs for bored frontier folk and space-navy people who might be out for a year or more. Anything you want they can get—anywhere—at a price."

"I'm not as naive as you think," I told her. "But go on. This syndicate, then, bred you?"

She nodded. "Bred me—and others."

That was interesting. "Others? Many others?"

She shrugged. "Who knows? We were raised independently."

"Yeah—but why? For what purpose?"

"The Confederacy has an elite force, bred to their jobs. They're called assassins, although they don't often kill. Did you know that?"

"I know something about them, yes," I admitted rather evasively.

"Well, how do you think the Four Lords got stuck here? Or most of the rest of the people, for that matter? *They*— the assassins—got them. The assassins are bred for the job, as I said, so they're almost impossible to corrupt. They love their work, and do nothing else. Their true identities aren't even known to the bureaus that employ them, and any time one is contacted, that contact is brief. After the job is done, all memory of them is wiped from even Security's minds and general records. Their anonymity is the one thing the Four Lords have never broken. Those men and women are the *only* people the high-ranking members of the Brethren, as the organization usually calls itself, are scared of. The only ones. Only one has ever been exposed and corrupted—and *he's* one of the Four Lords!"

"Marek Kreegan of Lilith," I responded. "He's dead, you know."

Her head shot up. "Dead! How?"

"A Confederacy assassin got him, it seems."

"You see, then?"

I shook my head. "No, I don't see at all. What's all this leading to?"

"The Four Lords, the entire Brethren, need people who can identify and kill these assassins before they themselves are killed. They've tried every way in the universe to crack the system, and been frustrated every time. Even Kreegan couldn't help them, for no assassin ever knows enough of the security system, which is changing anyway all the time, to break it. So, the Brethren figured, if they couldn't expose the system, they'd breed their own. Assassin killers, you might say."

I had to laugh. "*You* are an assassin killer?"

She shook her head. "No, not me. Kira. She's amazing, Park. Amazing. She learns almost anything from one lesson, and never forgets. She's got total control of her— our—body. Total. She is an analytical killing machine, and brilliant." She was saying this admiringly, but as if she were talking about someone else entirely. It was eerie. And, of course, it raised more questions than it solved.

If Zala were telling the truth, then Koril already *knew* what she was—he'd have to. And Korman probably would, too. Why didn't they? Or if they did, why all the charade? Something definitely smelled funny now, and Zala was the first suspect. She hadn't exactly proved reliable in the past.

"Zala, why two of you?" I asked. "Why *both* you and Kira?"

"Oh, that's supposed to be a safeguard if we were caught. They couldn't psych Kira, only me. They couldn't wipe her—only me."

"That only makes sense if you don't know about her yourself," I pointed out. "And of course you *had* to know."

"Oh, sure. But she's real strong. I don't really understand it, but Kira says that there's really only one of us, at least as far as memories and stuff is concerned. She can shut me off, and sometimes she does. One time I can remember a lot of things, then I can't—and sometimes I don't even know what I used to know until I know it again, if that makes any sense."

Oddly enough, it did, and it rang true. I had no idea of the biology of it—I certainly would have said two such personalities in one brain was impossible if an example wasn't sitting in front of me. But somehow, those syndicate biologists had done it. A master assassin, at least as good as the Confederacy's. Maybe better, I reflected sourly. There certainly was a mortality rate in my business, and sometimes it was impossible to explain. But if this dominant personality had all the keys to the memory core, a total understanding and command of what went on in there—which was more than anybody else did—it could literally reserve sections to itself. And add sections as needed too, I reflected. So you could get to know Zala, and hypno her, and put her under psych or mind control, and it wouldn't make a damned bit of difference.

"Kira seems to be satisfied to let you live your life, though," I pointed out. "Most of the time she just seems along for the ride."

Zala nodded. "That's right. But she's not asleep or anything like that. She's right here with me. She says that's the
way we were—well, *designed*, although that makes us seem
like some kind of creepy machine."

I nodded. "So when I talk to you I'm talking to her—but
when *you* talk to *me* it can be just you."

"That's about it," she agreed.

"And so how'd you wind up here, on Charon?"

"Well, Kira says it looked like a flute, but not anymore.
They never really told us. They just came in one day and
arrested me, that's all. *Oh!*" She suddenly started, and then
I watched that strange transformation take place in her.

Unlike my earlier perception, it really was more of a
mental than a physical thing, yet you could *see* it clearly.
What happened was more than a complete change of personality behind those big, brown eyes—Zala's hidden attributes were clearly displayed. In the Zala *persona* she looked
weak and ordinary, but as Kira the tremendous muscles
and the strength in them, matching the new strength in the
eyes, seemed to stand out. Although nothing really
changed, the transformation was startling.

"Hello, Kira," I said.

"Lacoch," she responded, her voice lower and very cool,
almost inhuman in its lack of tone. "I think it is time we
talked directly."

I relaxed back on my tail. "I'll agree to *that*. Uh—tell
me. Does Zala know what's going on when you are you?"

"When I permit," she replied. "I am permitting now.
There seems no reason not to."

"And when you don't—permit?"

"Then it's like she is asleep."

"Fair enough. You're willing to answer the rest of my
questions?"

"We'll see. There is no penalty in asking."

I had this odd feeling that *I* was trapped in the room,
not her. She had an unsettling effect on me from the start.
"First of all, did Zala tell the truth?"

"She told no falsehoods," Kira responded, which was not

really answering the question. I took note of that fact and
went on.

"This breeding of special agents like yourself—it was entirely on Takanna?"

She nodded. "Spread the project and you spread the risk
of detection. There is no need to cover up now, since the
project was discovered and has probably been obliterated
by now anyway."

That was interesting. "Do you know how it was finally
penetrated?"

She shook her head negatively. "I suspect that it was not.
I believe it was leaked—closed down by the Four Lords
themselves. Zala was not penetrated. We were betrayed. A
very few of us have been taken and sent here before by the
Confederacy. But the Confederacy should not have known
about me. The project was ended and totally destroyed
years before I was caught. Ended by the Four Lords themselves. I have no direct evidence, but I believe that I am
here also at the Lords' direction. Perhaps all remaining of
my kind are."

I thought about that. "Then in effect you were called in
to the boss in the only way they could call you in."

"It is the only possible explanation."

"All right, then, tell me—if that's true, why didn't the
current or former Lord of Charon know anything about
you? Korman thought you were a Confederacy assassin.
Koril says he didn't even know of you until I drew attention your way. And Koril's staff says they were very curious about you—but also had no idea as to your true nature. *Why didn't they know*, Za . . . Kira?"

"At the moment, only three possibilities come to mind,"
she replied. "Either Koril or Matuze *didn't* know, and only
one was pretending, or both do not know and this project
was either not passed on to the new Lords who took over
since for some reason, or they had some purpose in keeping
this information from them."

"Nobody contacted you?"

"Yes, I *was* contacted. In Bourget."

"By who?"

"Yatek Morah."

I felt the old blood flowing again. *Now* we were getting somewhere.

"When was this?"

"Less than two days after we arrived."

"Less than two days! But we were there five months before he showed himself!"

She nodded. "He instructed me in the use of the *wa*—while you were working mostly. He'd come almost every day at the start, then less often as the lessons became less instruction and more practice, as you should understand."

Yeah, I sure did. "Did you ask him what all this was for?"

"I asked him if he had a mission for me. He told me that the mission would come later, that I was now only to practice."

"And you never pressed him?"

"I do not question the orders of my superiors." It wasn't a brag, just a fact stated in that same flat, emotionless tone as the rest.

"So you were still without instructions that morning at Bourget?"

"I was. I expected to be contacted, and even made an effort to contact Morah, but he brushed me aside. I am still without orders."

"You were never in the cult?"

"No. I tried, certainly—but I was not permitted. None would even admit its existence, and it was well hidden. Of course, it was no trick to determine who was involved and where those meetings were, but since I was still learning the powers myself I had no desire to meet a superior challenge in them until I felt I was ready."

I nodded idly, mostly to myself. It all made a crazy kind of sense, but all the pieces didn't fit. Damn it, *did* Koril know, or didn't he? And, regardless, had *Korman* known, at least at the start? Morah certainly had. I needed more information—and fast.

"Tell me, Kira, who do you work for now? Whose instructions will you, must you take?"

She immediately saw the point of the question. "It is not so simple on Charon, which is why I wait and live through Zala. Here, as back home, there are factions in the Brethren, but there I was clearly on one side. Here are two coequal forces, it seems to me. Matuze ousted Koril, who was one of my Lords. Matuze has control now, but may or may not maintain it. Morah has helped me, for Matuze's faction. But realistically, I must serve Lord Koril. I am here. I have no orders, no instructions, from Morah, and I am not likely to get any. If I do not ally myself with Lord Koril against Lord Matuze, I will be killed. Logic, therefore, dictates that I serve Lord Koril. I am at his service."

The statement was so cold and emotionless I could hardly suppress a shudder. Here was someone without any sense of morality, scruples, even loyalty. It made absolutely no difference to her who she worked for.

It was time to talk to Koril.

"You've seen the recording," I said. "Any reaction?"

Koril sat back and looked thoughtful. "I vaguely remember the project," he responded after a long pause. "Very vaguely. It was started long before I was sent here, of course. But it was never considered successful. I swear to you I thought the whole operation was shut down and abandoned years ago. And this double mind thing—hell, it's unbelievable to *me*."

He sounded sincere, and I wanted to believe him. Very much.

"Still, *somebody* knew," I pointed out. "She—and others—have been working for the Brethren for years. Who knows how many and over how long? And somebody ordered it shut down. Turned her in, in fact, and arranged somehow to send her here."

Koril seemed deep in thought and only half talking to me. "The more I think about it, the more I can see a possible scenario. The project was closed down, if I remember, because its products scared the hell out of the Four Lords—particularly their top people back home. Killing machines . . . What the Zala persona said rang a bell. No loyalty. No emotions. The bottom line was, no controls. Anything that—inhuman—could be used not only against the Confederacy but also against other power centers of the Brethren. Hell, it was supposedly shut down about the time I got sent here. I only got told about it when I was on the Synod by an old planetary boss who liked to reminisce."

"But that was forty or more years ago," I noted. "She's not nearly two-thirds that old."

He nodded. "And that, my friend, means that somebody has kept the thing going *after* it was ordered closed. Somebody who kept the secret from just about everybody except his own immediate family. It would give that person a tremendous edge."

"She said something about the Triana family," I said.

He shrugged. "I don't know them, but it might be a real family and not a Brethren one. Still, you see what this means? A fifth Lord, a secret one, in the game for maybe forty years."

"Morah. It has to be Morah."

"I agree. And yet Morah closed down the thing and exposed at least one, maybe all, the remaining ones. Why?"

"Well, I can think of one reason," I told him.

"Huh?"

"With organic super-robots and an alien force behind him he didn't need them anymore. Not there, anyway."

"Perhaps. But why did he need them *here*? And why, once here, didn't he use her?"

He thought a moment. "Maybe he wasn't ready to use her yet."

It was my turn. "Huh?"

"Suppose there aren't many of these—people. Suppose there are only, maybe, four of them. You remember Morah's getaway in the square at Bourget?"

"The four-headed hydra."

"And now Kreegan's dead. Remember—Dumonia said it *wasn't* the assassin who got him. A fluke, he called it." He looked straight at me. "And Morah's seen, met with, talked with those aliens face to face."

I finally saw where he was going. "So Korman might *not* have known. Or Aeolia Matuze either."

He nodded. "The Confederacy might not be the only ones trying to knock off the Four Lords. In fact, the Confederacy might just be doing Yatek Morah a favor.

"Not Four Lords of the Diamond—but one."

CHAPTER FOURTEEN

Forced Decisions

"That girl—Zala or Kira or whoever she is—worries you, doesn't she?" Darva asked.

I nodded. "Not the Zala part. There's something even likable about Zala. But ever since Korman told me about the other part of her I've wanted to meet that part—and now that I have, I'm not sure I should have forced it."

"I guess I'll never understand you," she sighed. "You force her out, then get really unhappy about it. Why? Isn't Kira more or less the same type as you?"

I whirled and felt my blood pressure go up. I paused a moment to try and get control of myself. I was going to make a nasty remark and strong denial, but Darva had really hit the nail on the head. Admitting that to myself calmed me down.

"All right. Yes, in a way. Never that cold, that unemotional, but, yes, she *is* a lot like I used to be. The way I still really think of myself. But she's me stripped down to the least common denominator. No morality, no cause, no feelings of any sort. That's what those biotechs managed with that two-mind technique. She's able to shift all her emotions, morals, feelings into Zala. It gives Kira the mind of a computer, unencumbered by any traces of—well, humanity. Zala may be dumb, shallow, and not good for much, but she's all that's human in that body and brain. And, still, when I look at Kira, talk to her, I see—me." *I see a man I used to be, sitting up there, a third of a light-year off the Warden system*, I added to myself.

And, in fact, just how different *was* Kira from that man up there? Outside of assignments, psych blocked and mostly wiped, he was really nothing more than a Zala with money. A playboy in the haunts of the rich and powerful, contributing little and totally hedonistic. The only difference between Kira and me, deep down, was that when I got all that information back before a mission, like now, I still had at my base that other man, that playboy lover of fun. Kira, on the other hand, experienced everything vicariously and never felt that her cover was anything more than that—certainly not a part of her.

The technique by which Zala/Kira had been formed remained a mystery. The medics here had poked and probed and found nothing. Her brain, aside from the Warden organisms' odd grouping, appeared normal. Nothing in medical science could pinpoint the difference in any way. And yet it was not a psych technique, or some mental aberration—the *wa* showed clearly a true biological division there somewhere.

To look into a mirror, to see such a personality—the perfect assassin—and see in all its ugliness the perfection of those qualities you always prided yourself on, this was the problem. Nor did I have the faith, the moral certitude, any more that I was on the side of right, justice, and good. Charon and its viewpoints and my own experiences here had killed that certainty, and even though I was still, for now, on the same side, I was there because the opposition repelled me, not out of any lingering loyalty to the Confederacy ideal. Had this, I wondered, happened to the others, my counterparts on Lilith, Cerberus, and Medusa? I knew this—I was more completely human now than ever before, and both the weaker for it and yet, somehow, whole as Kira was not and might never be.

Explaining all this to Darva wasn't easy. Although it helped to share it and talk it out, the fact was she could never fully understand. She hadn't been raised to *believe*.

And that, in the end, was the bottom line of difference between Kira and me. I had been a believer who lost his faith but found his humanity. She had never believed in anything, and, because of that, could never find or even fully comprehend her own humanity. I had been literally reduced to the animal on Charon and been reborn a hu-

man. Kira was reduced to the machine and locked there
for all time.

In a sense, she'd forced me to take a good, hard look at
myself—and in the process, I was free. The last bonds
were cut. Like that little Cerberan, Dumonia, I severed my
last ties to my past and stayed allied with it only because,
for the moment, our interests coincided.

For the first time I reached back and examined myself,
and much to my surprise, was able to locate through my
own *wa* that tiny piece of organic goo in my brain. Still
there. From Lacoch to changeling to bunhar to changeling
again, it had somehow survived. So you're still listening,
my brother out there? My . . . Kira.

Koril looked grim-faced. His office was littered with reports and photos, and he wasn't pleased with whatever they
said.

He got straight to the point. "We have been compromised. After all these years, we've been compromised."

"Somebody got word out?"

He nodded. "Somehow. I'm not sure how. But this complex is doomed, Park. It's only a matter of time. Oh, it's
safe enough against ground assault, but once its location is
known they could bring in heavy stuff, off-planet stuff,
and fry hell out of us."

"Then why haven't they?"

He smiled. "Funny. Basically because the Confederacy
monitors the system so well. They don't have the heavy
weapons on Charon to do the job, and if they tried to get
them they'd be shot to hell in space. To hit us hard they'd
have to bring in one of their alien friends' vessels—and
that would force them into the open. But it's only a matter
of time until they work out some way to fool our Wardens."

"How much time?" I asked uneasily.

"Who knows? A day? A week? A month? A minute
from now? Whenever they can work it out. We can't take
the chance of its being long." He sat back in his chair, and
for the first time he looked very old, old and incredibly
tired. "Well, perhaps it's for the best. To end it, one way or

the other, once and for all. He looked up at me, the weight of his decision showing in his face. "You know, Park, for the first time I realize how I've been kidding myself all these years. I *enjoyed* this place. I loved the research, the peace, the lack of demands. I even loved being the rebel leader. It was far more of a challenge to be the opposition than to actually run the place. It's funny—always preparing but never acting. That's just what Dumonia was saying the other—son of a bitch!"

'What's the matter?"

"That old bastard! Outside of people directly under my control, Dumonia was the only one who knew precisely how to determine this base's location. He had to—his people stocked it. Why, I ought to . . ." He was turning so red I feared his rage, but he soon calmed down.

"Oh, hell," he said, "I guess he had a right. Without him I wouldn't have all this."

"You mean the *Cerberan* betrayed you?"

He nodded. "Had to be."

"But why?"

"Just to get me to move. Damn it, Park, I'm ready. I've been ready for over a year. You saw Bourget—just a little test. That's why Dumonia was here. We talked and talked and talked, and I gave him a hundred excuses, but hell, the man's a psych. He knew I would have to be pushed, and so he pushed."

I frowned. "Who *is* that man, anyway? Where does he get the resources and power he uses?"

"He's probably the most dangerous man in the Diamond, and that's saying something," Koril replied. "He could be Lord if he wanted, or just about anything else, I think. He's absolutely brilliant, particularly at making other powerful people do what he wants. Right now he has the Confederacy and who knows how much of the Diamond doing his bidding. What his motives are I can't say—but I know it's not power for its own sake. If he wanted to run things, he would. I asked him once why he was helping me and you know what he said? He said it was a relief from boredom! But, enough of him. He's kicked me hard now—and I have no choice but to act."

"You're going to try and retake control then?"

He nodded. "Now, I don't want to minimize anything. You're still new here—a little over a year total, I think. You still don't really appreciate what we're up against."

I waved my hands around. "This place is equipped to take the whole system, and your planetwide underground is effective. I can't see why you'd have a problem at this stage."

He smiled grimly. "Ah, but you see only the surface. First of all, we can't depend on the weapons here. Didn't you ever wonder why those troopers in Bourget had projectile weapons? I took a great risk with the laser stuff there. One small tabarwind and we'd have been blown to kingdom come."

"You know, ever since I've been on Charon I've heard about tabarwinds," I told him. "And yet they have to be rare. I never saw one, or met anyone who did."

"It only takes one to scare hell out of you. It's a whirling electrical storm that reaches from the ground to the ion layer surrounding the planet. Nobody knows what causes them, but they look like something out of the most fanatical of religious hells. There's even a religion based on them, if you can believe it. They just appear—no cause, no real reason we've ever found. They can be anywhere—except here, in the center of Gamush, for some reason. They follow no set path and no logic, and they vanish as quickly as they come. It can be a year between them—and then there can be dozens, even hundreds. Aside from the direct fury of the storm, almost anything electrical within a dozen or more kilometers of the storm just goes crazy. Overloads and explodes, often with a force beyond anything inherent in the exploding device. No sorcery, no force of will can stand against them. And electrical energy attracts them like a magnet."

"Sounds like an experience I can gladly skip," I told him truthfully.

"And they're more common than you think," Koril went on. "There are three right now in the north, and that's where we have to go."

I sighed. "I see. But reduced to those primitive weapons,

numbers mean even more—and I think you have them. If Bourget is any indication, the masses of people here really don't give a damn who runs things."

"As usual anywhere," Koril agreed. "Oh, it's certain that we could take as much as seventy percent of the north and the few settlements on Gamush without problems. Tukyan's hardly worth worrying about it's so primitive. I have enough powerful sorcs, trained and developed here, to carry the day, force the government to a few strongholds like Montlay and Cubera. But it makes no difference. As long as they hold the Castle they hold one of only two spaceports on the planet, and they hold the power really. The trade, the records—the whole economy. Holding that, they can disrupt the business of the planet. Things don't work right, people get hungry, or angry. And while we deteriorate sitting on our seven-tenths, they wait for reinforcements either from the other three Lords or, maybe, directly from the aliens. Basically, we take the countryside without the Castle and we take nothing we can hold. Take the Castle and the rest falls automatically into line."

"Then we must take the Castle."

Tulio Koril laughed. "Easier said than done, my rash young assassin. Far easier said than done."

We sat in a small briefing room, eight of us and Koril. I looked around at the faces there, but aside from two I didn't recognize any of them. The two I knew were Darva, of course, and Zala Embuay whose presence was unexplained. It was definitely Zala we were seeing, not Kira, but we all knew that Kira was present too.

The room was darkened, and a picture appeared on the screen of a huge, black circular stone building set atop a commanding mountain. Pagodalike, there were a series of stone porches around it at regular intervals almost all the way to the not quite flat top of the building.

"This is the Castle," Koril told us. "It is eighty meters high from ground level, but there are an additional forty meters below ground. The building is divided into fifteen levels, and has excellent drainage. Its walls are solid stone, a meter thick, reinforced with steel plating and mesh. Be-

neath it, inside the mountain, is a network of tunnels leading to remote, below-ground armories. You could probably
blow a nice hole in it with a laser canon, but you'd never
get a second chance at it. Even so, you would have to be a
genius to make that first hole, since the outer rock surface
is chemically coated with a clever armorite compound developed on Cerberus. It will deflect a laser and, if you're
not careful, reflect it back at you. Because of the coating,
the *wa* of the Castle is inert to us. It acts like a true physical barrier to the best *wa* sense. You can't throw a spell to
disperse anything or anybody behind it. Of course, they
can't do it to you either—but, remember, they don't have
to. They can hold on until reinforced either from other
areas or from space. That topmost area is a shuttle cradle."

I had to admit the place was most impressive, although I
knew of two dozen weapons that could bring it down. Of
course, none were available in the Warden Diamond—and
two would also destroy the planet.

"The top level is shuttle receiving," Koril continued,
"and there is a series of lifts around the exterior for moving
people and goods up and down, mostly by a clever counterweight system. The fourteenth floor is the living quarters
of the Lord of the Daimond, her servants and whatever
entourage she might permit. On the next eight floors below
are special troopers and a defense force, living quarters for
the rest of the top government and their staffs, and central
records. The bottom five floors, all below ground level, include a supply level and warehouse with tunnel access, a
special prison known as the dungeon, a reception level and
general offices, and more defensive and trooper personnel.
Additionally, on many of the upper levels there are governmental and experimental offices, labs, and the like. All in
all, quite a complex."

Koril flipped a switch, and a schematic of the building
came on.

"Get to know this. You will all have copies provided,
and I want you to know every passage, service corridor,
twist and turn in the place. Within the next two days I'll be
putting you to the test, showing blind areas on a computer
simulator. Better know your way around or you'll get

quickly lost. Speed is important, but I don't want any of you in there to get lost in any way, shape, or form."

The picture flipped again, showing the bottom level and the tunnel complex.

"This is the weak spot of the Castle, if it can be said to have one," the sorcerer went on. "If you look closely, you'll realize that this is more than a complex of tunnels and caves in a mountain. This is a maze. It is certainly possible to get into the maze more than two kilometers from the Castle itself, but once in you have even more problems. There are spells and sensors everywhere. Apparent rock walls show where there is clear space, and there are literally hundreds of rock plugs that can be—and are— shifted regularly, changing the entire maze. There is, literally, no way to know the configuration of the maze at any given time. At one time, several years ago, I *did* discover the key to it and sent in some of my best people. Most of them got into the Castle, but only a handful got out again—and none lived to get back to me. You understand the meaning of that. Many of them were top sorcs. The best. Therefore, should we manage to get *in*, we're *in*. We either take the Castle or we die. No alternatives."

That outlook was pretty grim, but we all could see his point. Still, somebody had a question—I couldn't tell who.

"How will we solve the maze?" the questioner sensibly asked.

"The only advantage I have is that I know the entire area. I know what sort of things are installed and what are not, and I can orient myself even to changed circumstances. Basically, I'm betting that I can solve the maze based on my prior knowledge. If I can't, it's all over."

There was a nervous shuffling in the room at that. We were all being asked to put our necks entirely in a noose made for Koril, and were totally dependent on Koril to keep that noose from tightening.

"Now, it's inevitable we'll trip something, bringing troopers and defense forces," Koril continued, "but these don't worry me and should not worry you. None are above the level of a low-grade apt, maybe VII tops and more likely IXs. The least of you is a VII, and most of us are far higher than that. They keep the troop grade low to prevent any possible internal revolts, of course. But don't kid yourself—also in the Castle are some incredibly powerful sorcs. The tops. The best we know. With luck, there'll be no more than four or five Synod members there—they roam about much of the time. But the odds are extremely good that there will be at least that number, and we can't discount Morah. We can only hope that he's out—and then try and rig things a bit our way."

"What about Matuze?" somebody else asked.

"She'll almost certainly be in. She rarely leaves, and never for any extended visits. Without her, of course, the Castle is valueless, but I feel certain the odds are with us on that much. As for Morah, we'll stir up a big dish of trouble in the south coast region, as far from the Castle as we can. With any luck, the fracas will bring him there. Then we enter the Castle. Finally, as a distraction, there will be a general uprising and a well-coordinated but futile attack upon the Castle itself. Our own movements will be determined both by events inside and by the shuttle schedule, which we most certainly know. It puts down at four every afternoon and remains for an hour. That means we launch our south coast diversion a day before we go in. We go in at five the next day. Once we're discovered, we're committed. We must accomplish everything before that shuttle returns the next afternoon. If not, if we're held in the lower areas through then, Aeolia need only take the shuttle up to the space station and we're dead." He paused a moment, then added, "Remember, you all volunteered for this."

Well, maybe we had—but there were a lot of ifs in this proposition. If all the attacks were coordinated. If Morah could be drawn off. If there were no more Synod members in residence than we could handle ourselves. If the shuttle kept its schedule. If Aeolia Matuze was home. And if we could think, fight, and ensorcel our way through that huge building in only one full day.

I looked at Darva in the gloom and knew she was thinking the same things I was. "I really wish you wouldn't come," I told her. "You're not strong enough for the sorcs and you're a knife at my throat. They kill you, they get me."

"I have other skills," she reminded me, "not the least of which is the weapons practice I've been through here. And I'm no more a knife at your throat than you are at mine. If you're going to take me with you I don't want to get it sitting out the action someplace."

I smiled and squeezed her hand. "All right, then. It's a team we are."

Her smile in return was weak. I knew she really thought we were going to die in this, and I understood that she was willing to go, particularly if it was in the pursuit of something important.

And, I think, she understood me as well. Hell, up to the last I'd never expected to be in on the end of this thing, not directly. As it was, I was going to have more fun than I'd had in the past ten years.

CHAPTER FIFTEEN

A Walk in the Dark

We could have used four months to train for the mission;
Koril gave us four days. Once he'd decided to move, he
decided to *move*, and that was that. He said he'd picked
each of us for a reason, but some reasons were easier
than others to figure out.

I seemed to have been included because Koril, like many
of the Brethren I'd hunted for most of my life, had a very
high opinion of Confederacy assassins, an opinion I'd tried
to reinforce in my conversations with him. I was surprised
he agreed to let Darva come, but as she had pointed out,
what she lacked in sorcerous powers she more than compensated for with close-quarters weaponry. She'd worked
hard developing those skills, and I wouldn't want to be in
the way if she wanted to go somewhere. If her opponent
were equal or weaker than she in control of the *wa* force,
or was prevented by one of us from using it, that opponent
was dead. Zala—or, rather, Kira—was a more interesting
choice, since I knew Koril trusted her no more than I did.
If she was on the level, of course, she'd be invaluable—but
she could also easily be our Trojan Horse, ready to betray
us once we were trapped inside the Castle.

The rest were his best sorcs, as illustrated by the "K"
sound that preceded their names, which they took when
admitted to that fraternity of the very best. It was like a
title or badge of rank—and when I finally realized that it
explained a lot. Of them all, only Morah had never taken a
sorc name.

Our party wasn't without interesting abilities. In addition
to Darva and myself, Ku, a small, dark man with a rodent-
like face, was also a changeling, although very human in

appearance. He was naturally nocturnal and, additionally, had some sort of built-in sonar system which would be very useful to us—along with his unnerving ability to stick to walls and ceilings like a fly. It was obvious that, if in fact someone else had made him a changeling or not, he'd adapted for himself some most useful attributes.

Kaigh was a large, hairy bearlike man who looked naturally mean, and perhaps was. I understood he was a former Confederacy frontier officer who'd found the possibilities for graft and extortion out there irresistible. Kimil was a typical civilized worlder, younger than Koril but otherwise undistinguished. Kindel was a small, wiry woman with wickedly long nails and a shaved head. Her cold, black eyes seemed too large for her head, and were constantly in nervous motion. Krugar was a woman of the civilized worlds, in early middle age and otherwise not very distinguished from any other civilized worlder. Of us all, I realized, only Darva was native to Charon.

Darva and I were the largest and most obvious targets, I realized that from the beginning. Over the months we had managed to scale ourselves down slowly to a more moderately tall 204 centimeters, still enough to tower over the others. Of course, our appearance, although very human, was still changeling enough to mark us. We were both damned strong and surprisingly agile, and we worked at it.

We left Koril's redoubt by air, in much the same manner as we'd arrived—but this time, inside the cabin of the great flying creature and not in its claws. Zala hadn't been too excited by the idea of the trip, but apparently had been calmed or sedated in some way by Kira. I found the trip as bumpy and uncomfortable as the first time, but took it in stride. We had a schedule to keep.

We did not, of course, dare land anywhere near the Castle. Since there were no legitimate landing areas for the big creatures we could use, we made do with an area more than forty kilometers southwest of the seat of Charon's government and managed to get the big thing back off the ground ourselves.

Our equipment was surprisingly spare. Koril had risked

laser pistols, with the understanding that we might have to get rid of them for any number of reasons. We also carried a small store of projectile weapons and ammunition, on which we'd practiced and been checked out at the redoubt's firing ranges long before. Darva never did quite get the art of laser pistol down well, but she was a whiz at the projectile pistols—just the reverse of me. In addition several of us, including Darva, carried that most ancient of weapons, the sword; others carried small but deadly daggers. The burly Kaigh, to my awe and fascination, carried what seemed to be a crossbow, a kind of early weapon I'd only read about but had never seen before.

We carried no papers or documents of any kind. All information had been hypnoed into our minds to save weight and problems. We all wore tough clothing of jungle green, a sort of forest version of the trooper uniforms, Darva's and mine having been specially cut and tailored for our peculiar requirements. Beyond some prepackaged food cakes and canteens, we had nothing else.

On the road we ate mostly by transmutation, a rather fascinating process. Just as Garal had changed fruit punch into acid and Korman had changed it back, so our own sorcs could take almost any vegetable matter in the jungle and make almost anything of it we desired. To this day I'm still not sure if we really were eating transmuted stuff or just leaves and the like we were fooled into believing was the good food it seemed to be. In the end, it probably made no difference. At least our bodies not only accepted the stuff but seemed to make good use of it.

We had two and a half days to reach the Castle, which was easy enough considering the distance involved. Still, the trek was through the rough of the jungle, and not even Darva and I were any longer prepared to feel completely at home there. As we approached the mountains, though, the jungle gave way first to thick forest and then to intermittent groves with bare glades and rocky outcrops. The going was steep, since we could hardly use the known roads, and tough. Much of the open spaces had to be negotiated at night. We had our first practice with Koril's little nocturnal vision spells, but still needed the more natural and nearly perfect night eyes of Ku to keep us from breaking our fool necks.

By the morning of the appointed day, we had made it to the place where we knew we'd be entering the caves. It was a good spot, really. Nearby, through a small grove of trees, was a sheer cliff and we were able to look out on the valley below. From any point we could see the top of the Castle, which looked even more fearsome in person than it did in any pictures.

We settled down to wait for the late afternoon, when the real work would begin. Standing short watches, we tried to get as much sleep as we could. With some interest I noticed that, somehow, Zala hadn't been included in the watch schedule.

I slept in short stretches, but couldn't really relax. I was simply too keyed up, although I knew that was an amateur's problem and wasn't supposed to happen to me. Early in the afternoon, before the start of one of Charon's interminable rains, I wandered down through the grove of trees to the cliffside and looked out, perhaps for the last time, on the landscape below.

And, finally, I saw a tabarwind.

The view across the valley was fifteen, maybe twenty kilometers at worst, although it was obscured by rain. The cloud cover remained above the line of hills on both sides, though, allowing fair visibility with no real resolution of fine detail on the ground. Still, there was no mistaking what I was seeing—I watched it form.

First a small area far off to the east seemed to flash on and off with upper-level lightning. But instead of the intermittent and irregular illumination within the clouds it grew quite regular and very strong, so strong that it was almost as if a bright light was shining in the center of the cloud mass. Still nothing had emerged from the cloud. Then, suddenly, the immediate area began to swirl around. I had seen something of the pattern before, although not with the central globe of increasingly steady light. Tornado, it was called, or sometimes cyclone.

From that bright center in the clouds long fingers of electricity shot down to the ground, and seconds later, reported their arrival to me with a series of loud booms that echoed back and forth across the valley. I couldn't make out much of what was under those bolts, but I felt relieved that it wasn't me.

Now, out of that bright, shining center a funnel shape seemed to emerge, not like a tornado but almost mathematically regular. A conical shape of charged—what?—moving down, surrounded by a maniacal dance of lightning all around. The yellowish cone began to change, darken, take on colors as it reached for and then touched the ground. Reds and oranges and purples swirled within but did not mix.

I could see where the ignorant might ascribe a supernatural power to such a thing. It was a swirl of color and forces, and as I watched, it flattened into an almost cylindrical shape and began to move.

Others, hearing the thunder, came and joined me at my watching place. The storm, although far off, was awesome, and everyone seemed magnetically attracted to its grim, erratic march across the valley. Everyone but Koril.

"I think it's time we went in," he said calmly.

A couple of us turned and looked in surprise at him. "But it's not nearly five yet," I noted.

He nodded. "They won't risk a shuttle landing with tabarwind conditions in the area. The automatic systems will close down completely for the duration so as not to attract the storm. That means no electricity or automatic watchdogs, no landings, nothing. And right now any laser charges are being hauled down the long tunnel away from the Castle. That means we'll be between the charges and the people who can use them, and that's fine with me. The storm's a godsend! Let's move!"

The tabarwind's almost hypnotic effect was hard to leave, but we all understood his urgency. We slipped on our packs and headed for an undistinguished grove of trees some sixty meters from our camp.

"The watch has retreated," Koril said, almost gloating.

"That'll make it easy. If we can get past the interior guard-post without being seen we'll be in without a trace."

The roar of the tabarwind sounded very close, and the wind picked up to almost gale force. "Hadn't we better ditch out laser pistols?" Kimil asked nervously.

"I think not," the chief sorcerer replied. "I'm willing to take the risk. With the luck we're having, it just might mean we have 'em and nobody else will."

The spell in the grove was a good one, tightly woven and nearly impossible to detect. Few knew that the Castle had any back entrances and exits in the first place, although nobody builds a fortress without both an escape system and a hidden route of supply. This was one of four such, and the second closest to the Castle itself—but the most direct. The closest in, and most used, of these back doors actually led *away* from the Castle to the underground storerooms in natural caverns in the mountain Though it would be the easiest to uncover and enter, an enemy force might never find the Castle from there.

Koril and two of our other sorcerers worked quickly on the spell, with a skill and ease I found fascinating and envi-able. I might have their potential, but I was a long way from having their skill.

Two of the trees seemed to shrivel, wither before our eyes, then they bent backward to reveal a solid metal door. Medusan metal, I knew—and totally inert to us. Both door and lock were beyond our powers, but not the rock in which the lock was imbedded. I watched as our advance team of sorcs sent their combined energies into and around the rock, and saw the *wa* of the rock respond as if it was some living thing, compressing back from the locking mechanism. In a matter of minutes a hole appeared on one side of the door large enough for an arm to go through. Koril nodded to himself, walked forward, reached in al-most to his elbow, and slid the door back. We could all see that the locking mechanism also slid back, still in place. No alarms had been tripped because the lock had not been tampered with.

Quickly we were inside the tunnel entrance, then waited there as the door returned to its original position and our wizards replicated the spells they had broken on the way in, moving the trees and the rock back into place. A Class 1 sorc could detect the tampering if he was in any way suspicious, but I sure couldn't.

With the door shut, we were suddenly encased in total darkness, but we were neither blind nor helpless. Ku scampered up the wall and stuck firmly to the top of the cave. He would travel with us that way and be our surprise insurance policy. As for us, we could see each other's distinctive *wa*—Zala's twin mind was particularly visible—thus providing us with our own outlines as well as the *wa* in the rock of the cave itself. The sight, uncomplicated by anything visual, was eerie, and useful—but not only to us. Anyone else could see us, too.

Ku in the lead proceeded slowly about five meters ahead of us. As silently as possible, in this configuration, we began our walk down that long, dark tunnel, most attention focused on Ku. Koril took the lead in our group, Darva remained the last, her attention less on Ku than on Zala, as agreed. This was, in fact, one of Koril's little master strokes. The weakest in power, Darva's *wa* was linked immutably to mine. If she saw anything unusual, she could signal me with a prearranged pinch code. If anybody tried anything on her, I'd know it immediately, too. Koril, I now understood, had good reasons for everything he did, including bringing both Darva and me along.

We rounded a turn in the tunnel and suddenly had some sight—a flickering torch not in the cave itself but coming from a small room just off it. Ku was a nervy bastard, I had to give him that much. He scampered on the cave roof right up to that door, which didn't reach his position, and peered cautiously in from his upside-down angle. Then, cautiously, he made his way back to Koril.

"Two troopers," he hissed to Koril in a voice barely audible to me in the middle of the group. "Repeaters with exploding bullets. Power's still off."

Koril nodded to him and appeared to be satisfied. Then, as Ku went on ahead once again, the man who used to own both cave and troopers stepped forward, almost to the open door itself, and raised his hands in what I knew was a power gesture. He seemed immobile, frozen but majestic, and yet the index finger of his outstretched right hand wriggled, telling us to proceed.

One at a time, as silently as we could, we approached Koril, then the door, then passed it, walking right under Ku. We could see the two men in the room, looking bored and occasionally glancing up at some device beyond our gaze. Neither seemed to notice us.

Once Darva was past, Koril himself finally moved, retaining his outstretched form and moving first sideways, then back to the far cave wall, past the door, under Ku, and to the rest of us waiting on the other side. Only then did he relax, move forward, and allowing Ku to go ahead once again, he led us down the tunnel and around another curve, back into the darkness once again. There was no need to explain what he had done. We all knew he had maintained the illusion of peace, quiet, and no intruders for the two men while we all passed.

We continued another forty or fifty meters when the cave opened up into a large, circular area—an obvious junction point. The trouble was, once you stepped into it the *wa* glowed brightly all around, indicating solid rock. We couldn't even tell where we'd entered. This, then, was the first of the maze traps, and a very good one it was.

The tunnel system had the intricate workings of a circuit diagram, as I knew from my earlier sessions with the diagrams and floor plans. It would be obvious to anyone getting this far that the solidness of the chamber was a blind, but you had no real clue as to which opening to take, even if you found it. Of the five tunnels that actually fed into the place, only one led towards the Castle. Another, of course, led back the way we had come. The other three were laced with very nasty traps and ultimately led to storage areas away from the Castle itself.

I slipped back to Darva. "How're you holding up?" I whispered.

"Fine, except I feel like I have to pee," she responded just as quietly. I patted her comfortingly and retook my position.

Koril looked around, then urged us back and again

stretched out his arms. He began to turn, slowly, for more than a minute, making three complete circles before he stopped. Finally he said, in a very low voice, "Somebody very good's done a nice job. They're all badly booby-trapped, and they've added a new cross-tunnel about ten meters out. Okay—follow me closely and *don't* get ahead of me. Ku, no more than a couple meters at a time."

With that he made his decision, pointed his finger, and some of the *wa* to his left dissolved a bit. He walked cautiously through it, allowed Ku to go on, then waited for the rest of us. The *wa* curtain, made of some thin strands of something or other that simulated rock but were easily penetrable, slid back into place.

Slowly, cautiously, we reformed and started down the new path. After only two or three meters, though, Koril gestured for us to stop.

"Dumb shits," Koril mumbled. "They ought to know better than to use offworlder traps." He pointed to the floor, and we all could sense what he meant. All around us was *wa*—in us, in the walls, floor, and roof. Everything shone with its distinctive *wa* pattern—except an area four meters long that ran the width of the cave on the floor right in front of Koril. Inert matter meant Medusan metal, and its very lack of any sight, including *wa*, outlined it perfectly.

Ku needed no prompting; he was already on the roof of the cave and working. I saw a small laser drill snap into place, and, soon after, he was affixing a ring to the roof with an instant-bonding cement. Darva and I, being the largest, carried the miscellaneous packs, and she was already ahead of me. The rope, made from some really nasty jungle vines in Koril's shops, tested out at over 500 kilos. For our sake I hoped it still did.

Kindel was nearest me, and I whispered to her, "What would we do without Ku?"

"Why, we'd turn another of us into something like him," she replied matter-of factly.

"Oh," was all I could manage, and turned back to watch the work. The system was simple enough—grab the rope and swing across the pressure-sensitive floor plate to the other side. It wasn't quite as easy as all that though—the roof of the cave was less than three meters high, while the plate was four across. Since the rope couldn't touch the plate, that meant you needed good speed and a slight jump at the end. It would be tricky indeed.

It was a nervous eternity as each of us made our crossing, but we were all trained professionals. We had only one close call, and no other problems. I made it very easily, almost to my surprise, and the thought struck me that, if Kira were a double agent, primed to betray us, she could do so very convincingly now. She didn't, though, demonstrating that nice timing and power she tried so hard to hide.

In fact, only the tiny Kindel needed several swings until she felt confident enough to let go, and, even then, only fast action by the Ku overhead pushed her the last few precious centimeters.

We all waited while Ku used his little laser tool to cut the knot and retrieve the rope, then return, cut off and bring back the ring also. Again, anyone who passed by would have to be looking for something to find any sign that we had been here.

Much of the rest of the tunnel was arranged with other traps, some easier to spot than others. A few were actually powered and thus not active, but most were basic, mechanical types that were bad enough. Each caused a little heart trouble but each had its answer in our packs, and none deterred us.

We found countless blind junctions too, and in each we had to rely on Koril's old experience and the probing sense of the top sorcs. Approaching one, though, we were held up by Koril from entering. We had reached areas close to the Castle—and now we were going to face the real problems.

For one thing, *this* junction had traffic; a fair amount by the sound of it. Troopers and maintenance personnel pushing dollies of various things to and fro, or so it seemed. There was never a lag of more than a minute or so between such sounds, hardly enough time to enter, determine the right path, and move on through.

Koril was still deeply in thought when the power returned. A band of light came alive all up and down the corridors, illuminating us dimly but completely—and illuminating the junction as well. We moved quickly back into the tunnel, just in time to miss four red-clad people emerging from another tunnel mouth on the run, pushing a large yellow cart filled with cases of something or other across the open space, and into another opening. They never glanced in our direction.

"Well, we made it a lot farther than I thought, thanks to the tabarwind," Koril sighed. "Now the real fun begins. We're less than fifty meters from the bottom floor of the Castle right now. These tunnels lead to the art storage rooms, the precious metals rooms, and the like. That one to the right, there, at two o'clock, leads to the Castle." He stopped, and we all froze as yet another team came through, this time with what sounded like a powered vehicle of some kind. As the last sounds were receeding, he continued.

"The booby traps have got to be down by now. I'm not sure anybody ever expected anyone to get this far undetected. I'm not sure *I* ever did. I've had an education in security myself these past hours. Now, I know you're all tired but we have to push on. I'm sure all this fuss is over the attack that has surely been launched by now, and all hell is breaking loose. That means they'll be coming up or down here any moment now. We can't stay here and we can't go on. I think—"

Just as he said that last a small powered tractor towing a trailer entered the junction point, paused a moment, then turned our way and started right toward us.

Pistols were out in a moment, and Koril hardly had time to hiss "Don't miss!" as the thing chugged into view. There were only two people in the cab, both dressed in maintenance red. We shot them so fast I can't even describe what they looked like. In another moment Ku dropped from the roof into the open cab, kicked the corpses out of the way, and brought the tractor to a stop.

"Quickly!" Koril said. "Park. Darva. Kaigh. You're the biggest and strongest. Get those crates off this thing!"

We hustled to do as instructed. The damned things were

heavy, but not beyond any two of us, and we had them off the trailer and to the side of the little chugging train in a couple of minutes. During that time we nervously ignored other traffic sounds behind us. We were just far enough around the bend, we hoped, not to be noticed—unless somebody else wanted to come up our way.

Koril wasted no time on sorcery. He opened his laser pistol to wide scan and disintegrated the crates to white powder, taking the risk that the electronic springlike sound would be unheard or obscured by traffic noise. Quickly we climbed into the back trailer. Ku then stuck the small service cab into reverse, backed out carefully into the junction point, made the turn, then moved into the tunnel that headed for the Castle. We never knew what was in those crates.

Ku drove like a madman and hardly hesitated when we approached some troopers and maintenance personnel on foot. To my surprise they just stepped against the wall and let us by without a glance. A little further on, we passed a similar tractor going the other way. Ku waved, so did the red-clad driver of the other vehicle, and we passed with a few centimeters to spare.

Koril laughed out loud. "The fools! They figure we're troopers. Well, we are! Weapons at the ready! This is gonna get hairy in a minute!"

With that, we entered the bottom floor of the Castle, a huge open area supported by rock pillars. Hundreds of men and women clad in red or black were there, and a number of vehicles and trailers were about.

We pulled in between some painted lines on the floor and Ku brought us to a stop. Koril, brimming with confidence, winked. "Now I'll show you why bureaucracy is so evil." He jumped down, holstered his pistol, and walked briskly towards a gold-braided black-clad trooper, an officer of some kind and by his *wa* a powerful man.

The former Lord of the Diamond walked right up to him, started talking to him, and the trooper nodded, then pointed and said something back. Koril saluted and returned to us, hardly suppressing a grin. "Okay—out! We don't have to walk up. We're going to take Lift 4."

A little numbly we complied, and followed him across the busy floor to the doors of a huge open lift. I wasn't used to such a primitive device, but remembered that Koril had said these were moved by counterweight, not by any electrical power. They had to be—otherwise in a power outage they would be useless.

We stood there, looking about nervously, not quite believing what we were doing and feeling we stuck out like a sore thumb in our green uniforms. I couldn't stand it any more than the rest, and eased up to Koril. "All right—how the hell did you manage this?"

He smiled and winked. "I just walked up to the chief operations officer there, told him we were a special security patrol ordered to defensive positions, and asked him for the quickest way to our station."

"And he told you?"

"Sure. Why not?"

I wasn't the only one shaking my head in wonder as the big lift descended, stopped, and form-fitted itself neatly into the indentation for it in the floor. There were a number of hand carts on it, mostly empty, with security troopers and maintenance personnel on them, all of whom paid us no mind whatsoever. I admit, though, that at least I, and almost certainly most of us, were close to being nervous wrecks at this point. Still, this was just the sort of stunt *I* might improvise if this were *my* old stamping grounds. I knew that our greatest danger until we got off wasn't from these faceless men and women but from somebody's nerve springing in our group and giving us away.

When the lift was cleared we stepped uneasily on, only to find that several troopers also came up, pushing carts with cases of what looked like ammunition for the projectile weapons and, possibly, laser pistol power packs. No sooner were they on than a loud gong sounded overhead, and we started up, one floor at a time. The system was obviously designed for slow ascent and descent. It would stop on every floor no matter what.

The next floor, and most of the others, were not open spaces like the warehouse level but instead opened on access corridors that went down a few meters, then branched off to the right and left. Security guards were visible on each level, wearing special color-coded passes which, I was acutely and suddenly aware, we did *not* have.

The troopers with us didn't seem to notice, but when one cart got off at the fifth level the security men *did* check badges. At the seventh level when the rest exited, badges were given an even greater scrutiny. Alone and rising, I shouted to Koril, "Badges!"

He nodded and patted his pistol in its holster. It was pretty clear that we'd have to take his lead and use brute force—and, once we did, all hell would break loose. As we cleared Level 9 he whispered, "Draw weapons and shoot as soon as you're able!"

At Level 10, the topmost point you could go on these lifts without full security clearance, eight armed security guards waited for us with very ugly-looking projectile weapons. Even if they didn't suspect us, and they probably did, they would be ready to shoot anyone on the lift at the slightest provocation.

As our heads came up over the floor and into the clear, I shouted, "Wait! Don't shoot!" The guards naturally hesitated at that, and that was all we needed. As our shoulders cleared we opened wide rapid fire with the laser pistols. None of them had a chance against such concentrated fire.

"Everybody off—fast!" Koril shouted. "When they don't give the go-ahead signal this thing'll drop like a stone!" We needed no other urging; the last of us was off before the lift leveled with the floor—and just in time, too. Apparently the guards above had the locking mechanism, and with no guard to throw it the big platform rumbled and dropped immediately from view.

Kaigh looked back at the gaping hole and shook his head. "Close." We all turned our attention back to Koril, who was looking around critically.

Finally he said, "This is the primary guard floor for the upper levels. There'll be some fifty, sixty people here even if the rest were drawn off by the outside attack. I doubt, though, if we could walk through to the main stair without getting slaughtered. Park, Darva, Kira—stay in the middle of our circle. No firing even if fired upon. Bluff, bravado, and conventional weapons will no longer get us anywhere."

We knew what he meant and quickly formed up, allowing the sorcs to surround us. But neither Darva nor I put down our weapons. In the last analysis, something was better than nothing. Still, we'd gone through this procedure, and for now, I was certainly willing to let the pros do what they did best. What bothered me most was that what they were going to do was form an actual circle as we moved. Should anyone in the circle fall, breaking contact, one of us would have to complete the connection and quickly. Otherwise, instead of the pooled power of the highly trained Class 1 sorcs assembled by Koril, there would be only individuals—possibly capable of protecting themselves, but hardly me.

The circle was formed quickly, but we didn't start right away. The concentration required to link the *wa* of so many powerful minds was enormous. Darva, Kira, and I looked around nervously, and I know they were wondering why our unseen enemy hadn't charged. I could see why with no difficulty. The entry corridor dead-ended about twenty meters in, and you had to turn either right or left. From the diagrams I knew we had to go left to get to where we had to go—and so would any defenders. With the lift behind us, troopers on all lower floors, and safety seals in place above, we couldn't retreat, not even climb up or down, nor could we remain for long or that lift would return with really nasty goodies just for us. Any defender would naturally prefer to stake out a route of inevitable march by an invader than attack in this confined space, where we had good shots ourselves.

"The *wa* is one," Koril chanted. "The *wa* is one." The others repeated the chant, again and again, until they were all in sync. It was eerie. Still, we'd all seen Tully Kokul, a mere 4 or 5, shrug off laser pistol shots aimed directly at him. This was an infinitely more powerful group—the combined wills and power of the best Charon had to offer outside of the Synod. In fact, I realized, this was exactly what the Synod itself was, and why these sorcs were here.

They would be the new Synod—if we survived a wall of bullets and who knew what else and then reached the Synod itself, one floor above and almost certainly waiting.

Even I could sense the enormous power of the circle Koril and the others had created. All around us was a wall of *wa*, acting magnetically. We would see how well it repelled—for we started to move.

Troopers were waiting for us down both halls, of course. As soon as we turned left, then right again to walk together in very tight quarters, the troops from the wing on the right moved in behind us. They were cool and quite professional, I had to give them that. They let us get ten meters or more down that long, seventy-meter straight path, before they opened up. Both Darva and I froze for a moment when they did, and almost killed us all—for the circle kept moving, steadily, as it had to.

Enough of those primitive but deadly missiles were fired from remote positions and from gun stations along the hallway that paint flew, hundreds of holes seemed to appear all around in the walls, and the air seemed to grow almost solid. Yet, as we continued to move, not a single one seemed able to strike us, either directly or by ricochet.

The circle, acting as one, stopped about halfway; the others were in a trancelike state, seemingly oblivious to the horror that was being unleashed on us. No matter what, none of the three of us in the middle could keep from flinching and ducking, and it took a mighty amount of will power to just stand there, and try and match the motions or lack of them that the sorcerers' circle made.

The reason they stopped was soon clear. A massive wall of *wa*-force emerged from the circle and reached out in all directions from us. It was an almost blinding, overwhelming sense of force and power, more power than I had ever felt before in anything or anybody. It was almost a living thing, like that tabarwind, but totally invisible to any who could not sense the *wa*. It struck out at those with the weapons in an ever-widening circle, touched those weapons and controlled them.

Sometime I will work out the physics of what they did,

but basically they did to the weapons what would have happened to Darva and me had we immediately tried to significantly reduce our mass after my final transformation. The reaction was similar, with much heat being generated—and in projectile weapons the ammunition always has an explosive charge.

One by one, as the force met them and took hold, those weapons started blowing up. Troopers screamed in pain, and several came charging right at us in blind fury, hoping to break the circle by sheer physical force. Our own weapons had not been affected. Picking our shots carefully and going between the shoulders of the sorc circle, we calmly shot the hell out of those attackers. There weren't very many after the first batch from front and rear. To make sure we wouldn't have any spell problems, we all used laser weapons. At this range, even Darva couldn't miss, and she seemed particularly proud of herself as she gave me a wink and a big grin. I glanced over at Kira, who was all grim and businesslike. Well, to hell with her. What good was it to be good at something if you couldn't enjoy your work?

We started moving once again, but we were all ready for it now. We inside the circle kept a clear line of fire, though, not only because of the threat of more hall attacks but also because we'd have to pass some of the gun stations and offices. From that close, a man could physically hurl himself into the circle.

Nobody did, though. We reached an abandoned gun platform at the base of a wide set of stairs. Wide—but not wide enough to accommodate a circle our size, and steep enough so that we couldn't really see much of anything on the next floor. Whoever designed this place had put a lot of thought into it.

I reached into my pack and brought out four small silvery globes, each with a thin metal band around its middle. Almost as if on an unspoken command, the circle broke and the sorcs took up the defensive positions at the end of the hall which, until a few moments ago, had been occupied by troopers—in some cases they had to push still smoldering bodies out of the way. At almost the same mo-

ment a trooper came down the stairs, opening fire. I heard
some yells, but Kira acted with blinding speed and sliced
the man almost in two. He collapsed in a bloody heap and
fell to the base of the stairs.

Without looking back at casualties, I rushed to the bottom of the stairs, twisted the ring on the first globe, and
threw it underhanded to the top. Without waiting, I did the
same for the second. The first went off before I could
manage the third. It produced such a bang and shock wave
I was almost knocked over. I took no chances, throwing
number three before the second went off, and number four
immediately after I'd regained my balance. Only then did I
look around.

Class 1 sorcs or not, they were human beings and they
had been startled and surprised by the gunman. Kaigh was
certainly dead, and Krugar was clutching her bloody side
near her right hip. Now we were seven—down to four good
sorcs, but what the hell else could we do?

We had already delayed too long for the concussion
grenades to be one hundred percent effective, and we had
to press on. It was Kira, who started the run up the stairs,
and we had no choice but to abandon Krugar and charge
up behind her, all weapons drawn. The only optimistic
thing I could think about at this point was, well, at least the
place wasn't sealed enough to permit a gas trap.

I half expected Kira to be gone by the time I made the
next floor, but there she was, two more dead troopers at
her feet. We were still theoretically three floors from Aeolia Matuze—if she was there at all—but we were now beyond the security cordon and into the offices, living quarters, and labs of the Synod and top bureaucrats.

The eleventh floor resembled a hotel complex with all
the doors shut tight. Nice, modern, comfortable—and because these were offices and quarters, it wasn't really possible to tell what was what. They changed a lot, as would
be expected.

Koril paused to take a breather. "Krugar is in good
enough shape to try some self-repair and maybe hold off

anybody coming at us from below," he said between puffs. "Whew! I'm not as young as I used to be, that's for sure." He sighed. "Well, I'm not worried about troopers anymore. I think we can probably walk straight down this hall with no problems—but shoot anything that moves anyway."

"You don't think they'll make any more attempts?" I asked him worriedly.

He shook his head. "They know that anybody who can get this far is no slouch. No. Any members of the Synod here will have retreated to the thirteenth floor reception area. They'll be waiting for us there."

I looked at the others. "Are you and the other three enough?"

He shrugged. "Depends on how many are there and who they are. We've been damned lucky so far. Let's hope our luck holds out."

It was preparedness, the training of the sorcs, and a lot of inside information as well as skill and brass that had brought us this far, but in the end Koril was right. We *had* been lucky, too. He was certainly right, also, about the rest of the way. None of those doors opened, and we were unobstructed in our walk to the eleventh and twelfth floors. We could all hear, though, the floors below being occupied as soon as we left. *They* had the lift system, after all. They just didn't want to shoot up the official quarters. The troopers had already failed—now it was up to their bosses. In one sense, I suspected that the troopers, particularly the officers, were now very much on our side. If we failed, their own failures would have to be accounted for to those very same bosses. No, I decided, for that reason more than any other, they'd stay out of the rest of this fight.

Koril paused at the bottom of the stairway to the thirteenth level. "All right—Ku, Kimil, Kindel, stick close to me. You know what you must do. The rest of you follow us up, but stay out of it. None of your weapons will mean much now."

We understood what he meant. Our part was at least theoretically finished. All we could do was needlessly guard the back door.

Koril took in a deep breath, let it out slowly, then turned and started slowly up the stairs. One by one the sorcs followed him, then Kira, Darva, and myself. I don't know what I was expecting to see at the top, but it wasn't a sumptuously furnished empty room.

The large chamber was entirely crimson. The ancient-looking chairs upholstered in some silken material were ornamented with metal studs of a bright golden color that were inlaid in the dark native woods; the tables were equally antique and polished to a mirrorlike sheen. The carpet, too, was crimson, although of some thick, plush hair that the *wa* said was not native to Charon. In the center was a golden path, marked by two golden stripes of colored cloth woven into the rest and leading up to a raised platform. The platform itself was almost like a stage, with a huge wooden throne in the center of the same polished material and upholstered in the same deep red, but this time encrusted with what looked like—and turned out to be—enormous precious stones from all over the known galaxy. Two slightly smaller and more recessed but similar chairs flanked the big one. Behind the whole thing, eleven similar chairs were arranged in a permanent semi-circle. The entire stage area was decorated with gold-embroidered crimson drapes, hanging loosely around the back and tied back at the front.

We all stood there gazing about the room. I couldn't suppress a low whistle. "Like something out of an ancient fairy tale," I remarked.

Koril looked around, his eyes ablaze. "More power than those ancient kings had is represented here," he responded seriously. "This is the seat of Charon's government. I used to sit on that throne, remember. I *know*." That wistful, almost dreamlike quality left his voice. "She's redecorated since I left, though. In a way it's too bad. I had some great works of art looted from the Confederacy's top museums on those draped walls. Still, all in all, it's a nice touch."

"Skip the interior decoration comments," Kira broke in. "Where the hell's the enemy?"

At that moment I detected slight movement behind the

thrones, and I saw Kira's laser pistol come up. Koril quickly forced her hand down. "No use in burning the place down—unless you have to," he told her. "You can't harm these with that toy."

From behind the chairs five shapes emerged. All wore gold-embroidered robes of that same crimson as the room, and all wore scarlet hoods as well. They looked eerie and impressive, as they were supposed to.

Koril smiled a bit and with a flick of the wrist beckoned his three associate sorcs together in line, hands linked.

The figures walked out to the front of the stage and stood there, also in a line but not touching one another. Three of the five were women. One was Korman I saw— the only familiar face. None looked particularly worried.

"Just the five of you?" Koril said pleasantly. "I'm shocked."

"More than enough for the lot of *you*," Korman responded for the group. "We don't spend quite as much time here as we did in your day, Tulio. We don't have to." With that, all five levitated a meter or so above the stage and moved out just beyond it. All of us gasped at this, for we all realized it was no Warden trick. They were really doing it.

"Parlor tricks, Dieter?" Koril scoffed. "I thought we were beyond *that*."

"No parlor trick," one of the women answered him. "We are not as you knew us, Tulio. We are immortal, as powerful in body as in *wa*, with minds clearer than your merely human minds could ever be."

"So *that's* how she kept your allegiance," Koril responded. "With the new model alien robot bodies. You serve her now because you are *programmed* to serve! No longer humans—but mere machines."

"We are not 'mere machines,' Tulio," Korman replied. "I'll admit I have never heard 'programmed' used as a curseword before, but you are wrong. We were among those who freely chose to throw you out, Tulio. Freely. And none of us has ever regretted it. Should we choose, we could leave this place. Really leave, Tulio. The *wa* within

us dies as it would in you, but leaves us alive and whole—
and more than human."

"May we—examine those fancy new clothes of yours?"
Koril asked, and all of us understood that he didn't mean
literally.

"Go ahead. We can fool any scanner, rig any test—but
look at us as we really are. Be our guest, Tulio—and the
rest of you. You are powerful ones indeed to have come
this far. But no tricks."

Koril had a pained expression. "Would I insult your
intelligence?" With that, all four of them reached out their
Warden senses to the five who still floated, impossibly, in
the air.

"You see our superiority," Korman continued, not so
much bragging as being rather matter of fact about it all.
"You are a good man, Tulio. You served Charon well and
the Brethren before that. Don't you see that the revolution
is *now*? Are you so old and blind and prejudiced that you
can't realize that your ideals can become reality now—out
there? With you?"

They were very, very confident, I thought. Almost un-
settlingly so, yet I also understood that this sort of overcon-
fidence can kill you. I had no idea what Koril had up his
sleeve at this point, but I motioned to Darva and we edged
away toward a far wall, well away from the area between
the two group of sorcs. Suddenly I had a thought, and
leaned over and whispered to her, "See that alcove to the
left of the stage? I bet that goes up to You-Know-Who."

She nodded. "Seems likely. When do you want to try for
it?"

"Good girl. But not until they've started doing whatever
they're doing. They'll probably ignore us—I hope. We're
certainly no threat to them."

"I'll follow your lead," she whispered, and we turned
back to watch whatever was going to happen.

"Well, Tulio?" Korman was saying. "It's yours. It's for
all four of you, in fact. Immortal, superior bodies—free to
escape this prison. Free to run an empire."

Koril smiled. "So it's an empire now, is it? And who
would I be in this? Lord—or preprogrammed servant?"

Korman shrugged. "Your old position is, of course, already taken. But you would lead the Synod, as a matter of course. You never really liked being Lord anyway."

Koril sighed. "That's true enough. And yet I feel I cannot take your offer for two reasons. I do not trust those alien friends of yours as much as you do—though I'm sure I would once I got my new, improved body. Without a guarantee you cannot give, that of an unmolested mind, I can hardly accept. And, as for the second reason—do you remember Jatik?"

Korman looked puzzled, then brightened for a moment. "Of course. Little weasel of a man. Sorc for Diamond Rock. As bizarre a psychopath as we've ever had here on Charon. Killed in the desert, if I remember."

Koril nodded. "Killed coming to me. But he made his report, Dieter, before he died. He saw those friends of yours, those aliens. Tell me, Dieter—what would a man like that find so terrifying that he would brand it pure evil? It is a question that has troubled me, and driven me on, these past several years. More than anything, it's why I'm here."

Korman laughed. "Evil? The Lord of Satan, Agent of the Destroyer asks *me* about evil? What would that little psycho know about evil, anyway? Different, yes—incredibly so. Alien in many senses of that word. But *evil?* The former Lord of the Diamond, Lord of the Most Sacred Order of Brethren talks of *evil?*" And again he laughed.

"Now!" Koril yelled. At that moment all laughing stopped as a wall of Warden force at least the equal of what I had seen below lashed out with blinding speed right at Korman. Taken aback, he had only a simple shield himself and so he burst into flame before our very eyes, flame so intense I could not bear to look at it.

The others, less intent on Koril's speech and less confident than their leader of their own powers—after all, all of them hadn't been able to kill Koril alone the last time, or even keep him prisoner—struck back. Ignoring the flaming Korman, who toppled to the floor and continued melting into an acrid puddle, each of *our* sorcs took on the four remaining head to head.

I wasn't sure how they had managed to melt a robot of the type that had penetrated Military Systems Command and outsmarted all the Confederacy's best security devices, but I wasn't about to stay around and ask questions. I moved slowly and cautiously towards that alcove, and Darva followed. We were, as we had hoped, totally ignored.

Still, I stopped when we reached the alcove and looked back. It was no longer just *wa* being traded, willpower against willpower. The Synod sorcs were coming straight on, but the four, under Koril's direction, began twisting, turning, forming a careful mathematical pattern. Such was its nature and intricacy that it actually began disturbing the air between the two sets of antagonists. Incredibly I saw ripples there, then crackles of real, visible energy—electrical bolts forming and shooting, at first randomly and then *laterally*.

"Oh, by the gods! They're creating their own tabarwind!" Darva exclaimed.

"Let's get the hell out of here!" I responded, and we ducked into the alcove.

Frankly, the place didn't match the exterior. It was dark and dank and smelly. There were all sorts of pieces of furniture and stuff as well as controls for the curtains and whatever else was in the room. Still, far in back was indeed a service corridor which ran in one direction to a lift, clearly visible. Obviously the service entrance. We picked the other direction, as roars and howls of thunder and the crackle of raw energy sounded behind us. What was happening in that room back there would have been the sight of a lifetime—but it would almost certainly have ended ours.

Sure enough, at the end of the corridor a wooden stair led upward. We both hesitated at the bottom, then Darva looked at me. "Where's Kira or Zala or whatever the hell she is?"

I shook my head. "I don't know. I didn't really notice. Back there, I suppose. Hell, forget her—now." I took the lead and walked slowly and carefully up the stairs, laser pistol drawn.

I reached the top, stopped, and waited for Darva. I don't know quite who or what I expected up there, but it sure as hell wasn't Yatek Morah.

CHAPTER SIXTEEN

Twists and Turns

Darva fired before I could stop her, but Morah merely shrugged off the shots and dissipated the energy harmlessly. He was still dressed as I remembered him—in his black trooper uniform, although he had added a red-lined cape of the same material. His eyes were still bizarre and almost impossible to look at.

"Put away those things," he told us, gesturing at the pistols. "They are of no use here—and there is no need for them."

I sighed and holstered mine. Darva, uncertain, did the same. I looked at him, then at Darva, and sized up the situation. "Does 'Darkquest' mean anything to you?"

Darva looked blank, but Morah actually chuckled. "Now where'd you learn *that* little phrase?"

"I'm it. Park Lacoch. The same boy Korman threw to the wolves a year ago."

Morah sounded genuinely amused. "And of what use is that information to me now? I already know the true nature of Embuay, and I also know the location of Koril's base."

"That may be true, but it's not my problem," I responded casually. "I was given a job to do, and the first chance I got I did it."

That comment, and my calm manner, seemed to give him pause. "You may be right at that."

"Look—I could've taken the safe way out at Bourget, but I didn't. I deliberately got myself caught and wound up a changeling. Whether or not you no longer need the information, it says something about me, I think. I've paid a pretty high price to be just a redundancy."

Darva looked at me strangely. "What the hell are you talking about?"

"Sorry, honey. I'm a bottom-line pragmatist. I'll explain it all to you later. Let's just say Morah and I aren't necessarily the opponents we might seem to be."

She looked at Morah with obvious distaste. "Your girl Zala sure wasn't any help to you, you know."

Morah nodded, and I felt a little relieved that she was at least going along with me for now.

"It *is* true that the girl's been something of a disappointment so far," the Chief of Security admitted. "Is she with you?"

"Back there—someplace," I told him. "We didn't exactly want to stick around for the fireworks."

"Yes, well, I can understand that," he responded, sounding a little nervous and preoccupied. "How many are down there?"

"Koril and three others, all damned good," I told him truthfully. "Plus your girl, of course, if she survived all that."

"Hmmm . . . Yes. I see . . ."

He looked and sounded worried, and it gave me no end of satisfaction to see such emotions in him. His appearance, manner, and those damnable eyes all carried such an air of overwhelming power that I would have sworn he was above such things.

"How come you aren't down helping out your fellow— whatevers?" Darva asked, sensing the same thing.

"I am not required to," he said simply. "I am not on the Synod."

"*What!* But Koril said—" I began, but he cut me short.

"I told you before I was Chief of Security. I just did not tell you *whose* security."

"Oh, gods!" Darva breathed. "He's working directly for *them*!"

Morah cocked his head. "The battle is over downstairs," he told us matter-of-factly. "We are about to have visitors.

I suggest we three all go into that room over there and remain *very* silent."

I hesitated a moment. "Who won?"

"If the Synod had won, we wouldn't have to get into this room, now would we?"

That was good enough for me. I followed him. Darva, shrugging, did the same. I knew she was still trying to figure out which side we were on now. As for me, I was trying to figure out Morah's motives in all this. Clearly, as chief representative of the aliens on Charon, it was in his best interest to keep Matuze on her throne. Yet, here we were, about to let Koril have her.

There wasn't time for questions, though; we barely got the door closed when we heard somebody slowly mounting that final stairway. The newcomer sounded tired, perhaps weak and wounded, but he came steadily on. One man. One only. I knew who it had to be.

We heard him pause at the top of the stairs, and I could visualize him looking around cautiously. Finally, he walked past our door and away from us, his footsteps receding.

I turned to Morah. "You're letting him have her."

"Perhaps. Perhaps not. But—wait!"

A second, quieter tread could be heard on the stairs. Whoever it was was far lighter and more cautious than the first. We held our breaths a moment, then Morah let out a small sigh and beckoned us back in the room. On the far side was a rather pretty landscape of some world I'd never seen. He pressed a neatly hidden stud on it and the painting moved down silently revealing a one-way mirror.

It was a huge, comfortable living room, beautifully furnished and with good use of open space. Sculpture and paintings were around as well, and I clearly recognized some as lost art treasures of man's past. Originals, too, I knew instinctively.

Sitting on a divan, dressed casually in slacks, sandals, and a purple sleeveless shirt, was Aeolia Matuze. Unmistakably Matuze, looking every bit as good as her pictures. Very casually relaxed, legs crossed, she was smoking a cigarette in a long holder. She looked neither worried nor apprehensive.

"I assume this is soundproof?" I said in a low tone to Morah.

He nodded. "Absolutely. But I have a one way mike connection in."

"She looks awfully good for her age," I noted. "Robot?"

"Oh, no. Spell. I don't think we're quite ready for a robot Lord of the Diamond as yet."

"Why not just make everybody robots?" Darva said acidly. "That would make your job obsolete."

"You misunderstand our motives," Morah replied, shaking off the sarcastic tone. "The robots are weapons, and, in a sense, bribes; but they have their limitations as well. As weapons and bribes, they are valuable for the superior abilities they give. But they are sure death for a people and a civilization because of what they take away. Someday, perhaps, you will understand that. But—watch."

"Do you know what's gonna happen?" Darva asked him.

He shook his head from side to side. "Not the slighest idea. But it should be—interesting. You see, those entire quarters are *wa*-inert. Not only is there no *wa* in anything, the chemical treatment dampens out any *wa* sense you might have. It is quite a complex treatment and has to be—imported, if you understand."

I nodded. "That's why you don't have it all over this place."

"That, and the fact that it's very hard to manufacture and doesn't work with many surfaces. Still—here we go."

Aeolia Matuze leaned forward and flicked some ashes into an ornate standing ash tray, then turned toward the door to our right. A figure entered, a figure only recognizable with effort.

His clothing was scorched, and his face—all his exposed skin—was blackened as if by prolonged desert exposure. He was a terrible, and terrifying sight. He stood there in the doorway unsteadily, and stared at the woman.

Aeolia Matuze looked up in surprise. "Toolie! Oh, you *poor* dear! Whatever did they *do* to you?"

"It's been a long time, Aeolia," said Tulio Koril wearily.

"Oh, my! Come! Sit down in a chair and relax! Can I get you a drink or anything?"

We were dumbfounded by the scene, but Koril just chuckled dryly. "Got some of that wine? The good white?"

She stood up, went over to a small bar, reached behind, took out a bottle, opened it, and poured him a large glass; then she took it over to him. He accepted it, drank some in big gulps, then slowly sipped it. It *did* seem to relax him.

Aeolia Matuze sat back on the couch so she was pretty well facing him, then just watched him. She showed no fear, no shock, or horror at her predecessor's visit, which of course implied that either there was something we didn't know going on or, at the very least, something Koril sure as hell didn't. I remembered Morah's comment that, in there, both of them were equals in *wa*, having none at all.

Aeolia Matuze looked genuinely concerned. "Tell me—the burns. Do they hurt much?"

He shrugged. "Not so bad. More stiff than anything else. I think I'm still in a little bit of shock, but it's nothing I can't handle."

She nodded and appeared satisfied. "You know, I loved you for years, but never more than today. What you did was impossible, Toolie. No other man alive could have made it up here."

"You knew I'd come back."

She nodded. "I knew that if anybody could, you would. Tell me, how did you get by the Synod? They could rip iron bars, shoot into space—why, you wouldn't believe it. And they still had all their powers!"

"That was your problem," Koril told her, taking another sip of wine. "If they didn't keep their *wa* power, they were valueless as Synod members. If they did, then they had to have the *wa* in their molecules as sure as you and me. And *wa* is *wa*."

"But they are virtually impervious!"

He chuckled. "Know what we're made of, Aeolia? Chemical. Know what rock is made of? More chemicals. The rule is that if you're matter you have to be made of *something*. Chemicals. A specific mix of chemicals. And once you know how something's put together, and you know there's *wa* in each molecule; that stuff, whatever it was, was no different than natural flesh. No different.

And I happened to have a sample of the stuff ahead of time. I had it analyzed. It actually surprised me. The movement of just one little atom in its basic material caused it to change into another equally bizarre substance—but one that burned and melted quite nicely. Isn't it nice, Aeolia, to know that even sorcery is nothing more than basic chemistry?"

She laughed, seemingly delighted with his explanation. "How clever of you! I'll bet the reception room's a mess."

"It'll need a little more than mere redecorating," he agreed. "At least I'm happy now you got those paintings out of there."

Darva shook her head wonderingly. "They're talking like they're old buddies! Wasn't he here to *kill* her?"

"Perhaps," Morah replied. "But they were married for twenty-seven years."

Both Darva's and my own mouth flew open but no sound came out.

". . . two left alive down there," Koril was saying. "They're in worse shape than I am. They're backstage, but I told them not to come up just yet."

Matuze looked satisfied. "Tell me, Toolie—why now? I thought you'd be stuck forever down there in your desert hideaway, particularly with all those *delicious* toys we allowed to get through."

That startled the sorcerer. "Allowed?"

She smiled sweetly. "Toolie! Who knows you better than I do? Do you *really* think you could have gotten all that stuff from offworld all this time without our help? It was far cheaper and easier to keep you occupied at what you love best than to try any all-out fight. In a few more months' time, your return would have been academic anyway. Our delicious little war is well underway."

Koril looked absolutely devastated by the obvious truth of what she was telling him. He had as much as admitted his failings to me. I now more than suspected that Dumonia had caught onto the plot and that had been why he'd finally decided to push. But Koril wasn't about to mention the Cerberan, I'll give him that.

"It has to do with evil, Aeolia. Evil."

She laughed. *"Evil?* What in the *world* are you talking about?"

And, once more, he repeated the words that seemed to have haunted him since they were first uttered by the hapless Jatik.

She listened intently, but without any obvious reaction. Finally, when he'd completed his story, she said, "That's the most utter and complete nonsense I've ever heard! They're—odd—I admit, but they're not *evil.* What *is* evil, anyway, except somebody's arbitrary idea of what's wrong? Isn't that what you fought the Confederacy about? Aren't *our* ideas evil by everyone else's standards? Do *you* feel evil, Toolie? I don't."

But Koril did not reply. Slowly he seemed to stiffen, then relax. The wineglass dropped from his fingers and bounced on the rug, spilling a little of the remainder.

"Toolie?" she inquired sweetly. "Toolie?" Getting no response, she stood up and went over to him, then bent down and examined him carefully. Satisfied, she nodded and looked around the empty room.

"Morah!" she snapped, her tone suddenly cold and imperious. "I know you're spying around here someplace! Clean up this mess and get this *garbage* out of my living room!"

"She *poisoned* him!" Darva gasped. "All this way and he lets her poison him!"

"No," I told her. "He surrendered. When he got all the way up here he just couldn't do it—and she knew it. She sure knew him, all right!"

Darva just shook her head sadly. "So simple. So powerful, so smart a man."

"Oddly enough, those are exactly the qualities in humans that are worth preserving," Morah added enigmatically. "You'll see. But—wait. The play isn't over yet."

Aeolia Matuze was up and striding around the room like a mad woman. "Morah! Somebody! Attend me! It will be necessary to arrange the executions of those below and those troops who failed me! Where the hell *is* everybody?"

"Here." A cold, female voice came from behind her. She

whirled and looked very surprised and not the least bit annoyed.

"Who the hell are *you*?" Aeolia Matuze snapped.

"We're the new Queen of Charon," Zala/Kira replied as she shot Aeolia Matuze three times. The Lord of Charon toppled and fell, a look of total surprise and bewilderment frozen forever on her face.

I looked at Morah. "She expected you to guard her."

He nodded. "She never could get it through her head who I worked for," he replied, as we watched the woman we both knew walk over, check Koril first, then Aeolia Matuze.

Yatek Morah sighed and turned away from the window. We did the same. "What now?" I asked him.

He smiled. "That depends on you. The remainder of Koril's surviving Class I's will pretty well fill out the Synod."

Darva turned and pointed back at the glass. "But *she's* not qualified to run Charon! Zala's a helpless wimp and Kira's a mechanized assassin!"

"I'm aware of that," Morah replied. "Think of this, Lacoch. You're the Confederacy's assassin. Don't bother to deny it. Nobody else in your batch showed any real promise. I arranged that whole sideshow at Bourget on that assumption." He made a backhanded gesture at the glass. "Her type is now obsolete. It has served its purpose. I've called the few surviving ones to the Diamond. The robots are better, more reliable, and harder to kill."

"Koril thought you wanted to be Supreme Lord of all the Diamond," I told him.

"That ambition had crossed my mind when I had my agents on Takanna keep a small version of this bioagent project going many years ago," he admitted. "However, that prospect no longer interests me. It has become rather—small. Petty, even. No longer worth going after. It has been so for quite some time."

"And Zala?"

He chuckled. "That's up to you. Kira is *extremely* good at what she does, but that's all she does. Zala—well, she trusts you. And she'll need the help of a lot of people she trusts to put things back together and get the government straightened out once more. You're an assassin. She's an assassin. It will be interesting to see who, in the end, is the better."

"You're offering me a shot at being Lord of Charon," I said, a little in awe of the possibilities. I turned to Darva. "Remember those dreams we had? Of changing things for the better, of a virgin continent for the changelings?"

She looked at me strangely. "You mean you'd *do* it? But it'd be on *his* terms and at *his* pleasure."

I turned to Morah. "From what I've seen I could have a very brief tenure myself."

"She was power-mad, you know. She was about to proclaim herself Supreme Goddess of a new, true, and only religion. She was no longer rational enough to do what she was supposed to do—run Charon. As for me and my employers, we frankly don't *care* how the humans run each other on Charon. Our motives—but no, that must wait. I know from reports from Lilith that you carry within you, perhaps still, a sort of organic transmitter. You will eliminate it, or I will. Then, I think, you can be told the whole story. Then you can make your own decisions. For now I must go and tend to our new queen."

For a while we just stood there, not saying anything to one another. Finally Darva asked, "Well? After all this, you're gonna do it? Or what?"

I smiled and kissed her, then looked back at the glass. Zala was there now, not Kira, and she was doing a happy little dance between the bodies. I stared at her, not quite knowing what to do next.

Finally I sighed and said, "Well, I'm of two minds about this . . ."

The man in the chair came out of it slowly. He lifted the probes from his head and pushed the apparatus away, but just sat there for a while, as if in a daze.

"Are you all right?" the computer asked him, sounding genuinely concerned.

"Yeah, as good as I'll ever be again, I guess. It gets worse and worse. Now I'm considering joining the enemy!"

"Differing circumstances, an additional year in an alien environment under trapped conditions—it is not totally unexpected. They are not you. They are different people."

The man chuckled mirthlessly. "Maybe. Maybe. At any rate—you saw and heard?"

"It is obvious. Do you wish to file a report and make a recommendation now?"

The man seemed startled. "Huh? No. Of course not! Some pieces are still missing, and while I'm pretty sure I know what is going on I'm still not at all sure how to stop it."

"Time is of the essence now," the computer reminded him. "You heard Matuze. A matter of months. That means they are probably all in place even now."

"And we've yet to find the aliens. We've yet to see what one looks like. We've yet to determine their defensive force and how near it is. Pretty near, I'd guess."

"I believe you do not wish to act," the computer responded. "You know why the aliens are here, their interest in the Warden Diamond specifically, the method by which the Confederacy is to be attacked and just about when—there is more than enough evidence to act."

"Evidence! Deduction! Not a shred of real evidence!"

"Considering the extreme circumstances and the consistency of the deductions on three worlds now, I'd say you were more than justified."

"*No!*" the man protested. "I want to be absolutely certain! There are millions of lives at stake here!"

"In the Warden Diamond. But there are thousands of times that at stake elsewhere."

"It's not as easy as you make it seem. That's why they just don't let *you* make the decisions. We still have *some* time. And maybe we can figure out some way so nobody has to die."

"You *have* changed," the computer chided. "I feel obligated to make an emergency summary report. You will add your conclusions."

"Not yet. All right—look. Let me get to the ship's library and labs for a day or so. I also want to check out communications. I have a strong feeling I can track the alien fleet."

"I don't believe you. You're just stalling. You have become assimilated with your counterparts."

"Three days. Even you will have to admit that three days won't hurt anything. Besides, the solution is so outrageous they wouldn't believe it now anyway. Even *you* must admit that much."

The computer actually hesitated a moment. Finally it said, "All right. Three days. What can you possibly expect to turn up in three days?"

"Just watch. And I'll want to run Medusa before we finish up."

"But Medusa is not complete."

"Makes no difference. Medusa's the key to it all. Be ready when I return."

He walked back, showered, dressed, then approached the security door that both interlocked him to and isolated him from the giant picket ship. He pressed the identplate; the door refused to open. Angrily, he turned and yelled at the empty air, "All right! Let me out, you bastard! We had an agreement!"

"Do you really know what you're going to do, or are you

just grasping at straws?" the computer's disembodied voice asked him.

"Look—am I a prisoner or the agent in charge?" he shot back angrily.

"You *will* come back?"

"Of course I will! Where the hell am I going to run?"

"What are you planning?"

"I'm—oh, let's just say I'm of two minds about it right now."

"Well . . ."

"Would I lie to you?"

There was a second pause, and then the door opened.

ABOUT THE AUTHOR

JACK L. CHALKER was born in Baltimore, Maryland, on December 17, 1944. He learned to read almost from the moment of entering school and, by working odd jobs ranging from engineering outdoor rock concerts in the sixties to computer typesetting, amassed a large SF/fantasy/horror book collection that today is ranked among the finest in private hands.

Chalker joined the Washington Science Fiction Association in 1958 and began publishing an amateur SF journal, *Mirage*, in 1960, and in 1963 founded the Baltimore Science Fiction Society. After high school, he set out to be a trial lawyer, but money problems caused him to switch to teaching as a career. He holds a bachelor's degree in history and English from Towson State College and an M.L.A. in the History of Ideas from Johns Hopkins University, and taught history and geography in the Baltimore city school system from 1966 until 1978 with time out for military service, until his writing career allowed him to become a full-time free-lance writer. Additionally, out of the amateur journals, he founded a publishing house, The Mirage Press, Ltd., producing over thirty books, mostly nonfiction, related to SF and fantasy, and, although no longer a major publisher, it still publishes an occasional book. His interests include computers, esoteric audio, travel, history and politics, lecturing on the SF field to private groups, universities, and such institutions as the Smithsonian. He is an active conservationist, a Sierra Club life member and National Parks supporter, and he has a passion for ferryboats, with the avowed goal of riding every one in the world. In fact, in 1978 he was married to Eva Whitley on an ancient ferryboat in midriver, and they have lived ever since in the Catoctin Mountain region of Maryland with their son.

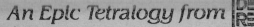
TA-50